THE BEST OF ELLERY QUEEN

THE BEST OF ELLERY QUEEN

*Four Decades of Stories from the
Mystery Masters*

Edited by Francis M. Nevins, Jr. and
Martin H. Greenberg

BEAUFORT BOOKS
Publishers · New York

Library of Congress Cataloging in Publication Data

Queen, Ellery.
The best of Ellery Queen.

1. Detective and mystery stories, American. I. Nevins,
Francis M.   II. Greenberg, Martin Harry.   III. Title.
PS3533.U4A6   1984   813'.52   84-21572
ISBN 0-8523-0246-3

Published in the United States by Beaufort Books Publishers,
New York.

Printed in the U.S.A.   First Edition

10   9   8   7   6   5   4   3   2   1

CONTENTS

INTRODUCTION

Francis M. Nevins, Jr.

ONE NOON HOUR during the late spring or early summer of 1928, two cousins in their early twenties met for lunch at an Italian restaurant in midtown Manhattan. Over the antipasto one of them—later neither could remember which—mentioned seeing an announcement in the morning *Times* about a $7,500 mystery novel writing contest sponsored jointly by *McClure's Magazine* and the publishing firm of Frederick A. Stokes. Before the meal was over the cousins had not only decided to enter the competition but had devised the nucleus of a plot. They worked frantically on evenings, weekends and holidays over the next several months, pushing themselves to complete the manuscript before the contest deadline of December 31, 1928. "I remember Manny Lee had to go to a wedding in Philadelphia during the time we were writing it," Fred Dannay recalled more than fifty years later. "And I had to go with him, to the wedding of a complete stranger, just so we wouldn't lose the time it took to get there and back on the train."

They finished the manuscript on December 30, turned it in the next day, and, as Dannay put it many decades later, "sat back with a sigh of relief to await the outcome." That was how Ellery Queen was born, both as a detective (and detective-story writer) within the novel and as the joint pseudonym of the authors.

Frederic Dannay and Manfred B. Lee were born in 1905, nine months and five blocks apart, in Brooklyn's teeming Brownsville district. "My family moved to the small upstate town of Elmira, New

York, when I was a baby," Dannay recalled in his seventies, "and the twelve years I spent there were a great gift. I lived a Tom Sawyer boyhood in one of Mark Twain's hometowns. My cousin stayed in Brooklyn and became streetwise, while I was sort of a country bumpkin." Dannay's best friend in Elmira was named Ellery. Meanwhile Manny Lee, growing up in Brownsville's rough environment, performed an inner emigration. "I knew I was going to be a writer from the time I was eight years old," he said near the end of his life. "I think boys of American Jewish background can't take the brutality of the streets and turn for refuge to books." In summers he went upstate to visit his cousin, and the boys spent their time competing against each other in games of one-upmanship which, in altered forms, they carried on throughout their more than forty years of literary collaboration.

In 1917 Dannay's family returned to Brooklyn, and that winter, while 12-year-old Fred was in bed suffering from an ear infection, an aunt visited his sickroom and handed him a book she'd borrowed from the neighborhood public library. It was Conan Doyle's *Adventures of Sherlock Holmes*, and it changed Dannay's life. Reading those fabulous stories so fired the boy's imagination that the next morning he slipped out of the house, wangled a card at the library and took home all the Sherlock Holmes books he could lay his hands on.

With his family's return to Brooklyn there developed a powerful friendship between Fred and Manny. "We were cousins," Fred said more than sixty years later, "but we were closer than brothers." They shared a passion for detective fiction, and as early as 1920, while attending Boys' High together, they began to play with the notion of writing mysteries themselves. Manny, the older cousin, graduated from Boys' High and, four years later, from New York University. Fred was forced by family financial reverses to quit high school before graduation and go to work. Through the 1920s he hopped from job to job like a kangaroo. In 1926 he married Mary Beck, the first of his three wives, and at the time of that fateful lunch in 1928 he was a copywriter and art director for a New York advertising agency. Manny meanwhile was making his living writing publicity releases for the Manhattan-based Pathé movie studio. The cousins' offices were only a few blocks apart and they met for lunch almost every day. That was how Ellery Queen was born.

With their backgrounds in advertising and publicity, they decided to take great pains over the name of their detective protagonist. "What we wanted," Dannay said on *The Dick Cavett Show* in 1978, "was a name which, once heard, read, or seen in print, would have a mnemonic value and remain in the person's memory." It had to be slightly unusual, easy to remember and rhythmic in sound, and after a few false starts like "James Griffen" and "Wilbur See," they had it.

The mystery novel contest was open to all, professionals as well as beginners, but in order to insure equal treatment of all entries the sponsors required that each manuscript had to be submitted under a pseudonym. Instead of picking a name out of hat, Dannay and Lee hit upon the brilliant idea of using "Ellery Queen" as their own joint by-line as well as the name of their detective, figuring that readers tended to remember the character's name, not the author's—Sherlock Holmes, not Doyle—and that the same name in both functions would make Ellery Queen literally unforgettable. How right they were!

In March of 1929, Fred and Manny phoned the Curtis Brown literary agency, which was administering the contest, and were told to come over right away and see a Mr. Rich. "Mr. Rich's office was absolutely cluttered," Dannay recalled, "mostly with manuscripts stacked more than waist-high everywhere on the floor. He said to us: 'Now this is not for public report, but, confidentially, you have won the contest, and it will be publicly reported in a few days, and I congratulate you.' So Manny and I walked out on Cloud Nine. And we said to ourselves: 'We have to commemorate this event.' So we went into Dunhill's [the famous New York tobacconist shop] and bought each other a pipe and had the initials EQ put on the stem of each pipe." But the public announcement never came, and when they called Mr. Rich again they found out why. "Since I last talked to you something terrible has happened," he told them. "*McClure's* has gone bankrupt."

The magazine's assets had been taken over by another magazine, *Smart Set*, whose editors had decided to award the prize to another manuscript more suited to that periodical's female readership. That was the bad news. The good news was that the editors at the Stokes company liked the Ellery Queen novel enough to publish it anyway, provided Fred and Manny would accept advances of $200 apiece.

Dannay in his seventies was philosophical about having won the contest only to lose it. As he told Dick Cavett: "We thought at the time that it was a terrible blow from fate. What we had planned to do was to pack up our families, give up our jobs, go to the south of France (where at that time there were many expatriate American writers), and write. And of course when we lost the contest and lost the first prize we had to stay with our jobs. And that actually was the best thing that ever happened to us. Because I think if we had gone to the south of France we'd have frittered the money away, produced no work, whereas the way it happened, we buckled down and started a career."

That career lasted for more than forty years, and the best short stories the cousins wrote during those years are collected here.

One of the reasons behind Ellery Queen's phenomenal success is that Dannay and Lee had no qualms about modifying the personality of their hero and altering the kind of books they wrote so as to keep up with changing times and tastes. Their work can be divided into four diverse periods, beginning with the years from 1929 to 1935 when Ellery Queen established himself as *the* American master detective *par excellence*.

At the time they created Ellery over that lunch table, the foremost detective novels in the United States were the best-selling Philo Vance books, written by art critic Willard Huntington Wright (1888-1939) under the pseudonym of S.S. Van Dine. Although superior in plotting, characterization and style, the early Queen novels were heavily influenced by the Van Dine blockbusters. The strict title pattern of the first-period Queen novels, *The* Adjective-of-Nationality Noun *Mystery*, comes from Van Dine's pattern, *The* Six-Letter-Word *Murder Case*. Each of the running characters in early Queen has a counterpart in Van Dine—blockheaded Sergeant Velie, for instance—stemming from dumb Sergeant Heath in the Vance cases. Ellery's father, Inspector Richard Queen of the NYPD, calls on his brilliant son for help in difficult crime puzzles much as District Attorney Markham called on that insufferable mandarin Philo Vance. And, of course, it was from Van Dine that Dannay and Lee borrowed the concept of the super-intellectual amateur detective, full of scholarly quotations, detached from people and interested only in abstract problems. We meet Ellery I, the Harvard-educated dilettante and bibliophile, in the early tales in this collection, which comes from the 1934 volume *The Adventures of Ellery Queen*, a title deliberately echoing that of the first Sherlock Holmes story collection. In their final phase as mystery writers, the

cousins developed a strong dislike for this first version of their character, whom Manny Lee ridiculed as "the biggest prig that ever came
down the pike." But on a smaller scale, the best of their Period One
short stories are like their early novels: richly plotted specimens of the
Golden Age deductive puzzle, bursting with bizarre circumstances,
conflicting testimony, enigmatic clues (including that uniquely
Queenian device, the dying message), alternative solutions, fireworks
displays of virtuoso reasoning, and a crackle of intellectual excitement.

What made the Ellery Queen novels and stories stand out from the
detective fiction of the time was the cousins' insistence on playing fair
with the reader. "We stressed fairness to the reader," Dannay said in
1979, "in the sense that . . . the reader had to know everything that the
detective knew, and therefore had an even chance of beating the
detective before the solution was given at the end of the book."

And they did play the game with scrupulous fairness, not only
presenting all the facts honestly (albeit with a great deal of trickiness on
occasion) but stopping most of the novels at a certain point to issue a
formal "Challenge to the Reader" to solve the puzzle ahead of Ellery.
The odds of course were stacked in favor of the house, and when Fred
Dannay once boasted to a *Look Magazine* interviewer that Queen was
always "completely fair to the reader," Manny Lee rightly interjected:
"We are fair to the reader only if he is a genius."

All nine of the novels about Ellery I are gems, from *The Roman Hat
Mystery* (1929) which launched his career; through *The Spanish Cape
Mystery* (1935) at the tail end of Period One, but my personal favorites
from this era are *The Greek Coffin Mystery* and *The Egyptian Cross
Mystery* (both 1932), top-of-the-line deductive puzzles which are as
fresh and intellectually stimulating today as they were half a century
ago.

By the mid-1930s Dannay and Lee were professional writers, making
excellent money not just from books but from two highly lucrative
media which had begun to buy their work at this time—the slick-paper
magazines like *Redbook* and *Cosmopolitan* and the movies. It was the
requirements of these markets which led to the reshaping of the
cousins' fictional universe and the launching of Ellery II.

In second-period Queen, between 1936 and 1940, the Van Dine
patterned titles vanish, and Ellery gradually loses his priggishness and

becomes more human. Here is how Dannay in 1979 described his and Lee's strategy. "We loosened the construction . . . we put more emphasis on character development and background; we put more emphasis on human-interest situations. And what we were doing, frankly, was to aim at getting magazine serialization, which paid very good money in those days, and to sell to the movies, which was the only other means of getting extra money."

Compared with the Period One classics, much of the cousins' output of the late 1930s suffers from intellectual thinness, a surfeit of so-called love interest (meaning tedious boy-meet-girl byplay), and characters tailored to please story editors at the slick magazine suites and the studios. But in the longer view they managed at least in part to open up the deductive puzzle and make room within its cerebral rigor for more of the virtues of mainstream storytelling. In several Period Two short adventures and in the novels *The Devil to Pay* and *The Four of Hearts* (both 1938), Ellery works as a Hollywood screenwriter, paralleling his creators' brief stints at Columbia, Paramount and M-G-M during these years. While on the west coast he becomes involved with lovely gossip columnist Paula Paris (a Thirties screwball comedy movie heroine of the first water), who figures in the two excellent sports whodunits of 1939 that represent Period Two in the present collection. The period came to an end with *The New Adventures of Ellery Queen* (1940), which brought together all the short cases of Ellery II plus a few leftovers from the early years.

By 1940 Fred and Mary Dannay and their young sons were living the suburban life in Great Neck, Long Island. Fred collected stamps and wrote poetry in odd moments, as he had since boyhood, and was close to reaching his ultimate goal as a book collector, namely owning a copy of every volume of detective-crime short stories ever published. Manny Lee, divorced from his first wife, was living with his daughters in a spacious Park Avenue apartment. In his own spare time Manny played the violin and hunted classical record albums for his collection. But there was little leisure for either cousin. They were putting in twelve-hour workdays at home and meeting once a week at a rented office to consolidate their material. Both men were chain smokers and their workplace atmosphere tended to be on the thick side. On the office floor they kept a tattered brown envelope labeled IDEAS.

And at that point they needed every idea they could come up with. Since June of 1939, when *The Adventures of Ellery Queen* series had debuted on the CBS radio network, they had had to turn out a script a week. It was a lucrative grind but one that left them no time for novels or short stories. In September 1940 the show left the air, and the next fifteen months were among the most fruitful in the cousins' lives. Dannay, the historian and bibliophile of the partnership, used his private library of crime and detective short story collections as the basis for editing *101 Years' Entertainment* (1941), the definitive anthology of short mystery fiction up to its own time. And when he found countless first-rate stories for which there was no room in that mammoth volume, he persuaded publisher Lawrence E. Spivak to launch *Ellery Queen's Mystery Magazine*, the premier periodical in the field, which Fred actively edited from its first issue, dated Fall 1941, until shortly before his death in 1982. It was also during these fifteen months that Dannay and Lee inaugurated their third and richest period as writers with *Calamity Town* (1942), which is subtitled "a novel" rather than "a problem in deduction" like the earliest Queen books. Ellery III is no longer a Philo Vance clone detached from the terrible events around him but a human being involved in horrors.

In their third period, which lasted until 1958 and embraced twelve Queen novels and two short-story collections, the cousins fused complex deductive puzzles with in-depth characterization, finely detailed evocations of place and mood, occasional ventures into a topsy-turvy Alice in Wonderland otherworld, and explorations into history, psychiatry and religion. The best novels of Period Three are *Calamity Town*, in which Ellery shares the emotional and criminal problems of the people in the "typical American town" of Wrightsville, U.S.A.; *Ten Days' Wonder* (1948) with its return to Wrightsville and its phantasmagoria of Biblical symbolism; *Cat of Many Tails* (1949) with its unforgettable images of New York City menaced by a heat wave, a mad strangler of what seem to be randomly chosen victims, and the threat of World War III; and *The Origin of Evil* (1951), in which Darwinian motifs underlie the clues and deductions.

In the first Queen story collection of the period, *Calendar of Crime* (1952), Ellery solves twelve puzzles, each thematically related to a particular month of the year. The tales had begun appearing in *Ellery Queen's Mystery Magazine* back in 1946, and even before then they had first seen life as scripts for the Queen radio series, which returned to the air in January 1942 and stayed on, with occasional short breaks, till May 1948. The best of the *Calendar* crimes deal with the months of January and December and are reprinted here. Like the other stories in the collection, they feature a young woman named Nikki Porter, Ellery's secretary and sort-of girlfriend, whom Dannay and Lee had created for the radio series and who also appears in the Queen novels *There Was an Old Woman* (1943) and *The Scarlet Letters* (1953).

By the time the Queen show had left radio for good, both Fred's life and Manny's had undergone radical changes. Mary Dannay died of cancer in 1945 after a long illness, and two years later Fred remarried and moved with his wife Hilda and his sons to a colonial house in Larchmont, a quiet New York suburb forty minutes by train from Manhattan. There he was again struck by tragedy when, in 1948, Hilda gave birth to their only child. Stephen Dannay was born prematurely at seven months, weighing less than two pounds and suffering from brain damage which, Fred said, was "so severe that the child, who had an absolutely angelic face, never walked and never talked. I was aware long before my wife that one of these days the tragedy would be capped by the death of that child. Actually he lived till he was six years old." No wonder there is so much sadness in Queen's third-period novels.

Manny Lee, meanwhile, had also remarried, this time to actress Kaye Brinker, whom he'd met on the Queen show. After that series left the air, the Lees and their by then sizable brood of children relocated in suburban Connecticut. Manny took to the life of a country gentleman as if to the manor born, buying a station wagon for the family, keeping chickens and cows, helping make butter and pasteurized milk for home use, declaring his 63-acre Roxbury property a game preserve, and adding to his record collection. In his workroom, a small converted cottage on his grounds that had been a schoolhouse back in the Revolutionary era, he carried on as Ellery Queen, collaborating with Fred by telephone. It was a productive but relaxed and varied existence, and Manny seemed to thrive on it.

When not busy on a novel, the cousins kept themselves and Ellery occupied in yet another market, that of the short-short story. The Sunday supplement magazine *This Week* paid them handsomely for a series of two dozen mini-puzzles that ran from 1949 till the early

Sixties. Most of these plus a few tales from other sources were collected in *QBI: Queen's Bureau of Investigation* (1955), from which four exceptionally clever exploits have been chosen for this book.

Period Three came to an end with *The Finishing Stroke* (1958), in which Fred and Manny nostalgically recreated the young manhood of Ellery himself. The book is set in 1929, shortly after publication of the author-detective's first novel—which happens to be titled *The Roman Hat Mystery*—and the signals are clear all through this elegy to "the lovely past" that the cousins were retiring as mystery writers. Manny began to take a more active role in Roxbury's civic life, serving a term as Justice of the Peace and beating his playwright neighbor Arthur Miller in an election for a seat on the Library Board. Fred sold the University of Texas his huge collection of detective short story volumes and wound up spending two semesters on campus as a professor of creative writing.

After five years of almost complete fictional inactivity, a fourth period opened with *The Player on the Other Side* (1963). These late Queens are marked by a zest for experiment within the strict deductive tradition and a retreat from all semblance of plausibility into what Fred liked to call "Fun and Games," i.e. a potpourri of stylized plots and characters and dozens of motifs recycled from earlier Queen material. Fred's favorite late Queen novel was the religiously allegorical *And On the Eighth Day* (1964), but most readers would probably opt for *The Player* and the later *Face to Face* (1967) from Period Four. The story collections *Queens Full* (1965) and *QED: Queen's Experiments in Detection* (1968) brought together most of the shorter Queen cases which hadn't appeared before in hardcover, and our present offering closes with three of the best from *QED* plus one that has never been in a previous Queen collection.

In the late 1960s Manny Lee suffered a series of heart attacks and, on doctor's orders, took off a great deal of weight. It didn't save him. On April 2, 1971, the 65-year-old Lee had another attack and died on the way to the Waterbury hospital. He never saw a copy of Ellery's last novel-length adventure, *A Fine and Private Place* (1971).

At first Fred planned to continue the Queen books, either alone or with a new partner. But then on the heels of Manny's death a new tragedy invaded Fred's life. In 1972 his second wife died of cancer just as his first wife had done 27 years before, and with her death Fred too began dying by inches. Until he met the third woman in his life—Rose Koppel, a recently widowed artist who worked at Manhattan's Ethical Culture School—and, in November 1975, married her.

He had always been a private person, so much so that often after almost thirty years many of his closest Larchmont neighbors had no idea what he did for a living. Rose de-privatized him, made it possible for him to enjoy the role of mystery fiction's Elder Statesman that time and deaths of his peers like John Dickson Carr, Agatha Christie and Rex Stout had bestowed on him.

In his seventies Frederic Dannay received more media exposure than in all his previous years. He abandoned the idea of writing more Ellery Queen novels, saying it would be disloyal to Manny's memory, but continued to edit *Ellery Queen's Mystery Magazine* as well as a huge number of crime-fiction anthologies. After his 75th birthday his own health began to fail and he was forced to curtail more and more work. He was hospitalized twice and then, late in the summer of 1982, a third time. That Labor Day weekend, his heart stopped. And in a very real sense, the detective tradition of the Golden Age died with him.

The best short cases of perhaps the greatest American mastersleuth of that tradition are assembled here. Read, enjoy, and be challenged.

THE GLASS-DOMED CLOCK

(1933)

OF ALL THE hundreds of criminal cases in the solution of which Mr. Ellery Queen participated by virtue of his self-imposed authority as son of the famous Inspector Queen of the New York Detective Bureau, he has steadfastly maintained that none offered a simpler diagnosis than the case which he has designated as "The Adventure of the Glass-Domed Clock." "So simple," he likes to say—sincerely!— "that a sophomore student in high school with the most elementary knowledge of algebraic mathematics would find it as easy to solve as the merest equation." He has been asked, as a result of such remarks, what a poor untutored first-grade detective on the regular police force—whose training in algebra might be something less than elementary—could be expected to make of such a "simple" case. His invariably serious response has been: "Amendment accepted. The resolution now reads: Anybody with common sense could have solved this crime. It's as basic as five minus four leaves one."

This was a little cruel, when it is noted that among those who had opportunity—and certainly wishfulness—to solve the crime was Mr. Ellery Queen's own father, the Inspector, certainly not the most stupid of criminal investigators. But then Mr. Ellery Queen, for all his mental prowess, is sometimes prone to confuse his definitions: *viz.*, his uncanny capacity for strict logic is far from the average citizen's common sense. Certainly one would not be inclined to term elementary a problem in which such components as the following figured: a pure purple amethyst, a somewhat bedraggled expatriate from Czarist Rus-

1

sia, a silver loving-cup, a poker game, five birthday encomiums, and of course that peculiarly ugly relic of early Americana catalogued as "the glass-domed clock"—among others! On the surface the thing seems too utterly fantastic, a maniac's howling nightmare. Anybody with Ellery's cherished "common sense" would have said so. Yet when he arranged those weird elements in their proper order and pointed out the "obvious" answer to the riddle—with that almost monastic intellectual innocence of his, as if everybody possessed his genius for piercing the veil of complexities!—Inspector Queen, good Sergeant Velie, and the others figuratively rubbed their eyes, the thing was so clear.

It began, as murders do, with a corpse. From the first the eeriness of the whole business struck those who stood about in the faintly musked atmosphere of Martin Orr's curio shop and stared down at the shambles that had been Martin Orr. Inspector Queen, for one, refused to credit the evidence of his old senses; and it was not the gory nature of the crime that gave him pause, for he was as familiar with scenes of carnage as a butcher and blood no longer made him squeamish. That Martin Orr, the celebrated little Fifth Avenue curio dealer whose establishment was a treasure-house of authentic rarities, had had his shiny little bald head bashed to red ruin—this was an indifferent if practical detail; the bludgeon, a heavy paperweight spattered with blood but wiped clean of fingerprints, lay not far from the body; so *that* much was clear. No, it was not the assault on Orr that opened their eyes, but what Orr had apparently done, as he lay gasping out his life on the cold cement floor of his shop, *after* the assault.

The reconstruction of events after Orr's assailant had fled the shop, leaving the curio dealer for dead, seemed perfectly legible: having been struck down in the main chamber of his establishment, toward the rear, Martin Orr had dragged his broken body six feet along a counter —the red trail told the story plainly—had by superhuman effort raised himself to a case of precious and semi-precious stones, had smashed the thin glass with a feeble fist, had groped about among the gem-trays, grasped a large unset amethyst, fallen back to the floor with the stone tightly clutched in his left hand, had then crawled on a tangent five feet past a table of antique clocks to a stone pedestal, raised himself again, and deliberately dragged off the pedestal the object it supported

—an old clock with a glass dome over it—so the clock fell to the floor by his side, shattering its fragile case into a thousand pieces. And there Martin Orr had died, in his left fist the amethyst, his bleeding right hand resting on the clock as if in benediction. By some miracle the clock's machinery had not been injured by the fall; it had been one of Martin Orr's fetishes to keep all his magnificent timepieces running; and to the bewildered ears of the little knot of men surrounding Martin Orr's corpse that gray Sunday morning came the pleasant *tick-tick-tick* of the no longer glass-domed clock.

Weird? It was insane!

"There ought to be a law against it," growled Sergeant Velie.

Dr. Samuel Prouty, Assistant Medical Examiner of New York County, rose from his examination of the body and prodded Martin Orr's dead buttocks—the curio dealer was lying face down—with his foot.

"Now here's an old coot," he said grumpily, "sixty if he's a day, with more real stamina than many a youngster. Marvelous powers of resistance! He took a fearful beating about the head and shoulders, his assailant left him for dead, and the old monkey clung to life long enough to make a tour about the place! Many a younger man would have died in his tracks."

"Your professional admiration leaves me cold," said Ellery. He had been awakened out of a pleasantly warm bed not a half-hour before to find Djuna, the Queens' gypsy boy-of-all-work, shaking him. The Inspector had already gone, leaving word for Ellery, if he should be so minded, to follow. Ellery was always so minded when his nose sniffed crime, but he had not had breakfast and he was thoroughly out of temper. So his taxicab had rushed through Fifth Avenue to Martin Orr's shop, and he had found the Inspector and Sergeant Velie already on the cluttered scene interrogating a grief-stunned old woman—- Martin Orr's aged widow—and a badly frightened Slavic giant who introduced himself in garbled English as the "ex-Duke Paul." The ex-Duke Paul, it developed, had been one of Nicholas Romanov's innumerable cousins caught in the whirlpool of the Russian revolution who had managed to flee the homeland and was eking out a none too fastidious living in New York as a sort of social curiosity. This was in 1926, when royal Russian expatriates were still something of a novelty in the land of democracy. As Ellery pointed out much later, this was not only 1926, but precisely Sunday, March the seventh, 1926, although at the time it seemed ridiculous to consider the specific date of any importance whatever.

"Who found the body?" demanded Ellery, puffing at his first cigarette of the day.

"His Nibs here," said Sergeant Velie, hunching his colossal shoulders. "*And* the lady. Seems like the Dook or whatever he is has been workin' a racket—been a kind of stooge for the old duck that was murdered. Orr used to give him commissions on the customers he brought in—and I understand he brought in plenty. Anyway, Mrs. Orr here got sort of worried when her hubby didn't come home last night from the poker game. . . ."

"Poker game?"

The Russian's dark face lighted up. "Yuss. Yuss. It is remarkable game. I have learned it since my sojourn in your so amazing country. Meester Orr, myself, and some others here play each week. Yuss." His face fell, and some of his fright returned. He looked fleetingly at the corpse and began to edge away.

"You played last night?" asked Ellery in a savage voice.

The Russian nodded. Inspector Queen said: "We're rounding 'em up. It seems that Orr, the Duke, and four other men had a sort of poker club, and met in Orr's back room there every Saturday night and played till all hours. Looked over that back room, but there's nothing there except the cards and chips. When Orr didn't come home Mrs. Orr got frightened and called up the Duke—he lives at some squirty little hotel in the Forties—the Duke called for her, they came down here this morning. . . . This is what they found." The Inspector eyed Martin Orr's corpse and the débris of glass surrounding him with gloom, almost with resentment. "Crazy, isn't it?"

Ellery glanced at Mrs. Orr; she was leaning against a counter, frozen-faced, tearless, staring down at her husband's body as if she could not believe her eyes. Actually, there was little to see: for Dr. Prouty had flung outspread sheets of a Sunday newspaper over the body, and only the left hand—still clutching the amethyst—was visible.

"Unbelievably so," said Ellery dryly. "I suppose there's a desk in the back room where Orr kept his accounts?"

"Sure."

"Any paper on Orr's body?"

4

"Paper?" repeated the Inspector in bewilderment. "Why, no."

"Pencil or pen?"

"No. Why, for heaven's sake?"

Before Ellery could reply, a little old man with a face like wrinkled brown papyrus pushed past a detective at the front door; he walked like a man in a dream. His gaze fixed on the shapeless bulk and the bloodstains. Then, incredibly, he blinked four times and began to cry. His wizened frame jerked with sobs. Mrs. Orr awoke from her trance; she cried: "Oh, Sam, Sam!" and putting her arms around the newcomer's racked shoulders, began to weep with him.

Ellery and the Inspector looked at each other, and Sergeant Velie belched his disgust. Then the Inspector grasped the crying man's little arm and shook him. "Here, stop that!" he said gruffly. "Who are you?"

The man raised his tear-stained face from Mrs. Orr's shoulder; he blubbered: "S-Sam Mingo, S-Sam Mingo, Mr. Orr's assistant. Who—who—Oh, I can't believe it!" and he buried his face in Mrs. Orr's shoulder again.

"Got to let him cry himself out, I guess," said the Inspector, shrugging. "Ellery, what the deuce do you make of it? I'm stymied."

Ellery raised his eyebrows eloquently. A detective appeared in the street-door escorting a pale, trembling man. "Here's Arnold Pike, Chief. Dug him out of bed just now."

Pike was a man of powerful physique and jutting jaw; but he was thoroughly unnerved and, somehow, bewildered. He fastened his eyes on the heap which represented Martin Orr's mortal remains and kept mechanically buttoning and unbuttoning his overcoat. The Inspector said: "I understand you and a few others played poker in the back room here last night. With Orr. What time did you break up?"

"Twelve-thirty." Pike's voice wabbled drunkenly.

"What time did you start?"

"Around eleven."

"Cripes," said Inspector Queen, "that's not a poker game, that's a game of tiddledywinks. . . . Who killed Orr, Mr. Pike?"

Arnold Pike tore his eyes from the corpse. "God, sir, I don't know."

"You don't, hey? All friends, were you?"

"Yes. Oh, yes."

"What's your business, Mr. Pike?"

"I'm a stock-broker."

"Why—" began Ellery, and stopped. Under the urging of two detectives, three men advanced into the shop—all frightened, all exhibiting evidences of hasty awakening and hasty dressing, all fixing their eyes at once on the paper-covered bundle on the floor, the streaks of blood, the shattered glass. The three, like the incredible ex-Duke Paul, who was straight and stiff and somehow ridiculous, seemed petrified; men crushed by a sudden blow.

A small fat man with brilliant eyes muttered that he was Stanley Oxman, jeweler. Martin Orr's oldest, closest friend. He could not believe it. It was frightful, unheard of. Martin murdered! No, he could offer no explanation. Martin had been a peculiar man, perhaps, but as far as he, Oxman, knew the curio dealer had not had an enemy in the world. And so on, and so on, as the other two stood by, frozen, waiting their turn.

One was a lean, debauched fellow with the mark of the ex-athlete about him. His slight paunch and yellowed eyeballs could not conceal the signs of a vigorous prime. This was, said Oxman, their mutual friend, Leo Gurney, the newspaper feature-writer. The other was J.D. Vincent, said Oxman—developing an unexpected streak of talkativeness which the Inspector fanned gently—who, like Arnold Pike, was in Wall Street—"a manipulator," whatever that was. Vincent, a stocky man with the gambler's tight face, seemed incapable of speech; as for Gurney, he seemed glad that Oxman had constituted himself spokesman and kept staring at the body on the cement floor.

Ellery sighed, thought of his warm bed, put down the rebellion in his breakfastless stomach, and went to work—keeping an ear cocked for the Inspector's sharp questions and the halting replies. Ellery followed the streaks of blood to the spot where Orr had ravished the case of gems. The case, its glass front smashed, little frazzled splinters framing the orifice, contained more than a dozen metal trays floored with black velvet, set in two rows. Each held scores of gems—a brilliant array of semi-precious and precious stones beautifully variegated in color. Two trays in the center of the front row attracted his eye particularly—one containing highly polished stones of red, brown, yellow, and green; the other a single variety, all of a subtranslucent quality, leek-green in color, and covered with small red spots. Ellery noted that both these trays were in direct line with the place where Orr's hand had smashed the glass case.

He went over to the trembling little assistant, Sam Mingo, who had quieted down and was standing by Mrs. Orr, clutching her hand like a child. "Mingo," he said, touching the man. Mingo started with a leap of his stringy muscles. "Don't be alarmed, Mingo. Just step over here with me for a moment." Ellery smiled reassuringly, took the man's arm, and led him to the shattered case.

And Ellery said: "How is it that Martin Orr bothered with such trifles as these? I see rubies here, and emeralds, but the others. . . . Was he a jeweler as well as a curio dealer?"

Orr's assistant mumbled: "No. N-no, he was not. But he always liked the baubles. The baubles, he called them. Kept them for love. Most of them are birthstones. He sold a few. This is a complete line."

"What are those green stones with the red spots?"

"Bloodstones."

"And this tray of red, brown, yellow, and green ones?"

"All jaspers. The common ones are red, brown, and yellow. The few green ones in the tray are more valuable. . . . The bloodstone is itself a variety of jasper. Beautiful! And . . ."

"Yes, yes," said Ellery hastily. "From which tray did the amethyst in Orr's hand come, Mingo?"

Mingo shivered and pointed a crinkled forefinger to a tray in the rear row, at the corner of the case.

"*All* the amethysts are kept in this one tray?"

"Yes. You can see for yourself—"

"Here!" growled the Inspector, approaching. "Mingo! I want you to look over the stock. Check everything. See if anything's been stolen."

"Yes, sir," said Orr's assistant timidly, and began to potter about the shop with lagging steps. Ellery looked about. The door to the back room was twenty-five feet from the spot where Orr had been assaulted. No desk in the shop itself, he observed, no paper about. . . .

"Well, son," said the Inspector in troubled tones, "it looks as if we're on the trail of something. I don't like it. . . . Finally dragged it out of these birds. I *thought* it was funny, this business of breaking up a weekly Saturday night poker game at half-past twelve. They had a fight!"

"Who engaged in fisticuffs with whom?"

"Oh, don't be funny. It's this Pike feller, the stockbroker. Seems

7

they all had something to drink during the game. They played stud, and Orr, with an ace-king-queen-jack showing, raised the roof off the play. Everybody dropped out except Pike; he had three sixes. Well, Orr gave it everything he had and when Pike threw his cards away on a big over-raise, Orr cackled, showed his hole-card—a deuce!—and raked in the pot. Pike, who'd lost his pile on the hand, began to grumble; he and Orr had words—you know how those things start. They were all pie-eyed, anyway, says the Duke. Almost a fist-fight. The others interfered, but it broke up the game."

"They all left together?"

"Yes. Orr stayed behind to clean up the mess in the backroom. The five others went out together and separated a few blocks away. Any one of 'em could have come back and pulled off the job before Orr shut up shop!"

"And what does Pike say?"

"What the deuce would you expect him to say? That he went right home and to bed, of course."

"The others?"

"They deny any knowledge of what happened after they left here last night. . . . Well, Mingo? Anything missing?"

Mingo said helplessly: "Everything seems all right."

"I thought so," said the Inspector with satisfaction. "This is a grudge kill, son. Well, I want to talk to these fellers some more. . . . What's eating you?"

Ellery lighted a cigarette. "A few random thoughts. Have you decided in your own mind why Orr dragged himself about the shop when he was three-quarters dead, broke the glass-domed clock, pulled an amethyst out of the gem-case?"

"That," said the Inspector, the troubled look returning, "is what I'm foggy about. I can't— 'Scuse me." He returned hastily to the waiting group of men.

Ellery took Mingo's lax arm. "Get a grip on yourself, man. I want to you to look at that smashed clock for a moment. Don't be afraid of Orr—dead men don't bite, Mingo." He pushed the little assistant toward the paper-covered corpse. "Now tell me something about that clock. Has it a history?"

"Not much of one. It's a h-hundred and sixty-nine years old. Not especially valuable. Curious piece because of the glass dome over it.

Happens to be the only glass-domed clock we have. That's all."

Ellery polished the lenses of his *pince-nez*, set the glasses firmly on his nose, and bent over to examine the fallen clock. It had a black wooden base, cirular, about nine inches deep, and scarified with age. On this the clock was set—ticking away cosily. The dome of glass had fitted into a groove around the top of the black base, sheathing the clock completely. With the dome unshattered, the entire piece must have stood about two feet high.

Ellery rose, and his lean face was thoughtful. Mingo looked at him in a sort of stupid anxiety. "Did Pike, Oxman, Vincent, Gurney, or Paul ever own this piece?"

Mingo shook his head. "No, sir. We've had it for many years. We couldn't get rid of it. Certainly *those* gentlemen didn't want it."

"Then none of the five ever tried to purchase the clock?"

"Of course not."

"Admirable," said Ellery. "Thank you." Mingo felt that he had been dismissed; he hesitated, shuffled his feet, and finally went over to the silent widow and stood by her side. Ellery knelt on the cement floor and with difficulty loosened the grip of the dead man's fingers about the amethyst. He saw that the stone was a clear glowing purple in color, shook his head as if in perplexity, and rose.

Vincent, the stocky Wall Street gambler with the tight face, was saying to the Inspector in a rusty voice: "—can't see why you suspect any of us. Pike particularly. What's in a little quarrel? We've always been good friends, all of us. Last night we were pickled—"

"Sure," said the Inspector gently. "Last night you were pickled. A drunk sort of forgets himself at times, Vincent. Liquor affects a man's morals as well as his head."

"Nuts!" said the yellow-eyeballed Gurney suddenly. "Stop sleuthing, Inspector. You're barking up the wrong tree. Vincent's right. We're all friends. It was Pike's birthday last week." Ellery stood very still. "We all sent him gifts. Had a celebration, and Orr was the cockiest of us all. Does that look like the preparation for a pay-off?"

Ellery stepped forward, and his eyes were shining. All his temper had fled by now, and his nostrils were quivering with the scent of the chase. "And when was this celebration held, gentlemen?" he asked softly.

Stanley Oxman puffed out his cheeks. "Now they're going to suspect a birthday blowout! Last Monday, mister. This past Monday. What of it?"

"This past Monday," said Ellery. "How nice. Mr. Pike, your gifts—"

"For God's sake. . . ." Pike's eyes were tortured.

"When did you receive them?"

"After the party, during the week. Boys sent them up to me. I didn't see any of them until last night, at the poker game."

The others nodded their heads in concert; the Inspector was looking at Ellery with puzzlement. Ellery grinned, adjusted his *pince-nez*, and spoke to his father aside. The weight of the Inspector's puzzlement, if his face was a scale, increased. But he said quietly to the white-haired broker: "Mr. Pike, you're going to take a little trip with Mr. Queen and Sergeant Velie. Just for a few moments. The others of you stay here with me. Mr. Pike, please remember not to try anything—foolish."

Pike was incapable of speech; his head twitched sidewise and he buttoned his coat for the twentieth time. Nobody said anything. Sergeant Velie took Pike's arm, and Ellery preceded them into the early-morning peace of Fifth Avenue. On the sidewalk he asked Pike his address, the broker dreamily gave him a street-and-number, Ellery hailed a taxicab, and the three men were driven in silence to an apartment-building a mile farther uptown. They took a self-service elevator to the seventh floor, marched a few steps to a door, Pike fumbled with a key, and they went into his apartment.

"Let me see your gifts, please," said Ellery without expression—the first words uttered since they had stepped into the taxicab. Pike led them to a den-like room. On a table stood four boxes of different shapes, and a handsome silver cup. "There," he said in a cracked voice.

Ellery went swiftly to the table. He picked up the silver cup. On it was engraved the sentimental legend:

> *To a True Friend*
> ARNOLD PIKE
> *March 1, 1876, to—*
> *J.D. Vincent*

"Rather macabre humor, Mr. Pike," said Ellery, setting the cup down, "since Vincent has had space left for the date of your demise." Pike began to speak, then shivered and clamped his pale lips together.

Ellery removed the lid of a tiny black box. Inside, imbedded in a cleft between two pieces of purple velvet, there was a man's signet-ring, a magnificent and heavy circlet the signet of which revealed the coat-of-arms of royalist Russia. "The tattered old eagle," murmured Ellery. "Let's see what our friend the ex-Duke has to say." On a card in the box, inscribed in minute script, the following was written in French:

> To my good friend Arnold Pike on his 50th birthday. March the first ever makes me sad. I remember that day in 1917— two weeks before the Czar's abdication—the quiet, then the storm. . . . But be merry, Arnold! Accept this signet-ring given to me by my royal Cousin, as a token of my esteem. Long life!
>
> *Paul*

Ellery did not comment. He restored ring and card to the box, and picked up another, a large flat packet. Inside there was a gold-tipped Morocco-leather wallet. The card tucked into one of the pockets said:

> "Twenty-one years of life's rattle
> And men are no longer boys
> They gird their loins for the battle
> And throw away their toys—
>
> "But here's a cheerful plaything
> For a white-haired old mooncalf,
> Who may act like any May-thing
> For nine years more and a half!"

"Charming verse," chuckled Ellery. "Another misbegotten poet. Only a newspaper man would indite such nonsense. This is Gurney's?"

"Yes," muttered Pike. "It's nice, isn't it?"

"If you'll pardon me," said Ellery, "it's rotten." He threw aside the wallet and seized a larger carton. Inside there was a glittering pair of patent-leather carpet slippers; the card attached read:

> Happy Birthday, Arnold! May We Be All Together On as Pleasant a March First to Celebrate Your 100th Anniversary!
>
> *Martin*

"A poor prophet," said Ellery dryly. "And what's this?" He laid the shoebox down and picked up a small flat box. In it he saw a gold-plated cigarette case, with the initials *A.P.* engraved on the lid. The accompanying card read:

Good luck on your fiftieth birthday. I look forward to your sixtieth on March first, 1936, for another bout of whoopee!

Stanley Oxman

"And Mr. Stanley Oxman," remarked Ellery, putting down the cigarette case, "was a little less sanguine than Martin Orr. His imagination reached no further than sixty, Mr. Pike. A significant point."

"I can't see—" began the broker in a stubborn little mutter, "why you have to bring my friends into it—"

Sergeant Velie gripped his elbow, and he winced. Ellery shook his head disapprovingly at the man-mountain. "And now, Mr. Pike, I think we may return to Martin Orr's shop. Or, as the Sergeant might fastidiously phrase it, the scene of the crime. . . . Very interesting. *Very* interesting. It almost compensates for an empty belly."

"You got something?" whispered Sergeant Velie hoarsely as Pike preceded them into a taxicab downstairs.

"Cyclops," said Ellery, "all God's chillun got something. But *I* got everything."

Sergeant Velie disappeared somewhere *en route* to the curio shop, and Arnold Pike's spirits lifted at once. Ellery eyed him quizzically. "One thing, Mr. Pike," he said as the taxicab turned into Fifth Avenue, "before we disembark. How long have you six men been acquainted?"

The broker sighed. "It's complicated. My only friend of considerable duration is Leo; Gurney, you know. Known each other for fifteen years. But then Orr and the Duke have been friends since 1918, I understand, and of course Stan Oxman and Orr have known each other—knew each other—for many years. I met Vincent about a year ago through my business affiliations and introduced him into our little clique."

"Had you yourself and the others—Oxman, Orr, Paul—been acquainted before this time two years ago?"

12

Pike looked puzzled. "I don't see . . . Why, no. I met Oxman and the Duke a year and a half ago through Orr."

"And that," murmured Ellery, "is so perfect that I don't care if I *never* have breakfast. Here we are, Mr. Pike."

They found a glum group awaiting their return—nothing had changed, except that Orr's body had disappeared, Dr. Prouty was gone, and some attempt at sweeping up the glass fragments of the domed clock had been made. The Inspector was in a fever of impatience, demanded to know where Sergeant Velie was, what Ellery had sought in Pike's apartment. . . . Ellery whispered something to him, and the old man looked startled. Then he dipped his fingers into his brown snuff-box and partook with grim relish.

The regal expatriate cleared his bull throat. "You have mystery re-solved?" he rumbled. "Yuss?"

"Your Highness," said Ellery gravely, "I have indeed mystery re-solved." He whirled and clapped his palms together; they jumped. "Attention, please! Piggot," he said to a detective, "stand at that door and don't let any one in but Sergeant Velie."

The detective nodded. Ellery studied the faces about him. If one of them was apprehensive, he had ample control of his physiognomy. They all seemed merely interested, now that the first shock of the tragedy had passed them by. Mrs. Orr clung to Mingo's fragile hand; her eyes did not once leave Ellery's face. The fat little jeweler, the journalist, the two Wall Street men, the Russian ex-duke . . .

"An absorbing affair," grinned Ellery, "and quite elementary, despite its points of interest. Follow me closely." He went over to the counter and picked up the purple amethyst which had been clutched in the dead man's hand. He looked at it and smiled. Then he glanced at the other object on the counter—the round-based clock, with the fragments of its glass dome protruding from the circular groove.

"Consider the situation. Martin Orr, brutally beaten about the head, managed in a last desperate living action to crawl to the jewel-case on the counter, pick out this gem, then go to the stone pedestal and pull the glass-domed clock from it. Whereupon, his mysterious mission accomplished, he dies.

"Why should a dying man engage in such a baffling procedure? There can be only one general explanation. He knows his assailant and is endeavoring to leave clues to his assailant's identity." At this point the Inspector nodded, and Ellery grinned again behind the curling smoke of his cigarette. "But such clues! Why? Well, what would you expect a dying man to do if he wished to leave behind him the name of his murderer? The answer is obvious: he would write it. But on Orr's body we find no paper, pen, or pencil; and no paper in the immediate vicinity. Where else might he secure writing materials? Well, you will observe that Martin Orr was assaulted at a spot twenty-five feet from the door of the back room. The distance, Orr must have felt, was too great for his failing strength. Then Orr couldn't write the name of his murderer except by the somewhat fantastic method of dipping his finger into his own blood and using the floor as a slate. Such an expedient probably didn't occur to him.

"He must have reasoned with rapidity, life ebbing out of him at every breath. Then—he crawled to the case, broke the glass, took out the amethyst. Then—he crawled to the pedestal and dragged off the glass-domed clock. Then—he died. So the amethyst and the clock were Martin Orr's bequest to the police. You can almost hear him say: 'Don't fail me. This is clear, simple, easy. Punish my murderer.'"

Mrs. Orr gasped, but the expression on her wrinkled face did not alter. Mingo began to sniffle. The others waited in total silence.

"The clock first," said Ellery lazily. "The first thing one thinks of in connection with a timepiece is time. Was Orr trying, then, by dragging the clock off the pedestal, to smash the works and, stopping the clock, so fix the time of his murder? Offhand a possibility, it is true; but if this was his purpose, it failed, because the clock didn't stop running after all. While this circumstance does not invalidate the time-interpretation, further consideration of the whole problem does. For you five gentlemen had left Orr in a body. The time of the assault could not possibly be so checked against your return to your several residences as to point inescapably to one of you as the murderer. Orr must have realized this, if he thought of it at all; in other words, there wouldn't be any particular *point* to such a purpose on Orr's part.

"And there is still another—and more conclusive—consideration that invalidates the time-interpretation; and that is, that Orr crawled *past* a table full of running clocks to get to this glass-domed one. If it had been time he was intending to indicate, he could have preserved his energies by stopping at this table and pulling down one of the many clocks upon it. But no—he deliberately passed that table to get to the *glass-domed* clock. So it wasn't time.

14

"Very well. Now, since the glass-domed clock is *the only one* of its kind in the shop, it must have been not time in the general sense but this particular timepiece in the specific sense by which Martin Orr was motivated. But what could this particular timepiece possibly indicate? In itself, as Mr. Mingo has informed me, it has no personal connotation with any one connected with Orr. The idea that Orr was leaving a clue to a clockmaker is unsound; none of you gentlemen follows that delightful craft, and certainly Mr. Oxman, the jeweler, could not have been indicated when so many things in the gem-case would have served."

Oxman began to perspire; he fixed his eyes on the jewel in Ellery's hand.

"Then it wasn't a professional meaning from the clock, as a clock," continued Ellery equably, "that Orr was trying to convey. But what is there about this particular clock which is different from the other clocks in the shop?" Ellery shot his forefinger forward. "This particular clock has a glass dome over it!" He straightened slowly. "Can any of you gentlemen think of a fairly common object almost perfectly suggested by a glass-domed clock?"

No one answered, but Vincent and Pike began to lick their lips. "I see signs of intelligence," said Ellery. "Let me be more specific. What is it—I feel like Sam Lloyd!—that has a base, a glass dome, and ticking machinery inside the dome?" Still no answer. "Well," said Ellery, "I suppose I should have expected reticence. Of course, *it's a stock-ticker!*"

They stared at him, and then all eyes turned to examine the whitening faces of J. D. Vincent and Arnold Pike. "Yes," said Ellery, "you may well gaze upon the countenances of the *Messieurs* Vincent and Pike. For they are the only two of our little cast who are connected with stock-tickers: Mr. Vincent is a Wall Street operator, Mr. Pike is a broker." Quietly two detectives left a wall and approached the two men.

"Whereupon," said Ellery, "we lay aside the glass-domed clock and take up this very fascinating little bauble in my hand." He held up the amethyst. "A purple amethyst—there are bluish-violet ones, you know. What could this purple amethyst have signified to Martin Orr's frantic brain? The obvious thing is that it is a jewel. Mr. Oxman looked disturbed a moment ago; you needn't be, sir. The jewelry significance of this amethyst is eliminated on two counts. The first is that the tray on which the amethysts lie is in a corner at the rear of the shattered case. It was necessary for Orr to reach far into the case. If it was a jewel he sought, why didn't he pick any one of the stones nearer to his palsied hand? For any single one of them would connote 'jeweler.' But no; Orr went to the excruciating trouble of ignoring what was close at hand—as in the business of the clock—and deliberately selected something from an inconvenient place. Then the amethyst did not signify a jeweler, but something else.

"The second is this, Mr. Oxman: certainly Orr knew that the stock-ticker clue would not fix guilt on *one* person; for two of his cronies are connected with stocks. On the other hand, did Orr have two assailants rather than one? Not likely. For if by the amethyst he meant to connote you, Mr. Oxman, and by the glass-domed clock he meant to connote either Mr. Pike or Mr. Vincent, he was still leaving a wabbly trail; for we still would not know whether Mr. Pike or Mr. Vincent was meant. Did he have *three* assailants, then? You see, we are already in the realm of fantasy. No, the major probability is that, since the glass-domed clock cut the possibilities down to two persons, the amethyst was meant to single out one of those two.

"How does the amethyst pin one of these gentlemen down? What significance besides the obvious one of jewelry does the amethyst suggest? Well, it is a rich purple in color. Ah, but one of your coterie fits here: His Highness the ex-Duke is certainly one born to the royal purple, even if it is an ex-ducal purple, as it were. . . ."

The soldierly Russian growled: "I am *not* Highness. You know nothing of royal address!" His dark face became suffused with blood, and he broke into a volley of guttural Russian.

Ellery grinned. "Don't excite yourself—Your Grace, is it? *You* weren't meant. For if we postulate you, we again drag in a third person and leave unsettled the question of which Wall Street man Orr meant to accuse; we're no better off than before. Avaunt, royalty!

"Other possible significances? Yes. There is a species of humming-bird, for instance, known as the amethyst. Out! We have no aviarists here. For another thing, the amethyst was connected with ancient Hebrew ritual—an Orientalist told me this once—breastplate decoration of the high priest, or some such thing. Obviously inapplicable here. No, there is only one other possible application." Elley turned to the stocky gambler. "Mr. Vincent, what is your birthdate?"

Vincent stammered: "November s-second."

"Splendid. That eliminates *you*." Ellery stopped abruptly. There was a stir at the door and Sergeant Velie barged in with a very grim face. Ellery smiled. "Well, Sergeant, was my hunch about motive correct?"

Velie said: "And how. He forged Orr's signature to a big check. Money-trouble, all right. Orr hushed the matter up, paid, and said he'd collect from the forger. The banker doesn't even know who the forger is."

"Congratulations are in order, Sergeant. Our murderer evidently wished to evade repayment. Murders have been committed for less vital reasons." Ellery flourished his *pince-nez*. "I said, Mr. Vincent, that you are eliminated. Eliminated because the only other significance of the amethyst left to us is that it is a *birthstone*. But the November birth-stone is a topaz. On the other hand, Mr. Pike has just celebrated a birthday which. . . ."

And with these words, as Pike gagged and the others broke into excited gabble, Ellery made a little sign to Sergeant Velie, and himself leaped forward. But it was not Arnold Pike who found himself in the crushing grip of Velie and staring into Ellery's amused eyes.

It was the newspaper man, Leo Gurney.

"As I said," explained Ellery later, in the privacy of the Queens' living-room and after his belly had been comfortably filled with food, "this has been a ridiculously elementary problem." The Inspector toasted his stockinged feet before the fire, and grunted. Sergeant Velie scratched his head. "You don't think so?"

"But look. It was evident, when I decided what the clues of the clock and the amethyst were intended to convey, that Arnold Pike was the man meant to be indicated. For what is the month of which the amethyst is the birth-stone? *February*—in both the Polish and Jewish birth-stone systems, the two almost universally recognized. Of the two men indicated by the clock-clue, Vincent was eliminated because his birthstone is a topaz. Was Pike's birthday then in February? Seemingly not, for he celebrated it—this year, 1926—in March! March first, observe. What could this mean? Only one thing: since Pike was the sole remaining possibility, then his birthday *was* in February, but on the *twenty-ninth*, on Leap Day, as it's called, and 1926 not being a Leap Year, Pike chose to celebrate his birthday on the day on which it would ordinarily fall, March first.

"But this meant that Martin Orr, to have left the amethyst, must have known Pike's birthday to be in February, since he seemingly left the February birthstone as a clue. Yet what did I find on the card accompanying Orr's gift of carpet-slippers to Pike last week? 'May we all be together on as pleasant a *March first* to celebrate your hundredth anniversary.' But if Pike is fifty years old in 1926, he was born in 1876—a Leap Year—and his hundredth anniversary would be 1976, also a Leap Year. They *wouldn't* celebrate Pike's birthday on his hundredth anniversary on March first! Then Orr *didn't* know Pike's real birthday was February twenty-ninth, or he would have said so on the card. He thought it was March.

"But the person who left the amethyst sign *did* know Pike's birth-month was February, since he left February's birth-stone. We've just established that Martin Orr didn't know Pike's birth-month was February, but thought it was March. Therefore Martin Orr was not the one who selected the amethyst.

"Any confirmation? Yes. The birth-stone for March in the Polish system is the bloodstone; in the Jewish it's the jasper. But both these stones were nearer a groping hand than the amethysts, which lay in a tray at the back of the case. In other words, whoever selected the amethyst deliberately ignored the March stones in favor of the February stone, and therefore knew that Pike was born in February, not in March. But had Orr selected a stone, it would have been bloodstone or jasper, since he believed Pike *was* born in March. Orr eliminated again.

"But if Orr did not select the amethyst, as I've shown, then what have we? Palpably, a frame-up. Some one arranged matters to make us believe that Orr himself had selected the amethyst and smashed the clock. You can see the murderer dragging poor old Orr's dead body around, leaving the blood-trail on purpose. . . ."

Ellery sighed. "I never did believe Orr left those signs. It was all too pat, too slick, too weirdly unreal. It is conceivable that a dying man will leave one clue to his murderer's identity, but *two.* . . ." Ellery shook his head.

"If Orr didn't leave the clues, who did? Obviously the murderer. But the clues deliberately led to Arnold Pike. Then Pike couldn't be the murderer, for certainly he would not leave a trail to himself had he killed Orr.

"Who else? Well, one thing stood out. Whoever killed Orr, framed Pike, and really selected that amethyst, knew Pike's birthday to be in

February. Orr and Pike we have eliminated. Vincent didn't know Pike's birthday was in February, as witness his inscription on the silver cup. Nor did our friend the ex-Duke, who also wrote 'March the first' on his card. Oxman didn't—he said they'd celebrate Pike's sixtieth birthday on March first, 1936—a Leap Year, observe, when Pike's birthday would be celebrated on February twenty-ninth. . . . Don't forget that we may accept these cards' evidence as valid; the cards were sent before the crime, and the crime would have no connection in the murderer's mind with Pike's five birthday-cards. The flaw in the murderer's plot was that he assumed—a natural error—that Orr and perhaps the others, too, knew Pike's birthday really fell on Leap Day. And he never did see the cards which proved the others didn't know, because Pike himself told us that after the party Monday night he did not see any of the others until last night, the night of the murder."

"I'll be fried in lard," muttered Sergeant Velie, shaking his head.

"No doubt," grinned Ellery. "But we've left some one out. How about Leo Gurney, the newspaper feature-writer? His stick o' doggerel said that Pike wouldn't reach the age of twenty-one for another nine and a half years. Interesting? Yes, and damning. For this means he considered facetiously that Pike was at the time of writing eleven and a half years old. But how is this possible, even in humorous verse? It's possible only if Gurney knew that Pike's birthday falls on February twenty-ninth, which occurs only once in four years! Fifty divided by four is twelve and a half. But since the year 1900 for some reason I've never been able to discover, was not a Leap Year, Gurney was right, and actually Pike had celebrated only 'eleven and a half' birthdays."

And Ellery drawled: "Being the only one who knew Pike's birthday to be in February, then Gurney was the only one who could have selected the amethyst. Then Gurney arranged matters to make it seem that Orr was accusing Pike. Then Gurney was the murderer of Orr. . . .

"Simple? As a child's sum!"

THE BEARDED LADY

(1934)

MR. PHINEAS MASON, attorney-at-law—of the richly, almost indigestibly respectable firm of *Dowling, Mason & Coolidge*, 40 Park Row—was a very un-Phineaslike gentleman with a chunky nose and wrinkle-bedded eyes which had seen thirty years of harassing American litigation and looked as if they had seen a hundred. He sat stiffly in the lap of a chauffeur-driven limousine, his mouth making interesting sounds.

"And now," he said in an angry voice, "there's actually been murder done. I can't imagine what the world is coming to."

Mr. Ellery Queen, watching the world rush by in a glaring Long Island sunlight, mused that life was like a Spanish wench: full of surprises, none of them delicate and all of them stimulating. Since he was a monastic who led a riotous mental existence, he liked life that way; and since he was also a detective—an appellation he cordially detested—he got life that way. Nevertheless, he did not vocalize his reflections: Mr. Phineas Mason did not appear the sort who would appreciate fleshly metaphor.

He drawled: "The world's all right; the trouble is the people in it. Suppose you tell me what you can about these curious Shaws. After all, you know, I shan't be too heartily received by your local Long Island constabulary; and since I foresee difficulties, I should like to be forearmed as well."

Mason frowned. "But McC. assured me—"

"Oh, bother J. J.! He has vicarious delusions of grandeur. Let me

20

warn you now, Mr. Mason, that I shall probably be a dismal flop. I don't go about pulling murderers out of my hat. And with your Cossacks trampling the evidence—"

"I warned them," said Mason fretfully. "I spoke to Captain Murch myself when he telephoned this morning to inform me of the crime." He made a sour face. "They won't even move the body, Mr. Queen. I wield—ah—a little local influence, you see."

"Indeed," said Ellery, adjusting his *pince-nez*; and he sighed. "Very well, Mr. Mason. Proceed with the dreary details."

"It was my partner, Coolidge," began the attorney in a pained voice, "who originally handled Shaw's affairs. John A. Shaw, the millionaire. Before your time, I daresay. Shaw's first wife died in childbirth in 1895. The child—Agatha; she's a divorcee now, with a son of eight—of course survived her mother; and there was one previous child, named after his father. John's forty-five now. . . . At any rate, old John Shaw remarried soon after his first wife's death, and then shortly after his second marriage died himself. This second wife, Maria Paine Shaw, survived her husband by a little more than thirty years. She died only a month ago."

"A plethora of mortalities," murmured Ellery, lighting a cigarette. "So far, Mr. Mason, a prosaic tale. And what has the Shaw history to do—"

"Patience," sighed Mason. "Now old John Shaw bequeathed his entire fortune to this second wife, Maria. The two children, John and Agatha, got nothing, not even trusts; I suppose old Shaw trusted Maria to take care of them."

"I scent the usual story," yawned Ellery. "She didn't? No go between stepmother and acquired progeny?"

The lawyer wiped his brow. "It was horrible. They fought for thirty years like—like savages. I will say, in extenuation of Mrs. Shaw's conduct, that she had provocation. John's always been a shiftless, unreliable beggar: disrespectful, profligate, quite vicious. Nevertheless she's treated him well in money matters. As I said, he's forty-five now; and he hasn't done a lick of work in his life. He's a drunkard, too."

"Sounds charming. And Sister Agatha, the divorcee?"

"A feminine edition of her brother. She married a fortune-hunter as worthless as herself; when he found out she was penniless he deserted

21

her and Mrs. Shaw managed to get her a quiet divorce. She took Agatha and her boy, Peter, into her house and they've been living there ever since, at daggers' points. Please forgive the—ah—brutality of the characterizations; I want you to know these people as they are."

"We're almost intimate already," chuckled Ellery.

"John and Agatha," continued Mason, biting the head of his cane, "have been living for only one event—their stepmother's death. So that they might inherit, of course. Until a certain occurrence a few months ago Mrs. Shaw's will provided generously for them. But when that happened—"

Mr. Ellery Queen narrowed his gray eyes. "You mean—?"

"It's complicated," sighed the lawyer. "Three months ago there was an attempt on the part of someone in the household to poison the old lady!"

"Ah!"

"The attempt was unsuccessful only because Dr. Arlen—Dr. Terence Arlen is the full name—had suspected such a possibility for years and had kept his eyes open. The cyanide—it was put in her tea—didn't reach Mrs. Shaw but killed a house-cat. None of us, of course, knew who had made the poisoning attempt. But after that Mrs. Shaw changed her will."

"Now," muttered Ellery, "I *am* enthralled. Arlen, eh? That creates a fascinating mess. Tell me about Arlen, please."

"Rather mysterious old man with two passions: devotion to Mrs. Shaw and a hobby of painting. Quite an artist, too, though I know little about such things. He lived in the Shaw house about twenty years. Medico Mrs. Shaw picked up somewhere; I think only she knew his story, and he's always been silent about his past. She put him on a generous salary to live in the house and act as the family physician; I suspect it was rather because she anticipated what her stepchildren might attempt. And then too it's always seemed to me that Arlen accepted this unusual arrangement so tractably in order to pass out of—ah—circulation."

They were silent for some time. The chauffeur swung the car off the main artery into a narrow macadam road. Mason breathed heavily.

"I suppose you're satisfied," murmured Ellery at last through a fat smoke-ring, "that Mrs. Shaw died a month ago of natural causes?"

"Heavens, yes!" cried Mason. "Dr. Arlen wouldn't trust his own judgment, we were so careful; he had several specialists in, before and after her death. But she died of the last of a series of heart-attacks; she was an old woman, you know. Something-thrombosis, they called it." Mason looked gloomy. "Well, you can understand Mrs. Shaw's natural reaction to the poisoning episode. 'If they're so depraved,' she told me shortly after, 'that they'd attempt my *life*, they don't deserve any consideration at my *hands*.' And she had me draw up a new will, cutting both of them off without a cent."

"There's an epigram," chuckled Ellery, "worthy of a better cause."

Mason tapped on the glass. "Faster, Burroughs." The car jolted ahead. "In looking about for a beneficiary, Mrs. Shaw finally remembered that there was someone to whom she could leave the Shaw fortune without feeling that she was casting it to the winds. Old John Shaw had had an elder brother, Morton, a widower with two grown children. The brothers quarrelled violently and Morton moved to England. He lost most of his money there; his two children, Edith and Percy, were left to shift for themselves when he committed suicide."

"These Shaws seem to have a penchant for violence."

"I suppose it's in the blood. Well, Edith and Percy both had talent of a sort, I understand, and they went on the London stage in a brother-and-sister music-hall act, managing well enough. Mrs. Shaw decided to leave her money to this Edith, her niece. I made inquiries by correspondence and discovered that Edith Shaw was now Mrs. Edythe Royce, a childless widow of many years' standing. On Mrs. Shaw's decease I cabled her and she crossed by the next boat. According to Mrs. Royce, Percy—her brother—was killed in an automobile accident on the Continent a few months before; so she had no ties whatever."

"And the will—specifically?"

"It's rather queer," sighed Mason. "The Shaw estate was enormous at one time, but the depression whittled it down to about three hundred thousand dollars. Mrs. Shaw left her niece two hundred thousand outright. The remainder, to his astonishment," and Mason paused and eyed his tall young companion with a curious fixity, "was put in trust for Dr. Arlen."

"Arlen!"

"He was not to touch the principal, but was to receive the income from it for the remainder of his life. Interesting, eh?"

"That's putting it mildly. By the way, Mr. Mason, I'm a suspicious bird. This Mrs. Royce—you're satisfied she *is* a Shaw?"

The lawyer started; then he shook his head. "No, no, Queen, that's the wrong tack. There can be absolutely no question about it. In the first place she possesses the marked facial characteristics of the Shaws; you'll see for yourself; although I will say that she's rather—well, rather a character, rather a character! She came armed with intimate possessions of her father, Morton Shaw; and I myself, in company with Coolidge, questioned her closely on her arrival. She convinced us utterly, from her knowledge of *minutiae* about her father's life and Edith Shaw's childhood in America—knowledge impossible for an outsider to have acquired—that she *is* Edith Shaw. We were more than cautious, I assure you; especially since neither John nor Agatha had seen her since childhood."

"Just a thought." Ellery leaned forward. "And what was to be the disposition of Arlen's hundred-thousand-dollar trust on Arlen's death?"

The lawyer gazed grimly at the two rows of prim poplars flanking a manicured driveway on which the limousine was now noiselessly treading. "It was to be equally divided between John and Agatha," he said in a careful voice. The car rolled to a stop under a coldly white *porte-cochère*.

"I see," said Ellery. For it was Dr. Terence Arlen who had been murdered.

A country trooper escorted them through high Colonial halls into a remote and silent wing of the ample old house, up a staircase to a dim cool corridor patrolled by a nervous man with a bull neck.

"Oh, Mr. Mason," he said eagerly, coming forward. "We've been waiting for you. This is Mr. Queen?" His tone changed from unguent haste to abrasive suspicion.

"Yes, yes. Murch of the county detectives, Mr. Queen. You've left everything intact, Murch?"

The detective grunted and stepped aside. Ellery found himself in the study of what appeared to be a two-room suite; beyond an open door he could see the white counterpane of a bird's-eye-maple four-poster. A hole at some remote period had been hacked through the ceiling and covered with glass, admitting sunlight and coverting the room into a sky-light studio. The trivia of a painter's paraphernalia lay in confusion about the room, overpowering the few medical implements. There were easels, paintboxes, a small dais, carelessly draped smocks, a profusion of daubs in oils and watercolors on the walls.

A little man was kneeling beside the outstretched figure of the dead doctor—a long brittle figure frozen in death, capped with curiously lambent silver hair. The wound was frank and deep: the delicately chased haft of a stiletto protruded from the man's heart. There was very little blood.

Murch snapped: "Well, Doc, anything else?"

The little man rose and put his instruments away. "Died instantly from the stab-wound. Frontal blow, as you see. He tried to dodge at the last instant, I should say, but wasn't quick enough." He nodded and reched for his hat and quietly went out.

Ellery shivered a little. The studio was silent, and the corridor was silent, and the wing was silent; the whole house was crushed under the weight of a terrific silence that was almost uncanny. There was something indescribably evil in the air. . . . He shook his shoulders impatiently. "The stiletto, Captain Murch. Have you identified it?"

"Belonged to Arlen. Always right here on this table."

"No possibility of suicide, I suppose."

"Not a chance, Doc said."

Mr. Phineas Mason made a retching sound. "If you want me, Queen—" He stumbled from the room, awakening dismal echoes.

The corpse was swathed in a paint-smudged smock above pajamas; in the stiff right hand a paint-brush, its hairs stained jet-black, was still clutched. A color-splashed palette had fallen face down on the floor near him. . . . Ellery did not raise his eyes from the stiletto. "Florentine, I suppose. Tell me what you've learned so far, Captain," he said absently. "I mean about the crime itself."

"Damned little," growled the detective. "Doc says he was killed about two in the morning—about eight hours ago. His body was found at seven this a.m. by a woman named Krutch, a nurse in the house here for a couple of years. Nice wench, by God! Nobody's got an alibi for the time of the murder, because according to their yarns they were all sleeping, and they all sleep separately. That's about the size of it."

"Precious little, to be sure," murmured Ellery. "By the way, Captain, was it Dr. Arlen's custom to paint in the wee hours?"

"Seems so. I thought of that, too. But he was a queer old cuss and when he was hot on something he'd work for twenty-four hours at a clip."

"Do the others sleep in this wing?"

"Nope. Not even the servants. Seems Arlen liked privacy, and whatever he liked the old dame—Mrs. Shaw, who kicked off a month ago—said 'jake' to." Murch went to the doorway and snapped: "Miss Krutch."

She came slowly out of Dr. Arlen's bedroom—a tall fair young woman who had been weeping. She was in nurse's uniform and there was nothing in common between her name and her appearance. In fact, as Ellery observed with appreciation, she was a distinctly attractive young woman with curves in precisely the right places. Miss Krutch, despite her tears, was the first ray of sunshine he had encountered in the big old house.

"Tell Mr. Queen what you told me," directed Murch curtly.

"But there's so little," she quavered. "I was up before seven, as usual. My room's in the main wing, but there's a storeroom here for linen and things. . . . As I passed I—I saw Dr. Arlen lying on the floor, with the knife sticking up— The door was open and the light was on. I screamed. No one heard me. This is so far away. . . . I screamed and screamed and then Mr. Shaw came running, and Miss Shaw. Th-that's all."

"Did any of you touch the body, Miss Krutch?"

"Oh, no, sir!" She shivered.

"I see," said Ellery, and raised his eyes from the dead man to the easel above, casually, and looked away. And then instantly he looked back, his nerves tingling. Murch watched him with a sneer.

"How," jeered Murch, "d'ye like that, *Mr.* Queen?"

Ellery sprang forward. A smaller easel near the large one supported a picture. It was a cheap "processed" oil painting, a commercial copy of Rembrandt's famous self-portrait group, *The Artist and His Wife*. Rembrandt himself sat in the foreground, and his wife stood in the background. The canvas on the large easel was a half-finished replica of this painting. Both figures had been completely sketched in by Dr. Arlen and brushwork begun: the lusty smiling mustached artist in his gayly plumed hat, his left arm about the waist of his Dutch-garbed wife.

And on the woman's chin there was painted a beard.

Ellery gaped from the processed picture to Dr. Arlen's copy. But the one showed a woman's smooth chin, and the other—the doctor's—a squarish, expertly stroked black beard. And yet it had been daubed in hastily, as if the old painter had been working against time.

"Good heavens!" exclaimed Ellery, glaring. "That's insane!"

"Think so?" said Murch blandly. "Me, I don't know. I've got a notion about it." He growled at Miss Krutch: "Beat it," and she fled from the studio, her long legs twinkling.

Ellery shook his head dazedly and sank into a chair, fumbling for a cigarette. "That's a new wrinkle to me, Captain. First time I've ever encountered in a homicide an example of the beard-and-mustache school of art—you've seen the pencilled hair on the faces of men and women in billboard advertisements? It's—" and then his eyes narrowed as something leaped into them and he said abruptly: "Is Miss Agatha Shaw's boy—that Peter—in the house?"

Murch, smiling secretly as if he were enjoying a huge jest, went to the hallway door and roared something. Ellery got out of the chair and ran across the room and returned with one of the smocks, which he flung over the dead man's body.

A small boy with frightened yet inquisitive eyes came slowly into the room, followed by one of the most remarkable creatures Ellery had ever seen. This apparition was a large stout woman of perhaps sixty, with lined rugged features—so heavy they were almost wattled—painted, bedaubed, and varnished with an astounding cosmetic technique. Her lips, gross as they were, were shaped by rouge into a perfect and obscene cupid's-bow; her eyebrows had been tweezed to incredible thinness; round rosy spots punctuated her sagging cheeks; and the whole rough heavy skin was floury with white powder.

But her costume was even more amazing than her face. For she was rigged out in Victorian style—a tight-waisted garment, almost bustle-hipped, full wide shirts that reached to her thick ankles, a deep and shiny bosom, and an elaborate boned lace choker-collar. . . . And then Ellery remembered that, since this must be Edythe Shaw Royce, there was at least a partial explanation for her eccentric appearance: she was an old woman, she came from England, and she was no doubt still basking in the vanished glow of her girlhood theatrical days.

"Mrs. Royce," said Murch mockingly, "*and* Peter."

"How d'ye do," muttered Ellery, tearing his eyes away. "Uh—Peter."

The boy, a sharp-featured and skinny little creature, sucked his dirty forefinger and stared.

"Peter!" said Mrs. Royce severely. Her voice was quite in tune with her appearance: deep and husky and slightly cracked. Even her hair, Ellery noted with a wince, was nostalgic—a precise deep brown, frankly dyed. Here was one female, at least, who did not mean to yield to old age without a determined struggle, he thought. "He's frightened. Peter!"

"Ma'am," mumbled Peter, still staring.

"Peter," said Ellery," look at that picture." Peter did so, reluctantly. "Did you put that beard on the face of the lady in the picture, Peter?"

Peter shrank against Mrs. Royce's voluminous skirts. "N-no!"

"Curious, isn't it?" said Mrs. Royce cheerfully. "I was remarking about that to Captain Burch—Murch only this morning. I'm sure Peter wouldn't have drawn the beard on *that* one. He'd learned his lesson, hadn't you, Peter?" Ellery remarked with alarm that the extraordinary woman kept screwing her right eyebrow up and drawing it deeply down, as if there were something in her eye that bothered her.

"Ah," said Ellery. "Lesson?"

"You see," went on Mrs. Royce, continuing her ocular gymnastics with unconscious vigor, "it was only yesterday that Peter's mother caught him drawing a beard with chalk on one of Dr. Arlen's paintings in Peter's bedroom. Dr. Arlen gave him a round hiding, I'm afraid, and himself removed the chalk-marks. Dear Agatha was *so* angry with poor Dr. Arlen. So you didn't do it, did you, Peter?"

"Naw," said Peter, who had become fascinated by the bulging smock on the floor.

"Dr. Arlen, eh?" muttered Ellery. "Thank you," and he began to pace up and down as Mrs. Royce took Peter by the arm and firmly removed him from the studio. A formidable lady, he thought, with her vigorous room-shaking tread. And he recalled that she wore flat-heeled shoes and had, from the ugly swelling of the leather, great bunions.

"Come on," said Murch suddenly, going to the door.

"Where?"

"Downstairs." The detective signalled a trooper to guard the studio and led the way. "I want to show you," he said as they made for the main part of the house, "the reason for the beard on that dame-in-the-picture's jaw."

"Indeed?" murmured Ellery, and said nothing more. Murch paused in the doorway of a pale Colonial livingroom and jerked his head.

Ellery looked in. A hollow-chested, cadaverous man in baggy tweeds sat slumped in a Cogswell chair staring at an empty glass in his hand, which was shaking. His eyes were yellow-balled and shot with blood, and his loose skin was a web of red veins.

"That," said Murch contempuously and yet with a certain triumph, "is Mr. John Shaw."

Ellery noted that Shaw possessed the same heavy features, the same fat lips and rock-hewn nose, as the wonderful Mrs. Royce, his cousin; and for that matter, as the dour and annoyed-looking old pirate in the portrait over the fireplace who was presumably his father.

And Ellery also noted that on Mr. John Shaw's unsteady chin there was a bedraggled, pointed beard.

Mr. Mason, a bit greenish about the jowls, was waiting for them in a sombre reception-room. "Well?" he asked in a whisper, like a supplicant before the Cumæan Sibyl.

"Captain Murch," murmured Ellery, "has a theory."

The detective scowled. "Plain as day. It's John Shaw. It's my hunch Dr. Arlen painted that beard as a clue to his killer. The only one around here with a beard is Shaw. It ain't evidence, I admit, but it's something to work on. And believe you me," he said with a snap of his brown teeth, "I'm going to work on it!"

"John," said Mason slowly. "He certainly has motive. And yet I find it difficult to. . . ." His shrewd eyes flickered. "Beard? What beard?"

"There's a beard painted on the chin of a female face upstairs," drawled Ellery, "the face being on a Rembrandt Arlen was copying at the time he was murdered. That the good doctor painted the beard himself is quite evident. It's expertly stroked, done in black oils, and in his dead hand there's still the brush tipped with black oils. There isn't any one else in the house who paints, is there?"

"No," said Mason uncomfortably.

"Voilà."

"But even if Arlen did such a—a mad thing," objected the lawyer, "how do you know it was just before he was attacked?"

"Aw," growled Murch, "when the hell else would it be?"

"Now, now, Captain," murmured Ellery, "let's be scientific. There's a perfectly good answer to your question, Mr. Mason. First, we all agree that Dr. Arlen couldn't have painted the beard *after* he was attacked; he died instantly. Therefore he must have painted it before he was attacked. The question is: How long before? Well, why did Arlen paint the beard at all?"

"Murch says as a clue to his murderer," muttered Mason. "But such a—a fantastic legacy to the police! It looks deucedly odd."

"What's odd about it?"

"Well, for heaven's sake," exploded Mason, "if he wanted to leave a clue to his murderer, why didn't he write the murderer's name on the canvas? He had the brush in his hand. . . ."

"Precisely," murmured Ellery. "A very good question, Mr. Mason. Well, why didn't he? If he was alone—that is, if he was *anticipating* his murder—he certainly would have left us a written record of his concrete suspicions. The fact that he left no such record shows that he didn't anticipate his murder before the appearance of his murderer. Therefore he painted the beard *while his murderer was present*. But now we find an explanation for the painted beard as a clue. With his murderer present, he *couldn't* paint the name; the murderer would have noticed it and destroyed it. Arlen was forced, then, to adopt a subtle means: leave a clue that would escape his killer's attention. Since he was painting at the time, he used a painter's means. Even if his murderer noticed it, he probably ascribed it to Arlen's nervousness; although the chances are he didn't notice it."

Murch stirred. "Say, listen—"

"But a beard on a woman's face," groaned the lawyer. "I tell you—"

"Oh," said Ellery dreamily, "Dr. Arlen had a precedent."

"Precedent?"

"Yes; we've found, Captain Murch and I, that young Peter in his divine innocence had chalked a beard and mustache on one of Dr. Arlen's daubs which hangs in Peter's bedroom. This was only yesterday. Dr. Arlen whaled the tar out of him for this horrible crime *vers l'art*, no doubt justifiably. But Peter's beard-scrawl must have stuck in the doctor's mind; threshing about wildly in his mind while his murderer talked to him, or threatened him, the beard business popped out at him. Apparently he felt that it told a story, because he used it. And there, of course, is the rub."

"I stil say it's all perfectly asinine," grunted Mason.

"Not asinine," said Ellery. "Interesting. He painted a beard on the chin of Rembrandt's wife. Why Rembrandt's wife, in the name of all that's wonderful?—a woman dead more than two centuries! These Shaws aren't remote descendants. . .''

"Nuts," said Murch distinctly.

"Nuts," said Ellery, "is a satisfactory word under the circumstances, Captain. Then a grim jest? Hardly. But if it wasn't Dr. Arlen's grisly notion of a joke, what under heaven was it? What did Arlen mean to convey?''

"If it wasn't so ridiculous," muttered the lawyer, "I'd say he was pointing to—Peter.''

"Nuts and double-nuts," said Murch, "begging your pardon, Mr. Mason. The kid's the only one, I guess, that's got a real alibi. It seems his mother's nervous about him and she always keeps his door locked from the outside. I found it that way myself this morning. And he couldn't have got out through the window.''

"Well, well," sighed Mason, "I'm sure I'm all at sea. John, eh. . . . What do *you* think, Mr. Queen?''

"Much as I loathe argument," said Ellery, "I can't agree with Brother Murch.''

"Oh, yeah?" jeered Murch. "I suppose you've got reasons?''

"I suppose,' said Ellery, "I have; not the least impressive of which is the dissimilar shapes of the real and painted beards.''

The detective glowered. "Well, if he didn't mean John Shaw by it, what the hell did he mean?''

Ellery shrugged. "If we knew that, my dear Captain, we should know everything.''

"Well," snarled Murch, "I think it's spinach, and I'm going to haul Mr. John Shaw down to county headquarters and pump the old bastard till I *find* it's spinach.''

"I shouldn't do that, Murch," said Ellery quickly. "If only for—''

"I know my duty," said the detective with a black look, and he stamped out of the reception-room.

John Shaw, who was quietly drunk, did not even protest when Murch shoved him into the squad car. Followed by the county morgue-truck bearing Dr. Arlen's body, Murch vanished with his prey.

Ellery took a hungry turn about the room, frowning. The lawyer sat in a crouch, gnawing his fingernails. And again the room, and the house, and the very air were charged with silence, an ominous silence.

"Look here," said Ellery sharply, "there's something in this business you haven't told me yet, Mr. Mason."

The lawyer jumped, and then sank back biting his lips. "He's such a worrisome creature," said a cheerful voice from the doorway and they both turned, startled, to find Mrs. Royce beaming in at them. She came in with the stride of a grenadier, her bosom joggling. And she sat down by Mason's side and with daintiness lifted her capacious skirts with both hands a bit above each fat knee. "I know what's troubling you, Mr. Mason!"

The lawyer cleared his throat hastily. "I assure you—"

"Nonsense! I've excellent eyes. Mason, you haven't introduced this nice young man." Mason mumbled something placative. "Queen, is it? Charmed, Mr. Queen. First sample of reasonably attractive American I've seen since my arrival. I can appreciate a handsome man; I was on the London stage for many years. And really," she thundered in her formidable baritone, "I wasn't so ill-looking myself!"

"I'm sure of that," murmured Ellery. "But what—"

"Mason's afraid for me," said Mrs. Royce with a girlish simper. "A most conscientious barrister! He's simply petrified with fear that whoever did for poor Dr. Arlen will select me as his next victim. And *I* tell him now, as I told him a few moments ago when you were upstairs with that dreadful Murch person, that for one thing I shan't be such an easy victim—" Ellery could well believe *that*—"and for another I don't believe either John or Agatha, which is what's in Mason's mind—don't deny it, Mason!—was responsible for Dr. Arlen's death."

"I never—" began the lawyer feebly.

"Hmm," said Elery. "What's *your* theory, Mrs. Royce?"

"Some one out of Arlen's past," boomed the lady with a click of her jaws as a punctuation mark. "I understand he came here twenty years ago under most mysterious circumstances. He may have murdered somebody, and that somebody's brother or some one has returned to avenge—"

"Ingenious," grinned Ellery. "As tenable as Murch's, Mr. Mason."

The lady sniffed. "He'll release Cousin John soon enough," she said complacently. "John's stupid enough under ordinary circumstances, you know, but when he's drunk—! There's no evidence, is there? A cigarette if you please, Mr. Queen."

Ellery hastened to offer his case. Mrs. Royce selected a cigarette with a vast paw, smiled roguishly as Ellery held a match, and then withdrew the cigarette and blew smoke, crossing her legs as she did so. She smoked almost in the Russian fashion, cupping her hand about the cigarette instead of holding it between two fingers. A remarkable woman! "Why are you so afraid for Mrs. Royce?" he drawled.

"Well—" Mason hesitated, torn between discretion and desire. "There may have been a double motive for killing Dr. Arlen, you see. That is," he added hurriedly, "*if* Agatha or John had anything to do—"

"Double motive?"

"One, of course, is the conversion of the hundred thousand to Mrs. Shaw's stepchildren, as I told you. The other.... Well, there is a proviso in connection with the bequest to Dr. Arlen. In return for offering him a home and income for the rest of his life, he was to continue to attend to the medical needs of the family, you see, with *special* attention to Mrs. Royce."

"Poor Aunt Maria," said Mrs. Royce with a tidal sigh. "She must have been a dear, dear person."

"I'm afraid I don't quite follow, Mr. Mason."

"I've a copy of the will in my pocket." The lawyer fished for a crackling document. "Here it is. 'And in particular to conduct monthly medical examinations of my niece, Edith Shaw—or more frequently if Dr. Arlen should deem it necessary—to insure her continued good health; a provision' (mark this, Queen!) '*a provision I am sure my stepchildren will appreciate.*' "

"A cynical addendum," nodded Ellery, blinking a little. "Mrs. Shaw placed on her trusted leech the responsibility for keeping you healthy, Mrs. Royce, suspecting that her dearly beloved stepchildren might be tempted to—er—tamper with your life. But why should they?"

For the first time something like terror invaded Mrs. Royce's massive face. She set her jaw and said, a trifle tremulously: "N-nonsense. I can't believe— Do you think it's possible they've already tr—"

"You don't feel ill, Mrs. Royce?" cried Mason, alarmed.

Under the heavy coating of powder her coarse skin was muddily pale. "No, I— Dr. Arlen was supposed to examine me for the first time tomorrow. Oh, if it's.... The food—"

"Poison was tried three months ago," quavered the lawyer. "On Mrs. Shaw, Queen, as I told you. Good God, Mrs. Royce, you'll have to be careful!"

"Come, come," snapped Ellery. "What's the point? Why should the Shaws want to poison Mrs. Royce, Mason?"

"Because," said Mason in a trembling voice, "in the event of Mrs. Royce's demise her estate is to revert to the original estate: which would automatically mean to John and Agatha." He mopped his brow.

Ellery heaved himself out of the chair and took another hungry turn about the somber room. Mrs. Royce's right eyebrow suddenly began to go up and down with nervousness.

"This needs thinking over," he said abruptly; and there was something queer in his eyes that made both of them stare at him with uneasiness. "I'll stay the night, Mr. Mason, if Mrs. Royce has no objection."

"Do," whispered Mrs. Royce in a tremble; and this time she was afraid, very plainly afraid. And over the rooms settled an impalpable dust, like a distant sign of approaching villainy. "Do you think they'll actually try . . . ?"

"It is entirely," said Ellery dryly, "within the realm of possiblity."

The day passed in a timeless haze. Unaccountably, no one came; the telephone was silent; and there was no word from Murch, so that John Shaw's fate remained obscure. Mason sat in a miserable heap on the front porch, a cigar cold in his mouth, rocking himself like a wizened old doll. Mrs. Royce retired, subdued, to her quarters. Peter was off somewhere in the gardens tormenting a dog; occasionally Miss Krutch's tearful voice reprimanded him ineffectually.

To Mr. Ellery Queen it was a painful, puzzling, and irritatingly evil time. He prowled the rambling mansion, a lost soul, smoking tasteless cigarettes and thinking. . . . That a blanket of menace hung over this house his nerves convinced him. It took all his willpower to keep his body from springing about at unheard sounds; moreover, his mind was distracted and he could not think clearly. A murderer was abroad; and this was a house of violent people.

He shivered and darted a look over his shoulder and shrugged and bent his mind fiercely to the problem at hand. . . . And after hours his thoughts grew calmer and began to range themselves in orderly rows, until it was evident that there was a beginning and an end. He grew quiet.

He smiled a little as he stopped a tiptoeing maid and inquired the location of Miss Agatha Shaw's room. Miss Shaw had wrapped herself thus far in a mantle of invisibility. It was most curious. A sense of rising drama excited him a little. . . .

A tinny female voice responded to his knock, and he opened the door to find a feminine Shaw as bony and unlovely as the masculine edition curled in a hard knot on a *chaise-longue*, staring balefully out the window. Her *négligé* was adorned with boa feathers and there were varicose veins on her swollen naked legs.

"Well," she said acidly, without turning. "What do you want?"

"My name," murmured Ellery, "is Queen, and Mr. Mason has called me in to help settle your—ah—difficulties."

She twisted her skinny neck slowly. "I've heard all about you. What do you want me to do, kiss you? I suppose it was you who instigated John's arrest. You're fools, the pack of you!"

"To the contrary, it was your worthy Captain Murch's exclusive idea to take your brother in custody, Miss Shaw. He's not formally arrested, you know. Even so, I advised strongly against it."

She sniffed, but she uncoiled the knot and drew her shapeless legs beneath her wrapper in a sudden consciousness of femininity. "Then sit down, Mr. Queen. I'll help all I can."

"On the other hand," smiled Ellery, seating himself in a gilt and Gallic atrocity, "don't blame Murch overly, Miss Shaw. There's a powerful case against your brother, you know."

"And me!"

"And," said Ellery regretfully, "you."

She raised her thin arms and cried: "Oh, how I hate this damned, damned house, that damned woman! She's the cause of all our trouble. Some day she's likely to get—"

"I suppose you're referring to Mrs. Royce. But aren't you being unfair? From Mason's story it's quite evident that there was no ghost of coercion when your stepmother willed your father's fortune to Mrs. Royce. They had never met, never corresponded, and your cousin was three thousand miles away. It's awkward for you, no doubt, but scarcely Mrs. Royce's fault."

"Fair! Who cares about fairness? She's taken our money away from us. And now we've got to stay here and—and be *fed* by her. It's intolerable, I tell you! She'll be here at least two years—trust her for that, the painted old hussy!—and all that time . . ."

"I'm afraid I don't understand. Two years?"

"That *woman's* will," snarled Miss Shaw, "provided that this precious cousin of ours come to live here and preside as mistress for a minimum of two years. That was her revenge, the despicable old witch! Whatever father saw in her . . . To 'provide a home for John and Agatha,' she said in the will, 'until they find a permanent solution of their problems.' How d'ye like that? I'll never forget those words. Our 'problems'! Oh, every time I think—" She bit her lip, eyeing him sidewise with a sudden caution.

Ellery sighed and went to the door. "Indeed? And if something should—er—drive Mrs. Royce from the house before the expiration of the required period?"

"We'd get the money, of course," she flashed with bitter triumph; her thin dark skin was greenish. "If something should happen—"

"I trust," said Ellery dryly, "that nothing will." He closed the door and stood for a moment gnawing his fingers, and then he smiled rather grimly and went downstairs to a telephone.

John Shaw returned with his escort at ten that night. His chest was hollower, his fingers shakier, his eyes bloodier; and he was sober. Murch looked like a thundercloud. The cadaverous man went into the living room and made for a full decanter. He drank alone, with steady mechanical determination. No one disturbed him.

"Nothing," growled Murch to Ellery and Mason.

At twelve the house was asleep.

The first alarm was sounded by Miss Krutch. It was almost one when she ran down the upper corridor screaming at the top of her voice: "Fire! Fire! Fire!" Thick smoke was curling about her slender ankles and the moonlight shining through the corridor-window behind her silhouetted her long plump trembling shanks through the thin nightgown.

The corridor erupted, boiled over. Doors crashed open, dishevelled heads protruded, questions were shrieked, dry throats choked over the bitter smoke. Mr. Phineas Mason, looking a thousand years old without his teeth, fled in a cotton nightshirt toward the staircase.

Murch came pounding up the stairs, followed by a bleary, bewildered John Shaw. Scrawny Agatha in silk pajamas staggered down the hall with Peter, howling at the top of his lusty voice, in her arms. Two servants scuttled downstairs like frantic rats.

But Mr. Ellery Queen stood still outside the door of his room and looked quietly about, as if searching for someone.

"Murch," he said in a calm, penetrating voice.

The detective ran up. "The fire!" he cried wildly. "Where the hell's the fire?"

"Have you seen Mrs. Royce?"

"Mrs. Royce? Hell, no!" He ran back up the hall, and Ellery followed on his heels, thoughtfully. Murch tried the knob of a door; the door was locked. "God, she may be asleep, or overcome by—"

"Well, then," said Ellery through his teeth as he stepped back, "stop yowling and help me break this door down. We don't want her frying in her own lard, you know."

In the darkness, in the evil smoke, they hurled themselves at the door. . . . At the fourth assault it splintered off its hinges and Ellery sprang through. An electric torch in his hand flung its powerful beam about the room, wavered. . . . Something struck it from Ellery's hand, and it splintered on the floor. The next moment Ellery was fighting for his life.

His adversary was a brawny, panting demon with muscular fingers that sought his throat. He wriggled about, coolly, seeking an armhold. Behind him Murch was yelling: "Mrs. Royce! It's only us!"

Something sharp and cold flicked over Ellery's cheek and left a burning line. Ellery found a naked arm. He twisted, hard, and there was a clatter as steel fell to the floor. Then Murch came to his senses and jumped in. A county trooper blundered in, fumbling with his electric torch. . . . Ellery's fist drove in, hard, to a fat stomach. Fingers relaxed from his throat. The trooper found the electric switch. . . .

Mrs. Royce, trembling violently, lay on the floor beneath the two men. On a chair nearby lay, in a mountain of Victorian clothing, a very odd and solid-looking contraption that might have been a rubber *brassière*. And something was wrong with her hair; she seemed to have been partially scalped.

Ellery cursed softly and yanked. Her scalp came away in a piece, revealing a pink gray-fringed skull.

"She's a man!" screamed Murch.

"Thus," said Ellery grimly, holding Mrs. Royce's throat firmly with one hand and with the other dabbing at his bloody cheek, "vindicating the powers of thought."

"I still don't understand," complained Mason the next morning, as his chauffeur drove him and Ellery back to the city, "how you guessed, Queen."

Ellery raised his eyebrows. "Guessed? My dear Mason, that's considered an insult at the Queen hearth. There was no guesswork whatever involved. Matter of pure reasoning. And a neat job, too," he added reflectively, touching the thin scar on his cheek.

"Come, come, Queen," smiled the lawyer, "I've never really believed McC.'s panegyrics on what he calls your uncanny ability to put two and two together; and though I'm not unintelligent and my legal training gives me a mental advantage over the layman and I've just been treated presumably to a demonstration of your—er—powers, I'll be blessed if I yet believe."

"A sceptic, eh?" said Ellery, wincing at the pain in his cheek. "Well, then, let's start where I started—with the beard Dr. Arlen painted on the face of Rembrandt's wife just before he was attacked. We've agreed that he deliberately painted in the beard to leave a clue to his murderer. What could he have meant? He was not pointing to a *specific* woman, using the beard just as an attention-getter; for the woman in the painting was the wife of Rembrandt, a historical figure and as far as our *personæ* went an utter unknown. Nor could Arlen have meant to point to a woman with a beard *literally*; for this would have meant a freak, and there were no freaks involved. Nor was he pointing to a bearded man, for there was *a man's face* on the painting which he left untouched; had he meant to point to a bearded man as his murderer—that is, to John Shaw—he would have painted the beard on Rembrandt's beardless face. Besides, Shaw's is a vandyke, a pointed beard; and the beard Arlen painted was squarish in shape. . . . You see how exhaustive it is possible to be, Mason."

"Go on," said the lawyer intently.

"The only possible conclusion, then, all others having been eliminated, was that Arlen meant the beard *merely to indicate masculinity*, since facial hair is one of the few exclusively masculine characteristics left to our sex by dear, dear Woman. In other words, by painting a beard on a woman's face—any woman's face, mark—Dr. Arlen was virtually saying: 'My murderer is a person who seems to be a woman but is really a man.' "

"Well, I'll be damned!" gasped Mason.

"No doubt," nodded Ellery. "Now, 'a person who seems to be a woman but is really a man' suggests, surely, impersonation. The only actual stranger at the house was Mrs. Royce. Neither John nor Agatha could be impersonators, since they were both well-known to Dr. Arlen as well as to you; Arlen had examined them periodically, in fact, for years as the personal physician of the household. As for Miss Krutch, aside from her unquestionable femininity—a ravishing young woman, my dear Mason—she could not possibly have had motive to be an impersonator.

"Now, since Mrs. Royce seemed the likeliest possibility, I thought over the infinitesimal phenomena I had observed connected with her person—that is, appearance and movements. I was amazed to find a vast number of remarkable confirmations!"

"Confirmations?" echoed Mason, frowning.

"Ah, Mason, that's the trouble with sceptics; they're so easily confounded. Of course! Lips constitute a strong difference between the sexes: Mrs. Royce's were shaped meticulously into a perfect Cupid's-bow with lipstick. Suspicious in an old woman. The general overuse of cosmetics, particularly the heavy application of face powder: *very* suspicious, when you consider that overpowdering is not common among genteel old ladies and also that a man's skin, no matter how closely and frequently shaved, is undisguisably coarser.

"Clothes? Really potent confirmation. Why on earth that outlandish Victorian get-up? Here was presumably a woman who had been on the stage, presumably a woman of the world, a sophisticate. And yet she wore those horrible doodads of the '90s. Why? Obviously, to swathe and disguise a padded figure—impossible with women's thin, scanty, and clinging modern garments. And the collar—ah, the collar! That was his inspiration. A choker, you'll recall, concealing the entire neck? But since a prominent Adam's-apple is an inescapable heritage of the male, a choker-collar becomes virtually a necessity in a female impersonation. Then the baritone voice, the vigorous movements, the mannish stride, the flat shoes. . . . The shoes were especially illuminating. Not only were they flat, but they showed signs of great bunions—and a man wearing woman's shoes, no matter how large, might well be expected to grow those painful excrescences."

"Even if I grant all that," objected Mason, "still they're generalities at best, might even be coincidences when you're arguing from a conclusion. Is that all?" He seemed disappointed.

"By no means," drawled Ellery. "These were, as you say, the generalities. But your cunning Mrs. Royce was addicted to three habits which are exclusively masculine, without argument. For one thing, when she sat down on my second sight of her she elevated her skirts at the knees with both hands; that is, one to each knee. Now that's precisely what a man does when he sits down: raises his trousers; to prevent, I suppose, their bagging at the knees."

"But—"

"Wait. Did you notice the way she screwed up her right eyebrow constantly, raising it far up and then drawing it far down? What could this have been motivated by except the lifelong use of a monocle? And a monocle is masculine. . . . And finally, her peculiar habit, in removing a cigarette from her lips, of cupping her hand about it rather than withdrawing it between the forefinger and middle finger, as most cigarette smokers do. But the cupping gesture is precisely the result of *pipe smoking*, for a man cups his hands about the bowl of a pipe in taking it out of his mouth. Man again. When I balanced these three specific factors on the same side of the scale as those generalities, I felt certain Mrs. Royce was a male.

"What male? Well, that was simplest of all. You had told me, for one thing, that when you and your partner Coolidge quizzed her she had shown a minute knowledge of Shaw history and specifically of Edith Shaw's history. On top of that, it took histrionic ability to carry off this female impersonation. Then there was the monocle deduction—England, surely? And the strong family resemblance. So I knew that 'Mrs. Royce,' being a Shaw undoubtedly, and an English Shaw to boot, was the other Shaw of the Morton side of the family—that is, Edith Shaw's brother Percy!"

"But she—he, I mean," cried Mason, "had told me Percy Shaw died a few months ago in Europe in an automobile jaccident!"

"Dear, dear," said Ellery sadly, "and a lawyer, too. She lied, that's all!—I mean 'he,' confound it. Your legal letter was addressed to Edith

Shaw, and Percy received it, since they probably shared the same establishment. If he received it, it was rather obvious, wasn't it, that it was Edith Shaw who must have died shortly before; and that Percy had seized the opportunity to gain a fortune for himself by impersonating her?"

"But why," demanded Mason, puzzled, "did he kill Dr. Arlen? He had nothing to gain—Arlen's money was destined for Shaw's cousins, not for Percy Shaw. Do you mean there was some past connection—"

"Not at all," murmured Ellery. "Why look for past connections when the motive's slick and shiny at hand? If Mrs. Royce was a man, the motive was at once apparent. Under the terms of Mrs. Shaw's will Arlen was periodically to examine the family, with particular attention to Mrs. Royce. And Agatha Shaw told me yesterday that Mrs. Royce was constrained by will to remain in the house for two years. Obviously, then, the only way Percy Shaw could avert the cataclysm of being examined by Dr. Arlen and his disguise penetrated—for a doctor would have seen the truth instantly on examination, of course—was to kill Arlen. Simple, *nein*?"

"But the beard Arlen drew—that meant he *had* seen through it?"

"Not unaided. What probably happened was that the imposter, knowing the first physical examination impended, went to Dr. Arlen the other night to strike a bargain, revealing himself as a man. Arlen, an honest man, refused to be bribed. He must have been painting at the time and, thinking fast, unable to rouse the house because he was so far away from the others, unable to paint his assailant's name because 'Mrs. Royce' would see it and destroy it, thought of Peter's beard, made the lightning connection, and calmly painted it while 'Mrs. Royce' talked to him. Then he was stabbed."

"And the previous poisoning attempt on Mrs. Shaw?"

"That," said Ellery, "undoubtedly lies between John and Agatha."

Mason was silent, and for some time they rode in peace. Then the lawyer stirred, and sighed, and said: "Well, all things considered, I suppose you should thank Providence. Without concrete evidence—your reasoning was unsupported by legal evidence, you realize that, of course, Queen—you could scarcely have accused Mrs. Royce of being a man, could you? Had you been wrong, what a beautiful suit she could have brought against you! That fire last night was an act of God."

"I am," said Ellery calmly, "above all, my dear Mason, a man of free will. I appreciate acts of God when they occur, but I don't sit around waiting for them. Consequently . . ."

"You mean—" gasped Mason, opening his mouth wide.

"A telephone call, a hurried trip by Sergeant Velie, and smoke-bombs were the *materia* for breaking into Mrs. Royce's room in the dead of night," said Ellery comfortably. "By the way, you don't by any chance know the permanent address of—ah—Miss Krutch?"

THE MAD TEA-PARTY

(1934)

THE TALL YOUNG man in the dun raincoat thought that he had never seen such a downpour. It gushed out of the black sky in a roaring flood, gray-gleaming in the feeble yellow of the station lamps. The red tails of the local from Jamaica had just been drowned out in the west. It was very dark beyond the ragged blur of light surrounding the little railroad station, and unquestionably very wet. The tall young man shivered under the eaves of the platform roof and wondered what insanity had moved him to venture into the Long Island hinterland in such wretched weather. And where, damn it all, was Owen?

He had just miserably made up his mind to seek out a booth, telephone his regrets, and take the next train back to the City, when a lowslung coupé came splashing and snuffling out of the darkness, squealed to a stop, and a man in chauffeur's livery leaped out and dashed across the gravel for the protection of the eaves.

"Mr. Ellery Queen?" he panted, shaking out his cap. He was a blond young man with a ruddy face and sun-squinted eyes.

"Yes," said Ellery with a sigh. Too late now.

"I'm Millan, Mr. Owen's chauffeur, sir," said the man. "Mr. Owen's sorry he couldn't come down to meet you himself. Some guests— This way, Mr. Queen."

He picked up Ellery's bag and the two of them ran for the coupé. Ellery collapsed against the mohair in an indigo mood. Damn Owen and his invitations! Should have known better. Mere acquaintance, when it came to that. One of J.J.'s questionable friends. People were always pushing so. Put him up on exhibition, like a trained seal. Come,

43

come, Rollo; here's a juicy little fish for you! . . . Got vicarious thrills out of listening to crime yarns. Made a man feel like a curiosity. Well, he'd be drawn and quartered if they got him to mention crime once! But then Owen had said Emmy Willowes would be there, and he'd always wanted to meet Emmy. Curious woman, Emmy, from all the reports. Daughter of some blueblood diplomat who had gone to the dogs—in this case, the stage. Stuffed shirts, her tribe, probably. Atavi! There were some people who still lived in mediæval . . . Hmm. Owen wanted him to see "the house." Just taken a month ago. Ducky, he'd said. "Ducky!" The big brute . . .

The coupé splashed along in the darkness, its headlights revealing only remorseless sheets of speckled water and occasionally a tree, a house, a hedge.

Millan cleared his throat. "Rotten weather, isn't it, sir. Worst this spring. The rain, I mean."

Ah, the conversational chauffeur! thought Ellery with an inward groan. "Pity the poor sailor on a night like this," he said piously.

"Ha, ha," said Millan. "Isn't it the truth, though. You're a little late, aren't you, sir? That was the eleven-fifty. Mr. Owen told me this morning you were expected tonight on the nine-twenty."

"Detained," murmured Ellery, wishing he were dead.

"A case, Mr. Queen?" asked Millan eagerly, rolling his squinty eyes.

Even he, O Lord . . . "No, no. My father had his annual attack of elephantiasis. Poor dad! We thought for a bad hour there that it was the end."

The chauffeur gaped. Then, looking puzzled, he returned his attention to the soggy pelted road. Ellery closed his eyes with a sigh of relief.

But Millan's was a persevering soul, for after a moment of silence he grinned—true, a trifle dubiously—and said: "Lots of excitement at Mr. Owen's tonight, sir. You see, Master Jonathan—"

"Ah," said Ellery, starting a little. Master Jonathan, eh? Ellery recalled him as a stringy, hot-eyed brat in the indeterminate years between seven and ten who possessed a perfectly fiendish ingenuity for making a nuisance of himself. Master Jonathan . . . He shivered again, this time from apprehension. He had quite forgotten Master Jonathan.

"Yes, sir, Jonathan's having a birthday party tomorrow, sir—ninth, I think—and Mr. and Mrs. Owen've rigged up something special."

Millan grinned again, mysteriously. "Something very special, sir. It's a secret, y'see. The kid—Master Jonathan doesn't know about it yet. Will he be surprised!"

"I doubt it, Millan," groaned Ellery, and lapsed into a dismal silence which not even the chauffeur's companionable blandishments were able to shatter.

Richard Owen's "ducky" house was a large rambling affair of gables and ells and colored stones and bright shutters, set at the terminal of a winding driveway flanked by soldierly trees. It blazed with light and the front door stood ajar.

"Here we are, Mr. Queen!" cried Millan cheerfully, jumping out and holding the door open. "It's only a hop to the porch; you won't get wet, sir."

Ellery descended and obediently hopped to the porch. Millan fished his bag out of the car and bounded up the steps. "Door open 'n' everything," he grinned. "Guess the help are all watchin' the show."

"Show?" gasped Ellery with a sick feeling at the pit of his stomach.

Millan pushed the door wide open. "Step in, step in, Mr. Queen. I'll go get Mr. Owen . . . They're rehearsing, y'see. Couldn't do it while Jonathan was up, so they had to wait till he'd gone to bed. It's for tomorrow, y'see. And he was very suspicious; they had an awful time with him—"

"I can well believe that," mumbled Ellery. Damn Jonathan and all his tribe! He stood in a small foyer looking upon a wide brisk living room, warm and attractive. "So they're putting on a play. Hmm . . . Don't bother, Millan; I'll just wander in and wait until they've finished. Who am I to clog the wheels of Drama?"

"Yes, sir," said Millan with a vague disappointment; and he set down the bag and touched his cap and vanished in the darkness inside. The door closed with a click curiously final, shutting out both rain and nght.

Ellery reluctantly divested himself of his drenched hat and raincoat, hung them dutifully in the foyer-closet, kicked his bag into a corner, and sauntered into the living room to warm his chilled hands at the good fire. He stood before the flames soaking in heat, only half-conscious of the voices which floated through one of the two open doorways beyond the fireplace.

45

A woman's voice was saying in odd childish tones: "No, please go on! I won't interrupt you again. I dare say there may be *one.*"

"Emmy," thought Ellery, becoming conscious very abruptly. "What's going on here?" He went to the first doorway and leaned against the jamb.

An astonishing sight met him. They were all—as far as he could determine—there. It was apparently a library, a large bookish room done in the modern manner. The farther side had been cleared and a homemade curtain, manufactured out of starchy sheets and a pulley, stretched across the room. The curtain was open, and in the cleared space there was a long table covered with a white cloth and with cups and saucers and things on it. In an armchair at the head of the table sat Emmy Willowes, whimsically girlish in a pinafore, her gold-brown hair streaming down her back, her slim legs sheathed in white stockings, and black pumps with low heels on her feet. Beside her sat an apparition, no less: a rabbity creature the size of a man, his huge ears stiffly up, an enormous bow-tie at his furry neck, his mouth clacking open and shut as human sounds came from his throat. Beside the hare there was another apparition: a creature with an amiably rodent little face and slow sleepy movements. And beyond the little one, who looked unaccountably like a dormouse, sat the most remarkable of the quartet—a curious creature with shaggy eyebrows and features reminiscent of George Arliss's, at his throat a dotted bow-tie, dressed Victorianishly in a quaint waistcoat, on his head an extraordinary tall cloth hat in the band of which was stuck a placard reading: "For This Style 10/6."

The audience was composed of two women: an old lady with pure white hair and the stubbornly sweet facial expression which more often than not conceals a chronic acerbity; and a very beautiful young woman with full breasts, red hair, and green eyes. Then Ellery noticed that two domestic heads were stuck in another doorway, gaping and giggling decorously.

"The mad tea-party," thought Ellery, grinning. "I might have known, with Emmy in the house. Too good for that merciless brat!"

"They were learning to draw," said the little dormouse in a high-pitched voice, yawning and rubbing its eyes, "and they drew all manner of things—everything that begins with an M—"

"Why with an M?" demanded the woman-child.

"Why not?" snapped the hare, flapping his ears indignantly.

The dormouse began to doze and was instantly beset by the top-hatted gentleman, who pinched him so roundly that he awoke with a shriek and said: "—that begins with an M, such as mousetraps, and the moon, and memory, and muchness—you know you say things are 'much of a muchness'—did you ever see such a thing as a drawing of a muchness?"

"Really, now you ask me," said the girl, quite confused, "I don't think—"

"Then you shouldn't talk," said the Hatter tartly.

The girl rose in open disgust and began to walk away, her white legs twinkling. The dormouse fell asleep and the hare and the Hatter stood up and grasped the dormouse's little head and tried very earnestly to push it into the mouth of a monstrous teapot on the table.

And the little girl cried, stamping her right foot: "At any rate I'll never go *there* again. It's the stupidest tea-party I was ever at in all my life!"

And she vanished behind the curtain; an instant later it swayed and came together as she operated the rope of the pulley.

"Superb," drawled Ellery, clapping his hands. "*Brava,* Alice. And a couple of *bravi* for the zoological characters, Messrs. Dormouse and March Hare, not to speak of my good friend the Mad Hatter."

The Mad Hatter goggled at him, tore off his hat, and came running across the room. His vulturine features under the make-up were both good-humored and crafty; he was a stoutish man in his prime, a faintly cynical and ruthless prime. "Queen! When on earth did you come? Darned if I hadn't completely forgotten about you. What held you up?"

"Family matter. Millan did the honors. Owen, that's your natural costume, I'll swear. I don't know what ever possessed you to go into Wall Street. You were born to be the Hatter."

"Think so?" chuckled Owen, pleased. "I guess I always did have a yen for the stage; that's why I backed Emmy Willowes's *Alice* show. Here, I want you to meet the gang. Mother," he said to the white-haired old lady, "may I present Mr. Ellery Queen. Laura's mother, Queen—Mrs. Mansfield." The old lady smiled a sweet, sweet smile; but Ellery noticed that her eyes were very sharp. "Mrs. Gardner," continued Owen, indicating the buxom young woman with the red hair and green eyes. "Believe it or not, she's the wife of that hairy Hare over there. Ho, ho, ho!'

There was something a little brutal in Owen's laughter. Ellery bowed to the beautiful woman and said quickly: "Gardner? You're not the wife of Paul Gardner, the architect?"

"Guilty," said the March Hare in a cavernous voice; and he removed his head and disclosed a lean face with twinkling eyes. "How are you, Queen? I haven't seen you since I testified for your father in that Schultz murder case in the Village."

They shook hands. "Surprise," said Ellery. "This *is* nice. Mrs. Gardner, you have a clever husband. He set the defense by their respective ears with his expert testimony in that case."

"Oh, I've always said Paul is a genius," smiled the red-haired woman. She had a queer husky voice. "But he won't believe me. He thinks I'm the only one in the world who doesn't appreciate him."

"Now, Carolyn," protested Gardner with a laugh; but the twinkle had gone out of his eyes and for some odd reason he glanced at Richard Owen.

"Of course you remember Laura," boomed Owen, taking Ellery forcibly by the arm. "That's the Dormouse. Charming little rat, isn't she?"

Mrs. Mansfield lost her sweet expression for a fleeting instant; very fleeting indeed. What the Dormouse thought about being publicly characterized as a rodent, however charming, by her husband was concealed by the furry little head; when she took it off she was smiling. She was a wan little woman with tired eyes and cheeks that had already begun to sag.

"And this," continued Owen with the pride of a stock-raiser exhibiting a price milch-cow, "is the one and only Emmy. Emmy, meet Mr. Queen, that murder-smelling chap I've been telling you about. Miss Willowes."

"You see us, Mr. Queen," murmured the actress, "in character. I hope you aren't here on a professional visit? Because if you are, we'll get into mufti at once and let you go to work. I know *I've* a vicariously guilty conscience. If I were to be convicted of every mental murder I've committed, I'd need the nine lives of the Cheshire Cat. Those damn' critics—"

"The costume," said Ellery, not looking at her legs, "is most fetching. And I think I like you better as Alice." She made a charming Alice;

she was curved in her slimness, half-boy, half-girl. "Whose idea was this, anyway?"

"I suppose you think we're fools or nuts," chuckled Owen. "Here, sit down, Queen. Maud!" he roared. "A cocktail for Mr. Queen. Bring some more fixin's." A frightened domestic head vanished. "We're having a dress-rehearsal for Johnny's birthday party tomorrow; we've invited all the kids of the neighborhood. Emmy's brilliant idea; she brought the costumes down from the theatre. You know we closed Saturday night."

"I hadn't heard. I thought *Alice* was playing to S.R.O."

"So it was. But our lease at the *Odeon* ran out and we've our engagements on the road to keep. We open in Boston next Wednesday."

Slim-legged Maud set a pinkish liquid concoction before Ellery. He sipped slowly, succeeding in not making a face.

"Sorry to break this up," said Paul Gardner, beginning to take off his costume. "But Carolyn and I have a bad trip before us. And then tomorrow . . . The road must be an absolute washout."

"Pretty bad," said Ellery politely, setting down his three-quarters'-full glass.

"I won't hear of it," said Laura Owen. Her pudgy little Dormouse's stomach gave her a peculiar appearance, tiny and fat and sexless. "Driving home in this storm! Carolyn, you and Paul must stay over."

"It's only four miles, Laura," murmured Mrs. Gardner.

"Nonsense, Carolyn! More like forty on a night like this," boomed Owen. His cheeks were curiously pale and damp under the make-up. "That's settled! We've got more room than we know what to do with. Paul saw to that when he designed this development."

"That's the insidious part of knowing architects socially," said Emmy Willowes with a grimace. She flung herself in a chair and tucked her long legs under her. "You can't fool 'em about the number of available guest-rooms."

"Don't mind Emmy," grinned Owen. "She's the Peck's Bad Girl of show business: no manners at all. Well, well! This is great. How's about a drink, Paul?"

"No, thanks."

"You'll have one, won't you, Carolyn? Only good sport in the crowd." Ellery realized with a furious embarrassment that his host was, under the red jovial glaze of the exterior, vilely drunk.

She raised her heavily-lidded green eyes to his. "I'd love it, Dick."

They stared with peculiar hunger at each other. Mrs. Owen suddenly smiled and turned her back, struggling with her cumbersome costume.

And, just as suddenly, Mrs. Mansfield rose and smiled her unconvincing sweet smile and said in her sugary voice to no one in particular: *"Will* you all excuse me? It's been a trying day, and I'm an old woman. . . . Laura, my darling." She went to her daughter and kissed the lined, averted forehead.

Everybody murmured something; including Ellery, who had a headache, a slow pinkish fire in his vitals, and a consuming wishfulness to be far, far away.

Mr. Ellery Queen came to with a start and a groan. He turned over in bed, feeling very poorly. He had dozed in fits since one o'clock, annoyed rather than soothed by the splash of the rain against the bedroom windows. And now he was miserably awake, inexplicably sleepless, attacked by a rather surprising insomnia. He sat up and reached for his wrist-watch, which was ticking thunderously away on the night-table beside his bed. By the radium hands he saw that it was five past two.

He lay back, crossing his palms behind his head, and stared into the half-darkness. The mattress was deep and downy, as one had a right to expect of the mattress of a plutocrat, but it did not rest his tired bones. The house was cosy, but it dod not comfort him. His hostess was thoughtful, but uncomfortably woebegone. His host was a disturbing force, like the storm. His fellow-guests; Master Jonathan snuffling away in his junior bed—Ellery was positive that Master Jonathan snuffled. . . .

At two-fifteen he gave up the battle and, rising, turned on the light and got into his dressing-gown and slippers. That there was no book or magazine on or in the night-table he had ascertained before retiring. Shocking hospitality! Sighing, he went to the door and opened it and peered out. A small night-light glimmered at the landing down the hall. Everything was quiet.

And suddenly he was attacked by the strangest diffidence. He definitely did not want to leave the bedroom.

Analyzing the fugitive fear, and arriving nowhere, Ellery sternly reproached himself for an imaginative fool and stepped out into the hall. He was not habitually a creature of nerves, nor was he psychic; he laid the blame to lowered physical resistance due to fatigue, lack of sleep. This was a nice house with nice people in it. It was like a man, he thought, saying: "Nice doggie, nice doggie," to a particularly fearsome beast with slavering jaws. That woman with the sea-green eyes. Put to sea in a sea-green boat. Or was it pea-green... "No room! No room!" . . . "There's *plenty* of room," said Alice indignantly. . . . And Mrs. Mansfield's smile did make you shiver.

Berating himself bitterly for the ferment his imagination was in, he went down the carpeted stairs to the living room.

It was pitch-dark and he did not know where the light-switch was. He stumbled over a hassock and stubbed his toe and cursed silently. The library should be across from the stairs, next to the fireplace. He strained his eyes toward the fireplace, but the last embers had died. Stepping warily, he finally reached the fireplace-wall. He groped about in the rain-splattered silence, searching for the library door. His hand met a cold knob, and he turned the knob rather noisily and swung the door open. His eyes were oriented to the darkness now and he had already begun to make out in the mistiest black haze the unrecognizable outlines of still objects.

The darkness from beyond the door however struck him like a blow. It was darker darkness. . . . He was about to step across the sill when he stopped. It was the wrong room. Not the library at all. How he knew he could not say, but he was sure he had pushed open the door of the wrong room. Must have wandered orbitally to the right. Lost men in the dark forest. . . . He stared intently straight before him into the absolute, unrelieved blackness, sighed, and retreated. The door shut noisily again.

He groped along the wall to the left. A few feet. . . . There it was! The very next door. He paused to test his psychic faculties. No, all's well. Grinning, he pushed open the door, entered boldly, fumbled on the nearest wall for the switch, found it, pressed. The light flooded on to reveal, triumphantly, the library.

The curtain was closed, the room in disorder as he had last seen it before being conducted upstairs by his host.

He went to the built-in bookcases, scanned several shelves, hesitated between two volumes, finally selected *Huckleberry Finn* as good reading on a dour night, put out the light, and felt his way back across the living room to the stairway. Book tucked under his arm, he began

51

to climb the stairs. There was a footfall from the landing above. He looked up. A man's dark form was silhouetted below the tiny landing light.

"Owen?" whispered a dubious male voice.

Ellery laughed. "It's Queen, Gardner. Can't you sleep either?"

He heard the man sigh with relief. "Lord, no! I was just coming downstairs for something to read. Carolyn—my wife's asleep, I guess, in the room adjoining mine. How she can sleep—! There's something in the air tonight."

"Or else you drank too much," said Ellery cheerfully, mounting the stairs.

Gardner was in pajamas and dressing-gown, his hair mussed. "Didn't drink at all to speak of. Must be this confounded rain. My nerves are all shot."

"Something in that. Hardy believed, anyway, in the Greek unities. . . . If you can't sleep, you might join me for a smoke in my room, Gardner."

"You're sure I won't be—"

"Keeping me up? Nonsense. The only reason I fished about downstairs for a book was to occupy my mind with something. Talk's infinitely better than Huck Finn, though he does help at times. Come on."

They went to Ellery's room and Ellery produced cigarettes and they relaxed in chairs and chatted and smoked until the early dawn began struggling to emerge from behind the fine gray wet bars of the rain outside. Then Gradner went yawning back to his room and Ellery fell into a heavy, uneasy slumber.

He was on the rack in a tall room of the Inquisition and his left arm was bring torn out of his shoulder-socket. The pain was almost pleasant. Then he awoke to find Millan's ruddy face in broad daylight above him, his blond hair tragically dishevelled. He was jerking at Ellery's arm for all he was worth.

"Mr. Queen!" he was crying. "Mr. Queen! For God's sake, wake up!"

Ellery sat up quickly, startled. "What's the matter, Millan?"

"Mr. Owen, sir. He's—he's gone!"

Ellery sprang out of bed. "What d'ye mean, man?"

"Disappeared, Mr. Queen. We—we can't find him. Just gone. Mrs. Owen is all—"

"You go downstairs, Millan," said Ellery calmly, stripping off his pajama-coat, "and pour yourself a drink. Please tell Mrs. Owen not to do anything until I come down. And nobody's to leave or telephone. You understand?"

"Yes, sir," said Millan in a low voice, and blundered off.

Ellery dressed like a fireman, splashed his face, spat water, adjusted his necktie, and ran downstairs. He found Laura Owen in a crumpled négligé on the sofa, sobbing. Mrs. Mansfield was patting her daughter's shoulder. Master Jonathan Owen was scowling at his grandmother, Emmy Willowes silently smoked a cigarette, and the Gardners were pale and quiet by the gray-washed windows.

"Mr. Queen," said the actress quickly. "It's a drama, hot off the script. At least Laura Owens thinks so. Won't you assure her that it's all probably nothing?"

"I can't do that," smiled Ellery, "until I learn the facts. Owen's gone? How? When?"

"Oh, Mr. Queen," choked Mrs. Owen, raising a tear-stained face. "I know something—something dreadful's happened. I had a feeling— You remember last night, after Richard showed you to your room?"

"Yes."

"Then he came back downstairs and said he had some work to do in his den for Monday, and told me to go to bed. Everybody else had gone upstairs. The servants, too. I warned him not to stay up too late and I went up to bed. I—I was exhausted, and I fell right asleep—"

"You occupy one bedroom, Mrs. Owen?"

"Yes. Twin beds. I fell asleep and didn't wake up until a half-hour ago. Then I saw—" She shuddered and began to sob again. Her mother looked helpless and angry. "His bed hadn't been slept in. His clothes—the ones he'd taken off when he got into the costume—were still where he had left them on the chair by his bed. I was shocked, and ran downstairs; but he was gone. . . ."

"Ah," said Ellery queerly. "Then, as far as you know, he's still in that Mad Hatter's rig? Have you looked over his wardrobe? Are any of his regular clothes missing?"

"No, no; they're all here. Oh, he's dead. I know he's dead."

"Laura, dear, please," said Mrs. Mansfield in a tight quavery voice.

53

"Oh, mother, it's too horrible—"

"Here, here," said Ellery. "No hysterics. Was he worried about anything? Business, for instance?"

"No, I'm sure he wasn't. In fact, he said only yesterday things were picking up beautifully. And he isn't—isn't the type to worry, anyway."

"Then it probably isn't amnesia. He hasn't had a shock of some sort recently?"

"No, no."

"No possibility, despite the costume, that he went to his office?"

"No. He never goes down Saturdays."

Master Jonathan jammed his fists into the pockets of his Eton jacket and said bitterly: "I bet he's drunk again. Makin' mamma cry. I hope he *never* comes back."

"Jonathan!" screamed Mrs. Mansfield. "You go up to your room this very minute, do you hear, you nasty boy? This minute!"

No one said anything; Mrs. Owen continued to sob; so Master Jonathan thrust out his lower lip, scowled at his grandmother with unashamed dislike, and stamped upstairs.

"Where," said Ellery with a frown, "was your husband when you last saw him, Mrs. Owen? In this room?"

"In his den," she said with difficulty. "He went in just as I went upstairs. I saw him go in. That door, there." She pointed to the door at the right of the library door. Ellery started; it was the door to the room he had almost blundered into during the night in his hunt for the library.

"Do you think—" began Carolyn Gardner in her husky voice, and stopped. Her lips were dry, and in the gray morning light her hair did not seem so red and her eyes did not seem so green. There was, in fact, a washed-out look about her, as if all the fierce vitality within her had been quenched by what had happened.

"Keep out of this, Carolyn," said Paul Gardner harshly. His eyes were red-rimmed from lack of sleep.

"Come, come," murmured Ellery, "we may be, as Miss Willowes has said, making a fuss over nothing at all. If you'll excuse me . . . I'll have a peep at the den."

He went into the den, closing the door behind him, and stood with his back squarely against the door. It was a small room, so narrow that

54

it looked long by contrast; it was sparsely furnished and seemed a business-like place. There was a simple neatness about its desk, a modern severity about its furnishings that were reflections of the direct, brutal character of Richard Owen. The room was as trim as a pin; it was almost ludicrous to conceive of its having served at the scene of a crime.

Ellery gazed long and thoughtfully. Nothing out of place, so far as he could see; and nothing, at least perceptible to a stranger, added. Then his eyes wavered and fixed themselves upon what stood straight before him. That *was* odd. . . . Facing him as he leaned against the door was a bold naked mirror set flush into the opposite wall and reaching from floor to ceiling—a startling feature of the room's decorations. Ellery's lean figure, and the door behind him, were perfectly reflected in the sparkling glass. And there, above . . . In the mirror he saw, above the reflection of the door against which he was leaning, the reflection of the face of a modern electric clock. In the dingy grayness of the light there was a curious lambent quality about its dial. . . . He pushed away from the door and stared up. It was a chromium-and-onyx clock, about a foot in diameter, round and simple and startling.

He opened the door and beckoned Millan, who had joined the silent group in the living room. "Have you a step-ladder?"

Millan brought one. Ellery smiled, shut the door firmly, mounted the ladder, and examined the clock. Its electric outlet was behind, concealed from view. The plug was in the socket, as he saw at once. The clock was going; the time—he consulted his wrist-watch—was reasonably accurate. But then he cupped his hands as best he could to shut out what light there was and stared hard and saw that the numerals and the hands, as he had suspected, were radium-painted. They glowed faintly.

He descended, opened the door, gave the ladder into Millan's keeping, and sauntered into the living room. They looked up at him trustfully.

"Well," said Emmy Willowes with a light shrug, "has the Master Mind discovered the all-important clue? Don't tell us that Dickie Owe ͻ is out playing golf at the Meadowbrook links in that Mad Hatter's get up!"

"Well, Mr. Queen?" asked Mrs. Owen anxiously.

Ellery sank into an armchair and lighted a cigarette. "There's something curious in there. Mrs. Owen, did you get this house furnished?"

She was puzzled. "Furnished? Oh, no. We bought it, you know; brought all our own things."

"Then the electric above the door in the den is yours?"

"The clock?" They all stared at him. "Why, of course. What has that—"

"Hmm," said Ellery. "That clock has a disappearing quality, like the Cheshire Cat—since we may as well continue being Carrollish, Miss Willowes."

"But what can the clock possibly have to do with Richard's—being gone?" asked Mrs. Mansfield with asperity.

Ellery shrugged. *"Je n'sais.* The point is that a little after two this morning, being unable to sleep, I ambled downstairs to look for a book. In the dark I blundered to the door of the den, mistaking it for the library door. I opened it and looked in. But I saw nothing, you see."

"But how could you, Mr. Queen?" said Mrs. Gardner in a small voice; her breasts heaved. "If it was dark—"

"That's the curious part of it," drawled Ellery. "I *should* have seen something *because* it was so dark, Mrs. Gardner."

"But—"

"The clock over the door."

"Did you go in?" murmured Emmy Willowes, frowning. "I can't say I understand. The clock's above the door, isn't it?"

"There is a mirror facing the door," explained Ellery absently, "and the fact that it was so dark makes my seeing nothing quite remarkable. Because that clock has luminous hands and numerals. Consequently I should have seen their reflected glow very clearly indeed in that pitch-darkness. But I didn't, you see. I saw literally nothing at all."

They were silent, bewildered. Then Gardner muttered: "I still don't see—You mean something, somebody was standing in front of the mirror, obscuring the reflection of the clock?"

"Oh, no. The clock's above the door—a good seven feet or more from the floor. The mirror reaches to the ceiling. There isn't a piece of furniture in that room seven feet high, and certainly we may dismiss the possibility of an intruder seven feet or more tall. No, no, Gardner. It does seem as if the clock wasn't above the door at all when I looked in."

"Are you sure, young man?" snapped Mrs. Mansfield, "that you know what you're talking about? I thought we were concerned with my son-in-law's absence. And how on earth could the clock not have been there?"

Ellery closed his eyes. "Fundamental. *It was moved from its position.* Wasn't above the door when I looked in. After I left, it was returned."

"But why on earth," murmured the actress, "should any one want to move a mere clock from a wall, Mr. Queen? That's almost as nonsensical as some of the things in *Alice.*"

"That," said Ellery, "is the question I'm propounding to myself. Frankly I don't know." Then he opened his eyes. "By the way, has any one seen the Mad Hatter's hat?"

Mrs. Owen shivered. "No, that—that's gone, too."

"You've looked for it?"

"Yes. Would you like to look yours—"

"No, no, I'll take your word for it, Mrs. Owen. Oh, yes. Your husband has no enemies?" He smiled. "That's the routine question, Miss Willowes. I'm afraid I can't offer you anything startling in the way of technique."

"Enemies? Oh, I'm sure not," quavered Mrs. Owen. "Richard was—is strong and—and sometimes rather curt and contemptuous, but I'm sure no one would hate him enough to—to kill him." She shivered again and drew the silk of her négligé closer about her plump shoulders.

"Don't say that, Laura," said Mrs. Mansfield sharply. "I do declare, you people are like children! It probably has the simplest explanation."

"Quite possible," said Ellery in a cheerful voice. "It's the depressing weather, I suppose. . . . There! I believe the rain's stopped." They dully looked out the windows. The rain had perversely ceased and the sky was growing brighter. "Of course," continued Ellery, "there are certain possibilities. It's conceivable—I say conceivable, Mrs. Owen— that your husband has been . . . well, kidnaped. Now, now, don't look so frightened. It's a theory only. The fact that he has disappeared in the costume does seem to point to a very abrupt—and therefore possibly enforced—departure. You haven't found a note of some kind? Nothing in your letter-box? The morning mail—"

"Kidnaped," whispered Mrs. Owen feebly.

"Kidnaped?" breathed Mrs. Gardner, and bit her lip. But there was a brightness in her eye, like the brightness of the sky outdoors.

"No note, no mail," snapped Mrs. Mansfield. "Personally, I think this is ridiculous. Laura, this is your house, but I think I have a duty. . . . You should do one of two things. Either take this seriously and telephone the *regular* police, or forget all about it. *I'm* inclined to believe Richard got befuddled—he *had* a lot to drink last night, dear—and wandered off drunk somewhere. He's probably sleeping it off in a field somewhere and won't come back with anything worse than a bad cold."

"Excellent suggestion," drawled Ellery. "All except for the summoning of the *regular* police, Mrs. Mansfield. I assure you I possess—er—*ex officio* qualifications. Let's not call the police and say we did. If there's any explaining to do—afterward—I'll do it. Meanwhile, I suggest we try to forget all this unpleasantness and wait. If Mr. Owen hasn't returned by nightfall, we can go into conference and decide what measures to take. Agreed?"

"Sounds reasonable," said Gardner disconsolately. "May I—" he smiled and shrugged—"this *is* exciting!—telephone my office, Queen?"

"Lord, yes."

Mrs. Owen shrieked suddenly, rising and tottering toward the stairs. "Jonathan's birthday party! I forgot all about it! And all those children invited—What *will* I say?"

"I suggest," said Ellery in a sad voice, "that Master Jonathan is indisposed, Mrs. Owen. Harsh, but necessary. You might 'phone all the potential spectators of the mad tea-party and voice your regrets." And Ellery rose and wandered into the library.

It was a depressing day for all the lightening skies and the crisp sun. The morning wore on and nothing whatever happened. Mrs. Mansfield firmly tucked her daughter into bed, made her swallow a small dose of luminol from a big bottle in the medicine-chest, and remained with her until she dropped off to exhausted sleep. Then the old lady telephoned to all and sundry the collective Owen regrets over the unfortunate turn of events. Jonathan *would* have to run a fever when . . . Master Jonathan, apprised later by his grandmother of the *débâcle*, sent up an ululating howl of surprisingly healthy anguish that caused Ellery, poking about downstairs in the library, to feel prickles slither up and down his spine. It took the combined labors of Mrs. Mansfield,

Millan, the maid and the cook to pacify the Owen hope. A five-dollar bill ulltimately restored a rather strained *entente*. . . . Emmy Willowes spent the day serenely reading. The Gardners listlessly played two-handed bridge.

Luncheon was a dismal affair. No one spoke in more than monosyllables, and the strained atmosphere grew positively taut.

During the afternoon they wandered about, restless ghosts. Even the actress began to show signs of tension: she consumed innumerable cigarettes and cocktails and lapsed into almost sullen silence. No word came; the telephone rang only once, and then it was merely the local confectioner protesting the cancellation of the ice cream order. Ellery spent most of the afternoon in mysterious activity in the library and den. What he was looking for remained his secret. At five o'clock he emerged from the den, rather gray of face. There was a deep crease between his brows. He went out onto the porch and leaned against a pillar, sunk in thought. The gravel was dry; the sun had quickly sopped up the rain. When he went back into the house it was already dusk and growing darker each moment with the swiftness of the country nightfall.

There was no one about; the house was quiet, its miserable occupants having retired to their rooms. Ellery sought a chair. He buried his face in his hands and thought for long minutes, completely still.

And then at last something happened to his face and he went to the foot of the stairs and listened. No sound. He tiptoed back, reached for the telephone, and spent the next fifteen minutes in low-voiced, earnest conversation with someone in New York. When he had finished, he went upstairs to his room.

An hour later, while the others were downstairs gathering for dinner, he slipped down the rear stairway and out of the house unobserved even by the cook in the kitchen. He spent some time in the thick darkness of the grounds.

How it happened Ellery never knew. He felt its effects soon after dinner; and on retrospection he recalled that the others, too, had seemed drowsy at approximately the same time. It was a late dinner and a cold one, Owen's disappearance apparently having disrupted the culinary organization as well; so that it was not until a little after eight that the coffee—Ellery was certain later it had been the coffee—

was served by the trim-legged maid. The drowsiness came on less than half an hour later. They were seated in the living room, chatting dully about nothing at all. Mrs. Owen, pale and silent, had gulped her coffee thirstily; had called for a second cup, in fact. Only Mrs. Mansfield had been belligerent. She had been definitely of a mind, it appeared, to telephone the police. She had great faith in the local constabulary of Long Island, particularly in one Chief Naughton, the local prefect; and she left no doubt in Ellery's mind of *his* incompetency. Gardner had been restless and a little rebellious; he had tinkered with the piano in the alcove. Emmy Willowes had drawn herself into a slant-eyed shell, no longer amused and very, very quiet. Mrs. Gardner had been nervous. Jonathan packed off screaming to bed. . . .

It came over their senses like a soft insidious blanket of snow. Just a pleasant sleepiness. The room was warm, too, and Ellery rather hazily felt beads of perspiration on his forehead. He was half-gone before his dulled brain sounded a warning note. And then, trying in panic to rise, to use his muscles, he felt himself slipping, slipping into unconsciousness, his body as leaden and remote as Vega. His last conscious thought, as the room whirled dizzily before his eyes and he saw blearily the expressions of his companions, was that they had all been drugged. . . .

The dizziness seemed merely to have taken up where it had left off, almost without hiatus. Specks danced before his closed eyes and somebody was hammering petulantly at his temples. Then he opened his eyes and saw glittering sun fixed upon the floor at his feet. Good God, all night. . . .

He sat up groaning and feeling his head. The others were sprawled in various attitudes of labored-breathing coma about him—without exception. Some one—his aching brain took it in dully; it was Emmy Willowes—stirred and sighed. He got to his feet and stumbled toward a portable bar and poured himself a stiff, nasty drink of Scotch. Then, with his throat burning, he felt unaccountably better; and he went to the actress and pummeled her gently until she opened her eyes and gave him a sick, dazed, troubled look.

"What—when—"

"Drugged," croaked Ellery. "The crew of us. Try to revive these people, Miss Willowes, while I scout about a bit. And see if any one's shamming."

He wove his way a little uncertainly, but with purpose, toward the rear of the house. Groping, he found the kitchen. And there were the trim-legged maid and Millan and the cook unconscious in chairs about the kitchen table over cold cups of coffee. He made his way back to the living room, nodded at Miss Willowes working over Gardner at the piano, and staggered upstairs. He discovered Master Jonathan's bedroom after a short search; the boy was still sleeping—a deep natural sleep punctuated by nasal snuffles. Lord, he *did* snuffle! Groaning, Ellery visited the lavatory adjoining the master-bedroom. After a little while he went downstairs and into the den. He came out almost at once, haggard and wild-eyed. He took his hat from the foyer-closet and hurried outdoors into the warm sunshine. He spent fifteen minutes poking about the grounds; the Owen house was shallowly surrounded by timber and seemed isolated as a Western ranch. . . . When he returned to the house, looking grim and disappointed, the others were all conscious, making mewing little sounds and holding their heads like scared children.

"Queen, for God's sake," began Gardner hoarsely.

"Whoever it was used that luminol in the lavatory upstairs," said Ellery, flinging his hat away and wincing at a sudden pain in his head. "The stuff Mrs. Mansfield gave Mrs. Owen yesterday to make her sleep. Except that almost the whole of that large bottle was used. Swell sleeping draught! Make yourselves comfortable while I conduct a little investigation in the kitchen. I think it was the java." But when he returned he was grimacing. "No luck. *Madame la Cuisinière,* it seems, had to visit the bathroom at one period; Millan was out in the garage looking at the cars; and the maid was off somewhere, doubtless primping. Result: our friend the luminolist had an opportunity to pour most of the powder from the bottle into the coffeepot. Damn!"

"I *am* going to call the police!" cried Mrs. Mansfield hysterically, striving to rise. "We'll be murdered in our beds, next thing we know! Laura, I positively insist—"

"Please, please, Mrs. Mansfield," said Ellery wearily. "No heroics. And you would be of greater service if you went into the kitchen and checked the insurrection that's brewing there. The two females are on the verge of packing, I'll swear."

Mrs. Mansfield bit her lip and flounced off. They heard her no longer sweet voice raised in remonstrance a moment later.

"But, Queen," protested Gardner, "we can't go unprotected—"

"What I want to know in my infantile way," drawled Emmy Willowes from pale lips, "is who did it, and why. That bottle upstairs . . . It looks unconscionably like one of us, doesn't it?"

Mrs. Gardner gave a little shriek. Mrs. Owen sank back into her chair.

"One of us?" whispered the red-haired woman.

Ellery smiled without humor. Then his smile faded and he cocked his head toward the foyer. "What was that?" he snapped suddenly.

They turned, terror-stricken, and looked. But there was nothing to see. Ellery strode toward the front door.

"What is it now, for heaven's sake?" faltered Mrs. Owen.

"I thought I heard a sound—" He flung the door open. The early morning sun streamed in. Then they saw him stoop and pick up something from the porch and rise and look swiftly about outside. But he shook his head and stepped back, closing the door.

"Package," he said with a frown. "I *thought* someone . . . "

They looked blankly at the brown-paper bundle in his hands. "Package?" asked Mrs. Owen. Her face lit up. "Oh, it may be from Richard!" And then the light went out, to be replaced by fearful pallor. "Oh, do you think—?"

"It's addressed," said Ellery slowly, "to you, Mrs. Owen. No stamp, no postmark, written in pencil in disguised block-letters. I think I'll take the liberty of opening this, Mrs. Owen." He broke the feeble twine and tore away the wrapping of the crude parcel. And then he frowned even more deeply. For the package contained only a pair of large men's shoes, worn at the heels and soles—sport oxfords in tan and white.

Mrs. Owen rolled her eyes, her nostrils quivering with nausea. "Richard's!" she gasped. And she sank back, half-fainting.

"Indeed?" murmured Ellery. "How interesting. Not, of course, the shoes he wore Friday night. You're positive they're his, Mrs. Owen?"

"Oh, he *has* been kidnaped!" quavered Mrs. Mansfield from the rear doorway. "Isn't there a note, b-blood . . . "

"Nothing but the shoes. I doubt the kidnap theory now, Mrs. Mansfield. These weren't the shoes Owen wore Friday night. When did you see these last, Mrs. Owen?"

She moaned: "In his wardrobe closet upstairs only yesterday afternoon. Oh—"

"There. You see?" said Ellery cheerfully. "Probably stolen from the closet while we were all unconsicous last night. And now returned rather spectacularly. So far, you know, there's been no harm done. I'm afraid," he said with severity, "we're nursing a viper at our bosoms."

But they did not laugh. Miss Willowes said strangely: "Very odd. In fact, insane, Mr. Queen. I can't see the slightest purpose in it."

"Nor I, at the moment. Somebody's either playing a monstrous prank, or there's a devilishly clever and warped mentality behind all this." He retrieved his hat and made for the door.

"Wherever are you going?" gasped Mrs. Gardner.

"Oh, out for a thinking spell under God's blue canopy. But remember," he added quietly, "that's a privilege reserved to detectives. No one is to set foot outside this house."

He returned an hour later without explanation.

At noon they found the second package. It was a squarish parcel wrapped in the same brown paper. Inside there was a cardboard carton, and in the carton, packed in crumpled tissue-paper, there were two magnificent toy sailing-boats such as children race on summer lakes. The package was addressed to Miss Willowes.

"This is getting dreadful," murmured Mrs. Gardner, her full lips trembling. "I'm all goose-pimples."

"I'd feel better," muttered Miss Willowes, "if it was a bloody dagger, or something. Toy boats!" She stepped back and her eyes narrowed. "Now, look here, good people, I'm as much a sport as anybody, but a joke's a joke and I'm just a bit fed up on this particular one. Who's maneuvering these monkeyshines?"

"Joke," snarled Gardner. He was white as death. "It's the work of a madman, I tell you!"

"Now, now," murmured Ellery, staring at the green-and-cream boats. "We shan't get anywhere this way. Mrs. Owen, have you ever seen these before?"

Mrs. Owen, on the verge of collapse, mumbled: "Oh, my good dear God. Mr. Queen, I don't—Why, they're—they're Jonathan's!"

Ellery blinked. Then he went to the foot of the stairway and yelled: "Johnny! Come down here a minute."

Master Jonathan descended sluggishly, sulkily. "What you want?" he asked in a cold voice.

"Come here, son." Master Jonathan came with dragging feet. "When did you see these boats of yours last?"

"Boats!" shrieked Master Jonathan, springing into life. He pounced on them and snatched them away, glaring at Ellery. "My boats! Never seen such a place. My boats! You stole 'em!"

"Come, come," said Ellery, flushing, "be a good little man. When did you see them last?"

"Yest'day! In my toy chest! My boats! Scan'lous," hissed Master Jonathan, and fled upstairs, hugging his boats to his scrawny breast.

"Stolen at the same time," said Ellery helplessly. "By thunder, Miss Willowes, I'm almost inclined to agree with you. By the way, who bought those boats for your son, Mrs. Owen?"

"H-his father."

"Damn," said Ellery for the second time that impious Sunday, and he sent them all on a search of the house to ascertain if anything else were missing. But no one could find that anything had been taken.

It was when they came down from upstairs that they found Ellery regarding a small white envelope with puzzlement.

"Now what?" demanded Gardner wildly.

"Stuck in the door," he said thoughtfully. "Hadn't noticed it before. This *is* a queer one."

It was a rich piece of stationery, sealed with blue wax on the back and bearing the same pencilled scrawl, this time addressed to Mrs. Mansfield.

The old lady collapsed in the nearest chair, holding her hand to her heart. She was speechless with fear.

"Well," said Mrs. Gardner huskily, "open it."

Ellery tore open the envelope. His frown deepened. "Why," he muttered, "there's nothing at all inside!"

Gardner gnawed his fingers and turned away, mumbling. Mrs. Gardner shook her head like a dazed pugilist and stumbled toward the bar for the fifth time that day. Emmy Willowes's brow was dark as thunder.

"You know," said Mrs. Owen almost quietly, "that's mother's stationery." And there was another silence.

Ellery muttered: "Queerer and queerer. I *must* get this organized. . . . The shoes are a puzzler. The toy boats might be constructed as a gift;

64

yesterday was Jonathan's birthday; the boats are his—a distorted practical joke. . . ." He shook his head. "Doesn't wash. And this third —an envelope without a letter in it. That would seem to point to the envelope as the important thing. But the envelope's the property of Mrs. Mansfield. The only thing—ah, the wax!" He scanned the blue blob on the back narrowly, but it bore no seal-insignia of any kind.

"That," said Mrs. Owen again in the quiet unnatural voice, "looks like our wax, too, Mr. Queen, from the library."

Ellery dashed away, followed by a troubled company. Mrs. Owen went to the library desk and opened the top drawer.

"Was it here?" asked Ellery quickly.

"Yes," she said, and then her voice quivered. "I used it only Friday when I wrote a letter. Oh, good . . ."

There was not stick of wax in the drawer.

And while they stared at the drawer, the front doorbell rang.

It was a market-basket this time, lying innocently on the porch. In it, nestling crisp and green, were two large cabbages.

Ellery shouted for Gardner and Millan, and himself led the charge down the steps. They scattered, searching wildly through the brush and woods surrounding the house. But they found nothing. No sign of the bell-ringer, no sign of the ghost who had cheerfully left a basket of cabbages at the door as his fourth odd gift. It was as if he were made of smoke and materialized only for the instant he needed to press his impalpable finger to the bell.

They found the woman huddled in a corner of the living room, shivering and white-lipped. Mrs. Mansfield, shaking like an aspen, was at the telephone ringing for the local police. Ellery started to protest, shrugged, set his lips, and stooped over the basket.

There was a slip of paper tied by string to the handle of the basket. The same crude pencil-scrawl. . . . "Mr. Paul Gardner."

"Looks," muttered Ellery, "as if you're elected, old fellow, this time."

Gardner stared as if he could not believe his eyes. "Cabbages!"

"Excuse me," said Ellery curtly. He went away. When he returned he was shrugging. "From the vegetable-bin in the outside pantry, said Cook. She hadn't thought to look for missing *vegetables*, she told me with scorn."

Mrs. Mansfield was babbling excitedly over the telephone to a sorely puzzled officer of the law. When she hung up she was red as a newborn baby. "That will be *quite* enough of this crazy nonsense, Mr. Queen!" she snarled. And then she collapsed in a chair and laughed hysterically and shrieked: "Oh, I knew you were making the mistake of your life when you married that beast, Laura!" and laughed again like a madwoman.

The law arrived in fifteen minutes, accompanied by a howling siren and personified by a stocky brick-faced man in chief's stripes and a gangling young policeman.

"I'm Naughton," he said shortly. "What the devil's goin' on here?"

Ellery said: "Ah, Chief Naughton. I'm Queen's son—Inspector Richard Queen of Centre Street. How d'ye do?"

"Oh!" said Naughton. He turned on Mrs. Mansfield sternly. "Why didn't you say Mr. Queen was here, Mrs. Mansfield? You ought to know—"

"Oh, I'm sick of the lot of you!" screamed the old lady. "Nonsense, nonsense, nonsense from the instant this weekend began! First that awful actress-woman there, in her short skirt and legs and things, and then this—this—"

Naughton rubbed his chin. "Come over here, Mr. Queen, where we can talk like human beings. What the deuce happened?"

Ellery with a sigh told him. As he spoke, the Chief's face grew redder and redder. "You mean you're serious about this business?" he rumbled at last. "It sounds plain crazy to me. Mr. Owen's gone off his nut and he's playing jokes on you people. Good God, you can't take this thing serious!"

"I'm afraid," murmured Ellery, "we must. . . . What's that? By heaven, if that's another manifestation of our playful ghost—!" And he dashed toward the door while Naughton gaped and pulled it open, to be struck by a wave of dusk. On the porch lay the fifth parcel, a tiny one this time.

The two officers darted out of the house, flashlights blinking and probing. Ellery picked up the packet with eager fingers. It was addressed in the now familiar scrawl to Mrs. Paul Gardner. Inside were two identically shaped objects: chessmen, kings. One was white and the other was black.

"Who plays chess here?" he drawled.

"Richard," shrieked Mrs. Owen. "Oh, my God, I'm going mad!"

Investigation proved that the two kings from Richard Owen's chess-set were gone.

The local officers came back, rather pale and panting. They had found no one outside. Ellery was silently studying the two chessmen.

"Well?" said Naughton, drooping his shoulders.

"Well," said Ellery quietly. "I have the most brilliant notion, Naughton. Come here a moment." He drew Naughton aside and began to speak rapidly in a low voice. The others stood limply about, twitching with nervousness. There was no longer any pretense of self-control. If this was a joke, it was a ghastly one indeed. And Richard Owen looming in the background . . .

The Chief blinked and nodded. "You people," he said shortly, turning to them, "get into that library there." They gasped. "I mean it! The lot of you. This tomfoolery is going to stop right now."

"But, Naughton," gasped Mrs. Mansfield, "it couldn't be any of us who sent those things. Mr. Queen will tell you we weren't out of his sight today—"

"Do as I say, Mrs. Mansfield," snapped the officer.

They trooped, puzzled, into the library. The policeman rounded up Millan, the cook, the maid, and went with them. Nobody said anything; nobody looked at any one else. Minutes passed; a half-hour; an hour. There was the silence of the grave from beyond the door to the living room. They strained their ears. . . .

At seven-thirty the door was jerked open and Ellery and the Chief glowered in on them. "Everybody out," said Naughton shortly. "Come on, step on it."

"Out?" whispered Mrs. Owen. "Where? Where is Richard? What—"

The policeman herded them out. Ellery stepped to the door of the den and pushed it open and switched on the light and stood aside.

"Will you please come in here and take seats," he said dryly; there was a tense look in his face and he seemed exhausted.

Silently, slowly, they obeyed. The policeman dragged in extra chairs from the living room. They sat down. Naughton drew the shades. The policeman closed the door and set his back against it.

Ellery said tonelessly: "In a way this has been one of the most remarkable cases in my experience. It's been unorthodox from every angle. Utterly nonconforming. I think, Miss Willowes, the wish you expressed Friday night has come true. You're about to witness a slightly cock-eyed exercise in criminal ingenuity."

"Crim—" Mrs. Gardner's full lips quivered. "You mean—there's been a crime?"

"Quiet," said Naughton harshly.

"Yes," said Ellery in gentle tones, "there has been a crime. I might say—I'm sorry to say, Mrs. Owen—a major crime."

"Richard's d—"

"I'm sorry." There was a little silence. Mrs. Owen did not weep; she seemed dried out of tears. "Fantastic," said Ellery at last. "Look here." He sighed. "the crux of the problem was the clock. The Clock That Wasn't Where It Should Have Been, the clock with the invisible face. You remember I pointed out that, since I hadn't seen the reflection of the luminous hands in that mirror there, the clock must have been moved. That was a tenable theory. But it wasn't the *only* theory."

"Richard's dead," said Mrs. Owen, in wondering voice.

"Mr. Gardner," continued Ellery quickly, "pointed out the possibility: that the clock may still have been over this door, but that something or some one may have been standing in front of the mirror. I told you why that was impossible. But," and he went suddenly to the tall mirror, "there was still another theory which accounted for the fact that I hadn't seen the luminous hands' reflection. And that was: that when I opened the door in the dark and peered in and saw nothing, the clock was still there but the *mirror* wasn't!"

Miss Willowes said with a curious dryness: "But how could that be, Mr. Queen? That—that's silly."

"Nothing is silly, dear lady, until it is proved so. I said to myself: How could it be that the mirror wasn't there at that instant? It's apparently a solid part of the wall, a built-in section in this modern room." Something glimmered in Miss Willowes's eyes. Mrs. Mansfield was staring straight before her, hands clasped tightly in her lap. Mrs. Owen was looking at Ellery with glazed eyes, blind and deaf. "Then," said Ellery with another sigh, "there was the very odd nature of the packages which have been descending upon us all day like manna from heaven. I said this was a fantastic affair. Of course it must have occurred to you that some one was trying desperately to call our attention to the secret of the crime."

"Call our at—" began Gardner, frowning.

"Precisely. Now, Mrs. Owen," murmured Ellery softly, "the first package was addressed to you. What did it contain?" She stared at him without expression. There was a dreadful silence. Mrs. Mansfield suddenly shook her, as if she had been a child. She started, smiled vaguely; Ellery repeated the question.

And she said, almost brightly: "A pair of Richard's sport oxfords."

He winced. "In a word, *shoes*. Miss Willowes," and despite her nonchalances he stiffened a little, "you were the recipient of the second package. And what did that contain?"

"Jonathan's toy boats," she murmured.

"In a word, again—*ships*. Mrs. Mansfield, the third package was sent to you. It contained what, precisely?"

"Nothing." She tossed her head. "I still think this is the purest drivel. Can't you see you're driving my daughter—all of us—insane? Naughton, are you going to permit this farce to continue? If you know what's happened to Richard, for goodness' sake tell us!"

"Answer the question," said Naughton with a scowl.

"Well," she said defiantly, "a silly envelope, empty, and sealed with our own wax."

"And again in a word," drawled Ellery, "*sealing-wax*. Now, Gardner, to you fell the really whimsical fourth bequest. It was—?"

"Cabbage," said Gardner with an uncertain grin.

"Cabbages, my dear chap; there were two of them. And finally, Mrs. Gardner, you received what?"

"Two chessmen," she whispered.

"No, no. Not just two chessmen, Mrs. Gardner. Two *kings*." Ellery's gray eyes glittered. "In other words, in the order named we were bombarded with gifts..." he paused and looked at them, and continued softly, " '*of shoes and ships and sealing-wax, of cabbages and kings.*' "

There was the most extraordinary silence. Then Emmy Willows gasped: "The Walrus and the Carpenter. *Alice's Adventures in Wonderland!*"

"I'm ashamed of you, Miss Willowes. Where precisely does Tweedledee's Walrus speech come in Carroll's duology?"

A great light broke over her eager features. "*Through the Looking Glass!*"

"*Through the Looking Glass,*" murmured Ellery in the crackling silence that followed. "And do you know what the subtitle of *Through the Looking Glass* is?"

She said in an awed voice: "*And What Alice Found There.*"

"A perfect recitation, Miss Willowes. We were instructed, then, to go through the looking glass and, by inference, find something on the other side connected with the disappearance of Richard Owen. Quaint idea, eh?" He leaned forward and said brusquely: "Let me revert to my original chain of reasoning. I said that a likely theory was that the mirror didn't reflect the luminous hands because the mirror wasn't there. But since the wall at any rate is solid, the mirror itself must be movable to have been shifted out of place. How was this possible? Yesterday I sought for two hours to find the secret of that mirror—or should I say . . . looking glass?" Their eyes went with horror to the tall mirror set in the wall, winking back at them in the glitter of the bulbs. "And when I discovered the secret, I looked *through the looking glass* and what do you suppose I—a clumsy Alice, indeed!—found there?"

No one replied.

Ellery went swiftly to the mirror, stood on tiptoe, touched something, and something happened to the whole glass. It moved forward as if on hinges. He hooked his fingers in the crack and pulled. The mirror, like a door, swung out and away, revealing a shallow closet-like cavity.

The women with one breath screamed and covered their eyes.

The stiff figure of the Mad Hatter, with Richard Owen's unmistakable features, glared out at them—a dead, horrible, baleful glare.

Paul Gardner stumbled to his feet, choking and jerking at his collar. His eyes bugged out of his head. "O-O-Owen," he gasped. "Owen. He *can't* be here. I b-b-buried him myself under the big rock behind the house in the woods. Oh, my God." And he smiled a dreadful smile and his eyes turned over and he collapsed in a faint on the floor.

Ellery sighed. "It's all right now, De Vere," and the Mad Hatter moved and his features ceased to resemble Richard Owen's magically. "You may come out now. Admirable bit of statuary histrionics. And it turned the trick, as I thought it would. There's your man, Mr. Naughton. And if you'll question Mrs. Gardner, I believe you'll find that she's been Owen's mistress for some time. Gardner obviously found it out and killed him. Look out—there *she* goes, too!"

70

"What I can't understand," murmured Emmy Willowes after a long silence late that night, as she and Mr. Ellery Queen sat side by side in the local bound for Jamaica and the express for Pennsylvania Station, "is—" She stopped helplessly. "I can't understand so many things, Mr. Queen."

"It was simple enough," said Ellery wearily, staring out the window at the rushing dark countryside.

"But who is that man—that De Vere?"

"Oh, he! A Thespian acquaintance of mine temporarily 'at liberty.' He's an actor—does character bits. You wouldn't know him, I suppose. You see, when my deductions had led me to the looking glass and I examined it and finally discovered its secret and opened it, I found Owen's body lying there in the Hatter costume—"

She shuddered. "Much too realistic drama to my taste. Why didn't you announce your discovery at once?"

"And gain what? There wasn't a shred of evidence against the murderer. I wanted time to think out a plan to make the murderer give himself away. I left the body there—"

"You mean to sit there and say you knew Gardner did it all the time?" she demanded, frankly skeptical.

He shrugged. "Of course. The Owens had lived in that house barely a month. The spring on that compartment is remarkably well concealed; it probably would never be discovered unless you knew it existed and were looking for it. But I recalled that Owen himself had remarked Friday night that Gardner had designed 'this development.' I had it then, naturally. Who more likely than the architect to know the secret of such a hidden closet? Why he designed and had built a secret panel I don't know; I suppose it fitted into some architectural whim of his. So it had to be Gardner, you see." He gazed thoughtfully at the dusty ceiling of the car. "I reconstructed the crime easily enough. After we retired Friday night Gardner came down to have it out with Owen about Mrs. Gardner—a lusty wench, if I ever saw one. They had words; Gardner killed him. It must have been an unpremeditated crime. His first impulse was to hide the body. He couldn't take it out Friday night in that awful rain without leaving traces on his night-clothes. Then he remembered the panel behind the mirror. The body would be safe enough there, he felt, until he could remove it when the rain stopped and the ground dried to a permanent hiding-place; dig a grave, or whatnot. . . . He was stowing the body away in the closet when I opened the door of the den; that was why I didn't see the reflection of the clock. Then, while I was in the library, he closed the mirror-door and dodged upstairs. I came out quickly, though, and he decided to brazen it out; even pretended he thought I might be 'Owen' coming up.

"At any rate, Saturday night he drugged us all, took the body out, buried it, and came back and dosed himself with the drug to make his part as natural as possible. He didn't know I had found the body behind the mirror Saturday afternoon. When, Sunday morning, I found the body gone, I knew of course the reason for the drugging. Gardner by burying the body in a place unknown to anyone—without leaving, as far as he knew, even a clue to the fact that murder had been committed at all—was naturally doing away with the primary piece of evidence in any murder-case . . . the *corpus delicti*. . . . Well, I found the opportunity to telephone De Vere and instruct him in what he had to do. He dug up the Hatter's costume somewhere, managed to get a photo of Owen from a theatrical office, came down here. . . . We put him in the closet while Naughton's man was detaining you people in the library. You see, I had to build up suspense, make Gardner give himself away, break down his moral resistance. He had to be forced to disclose where he had buried the body; and he was the only one who could tell us. It worked."

The actress regarded him sidewise out of her clever eyes. Ellery sighed moodily, glancing away from her slim legs outstretched to the opposite seat. "But the most puzzling thing of all," she said with a pretty frown. "Those perfectly fiendish and fantastic packages. Who sent them, for heavens sake?"

Ellery did not reply for a long time. Then he said drowsily, barely audible above the clatter of the train: "You did, really."

"I?" She was so startled that her mouth flew open.

"Only in a manner of speaking," murmured Ellery, closing his eyes. "Your idea about running a mad tea party out of *Alice* for Master Jonathan's delectation—the whole pervading spirit of the Reverend Dodgson—started a chain of fantasy in my own brain, you see. Just opening the closet and saying that Owen's body had been there, or even getting De Vere to act as Owen, wasn't enough. I had to prepare Gardner's mind psychologically, fill him with puzzlement first, get him to realize after a while where the gifts with their implications were leading. . . . Had to torture him, I suppose. It's a weakness of mine. At any rate, it was an easy matter to telephone my father, the Inspector; and he sent Sergeant Velie down and I managed to smuggle all those things I'd filched from the house out into the woods behind and hand good Velie what I had. . . . He did the rest, packaging and all."

She sat up and measured him a severe glance. "*Mr.* Queen! Is that cricket in the best detective circles?"

He grinned sleepily. "I had to do it, you see. Drama, Miss Willowes. You ought to be able to understand that. Surround a murderer with things he doesn't understand, bewilder him, get him mentally punch-drunk, and then spring the knock-out blow, the crusher. . . . Oh, it was devilish clever of me, I admit."

She regarded him for so long and in such silence and with such supple twisting of her boyish figure that he stirred uncomfortably, feeling an unwilling flush come to his cheeks. "And what, if I may ask," he said lightly, "brings that positively lewd expression to your Peter Pannish face, my dear? Feel all right? Anything wrong? By George, how *do* you feel?"

"As Alice would say," she said softly, leaning a little toward him, "curiouser and curiouser."

MAN BITES DOG

(1939)

ANYONE OBSERVING THE tigerish pacings, the gnawings of lip, the contortions of brow, and the fierce melancholy which characterized the conduct of Mr. Ellery Queen, the noted sleuth, during those early October days in Hollywood, would have said reverently that the great man's intellect was once more locked in titantic struggle with the forces of evil.

"Paula," Mr. Queen said to Paula Paris, "I am going mad."

"I hope," said Miss Paris tenderly, "it's love."

Mr. Queen paced, swathed in yards of thought. Queenly Miss Paris observed him with melting eyes. When he had first encountered her, during his investigation of the double murder of Blythe Stuart and Jack Royle, the famous motion picture stars,* Miss Paris had been in the grip of a morbid psychology. She had been in deathly terror of crowds. "Crowd phobia," the doctors called it. Mr. Queen had cured her by the curious method of making love to her. And now she was infected by the cure.

"Is it?" asked Miss Paris, her heart in her eyes.

"Eh?" said Mr. Queen. "What? Oh, no. I mean—it's the World Series." He looked savage. "Don't you realize what's happening? The New York Giants and the New York Yankees are waging mortal combat to determine the baseball championship of the world, and I'm three thousand miles away!"

*Related in *The Four of Hearts*, by Ellery Queen. Frederick A. Stokes Company, 1938.

"Oh," said Miss Paris. Then she said cleverly: "You poor darling."

"Never missed a New York series before," wailed Mr. Queen. "Driving me cuckoo. And what a battle! Greatest series ever played. Moore and DiMaggio have done miracles in the outfield. Giants have pulled a triple play. Goofy Gomez struck out fourteen men to win the first game. Hubbell's pitched a one-hit shutout. And today Dickey came up in the ninth inning with the bases loaded, two out, and the Yanks three runs behind, and slammed a homer over the right-field stands!"

"Is that good?" asked Miss Paris.

"Good!" howled Mr. Queen. "It merely sent the series into a seventh game."

"Poor darling," said Miss Paris again, and she picked up her telephone. When she set it down she said: "Weather's threatening in the East. Tomorrow the New York Weather Bureau expects heavy rains."

Mr. Queen stared wildly. "You mean—"

"I mean that you're taking tonight's plane for the East. And you'll see your beloved seventh game day after tomorrow."

"Paula, you're a genius!" Then Mr. Queen's face fell. "But the studio, tickets . . . *Bigre*! I'll tell the studio I'm down with elephantiasis, and I'll wire dad to snare a box. With his pull at City Hall, he ought to—Paula, I don't know what I'd do . . ."

"You might," suggested Miss Paris, "kiss me . . . goodbye."

Mr. Queen did so, absently. Then he started. "Not at all! You're coming with me!"

"That's what I had in mind," said Miss Paris contentedly.

And so Wednesday found Miss Paris and Mr. Queen at the Polo Grounds, ensconced in a field box behind the Yankees' dugout.

Mr. Queen glowed, he revelled, he was radiant. While Inspector Queen, with the suspiciousness of all fathers, engaged Paula in exploratory conversation, Ellery filled his lap and Paula's with peanut hulls, consumed frankfurters and soda pop immoderately, made hypercritical comments on the appearance of the various athletes, derided the Yankees, extolled the Giants, evolved complicated fifty-cent bets with Detective-Sergeant Velie, of the Inspector's staff, and leaped to his feet screaming with fifty thousand other maniacs as the news came that Carl Hubbell, the beloved Meal Ticket of the Giants, would oppose Señor El Goofy Gomez, the ace of the Yankee staff, on the mound.

"Will the Yanks murder that apple today!" predicted the Sergeant, who was an incurable Yankee worshiper. "And will Goofy mow 'em down!"

"Four bits," said Mr. Queen coldly, "say the Yanks don't score three earned runs off Carl."

"It's a pleasure!"

"I'll take a piece of that, Sergeant," chuckled a handsome man to the front of them, in a rail seat. "Hi, Inspector. Swell day for it, eh?"

"Jimmy Connor!" exclaimed Inspector Queen. "The old Song-and-Dance Man in person. Say, Jimmy, you never met my son Ellery, did you? Excuse me. Miss Paris, this is the famous Jimmy Connor, God's gift to Broadway."

"Glad to meet you, Miss Paris," smiled the Song-and-Dance Man, sniffing at his orchidaceous lapel. "Read your *Seeing Stars* column, every day. Meet Judy Starr."

Miss Paris smiled, and the woman beside Jimmy Connor smiled back, and just then three Yankee players strolled over to the box and began to jeer at Connor for having had to take seats behind the hated Yankee dugout.

Judy Starr was sitting oddly still. She was the famous Judy Starr who had been discovered by Florenz Ziegfield—a second Marilyn Miller, the critics called her; dainty and pretty, with a perky profile and great honey-colored eyes, who had sung and danced her way into the heart of New York. Her day of fame was almost over now. Perhaps, thought Paula, staring at Judy's profile, that explained the pinch of her little mouth, the fine lines about her tragic eyes, the singing tension of her figure.

Perhaps. But Paula was not sure. There was immediacy, a defense against a palpable and present danger, in Judy Starr's tautness. Paula looked about. And at once her eyes narrowed.

Across the rail of the box, in the box at their left, sat a very tall, leather-skinned, silent and intent man. The man, too, was staring out at the field, in an attitude curiously like that of Judy Starr, whom he could have touched by extending his big, ropy, muscular hand across the rail. And on the man's other side there sat a woman whom Paula recognized instantly. Lotus Verne, the motion picture actress!

Lotus Verne was a gorgeous, full-blown redhead with deep mercury-colored eyes who had come out of Northern Italy Ludovica Vernicchi, changed her name, and flashed across the Hollywood skies in a picture called *Woman of Bali*, a color-film in which loving care had been lavished on the display possibilities of her dark, full, dangerous body. With fame, she had developed a passion for press-agentry, borzois in pairs, and tall brown men with muscles. She was arrayed in sun-yellow, and she stood out among the women in the field boxes like a butterfly in a mass of grubs. By contrast little Judy Starr, in her flame-colored outfit, looked almost old and dowdy.

Paula nudged Ellery, who was critically watching the Yankees at batting practice. "Ellery," she said softly, "who is that big, brown, attractive man in the next box?"

Lotus Verne said something to the brown man, and suddenly Judy Starr said something to the Song-and-Dance Man; and then the two women exchanged the kind of glance women use when there is no knife handy.

Ellery said absently: "Who? Oh! Thàt's Big Bill Tree."

"Tree?" repeated Paula, "Big Bill Tree?"

"Greatest left-handed pitcher major-league baseball ever saw," said Mr. Queen, staring reverently at the brown man. "Six feet three inches of bull-whip and muscle, with a temper as sudden as the hook on his curve ball and a change of pace that fooled the greatest sluggers of baseball for fifteen years. What a man!"

"Yes, isn't he?" smiled Miss Paris.

"Now what does that mean?" demanded Mr. Queen.

"It takes greatness to escort a lady like Lotus Verne to a ball game," said Paula, "to find your wife sitting within spitting distance in the next box, and to carry it off as well as your muscular friend Mr. Tree is doing."

"That's right," said Mr. Queen softly. "Judy Starr *is* Mrs. Bill Tree."

He groaned as Joe DiMaggio hit a ball to the clubhouse clock.

"Funny," said Miss Paris, her clever eyes inspecting in turn the four people before her: Lotus Verne, the Hollywood siren; Big Bill Tree, the ex-baseball pitcher; Judy Starr, Tree's wife; and Jimmy Connor, the Song-and-Dance Man, Mrs. Tree's escort. Two couples, two boxes . . . and no sign of recognition. "Funny," murmured Miss Paris. "From the way Tree courted Judy you'd have thought the marriage would outlast eternity. He snatched her from under Jimmy Connor's nose one night at the Winter Garden, drove her up to Greenwich at eighty miles an hour, and married her before she could catch her breath."

"Yes," said Mr. Queen politely. "Come on, you Giants!" he yelled, as the Giants trotted out for batting practice.

"And then something happened," continued Miss Paris reflectively. "Tree went to Hollywood to make a baseball picture, met Lotus Verne, and the wench took the overgrown country boy the way the over-grown country boy had taken Judy Starr. What a fall was there, my baseball-minded friend."

"What a wallop!" cried Mr. Queen enthusiastically, as Mel Ott hit one that bounced off the right-field fence.

"And Big Bill yammered for a divorce, and Judy refused to give it to him because she loved him, I suppose," said Paula softly—"and now this. How interesting."

Big Bill Tree twisted in his seat a little; and Judy Starr was still and pale, staring out of her tragic, honey-colored eyes at the Yankee bat-boy and giving him unwarranted delusions of grandeur. Jimmy Connor continued to exchange sarcastic greetings with Yankee play-ers, but his eyes kept shifting back to Judy's face. And beautiful Lotus Verne's arm crept about Tree's shoulders.

"I don't like it," murmured Miss Paris a little later.

"You don't like it?" said Mr. Queen. "Why, the game hasn't even started."

"I don't mean your game, silly. I mean the quadrangular situation in front of us."

"Look, darling," said Mr. Queen. "I flew three thousand miles to see a ball game. There's only one angle that interests me—the view from this box of the greatest li'l ol' baseball tussle within the memory of gaffers. I yearn, I strain, I hunger to see it. Play with your quadrangle, but leave me to my baseball."

"I've always been psychic," said Miss Paris, paying no attention. "This is—bad. Something's going to happen."

Mr. Queen grinned. "I know what. The deluge. See what's coming."

Someone in the grandstand had recognized the celebrities, and a sea of people was rushing down on the two boxes. They thronged the aisle behind the boxes, waving pencils and papers, and pleading. Big Bill

Tree and Lotus Verne ignored their pleas for autographs; but Judy Starr with a curious eagerness signed paper after paper with the yellow pencils thrust at her by people leaning over the rail. Good-naturedly Jimmy Connor scrawled his signature, too.

"Little Judy," sighed Miss Paris, setting her natural straw straight as an autograph-hunter knocked it over her eyes, "is flustered and unhappy. Moistening the tip of your pencil with your tongue is scarcely a mark of poise. Seated next to her Lotus-bound husband, she hardly knows what she's doing, poor thing."

"Neither do I," growled Mr. Queen, fending off an octopus which turned out to be eight pleading arms offering scorecards.

Big Bill sneezed, groped for a handkerchief, and held it to his nose, which was red and swollen. "Hey, Mac," he called irritably to a red-coated usher. "Do somethin' about this mob, huh?" He sneezed again. "Damn this hay-fever!"

"The touch of earth," said Miss Paris. "But definitely attractive."

"Should 'a' seen Big Bill the day he pitched that World Series final against the Tigers," chuckled Sergeant Velie. "He was sure attractive that day. Pitched a no-hit shutout!"

Inspector Queen said: "Ever hear the story behind that final game, Miss Paris? The night before, a gambler named Sure Shot McCoy, who represented a betting syndicate, called on Big Bill and laid down fifty grand in spot cash in return for Bill's promise to throw the next day's game. Bill took the money, told his manager the whole story, donated the bribe to a fund for sick ball players, and the next day shut out the Tigers without a hit."

"Byronic, too," murmured Miss Paris.

"So then Sure Shot, badly bent," grinned the Inspector, "called on Bill for the payoff. Bill knocked him down two flights of stairs."

"Wasn't that dangerous?"

"I guess," smiled the Inspector, "you could say so. That's why you see that plug-ugly with the smashed nose sitting over there right behind Tree's box. He's Mr. Terrible Turk, late of Cicero, and since that night Big Bill's shadow. You don't see Mr. Turk's right hand, because Mr. Turk's right hand is holding on to an automatic under his jacket. You'll notice, too, that Mr. Turk hasn't for a second taken his eyes off that pasty-cheeked customer eight rows up, whose name is Sure Shot McCoy."

Paula stared. "But what a silly thing for Tree to do!"

"Well, yes," drawled Inspector Queen, "seeing that when he popped Mr. McCoy Big Bill snapped two of the carpal bones of his pitching wrist and wrote finis to his baseball career."

Big Bill Tree hauled himself to his feet, whispered something to the Verne woman, who smiled coyly, and left his box. His bodyguard, Turk, jumped up; but the big man shook his head, waved aside a crowd of people, and vaulted up the concrete steps toward the rear of the grandstand.

And then Judy Starr said something bitter and hot and desperate across the rail to the woman her husband had brought to the Polo Grounds. Lotus Verne's mercurial eyes glittered, and she replied in a careless, insulting voice that made Bill Tree's wife sit up stiffly. Jimmy Connor began to tell the one about Walter Winchell and the Seven Dwarfs . . . loudly and fast.

The Verne woman began to paint her rich lips with short, vicious strokes of her orange lipstick; and Judy Starr's flame kid glove tightened on the rail between them.

And after a while Big Bill returned and sat down again. Judy said something to Jimmy Connor, and the Song-and-Dance Man slid over one seat to his right, and Judy slipped into Connor's seat; so that between her and her husband there was now not only the box rail but an empty chair as well.

Lotus Verne put her arm about Tree's shoulders again.

Tree's wife fumbled inside her flame suède bag. She said suddenly: "Jimmy, buy me a frankfurter."

Connor ordered a dozen. Big Bill scowled. He jumped up and ordered some, too. Connor tossed the vendor two one-dollar bills and waved him away.

A new sea deluged the two boxes, and Tree turned round, annoyed. "All right, all right, Mac," he growled at the redcoat struggling with the pressing mob. "We don't want a riot here. I'll take six. Just six. Let's have 'em."

There was a rush that almost upset the attendant. The rail behind the boxes was a solid line of fluttering hands, arms, and scorecards.

"Mr. Tree—said—six!" panted the usher; and he grabbed a pencil and card from one of the outstretched hands and gave them to Tree. The overflow of pleaders spread to the next box. Judy Starr smiled her best professional smile and reached for a pencil and card. A group of players on the field, seeing what was happening, ran over to the field rail and handed her scorecards, too, so that she had to set her half-consumed frankfurter down on the empty seat beside her. Big Bill set his frankfurter down on the same empty seat; he licked the pencil long and absently and began to inscribe his name in the stiff, laborious hand of a man unused to writing.

The attendant howled: "That's six, now! Mr. Tree said just six, so that's all!" as if God Himself had said six; and the crowd groaned, and Big Bill waved his immense paw and reached over to the empty seat in the other box to lay hold of his half-eaten frankfurter. But his wife's hand got there first and fumbled round; and it came up with Tree's frankfurter. The big brown man almsot spoke to her then; but he did not, and he picked up the remaining frankfurter, stuffed it into his mouth, and chewed away, but not as if he enjoyed its taste.

Mr. Ellery Queen was looking at the four people before him with a puzzled, worried expression. Then he caught Miss Paula Paris's amused glance and blushed angrily.

The groundkeepers had just left the field and the senior umpire was dusting off the plate to the roar of the crowd when Lotus Verne, who thought a double play was something by Eugene O'Neill, flashed a strange look at Big Bill Tree.

"Bill! Don't you feel well?"

The big ex-pitcher, a sickly blue beneath his tanned skin, put his hand to his eyes and shook his head as if to clear it.

"It's the hot dog," snapped Lotus. "No more for you!"

Tree blinked and began to say something, but just then Carl Hubbell completed his warming-up, Crosetti marched to the plate, Harry Danning tossed the ball to his second-baseman, who flipped it to Hubbell and trotted back to his position yipping like a terrier.

The voice of the crowd exploded in one ear-splitting burst. And then silence.

And Crosetti swung at the first ball Hubbell pitched and smashed it far over Joe Moore's head for a triple.

Jimmy Connor gasped as if someone had thrust a knife into his heart. But Detective-Sergeant Velie was bellowing: "What'd I tell you? It's gonna be a massacree!"

"What is everyone shouting for?" asked Paula.

Mr. Queen nibbled his nails as Danning strolled halfway to the pitcher's box. But Hubbell pulled his long pants up, grinning. Red Rolfe was waving a huge bat at the plate. Danning trotted back. Manager Bill Terry had one foot up on the edge of the Giant dugout, his chin on his fist, looking anxious. The infield came in to cut off the run.

Again fifty thousand people made no single little sound.

And Hubbell struck out Rolfe, DiMaggio, and Gehrig.

Mr. Queen shrieked his joy with the thousands as the Giants came whooping in. Jimmy Connor did an Indian war-dance in the box. Sergeant Velie looked aggrieved. Señor Gomez took his warm-up pitches, the umpire used his whiskbroom on the plate again, and Jo-Jo Moore, the Thin Man, ambled up with his war club.

He walked. Bartell fanned. But Jeep Ripple singled off Flash Gordon's shins on the first pitch; and there were Moore on third and Ripple on first, one out, and Little Mel Ott at bat.

Big Bill Tree got half out of his seat, looking surprised, and then dropped to the concrete floor of the box as if somebody had slammed him behind the ear with a fast ball.

Lotus screamed. Judy, Bill's wife, turned like a shot, shaking. People in the vicinity jumped up. Three red-coated attendants hurried down, preceded by the hard-looking Mr. Turk. The bench-warmers stuck their heads over the edge of the Yankee dugout to stare.

"Fainted," growled Turk, on his knees beside the prostrate athlete.

"Loosen his collar," moaned Lotus Verne. "He's so p-pale!!"

"Have to git him outa here."

"Yes. Oh, yes!"

The attendants and Turk lugged the big man off, long arms dangling in the oddest way. Lotus stumbled along beside him, biting her lips nervously.

"I think," began Judy in a quivering voice, rising.

But Jimmy Connor put his hand on her arm, and she sank back.

And in the next box Mr. Ellery Queen, on his feet from the instant Tree collapsed, kept looking after the forlorn procession, puzzled, mad about something; until somebody in the stands squawked: "SID-DOWN!" and he sat down.

"Oh, I knew something would happen," whispered Paula.

"Nonsense!" said Mr. Queen shortly. "Fainted, that's all."

Inspector Queen said: "There's Sure Shot McCoy not far off. I wonder if—"

"Too many hot dogs," snapped his son. "What's the matter with you people? Can't I see my ball game in peace?" And he howled: "Come o-o-on, Mel!"

Ott lifted his right leg into the sky and swung. The ball whistled into right field, a long long fly, Selkirk racing madly back after it. He caught it by leaping four feet into the air with his back against the barrier. Moore was off for the plate like a streak and beat the throw to Bill Dickey by inches.

"Yip-ee!" Thus Mr. Queen.

The Giants trotted out to their positions at the end of the first inning leading one to nothing.

Up in the press box the working gentlemen of the press tore into their chores, recalling Carl Hubbell's similar feat in the All-Star game when he struck out the five greatest batters of the American League in succession; praising Twinkletoes Selkirk for his circus catch; and incidentally noting that Big Bill Tree, famous ex-hurler of the National League, had fainted in a field box during the first inning. Joe Williams of the *World-Telegram* said it was excitement, Hype Igoe opined that it was a touch of sun—Big Bill never wore a hat—and Frank Graham of the Sun guessed it was too many frankfurters.

Paula Paris said quietly: "I should think, with your detective instincts, Mr. Queen, you would seriously question the 'fainting' of Mr. Tree."

Mr. Queen squirmed and finally mumbled: "It's coming to a pretty pass when a man's instincts aren't his own. Velie, go see what really happened to him."

"I wanna watch the game," howled Velie. "Why don't you go yourself, maestro?"

"And possibly," said Mr. Queen, "you ought to go too, dad. I have a hunch it may lie in your jurisdiction."

Inspector Queen regarded his son for some time. Then he rose and sighed: "Come along, Thomas."

Sergeant Velie growled something about some people always spoiling other people's fun and why the hell did he ever have to become a cop; but he got up and obediently followed the Inspector.

Mr. Queen nibbled his fingernails and avoided Miss Paris's accusing eyes.

The second inning was uneventful. Neither side scored.

As the Giants took the field again, an usher came running down the concrete steps and whispered into Jim Connor's ear. The Song-and-Dance Man blinked. He rose slowly. "Excuse me, Judy."

Judy grasped the rail. "It's Bill. Jimmy, tell me."

"Now, Judy—"

"Something's happened to Bill!" Her voice shrilled, and then broke. She jumped up. "I'm going with you."

Connor smiled as if he had just lost a bet, and then he took Judy's arm and hurried her away.

Paula Paris stared after them, breathing hard.

Mr. Queen beckoned the redcoat. "What's the trouble?" he demanded.

"Mr. Tree passed out. Some young doc in the crowd tried to pull him out of it at the office, but he couldn't, and he's startin' to look worried—"

"I knew it!" cried Paula as the man darted away. "Ellery Queen, are you going to sit here and do *nothing*?"

But Mr. Queen defiantly set his jaw. Nobody was going to jockey him out of seeing this battle of giants; no ma'am!

There were two men out when Frank Crosetti stepped up to the plate for his second time at bat, with the count two all, plastered a wicked single over Ott's head.

And, of course, Sergeant Velie took just that moment to amble down and say, his eyes on the field: "Better come along, Master Mind. The old man wouldst have a word with thou. Ah, I see Frankie's on first. Smack it, Red!"

Mr. Queen watched Rolfe take a ball. "Well?" he said shortly. Paula's lips were parted.

"Big Bill's just kicked the bucket. What happened in the second inning?"

"He's . . . *dead*?" gasped Paula.

Mr. Queen rose involuntarily. Then he sat down again. "Damn it," he roared, "it isn't fair. I won't go!"

"Suit yourself. Attaboy, Rolfe!" bellowed the Sergeant as Rolfe singled sharply past Bartell and Crosetti pulled up at second base. "Far's I'm concerned, it's open and shut. The little woman did it with her own little hands."

"Judy *Starr*?" said Miss Paris.

"Bill's wife?" said Mr. Queen. "What are you talking about?"

"That's right, little Judy. She poisoned his hot dog." Velie chuckled. "Man bites dog, and—zowie."

"Has she confessed?" snapped Mr. Queen.

"Naw. But you know dames. She gave Bill the business all right. C'mon, Joe! And I gotta go. What a life."

Mr. Queen did not look at Miss Paris. He bit his lip. "Here, Velie, wait a minute."

DiMaggio hit a long fly that Lieber caught without moving in his tracks, and the Yankees were retired without a score.

"Ah," said Mr. Queen. "Good old Hubbell." And as the Giants trotted in, he took a fat roll of bills from his pocket, climbed onto his seat, and began waving greenbacks at the spectators in the reserved seats behind the box. Sergeant Velie and Miss Parks stared at him in amazement.

"I'll give five bucks," yelled Mr. Queen, waving the money, "for every autograph Bill Tree signed before the game! In this box right here! Five bucks, gentlemen! Come and get it!"

"You nuts?" gasped the Sergeant.

The mob gaped, and then began to laugh, and after a few moments a pair of sheepish-looking men came down, and then two more, and finally a fifth. An attendant ran over to find out what was the matter.

"Are you the usher who handled the crowd around Bill Tree's box before the game, when he was giving autographs?" demanded Mr. Queen.

"Yes, sir. But, look we can't allow—"

"Take a gander at these five men.... You, bud? Yes, that's Tree's handwriting. Here's your fin. Next!" and Mr. Queen went down the line, handing out five-dollar bills with abandon in return for five dirty scorecards with Tree's scrawl on them.

"Anybody else?" he called out, waving his roll of bills.

But nobody else appeared, although there was ungentle badinage from the stands. Sergeant Velie stood there shaking his big head. Miss Paris looked intensely curious.

"Who didn't come down?" rapped Mr. Queen.

"Huh?" said the usher, his mouth open.

"There were six autographs. Only five people turned up. Who was the sixth man? Speak up!"

"Oh." The redcoat scratched his ear. "Say, it wasn't a man. It was a kid."

"A *boy*?

"Yeah, a little squirt in knee-pants."

Mr. Queen looked unhappy. Velie growled: "Sometimes I think society's takin' an awful chance lettin' you run around loose," and the two men left the box. Miss Paris, bright-eyed, followed.

"Have to clear this mess up in a hurry," muttered Mr. Queen. "Maybe we'll still be able to catch the late innings."

Sergeant Velie led the way to an office, before which a policeman was lounging. He opened the door, and inside they found the Inspector pacing. Turk, the thug, was standing with a scowl over a long still thing on a couch covered with newspapers. Jimmy Connor sat between the two women; and none of the three so much as stirred a foot. They were all pale and breathing heavily.

"This is Dr. Fielding," said Inspector Queen, indicating an elderly white-haired man standing quietly by a window. "He was Tree's physician. He happened to be in the park watching the game when the rumor reached his ears that Tree had collapsed. So he hurried up here to see what he could do."

Ellery went to the couch and pulled the newspaper off Bill Tree's still head. Paula crossed swiftly to Judy Starr and said: "I'm terribly sorry, Mrs. Tree," but the woman, her eyes closed, did not move. After a while Ellery dropped the newspaper back into place and said irritably: "Well, well, let's have it."

"A young doctor," said the Inspector, "got here before Dr. Fielding did, and treated Tree for fainting. I guess it was his fault—"

"Not at all," said Dr. Fielding sharply. "The early picture was compatible with fainting, from what he told me. He tried the usual restorative methods—even injected caffeine and picrotoxin. But there was no convulsion, and he didn't happen to catch the odor of bitter almonds."

"Prussic!" said Ellery. "Taken orally?"

"Yes. HCN—hydrocyanic acid, or prussic, as you prefer. I suspected it at once because—well," said Dr. Fielding in a grim voice, "because of something that occurred in my office only the other day."

"What was that?"

"I had a two-ounce bottle of hydrocyanic acid on my desk—I sometimes use it in minute quantities as a cardiac stimulant. Mrs. Tree," the doctor's glance flickered over the silent woman, "happened to be in my office, resting in preparation for a metabolism test. I left her alone. By a coincidence, Bill Tree dropped in the same morning for a physical check-up. I saw another patient in another room, returned, gave Mrs. Tree her test, saw her out, and came back with Tree. It was then I noticed the bottle, which had been plainly marked DANGER— POISON, was missing from my desk. I thought I had mislaid it, but now . . ."

"I didn't take it," said Judy Starr in a lifeless voice, still not opening her eyes. "I never even saw it."

The Song-and-Dance Man took her limp hand and gently stroked it.

"No hypo marks on the body," said Dr. Fielding dryly. "And I am told that fifteen to thirty minutes before Tree collapsed he ate a frankfurter under . . . peculiar conditions."

"I didn't!" screamed Judy. "I didn't do it!" She pressed her face, sobbing, against Connor's orchid.

Lotus Verne quivered. "She made him pick up her frankfurter. I saw it. They both laid their frankfurters down on that empty seat, and she picked up his. So he had to pick up hers. She poisoned her own frankfurter and then saw to it that he ate it by mistake. Poisoner!" She glared hate at Judy.

"Wench," said Miss Paris *sotto voce*, glaring hate at Lotus.

"In other words," put in Ellery impatiently, "Miss Starr is convicted on the usual two counts, motive and opportunity. Motive—her jealousy of Miss Verne and her hatred—an assumption—of Bill Tree, her husband. And opportunity both to lay hands on the poison in your office, Doctor, and to sprinkle some on her frankfurter, contriving to exchange hers for his while they were both autographing scorecards."

"She hated him," snarled Lotus. "And me for having taken him from her!"

"Be quiet, you," said Mr. Queen. He opened the corridor door and said to the policeman outside: "Look, McGillicuddy, or whatever your name is, go tell the announcer to make a speech over the loud-speaker system. By the way, what's the score now?"

"Still one to skunk," said the officer. "Them boys Hubbell an' Gomez are hot, what I mean."

"The announcer is to ask the little boy who got Bill Tree's autograph just before the game to come to this office. If he does, he'll receive a ball, bat, pitcher's glove, and an autographed picuture of Tree in uniform to hang over his itsy-bitsy bed. Scram!"

"Yes, *sir*," said the officer.

"King Carl pitching his heart out," grumbled Mr. Queen, shutting the door, "and me strangulated by this blamed thing. Well, dad, do you think, too, that Judy Starr dosed the frankfurter?"

"What else can I think?" said the Inspector absently. His ears were cocked for the faint crowd-shouts from the park.

"Judy Starr," replied his son, "didn't poison her husband any more than I did."

Judy looked up slowly, her mouth muscles twitching. Paula said, gladly: "You wonderful man!"

"She didn't?" said the Inspector, looking alert.

"The frankfurter theory," snapped Mr. Queen, "is too screwy for words. For Judy to have poisoned her husband, she had to unscrew the cap of a bottle and douse her hot dog on the spot with the hydrocyanic acid. Yet Jimmy Connor was seated by her side, and in the only period in which she could possibly have poisoned the frankfurter a group of Yankee ball players was *standing before her* across the field rail getting her autograph. Were they all accomplices? And how could she have known Big Bill would lay his hot dog on that empty seat? The whole thing is absurd."

A roar from the stands made him continue hastily: "There was one plausible theory that fitted the facts. When I heard that Tree had died of poisoning, I recalled that at the time he was autographing the six scorecards, *he had thoroughly licked the end of a pencil* which had been handed to him with one of the cards. It was possible then, that the pencil he licked had been poisoned. So I offered to buy the six autographs."

Paula regarded him tenderly, and Velie said: "I'll be so-and-so if he didn't."

"I didn't expect the poisoner to come forward, but I knew the innocent ones would. Five claimed the money. The sixth, the missing one, the usher informed me, had been a small boy."

"A kid poisoned Bill?" growled Turk, speaking for the first time. "you're crazy from the heat."

"In spades," added the Inspector.

"Then why didn't the boy come forward?" put in Paula quickly. "Go on, darling!"

"He didn't come forward, not because he was guilty but because he wouldn't sell Bill Tree's autograph for anything. No, obviously a hero-worshiping boy wouldn't try to poison the great Bill Tree. Then, just as obviously, he didn't realize what he was doing. Consequently, he must have been an innocent tool. The question was—and still is—of whom?"

"Sure Shot," said the Inspector slowly.

Lotus Verne sprang to her feet, her eyes glittering. "Perhaps Judy Starr didn't poison that frankfurter, but if she didn't then she hired that boy to give Bill—"

Mr. Queen said disdainfully: "Miss Starr didn't leave the box once." Someone knocked on the corridor door and he opened it. For the first time he smiled. When he shut the door they saw that his arm was about the shoulders of a boy with brown hair and quick clever eyes. The boy was clutching a scorecard tightly.

"They say over the announcer," mumbled the boy, "that I'll get a autographed pi'ture of Big Bill Tree if . . ." He stopped, abashed at their strangely glinting eyes.

"And you'll certainly get it, too," said Mr. Queen heartily. "What's your name, sonny?"

"Fenimore Feigenspan," replied the boy, edging toward the door. "Gran' Concourse, Bronx. Here's the scorecard. How about the pi'ture?"

"Let's see that, Fenimore," said Mr. Queen. "When did Bill Tree give you this autograph?"

"Before the game. He said he'd on'y give six—"

"Where's the pencil you handed him, Fenimore?"

The boy looked suspicious, but he dug into a bulging pocket and brought forth one of the ordinary yellow pencils sold at the park with scorecards. Ellery took it from him gingerly, and Dr. Fielding took it from Ellery, and sniffed its tip. He nodded, and for the first time a look

89

of peace came over Judy Starr's still face and she dropped her head tiredly to Connor's shoulder.

Mr. Queen ruffled Fenimore Feigenspan's hair. "That's swell, Fenimore. Somebody gave you that pencil while the Giants were at batting practice, isn't that so?"

"Yeah." The boy stared at him.

"Who was it?" asked Mr. Queen lightly.

"I dunno. A big guy with a coat an' a turned-down hat an' a mustache, an' big black sun-glasses. I couldn't see his face good. Where's my pi'ture? I wanna see the game!"

"Just where was it that this man gave you the pencil?"

"In the—" Fenimore paused, glancing at the ladies with embarrassment. Then he muttered: "Well, I hadda go, an' this guy says—in there—he's ashamed to ask her for her autograph, so would I do it for him—"

"What? What's that?" exclaimed Mr. Queen. "Did you say 'her'"

"Sure," said Fenimore. "The dame, he says, wearin' the red hat an' red dress an' red gloves in the field box near the Yanks dugout, he says. He even took me outside an' pointed down to where she was sittin'. Say!" cried Fenimore, goggling. "That's her! That's the dame!" and he levelled a grimy forefinger at Judy Starr.

Judy shivered and felt blindly for the Song-and-Dance Man's hand.

"Let me get this straight, Fenimore," said Mr. Queen softly. "This man with the sun-glasses asked you to get this lady's autograph for him, and gave you the pencil and scorecard to get it with?"

"Yeah, an' two bucks too, sayin' he'd meet me after the game to pick up the card, but—"

"But you didn't get the lady's autograph for him, did you? You went down to get it, and hung around waiting for your chance, but then you spied Big Bill Tree, your hero, in the next box and forgot all about the lady, didn't you?"

The boy shrank back. "I didn't mean to, honest, Mister. I'll give the two bucks back!"

"And seeing Big Bill there, your hero, you went right over to get *his* autograph for *yourself*, didn't you?" Fenimore nodded, frightened. "You gave the usher the pencil and scorecard this man with the scorecard this man with the sun-glasses had handed you, and the usher turned the pencil and scorecard over to Bill Tree in the box—wasn't that the way it happened?''

"Y-yes, sir, an'..." Fenimore twisted out of Ellery's grasp, "an' so I—I gotta go." And before anyone could stop him he was indeed gone, racing down the corridor like the wind.

The policeman outside shouted, but Ellery said: "Let him go, officer," and shut the door. Then he opened it again and said: "How's she stand now?"

"Dunno exactly, sir. Somethin' happened out there just now. I think the Yanks scored."

"Damn," groaned Mr. Queen, and he shut the door again.

"So it was Mrs. Tree who was on the spot, not Bill," scowled the Inspector. "I'm sorry, Judy Starr... Big man with a coat and hat and mustache and sun-glasses. Some description!"

"Sounds like a phony to me," said Sergeant Velie.

"If it was a disguise, he dumped it somewhere," said the Inspector thoughtfully. "Thomas, have a look in the Men's Room behind the section where we were sitting. And Thomas," he added in a whisper, "find out what the score is." Velie grinned and hurried out. Inspector Queen frowned. "Quite a job finding a killer in a crowd of fifty thousand people."

"Maybe," said his son suddenly. "maybe it's not such a job after all. . . . What was used to kill? Hydrocyanic acid. Who was intended to be killed? Bill Tree's wife. Any connection between anyone in the case and hydrocyanic acid? Yes—Dr. Fielding 'lost' a bottle of it under suspicious circumstances. Which were? That Bill Tree's wife could have taken that bottle . . . or *Bill Tree himself.*"

"Bill Tree?" gasped Paula.

"Bill?" whispered Judy Starr.

"Quite! Dr. Fielding didn't miss the bottle until *after* he had shown you, Miss Starr, out of his office. He then returned to his office with your husband. Bill could have slipped the bottle into his pocket as he stepped into the room."

"Yes, he could have," muttered Dr. Fielding.

"I don't see," said Mr. Queen, "how we can arrive at any other conclusion. We knew his wife was intended to be the victim today, so obviously she didn't steal the poison. The only other person who had opportunity to steal it was Bill himself."

The Verne woman sprang up. "I don't believe it! It's a frame-up to protect *her*, now that Bill can't defend himself!"

"Ah, but didn't he have motive to kill Judy?" asked Mr. Queen. "Yes, indeed; she wouldn't give him the divorce he craved so that he could marry *you*. I think, Miss Verne, you would be wiser to keep the peace.... Bill had opportunity to steal the bottle of poison in Dr. Fielding's office. He also had opportunity to hire Fenimore today, for he was the *only* one of the whole group who left those boxes during the period when the poisoner must have searched for someone to offer Judy the poisoned pencil.

"All of which fits for what Bill had to do—get to where he had cached his disguise, probably yesterday; look for a likely tool; find Fenimore, give him his instructions and the pencil; get rid of the disguise again; and return to his box. And didn't Bill know better than anyone his wife's habit of moistening a pencil with her tongue—a habit she probably acquired from *him*?"

"Poor Bill," murmured Judy Starr brokenly.

"Women," remarked Miss Paris, "are *fools*."

"There were other striking ironies," replied Mr. Queen. "For if Bill hadn't been suffering from a hay-fever attack, he would have smelled the odor of bitter almonds when his own poisoned pencil was handed to him and stopped in time to save his worthless life. For that matter, if he hadn't been Fenimore Feigenspan's hero, Fenimore would not have handed him his own poisoned pencil in the first place.

"No," said Mr. Queen gladly, "putting it all together, I'm satisfied that Mr. Big Bill Tree, in trying to murder his wife, very neatly murdered himself instead."

"That's all very well for *you*, said the Inspector disconsolately. "But *I* need proof."

"I've told you how it happened," said his son airily, making for the door. "Can any man do more? Coming, Paula?"

But Paula was already at a telephone, speaking guardedly to the New York office of the syndicate for which she worked, and paying no more attention to him than if he had been a worm.

"What's the score? What's been going on?" Ellery demanded of the world at large as he regained his box seat. "Three to three! What the devil's got into Hubbell, anyway? How'd the Yanks score? What inning is it?"

"Last of the ninth," shrieked somebody. "The Yanks got three runs in the eighth on a walk, a double, and DiMag's homer! Danning homered in the sixth with Ott on base! Shut up!"

Bartell singled over Gordon's head. Mr. Queen cheered.

Sergeant Velie tumbled into the next seat. "Well, we got it," he puffed. "Found the whole outfit in the Men's Room—coat, hat, fake mustache, glasses and all. What's the score?"

"Three-three. Sacrifice, Jeep!" shouted Mr. Queen.

"There was a rain-check in the coat pocket from the sixth game, with Big Bill's box number on it. So there's the old man's proof. Chalk up another win for you."

"Who cares . . . *Zowie!*"

Jeep Ripple sacrificed Bartell successfully to second.

"Lucky stiff," howled a Yankee fan nearby. "That's the breaks. See the breaks they get? See?"

"And another thing," said the Sergeant, watching Mell Ott stride to the plate. "Seein' as how all Big Bill did was cross himself up, and no harm done except to his own carcass, and seein' as how organized baseball could get along without a murder, and seein' as how thousands of kids like Fenimore Feigenspan worship the ground he walked on—"

"Sew it up, Mel!" bellowed Mr. Queen.

"—and seein' as how none of the newspaper guys know what happened, except that Bill passed out of the picture after a faint, and seein' as everybody's only too glad to shut their traps—"

Mr. Queen awoke suddenly to the serious matters of life. "What's that? What did you say?"

"Strike him out, Goofy!" roared the Sergean to Señor Gomez, who did not hear. "As I was sayin', it ain't cricket, and the old man would be broke out of the force if the big cheese heard about it . . ."

Someone puffed up behind them, and they turned to see Inspector Queen, red-faced as if after a hard run, scrambling into the box with the assistance of Miss Paula Paris, who looked cool, serene, and star-eyed as ever.

"Dad!" said Mr. Queen, staring. "With a murder on your hands, how can you—"

"Murder?" panted Inspector Queen. "What murder?" And he winked at Miss Paris, who winked back.

"But Paula was telephoning the story—"

"Didn't you hear?" said Paula in a coo, setting her straw straight and slipping into the seat beside Ellery's. "I fixed it all up with your dad. Tonight all the world will know is that Mr. Bill Tree died of heart failure."

They all chuckled then—all but Mr. Queen, whose mouth was open.

"So now," said Paula, "your dad can see the finish of your precious game just as well as *you*, you selfish oaf!"

But Mr. Queen was already fiercely rapt in contemplation of Mel Ott's bat as it swung back and Señor Gomez's ball as it left the Señor's hand to streak toward the plate.

MIND OVER MATTER

(1939)

PAULA PARIS FOUND Inspector Richard Queen of the Homicide Squad inconsolable when she arrived in New York. She understood how he felt, for she had flown in from Hollywood expressly to cover the heavyweight fight between Champion Mike Brown and Challenger Jim Coyle, who were signed to box fifteen rounds at the Stadium that night for the championship of the world.

"You poor dear," said Paula. "And how about you, Master Mind? Aren't you disappointed, too, that you can't buy a ticket to the fight?" she asked Mr. Ellery Queen.

"I'm a jinx," said the great man gloomily. "If I went, something catastrophic would be sure to happen. So why should I want to go?"

"I thought witnessing catastrophes was why people *go* to fights."

"Oh, I don't mean anything gentle like a knockout. Something grimmer."

"He's afraid somebody will knock somebody off," said the Inspector.

"Well, doesn't somebody always?" demanded his son.

"Don't pay any attention to him, Paula," said the Inspector impatiently. "Look, you're a newspaperwoman. Can you get me a ticket?"

"You may as well get me one, too," groaned Mr. Queen.

So Miss Paris smiled and telephoned Phil Maguire, the famous sports editor, and spoke so persuasively to Mr. Maguire that he picked them up that evening in his cranky little sports roadster and they all drove uptown to the Stadium together to see the brawl.

"How do you figure the fight, Maguire?" asked Inspector Queen respectfully.

"On this howdedo," said Maguire, "Maguire doesn't care to be quoted."

"Seems to me the champ ought to take this boy Coyle."

Maguire shrugged. "Phil's sour on the champion," laughed Paula. "Phil and Mike Brown haven't been cuddly since Mike won the title."

"Nothing personal, y'understand," said Phil Maguire. "Only, remember Kid Berès? The Cuban boy. This was in the days when Ollie Stearn was finagling Mike Brown into the heavy sugar. So this fight was a fix, see, and Mike knew it was a fix, and the Kid knew it was a fix, and everybody knew it was a fix and that Kid Berès was supposed to lay down in the sixth round. Well, just the same Mike went out there and sloughed into the Kid and half-killed him. Just for the hell of it. The Kid spent a month in the hospital and when he came out he was only half a man." And Maguire smiled his crooked smile and pressed his horn gently at an old man crossing the street. Then he started, and said: "I guess I just don't like the champ."

"Speaking of fixes . . ." began Mr. Queen.

"Were we?" asked Maguire innocently.

"If it's on the level," predicted Mr. Queen gloomily, "Coyle will murder the champion. Wipe the ring up with him. That big fellow wants the title."

"Oh, sure."

"Damn it," grinned the Inspector, "who's going to win tonight?"

Maguire grinned back. "Well, you know the odds. Three to one on the champ."

When they drove into the parking lot across the street from the Stadium, Maguire grunted: "Speak of the devil." He had backed the little roadster into a space beside a huge twelve-cylinder limousine the color of bright blood.

"Now what's that supposed to mean?" asked Paula Paris.

"This red locomotive next to Lizzie?" Maguire chuckled. "It's the champ's. Or rather, it belongs to his manager, Ollie Stearn. Ollie lets Mike use it. Mike's car's gone down the river."

"I thought the champion was wealthy," said Mr. Queen.

"Not any more. All tangled up in litigation. Dozens of judgments wrapped around his ugly ears."

"He ought to be hunk after tonight," said the Inspector wistfully. "Pulling down more than a half a million bucks for his end!"

"He won't collect a red cent of it," said the newspaperman. "His loving wife—you know Ivy, the ex-strip tease doll with the curves and detours?—Ivy and Mike's creditors will grab it all off. Come on."

Mr. Queen assisted Miss Paris from the roadster and tossed his camel's-hair topcoat carelessly into the back seat.

"Don't leave your coat there, Ellery," protested Paula. "Some one's sure to steal it."

"Let 'em. It's an old rag. Don't know what I brought it for, anyway, in this heat."

"Come on, come on," said Phil Maguire eagerly.

From the press section at ringside the stands were one heaving mass of growling humanity. Two bantamweights were fencing in the ring.

"What's the trouble?" demanded Mr. Queen alertly.

"Crowd came out to see heavy artillery, not popguns," explained Maguire. "Take a look at the card."

"Six prelims," muttered Inspector Queen. "And all good boys, too. So what are these muggs beefing about?"

"Bantams, welters, lightweights, and one middleweight bout to wind up."

"So what?"

"So the card's too light. The fans came here to see two big guys slaughter each other. They don't want to be annoyed by a bunch of gnats—even good gnats. . . . Hi, Happy."

"Who's that?" asked Miss Paris curiously.

"Happy Day," the Inspector answered for Maguire. "Makes his living off bets. One of the biggest plungers in town."

Happy Day was visible a few rows off, an expensive Panama resting on a fold of neck-fat. He had a puffed face the color of cold rice pudding, and his eyes were two raisins. He nodded at Maguire and turned back to watch the ring.

"Normally, Happy's face is like a raw steak," said Maguire. "He's worried about something."

"Perhaps," remarked Mr. Queen darkly, "the gentleman smells a mouse."

Maguire glanced at the great man sidewise, and then smiled. "And there's Mrs. Champ herself. Ivy Brown. Some stuff, hey, men?"

The woman prowled down the aisle on the arm of a wizened,

wrinkled little man who chewed nervously on a long green cold cigar. The champion's wife was a full-blown animal with a face like a Florentine cameo. The little man handed her into a seat, bowed elaborately, and hurried off.

"Isn't the little guy Ollie Stearn, Brown's manager?" asked the Inspector.

"Yes," said Maguire. "Notice the act? Ivy and Mike Brown haven't lived together for a couple of years, and Ollie thinks it's lousy publicity. So he pays a lot of attention in public to the champ's wife. What d'ye think of her, Paula? The woman's angle is always refreshing."

"This may sound feline," murmured Miss Paris, "but she's an overdressed harpie with the instincts of a she-wolf who never learned to apply makeup properly. Cheap—very cheap."

"Expensive—very expensive. Mike's wanted a divorce for a long time, but Ivy keeps rolling in the hay—and Mike's made plenty of hay in his time. Say, I gotta go to work."

Maguire bent over his typewriter.

The night deepened, the crowd rumbled, and Mr. Ellery Queen, the celebrated sleuth, felt uncomfortable. Specifically, his six-foot body was taut as a violin-string. It was a familiar but always menacing phenomenon. It meant that there was murder in the air.

The challenger appeared first. He was met by a roar, like the roar of a river at flood-tide bursting its dam.

Miss Paris gasped with admiration. "Isn't he the one!"

Jim Coyle was the one—an almost handsome giant six feet and a half tall, with preposterously broad shoulders, long smooth muscles, and a bronze skin. He rubbed his unshaven cheeks and grinned boyishly at the frantic fans.

His manager, Barney Hawks, followed him into the ring. Hawks was a big man, but beside the fighter he appeared puny.

"Hercules in trunks," breathed Miss Paris. "Did you ever see such a body, Ellery?"

"The question more properly is," said Mr. Queen jealously, "can he keep that body off the floor? That's the question, my girl."

"Plenty fast for a big man," said Maguire. "Faster than you'd think, considering all that bulk. Maybe not as fast as Mike Brown, but Jim's got height and reach in his favor, and he's strong as a bull. The way Firpo was."

"Here comes the champ!" exclaimed Inspector Queen.

A large ugly man shuffled down the aisle and vaulted into the ring. His manager—the little wizened, wrinkled man—followed him and stood bouncing up and down on the canvas, still chewing the unlit cigar.

"Boo-oo-oo!"

"They're booing the champion!" cried Paula. "Phil, why?"

"Because they hate his guts," smiled Maguire. "They hate his guts because he's an ornery, brutal, crooked slob with the kick of a mule and the soul of a pretzel. That's why, darlin'."

Brown stood six feet two inches, anatomically a gorilla, with a broad hairy chest, long arms, humped shoulders, and large flat feet. His features were smashed, cruel. He paid no attention to the hostile crowd, to his taller, bigger, younger opponent. He seemed detatched, indrawn, a subhuman figting machine.

But Mr. Queen, whose peculiar genius it was to notice minutiae, saw Brown's powerful mandibles working ever so slightly beneath his leathery cheeks.

And again Mr. Queen's body tightened.

When the gong clamored for the start of the third round, the champion's left eye was a purple slit, his lips were cracked and bloody, and his simian chest rose and fell in gasps.

Thirty seconds later he was cornered, a beaten animal, above their heads. They could see the ragged splotches over his kidneys, blooming above his trunks like crimson flowers.

Brown crouched, covering up, protecting his chin. Big Jim Coyle streaked forward. The giant's gloves sank into Brown's body. The champion fell forward and pinioned the long bronze merciless arms.

The referee broke them. Brown grabbed Coyle again. They danced.

The crowd began singing *The Blue Danube*, and the referee stepped between the two fighters again and spoke sharply to Brown.

"The dirty double-crosser," smiled Phil Maguire.

"Who? What d'ye mean?" asked Inspector Queen, puzzled.

"Watch the payoff."

The champion raised his battered face and lashed out feebly at Coyle with his soggy left glove. The giant laughed and stepped in.

The champion went down.

"Pretty as a picture," said Maguire admiringly.

At the count of nine, with the bay of the crowd in his flattened ears, Mike Brown staggered to his feet. The bulk of Coyle slipped in, shadowy, and pumped twelve solid, lethal gloves into Brown's body. The champion's knees broke. A whistling six-inch uppercut to the point of the jaw sent him toppling to the canvas.

This time he remained there.

"But he made it look kosher," drawled Maguire.

The Stadium howled with glee and the satiation of bloodlust. Paula looked sickish. A few rows away Happy Day jumped up, stared wildly about, and then began shoving through the crowd.

"Happy isn't happy any more," sang Maguire.

The ring was boiling with police, handlers, officials. Jim Coyle was half-drowned in a wave of shouting people; he was laughing like a boy. In the champion's corner Ollie Stearn worked slowly over the twitching torso of the unconscious man.

"Yes, sir," said Phil Maguire, rising and stretching, "that was as pretty a dive as I've seen, brother, and I've seen some beauts in my day."

"See here, Maguire," said Mr. Queen, nettled. "I have eyes, too. What makes you so cocksure Brown just tossed his title away?"

"You may be Einstein on Centre Street," grinned Maguire, "but here you're just another palooka, Mr. Queen."

"Seems to me," argued the Inspector in the bedlam, "Brown took an awful lot of punishment."

"Oh, sure," said Maguire mockingly. "Look, you boobs. Mike Brown has as sweet a right hand as the game has ever seen. Did you notice him use his right on Coyle tonight—even once?"

"Well," admitted Mr. Queen, "no."

"Of course not. Not a single blow. And he had a dozen openings, especially in the second round. And Jimmy Coyle still carries his guard too low. But what did Mike do? Put his deadly right into cold storage, kept jabbing away with that silly left of his—it couldn't put Paula

100

away!—covering up, clinching, and taking one hell of a beating... Sure, he made it look good. But your ex-champ took a dive just the same!"

They were helping the gorilla from the ring. He looked surly and tired. A small group followed him, laughing. Little Ollie Stearn kept pushing people aside fretfully. Mr Queen spied Brown's wife, the curved Ivy, pale and furious, hurrying after them.

"It appears," sighed Mr. Queen, "that I was in error."

"What?" asked Paula.

"Hmm. Nothing."

"Look," said Maguire. "I've got to see a man about a man, but I'll meet you folks in Coyle's dressing-room and we'll kick a few gongs around. Jim's promised to help a few of the boys warm up some hot spots."

"Oh, I'd love it!" cried Paula. "How do we get in, Phil?"

"What have you got a cop with you for? Show her, Inspector."

Maguire's slight figure slouched off. The great man's scalp prickled suddenly. He frowned and took Paula's arm.

The new champion's dressing-room was full of smoke, people, and din. Young Coyle lay on a training table like Gulliver in Lilliput, being rubbed down. He was answering questions good-humoredly, grinning at cameras, flexing his shoulder-muscles. Barney Hawks was running about with his collar loosened handing out cigars like a new father.

The crowd was so dense it overflowed into the adjoining shower-room. There were empty bottles on the floor and near the shower-room window, pushed into a corner, five men were shooting craps with enormous sobriety.

The Inspector spoke to Barney Hawks, and Coyle's manager introduced them to the champion, who took one look at Paula and said: "Hey, Barney, how about a little privacy!"

"Sure, sure. You're the champ now, Jimmy-boy!"

"Come on, you guys, you got enough pictures to last you a lifetime. What did he say your name is, beautiful? Paris? That's a hell of a name."

"Isn't yours Couzzi?" asked Paula coolly.

"Socko," laughed the boy. "Come on, clear out, guys. This lady and I got some sparring to do. Hey, lay off the liniment, Louie. He didn't hardly touch me."

Coyle slipped off the rubbing table, and Barney Hawks began shooing men out of the shower-room, and finally Coyle grabbed some towels, winked at Paula, and went in, shutting the door. They heard the cheerful hiss of the shower.

Five minutes later Phil Maguire strolled in. He was perspiring and a little wobbly.

"Heil, Hitler," he shouted. "Where's the champ?"

"Here I am," said Coyle, opening the shower-room door and rubbing his bare chest with a towel. There was another towel draped around his loins. "Hya, Phil-boy. Be dressed in a shake. Say, this doll your Mamie? If she ain't, I'm staking out my claim."

"Come on, come on, champ. We got a date with Fifty-second Street."

"Sure! How about you, Barney? You joining us?"

"Go ahead and play," said his manager in a fatherly tone. "Me, I got money business with the management." He danced into the shower-room, emerged with a hat and a camel's-hair coat over his arm, kissed his hand affectionately at Coyle, and lumbered out.

"You're not going to stay in here while he dresses?" said Mr. Queen petulantly to Miss Paris. "Come on—you can wait for your hero in the hall."

"Yes, sir," said Miss Paris submissively.

Coyle guffawed. "Don't worry, fella. I ain't going to do you out of nothing. There's plenty of broads."

Mr. Queen piloted Miss Paris firmly from the room. "Let's meet them at the car," he said in a curt tone.

Miss Paris murmured: "Yes, *sir*."

They walked in silence to the end of the corridor and turned a corner into an alley which led out of the Stadium and into the street. As they walked down the alley Mr. Queen could see through the shower--room window into the dressing-room: Maguire had produced a bottle and he, Coyle, and the Inspector were raising glasses. Coyle in his athletic underwear was—well . . .

Mr. Queen hurried Miss Paris out of the alley and across the street to the parking lot. Cars were slowly driving out. But the big red limousine

102

belonging to Ollie Stearn still stood beside Maguire's roadster.

"Ellery," said Paula softly, "you're such a fool."

"Now, Paula, I don't care to discuss—"

"What do you think I'm referring to? It's your topcoat, silly. Didn't I warn you someone would steal it?

Mr. Queen glanced into the roadster. His coat was gone. "Oh, that. I was going to throw it away, anyway. Now look, Paula, if you think for one instant that I could be jealous of some oversized . . . Paula! What's the matter?

Paula's cheeks were gray in the brilliant arc-light. She was pointing a shaky forefinger at the blood-red limousine.

"In—in there . . . Isn't that—Mike Brown?"

Mr. Queen glanced quickly into the rear of the limousine. Then he said: "Get into Maguire's car, Paula, and look the other way."

Paula crept into the roadster, shaking.

Ellery opened the rear door of Stearn's car.

Mike Brown tumbled out of the car to his feet, and lay still.

And after a moment the Inspector, Maguire and Coyle strolled up, chuckling over something Maguire was relating in a thick voice.

Maguire stopped. "Say. Who's that?"

Coyle said abruptly: 'Isn't that Mike Brown?"

The Inspector said: "Out of the way, Jim." He knelt beside Ellery.

And Mr. Queen raised his head. "Yes, it's Mike Brown. Someone's used him for a pin-cushion."

Phil Maguire yelped and ran for a telephone. Paula Paris crawled out of Maguire's roadster and blundered after him, remembering her profession.

"Is he . . . is he—"began Jim Coyle, gulping.

"The long count," said the Inspector grimly. "Say, is that girl gone? Here, help me turn him over."

They turned him over. He lay staring up into the blinding arc-light. He was completely dressed; his fedora was still jammed about his ears and a gray tweed topcoat was wrapped about his body, still buttoned. He had been stabbed ten times in the abdomen and chest, through his topcoat. There had been a great deal of bleeding; his coat was sticky and wet with it.

103

"Body's warm," said the Inspector. "This happened just a few minutes ago." He rose from the dust and stared unseeingly at the crowd which had gathered.

"Maybe," began the champion, licking his lips, "maybe—"

"Maybe what, Jim?" asked the Inspector, looking at him.

"Nothing, nothing."

"Why don't you go home? Don't let this spoil your night, kid."

Coyle set his jaw. "I'll stick around."

The Inspector blew a police whistle.

Police came, and Phil Maguire and Paula Paris returned, and Ollie Stearn and others appeared from across the street, and the crowd thickened, and Mr. Ellery Queen crawled into the tonneau of Stearn's car.

The rear of the red limousine was a shambles. Blood stained the mohair cushions, the floor-rug, which was wrinkled and scuffed. A large coat-button with a scrap of fabric still clinging to it lay on one of the cushions, beside a crumpled camel's-hair coat.

Mr. Queen seized the coat. The button had been torn from it. The front of the coat, like the front of the murdered man's coat, was badly bloodstained. But the stains had a pattern. Mr. Queen laid the coat on the seat, front up, and slipped the buttons through the button-holes. Then the bloodstains met. When he unbuttoned the coat and separated the two sides of the coat the stains separated, too, and on the side where the buttons were the blood traced a straight edge an inch outside the line of buttons.

The Inspector poked his head in. "What's that thing?"

"The murderer's coat."

"Let's see that!"

"It won't tell you anything abut its wearer. Fairly cheap coat, label's been ripped out—no identifying marks. Do you see what must have happened in here, dad?"

"What?"

"The murder occurred, of course, in this car. Either Brown and his killer got into the car simultaneously, or Brown was here first and then his murderer came, or the murderer was skulking in here, waiting for Brown to come. In any event, the murderer wore this coat."

"How do you know that?"

"Because there's every sign of a fierce struggle, so fierce Brown managed to tear off one of the coat-buttons of his assailant's coat. In the course of the struggle Brown was stabbed many times. His blood flowed freely. It got all over not only his own coat but the murderer's as well. From the position of the bloodstains the murderer's coat must have been buttoned at the time of the struggle, which means he wore it."

The Inspector nodded. "Left it behind because he didn't want to be seen in a bloody coat. Ripped out all identifying marks."

From behind the Inspector came Paula's tremulous voice. "Could that be *your* camel's-hair coat, Ellery?"

Mr. Queen looked at her in an odd way. "No, Paula."

"What's this?" demanded the Inspector.

"Ellery left his topcoat behind in Phil's car before the fight," Paula explained. "I told him somebody would steal it, and somebody did. And now there's a camel's-hair coat—in this car."

"It isn't mine." said Mr. Queen patiently. "Mine has certain distinguishing characteristics which don't exist in this one—a cigarette burn at the second buttonhole, a hole in the right pocket."

The Inspector shrugged and went away.

"Then your coat's being stolen has nothing to do with it?" Paula shivered. "Ellery, I could use a cigarette."

Mr. Queen obliged. "On the contrary. The theft of my coat has everything to do with it."

"But I don't understand. You just said—"

Mr. Queen held a match to Miss Paris's cigarette and stared intently at the body of Mike Brown.

Ollie Stearn's chauffeur, a hard-looking customer, twisted his cap and said: "Mike tells me after the fight he won't need me. Tells me he'll pick me up on the Grand Concourse. Said he'd drive himself."

"Yes?"

"I was kind of—curious. I had a hot dog at the stand there and I—watched. I seen Mike come over and climb into the back—"

"Was he alone?" demanded the Inspector.

"Yeah. Just got in and sat there. A couple of drunks come along then and I couldn't see good. Only seemed to me somebody else come over and got into the car after Mike."

"Who? Who was it? Did you see?"

The chauffeur shook his head. "I couldn't see good. I don't know. After a while I thought it ain't my business, so I walks away. But when I heard police sirens I come back."

"The one who came after Mike Brown got in," said Mr. Queen with a certain eagerness. "That person was wearing a coat, eh?"

"I guess so. Yeah."

"You didn't witness anything else that occurred?" persisted Mr. Queen.

"Nope."

"Doesn't matter, really," muttered the great man. "Line's clear. Clear as the sun. Must be that—"

"What are you mumbling about?" demanded Miss Paris in his ear.

Mr. Queen started. "Was I mumbling?" He shook his head.

Then a man from Headquarters came up with a dudish little fellow with frightened eyes who babbled he didn't know nothing, nothing, he didn't know nothing; and the Inspector said: "Come on, Oetjens. You were heard shooting off your mouth in that gin-mill. What's the dope?"

And the little fellow said shrilly: "I don't want no trouble, no trouble. I only said—"

"Yes?"

"Mike Brown looked me up this morning," muttered Oetjens, "and he says to me, he says, 'Hymie,' he says, 'Happy Day knows you, Happy Day takes a lot of your bets,' he says, 'so go lay fifty grand with Happy on Coyle to win by a K.O.,' Mike says. 'You lay that fifty grand for *me*, get it?' he says. And he says, 'If you shoot your trap off to Happy or anyone else that you bet fifty grand for me on Coyle,' he says, 'I'll rip your heart out and break your hands and give you the thumb,' he says, and a lot more, so I laid the fifty grand on Coyle to win by a K.O. and Happy took the bet at twelve to five, he wouldn't give no more."

Jim Coyle growled: "I'll break your neck, damn you."

"Wait a minute, Jim—"

"He's saying Brown took a dive!" cried the champion. "I licked Brown fair and square. I beat the hell out of him fair and square!"

"You thought you beat the hell out of him fair and square," muttered Phil Maguire. "But he took a dive, Jim. Didn't I tell you, Inspector? Laying off that right of his—"

106

"It's a lie! Where's my manager? Where's Barney? They ain't going to hold up the purse on this fight!" roared Coyle. "I won it fair—I won the title fair!"

"Take it easy, Jim," said the Inspector. "Everybody knows you were in there leveling tonight. Look here, Hymie, did Brown give you the cash to bet for him?"

"He was busted," Oetjens cringed. "I just laid the bet on the cuff. The payoff don't come till the next day. So I knew it was okay, because with Mike himself betting on Coyle the fight was in the bag—"

"I'll cripple you, you tinhorn!" yelled young Coyle.

"Take it easy, Jim," soothed Inspector Queen. "So you laid the fifty grand on the cuff, Hymie, and Happy covered the bet at twelve to five, and you knew it would come out all right because Mike was going to take a dive, and then you'd collect a hundred and twenty thousand dollars and give it to Mike, is that it?"

"Yeah, yeah. But that's all, I swear—"

"When did you see Happy last, Hymie?"

Oetjens looked scared and began to back away. His police escort had to shake him a little. But he shook his head stubbornly.

"Now it couldn't be," asked the Inspector softly, "that somehow Happy got wind that you'd laid that fifty grand, not for yourself, but for Mike Brown, could it? It couldn't be that Happy found out it was a dive, or suspected it?" The Inspector said sharply to a detective: "Find Happy Day."

"I'm right here," said a bass voice from the crowd; and the fat gambler waded through and said hotly to Inspector Queen: "So I'm the sucker, hey? I'm supposed to take the rap, hey?"

"Did you know Mike Brown was set to take a dive?"

"No!"

Phil Maguire chuckled.

And little Ollie Stearn, pale as his dead fighter, shouted: "Happy done it, Inspector! He found out, and he waited till after the fight, and when he saw Mike laying down he came out here and gave him the business! That's the way it was!"

"You lousy rat," said the gambler. "How do I know you didn't do it yourself? He wasn't taking no dive you couldn't find out about! Maybe you stuck him up because of that fancy doll of his. Don't tell *me*. I know all about you and that Ivy broad. I know—"

"Gentlemen, gentlemen," said the Inspector with a satisfied smile, when there was a shriek and Ivy Brown elbowed her way through the jam and flung herself on the dead body of her husband for the benefit of the press.

And as the photographers joyously went to work, and Happy Day and Ollie Stearn eyed each other with hate, and the crowd milled around, the Inspector said happily to his son: "Not too tough. Not too tough. A wrap-up. It's Happy Day, all right, and all I've got to do is find—"

The great man smiled and said: "You're riding a dead nag."

"Eh?"

"You're wasting your time."

The Inspector ceased to look happy. "What am I supposed to be doing, then? You tell me. You know it all."

"Of course I do, and of course I shall," said Mr. Queen. "What are you to do? Find my coat."

"Say, what *is* this about your damn' coat?" growled the Inspector.

"Find my coat, and perhaps I'll find your murderer."

It was a peculiar sort of case. First there had been the ride to the Stadium, and the conversation about how Phil Maguire didn't like Mike Brown, and then there was the ringside gossip, the preliminaries, the main event, the champion's knockout, and all the rest of—all unimportant, all stodgy little details . . . until Mr. Queen and Miss Paris strolled across the parking lot and found two things—or rather, lost one thing—Mr. Queen's coat—and found another—Mike Brown's body; and so there was an important murder-case, all nice and shiny.

And immediately the great man began nosing about and muttering about his coat, as if an old and shabby topcoat being stolen could possibly be more important that Mike Brown lying there in the gravel of the parking space full of punctures, like an abandoned tire, and Mike's wife, full of more curves and detours than the Storm King highway, sobbing on his chest and calling upon Heaven and the New York press to witness how dearly she had loved him, poor dead gorilla.

So it appeared that Mike Brown had had a secret rendezvous with someone after the fight, because he had got rid of Ollie Stearn's chauffeur, and the appointment must have been for the interior of

Ollie Stearn's red limousine. And whoever he was, he came, and got in with Mike, and there was a struggle, and he stabbed Mike almost a dozen times with something long and sharp, and then fled, leaving his camel's-hair coat behind, because with blood all over its front it would have given him away.

That brought up the matter of the weapon, and everybody began nosing about, including Mr. Queen, because it was a cinch the murderer might have dropped it in his flight. And, sure enough, a radio-car man found it in the dirt under a parked car—a long, evil-looking stiletto with no distinguishing marks whatever and no fingerprints except the fingerprints of the radio-car man. But Mr. Queen persisted in nosing even after that discovery, and finally the Inspector asked him peevishly: "What are you looking for now?"

"My coat," explained Mr. Queen. "Do you see anyone with my coat?"

But there was hardly a man in the crowd with a coat. It was a warm night.

So finally Mr. Queen gave up his queer search and said: "I don't know what you good people are going to do, but, as for me, I'm going back to the Stadium."

"For heaven's sake, what for?" cried Paula.

"To see if I can find my coat," said Mr. Queen patiently.

"I told you you should have taken it with you!"

"Oh, no," said Mr. Queen. "I'm glad I didn't. I'm glad I left it behind in Maguire's car. I'm glad it was stolen."

"But why, you exasperating idiot?"

"Because now," replied Mr. Queen with a cryptic smile, "I have to go looking for it."

And while the morgue wagon carted Mike Brown's carcass off, Mr. Queen trudged back across the dusty parking lot and into the alley which led to the Stadium dressing-rooms. And the Inspector, with a baffled look, herded everyone—with special loving care and attention for Mr. Happy Day and Mr. Ollie Stearn and Mrs. Ivy Brown—after his son. He didn't know what else to do.

And finally they were assembled in Jim Coyle's dressing room, and Ivy was weeping into more cameras, and Mr. Queen was glumly contemplating Miss Paris's red straw hat, that looked like a pot, and there was

109

a noise at the door and they say Barney Hawks, the new champion's manager, standing on the threshold in the company of several officials and promoters.

"What ho," said Barney Hawks with a puzzled glance about. "You still here, champ? What goes on?"

"Plenty goes on," said the champ savagely. "Barney, did you know Brown took a dive tonight?"

"What? What's this?" said Barney Hawks, looking around virtuously. "Who says so, the dirty liar? My boy won that title on the up and up, gentlemen! He beat Brown fair and square."

"Brown threw the fight?" asked one of the men with Hawks, a member of the Boxing Commission. "Is there any evidence of that?"

"The hell with that," said the Inspector politely. "Barney, Mike Brown is dead."

Hawks began to laugh, then he stopped laughing and sputtered: "What's this? What's this? What's the gageroo? Brown dead?"

Jim Coyle waved his huge paw tiredly. "Somebody bumped him off tonight, Barney. In Stearn's car across the street."

"Well, I'm a bum, I'm a bum," breathed his manager, staring. "So Mike got his, hey? Well, well. Tough. Loses his title and his life. Who done it, boys?"

"Maybe you didn't know my boy was dead!" shrilled Ollie Stearn. "Yeah, you put on a swell act, Barney! Maybe you fixed it with Mike so he'd take a dive so your boy could win the title! Maybe you—"

"There's been another crime committed here tonight," said a mild voice, and they all looked wonderingly around to find Mr. Ellery Queen advancing toward Mr. Hawks.

"Hey?" said Coyle's manager, staring stupidly at him.

"My coat was stolen."

"Hey?" Hawks kept gaping.

"And, unless my eyes deceive me, as the phrase goes," continued the great man, stopping before Barney Hawks, "I've found it again."

"Hey?"

"On your arm." And Mr. Queen gently removed from Mr. Hawks' arm a shabby camel's-hair topcoat, and unfolded it, and examined it. "Yes. My very own."

Barney Hawks turned green in the silence.

Something sharpened in Mr. Queen's silver eyes, and he bent over the camel's-hair coat again. He spread out the sleeves and examined the armhole seams. They had burst. As had the seam at the back of the coat. He looked up and at Mr. Hawks reproachfully.

"The least you might have done,"he said, "is to have returned my property in the same condition in which I left it."

"Your coat?" said Barney Hawks damply. Then he shouted: "What the hell is this? That's my coat! My camel's-hair coat!"

"No," Mr. Queen dissented respectfully, "I can prove this to be mine. You see, it has a telltake cigarette burn at the second buttonhole, and a hole in the right-hand pocket."

"But—I found it where I left it! It was here all the time! I took it out of here after the fight and went up to the office to talk to these gentlemen and I've been—" The manager stopped, and his complexion faded from green to white. "Then where's my coat?" he asked slowly.

"Will you try this on?" asked Mr. Queen with the deference of a clothing salesman, and he took from a detective the bloodstained coat they had found abandoned in Ollie Stearn's car.

Mr. Queen held the coat up before Hawks; and Hawks said thickly: "All right. It's my coat. I guess it's my coat, if you say so, So what?"

"So," replied Mr. Queen, "someone knew Mike Brown was broke, that he owed his shirt, that not even his lion's share of the purse tonight would suffice to pay his debts. Someone persuaded Mike Brown to throw the fight tonight, offering to pay him a large sum of money, I suppose, for taking the dive. That money no one would know about. That money would not have to be turned over to the clutches of Mike Brown's loving wife and creditors. That money would be Mike Brown's own. So Mike Brown said yes, realizing that he could make more money, too, by placing a large bet with Happy Day through the medium of Mr. Oetjens. And with this double nest-egg he could jeer at the unfriendly world.

"And probably Brown and his tempter conspired to meet in Stearn's car immediately after the fight for the pay-off, for Brown would be insistent about that. So Brown sent the chauffeur away, and sat in the car, and the tempter came to keep the appointment—armed not with the pay-off money but with a sharp stiletto. And by using the stiletto he saved himself a tidy sum—the sum he'd promised Brown—and also made sure Mike Brown would never be able to tell the wicked story to the wicked world."

Barney Hawks licked his dry lips. "Don't look at me, Mister. You got nothing on Barney Hawks. I don't know nothing about this."

And Mr. Queen said, paying no attention whatever to Mr. Hawks: "A pretty problem, friends. You see, the tempter came to the scene of the crime in a camel's-hair coat, and he had to leave the coat behind because it was bloodstained and would have given him away. Also, in the car next to the murder-car lay, quite defenseless, my own poor camel's-hair coat, its only virtue the fact that it was stained with no man's blood.

"We found a coat abandoned in Stearn's car and my coat, in the next car, stolen. Coincidence? Hardly. The murderer certainly took my coat to replace the coat he was forced to leave behind."

Mr. Queen paused to refresh himself with a cigarette, glancing whimsically at Miss Paris, who was staring at him with a soul-satisfying worship. Mind over matter, thought Mr. Queen, remembering with special satisfaction how Miss Paris had stared at Jim Coyle's muscles. Yes, sir, mind over matter.

"Well?" said Inspector Queen. "Suppose this bird did take your coat? What of it?"

"But that's exactly the point," mourned Mr. Queen. "He took my poor, shabby, worthless coat. Why?"

"Why?" echoed the Inspector blankly.

"Yes, why? Everything in this world is activated by a reason. Why did he take my coat?"

"Well, I—I suppose to wear it."

"Very good," applauded Mr. Queen, playing up to Miss Paris. "Precisely. If he took it he had a reason, and since its only function under the circumstances could have been its wearability, so to speak, he took it to wear it." He paused, then murmured: "But why should he want to wear it?"

The Inspector looked angry. "See here, Ellery—" he began.

"No, dad, no," said Mr. Queen gently. "I'm talking with a purpose. There's a point. *The* point. You might say he had to wear it because he'd got blood on his suit *under* the coat and required a coat to hide the bloodstained suit. Or mightn't you?"

"Well, sure," said Phil Maguire eagerly. "That's it."

"You may be an Einstein in your sports department, Mr. Maguire, but here you're just a palooka. No," said Mr. Queen, shaking his head sadly, "that's not it. He couldn't possibly have got blood on his suit. The coat shows that at the time he attacked Brown he was wearing it buttoned. If the topcoat was buttoned, his suit didn't catch any of Brown's blood."

"He certainly didn't need a coat because of the weather," muttered Inspector Queen.

"True. It's been warm all evening. You see," smiled Mr. Queen, "what a cute little thing it is. He'd left his own coat behind, its labels and other identifying marks taken out, unworried about its being found—otherwise he would have hidden it or thrown it away. Such being the case, you would say he'd simply make his escape in the clothes he was wearing *beneath* the coat. But he didn't. He stole another coat, my coat, for his escape." Mr. Queen coughed gently. "So surely it's obvious that if he stole my coat for his escape, he *needed* my coat for his escape? That if he escaped without my coat he would be *noticed*?"

"I don't get it," said the Inspector. "He'd be noticed? But if he was wearing ordinary clothing—"

"Then obviously he wouldn't need my coat," nodded Mr. Queen.

"Or—say! If he was wearing a uniform of some kind—say he was a Stadium attendant—"

"Then still obviously he wouldn't need my coat. A uniform would be a perfect guarantee that he'd pass in the crowds unnoticed." Mr. Queen shook his head. "No, there's only one answer to this problem. I saw it at once, of course." He noted the Inspector's expression and continued hastily: "And that was: If the murderer had been wearing clothes—*any* normal body-covering—beneath the bloodstained coat, he could have made his escape in those clothes. But since he didn't, it can only mean that he *wasn't* wearing clothes, you see, and that's why he needed a coat not only to come to the scene of the crime, but to escape from it as well."

There was another silence, and finally Paula said: "Wasn't wearing clothes? A . . . naked man? Why, that's like something out of Poe!"

"No," smiled Mr. Queen, "merely something out of the Stadium. You see, we had a classification of gentlemen in the vicinity tonight who wore no—or nearly no—clothing. In a word, the gladiators. Or, if you choose, the pugilists. . . . Wait!" he said swiftly. "This is an extraordinary case, chiefly because I solved the hardest part of it almost the instant I knew there was a murder. For the instant I discovered that

113

Brown had been stabbed, and that my coat had been stolen by a murderer who left his own behind, I knew that the murderer could have been *only one of thirteen men* . . . the thirteen living prizefighters left after Brown was killed. For you'll recall there were fourteen fighters in the Stadium tonight—twelve distributed among six preliminary bouts, and two in the main bout.

"Which of the thirteen living fighters had killed Brown? That was my problem from the beginning. And so I had to find my coat, because it was the only concrete connection I could discern between the murderer and his crime. And now I've found my coat, and now I know which of the thirteen murdered Brown."

Barney Hawks was speechless, his jaws agape.

"I'm a tall, fairly broad man. In fact, I'm six feet tall," said the great man. "And yet the murderer, in wearing my coat to make his escape, burst its seams at the armholes and back! That meant he was a big man, a much bigger man that I, much bigger and broader.

"Which of the thirteen fighters on the card tonight were bigger and broader than I? Ah, but it's been a very light card—bantamweights, welterweights, lightweights, middleweights! Therefore none of the twelve preliminary fighters could have murdered Brown. Therefore only one fighter was left—a man six and a half feet tall, extremely broad-shouldered and broad-backed, a man who had every motive— the greatest motive—to induce Mike Brown to throw the fight tonight!"

And this time the silence was ghastly with meaning. It was broken by Jim Coyle's lazy laugh. "If you mean me, you must be off your nut. Why, I was in that shower-room taking a shower at the time Mike was bumped off!"

"Yes, I mean you, Mr. Jim Coyle Stiletto-Wielding Couzzi," said Mr. Queen clearly, "and the shower-room was the cleverest part of your scheme. You went into the shower-room in full view of all of us, with towels, shut the door, turned on the shower, slipped a pair of trousers over your bare and manly legs, grabbed Barney Hawks's camel's-hair coat and hat which were hanging on a peg in there, and then ducked out the shower-room window into the alley. From there it was a matter of seconds to the street and the parking lot across the street. Of course, when you stained Hawks's coat during the commission of your crime, you couldn't risk coming back in it. And you had to have a coat—a buttoned coat—to cover your nakedness for the return trip. So you stole mine, for which I'm very grateful, because otherwise—Grab him, will you? My right isn't very good," said Mr. Queen, employing a dainty and beautiful bit of footwork to escape Coyle's sudden homicidal lunge in his direction.

And while Coyle went down under an avalanche of flailing arms and legs, Mr. Queen murmured apologetically to Miss Paris: "After all, darling, he *is* the heavyweight champion of the world."

THE INNER CIRCLE

(1947)

IF YOU ARE an Eastern alumnus who has not been to New York since last year's All-University Dinner, you will be astounded to learn that the famous pickled-pine door directly opposite the elevators on the thirteenth floor of your Alumni Club in Murray Hill is now inscribed: LINEN ROOM.

Visit The Alumni Club on your next trip to Manhattan and see for yourself. On the door now consigned to napery, in the area where the stainless steel medallion of Janus glistened for so long, you will detect a ghostly circumference some nine inches in diameter—all that is left of the Januarians. Your first thought will of course be that they have removed to more splendid quarters. Undeceive yourself. You may search from cellar to sundeck and you will find no crumb's trace of either Janus or his disciples.

Hasten to the Steward for an explanaton and he will give you one as plausable as it will be false.

And you will do no better elsewhere.

The fact is, only a very few share the secret of The Januarians' obliteration, and these have taken a vow of silence. And why? Because Eastern is a young—a very young—temple of learning; and there are calamities only age can weather. There is more to it that even that. The cataclysm of events struck at the handiwork of the Architects themselves, that legendary band who built the tabernacle and created the holy canons. So Eastern's shame is kept steadfastly covered with silence; and if we uncover its bloody stones here, it is only because the very first word on the great seal of Eastern University is: *Veritas*.

116

To a Harvard man, "Harvard '13" means little more than "Harvard '06" or "Harvard '79", unless "Harvard '13" happens to be his own graduating class. But to an Eastern man, of whatever vintage "Eastern '13" is *sui generis*. Their names bite deep into the strong marble of The Alumni Club lobby. A member of the Class is traditionally The Honorable Mr. Honorary President of The Eastern Alumni Association. To the last man they carry gold, lifetime, non-cancelable passes to Eastern football games. At the All-University Dinner, Eastern '13 shares the Cancellor's parsley-decked table. The twined-elbow Rite of the Original Libation, drunk in foaming beer (the second most sacred canon), is dedicated to that Class and no other.

One may well ask why this exaltaton of Eastern '13 as against, for example, Eastern '98? The answer is that there was no Eastern '12, and Eastern '98 never existed. For Eastern U. was not incorporated under the laws of the State of New York until A.D. 1909, from which it solemnly follows that Eastern '13 was the university's very first graduating class.

It was Charlie Mason who said they must be gods, and it was Charlie Mason who gave them Janus. Charlie was destined to forge a chain of one hundred and twenty-three movie houses which bring Abbott and Costello to millions; but in those days Charlie was a lean weaver of dreams, the Class Poet, an antiquarian with a passion for classical allusion. Eastern '13 met on the eve of graduation in the Private Party Room of McElvy's Brauhaus in Riverdale, and the air was boiling with pipe smoke, malt fumes, and motions when Charlie rose to make his historic speech.

"Mr. Chairman," he said to Bill Updike, who occupied the Temporary Chair. "Fellows," he said to the nine others. And he paused.

Then he said: *"We are the First Alumni."*

He paused again.

"The eyes of the future are on us." (Stan Jones was taking notes, as Recording Secretary of the Evening, and we have Charlie's address verbatim. You have seen it in The Alumni club lobby, under glass. Brace yourself: It, too, has vanished.)

"What we do here tonight, therefore, will initiate a whole codex of Eastern tradition."

And now, the Record records, there was nothing to be heard in that smoky room but the whizz of the electric fan over the lithograph of Woodrow Wilson.

"I have no hesitation in saying—out loud!—that we men in this room, tonight... that we're... Significant. Not as individuals! But as the Class of '13." And then Charlie drew himself up and said quietly: *"They will remember us and we must give them something to remember"* (the third sacred canon).

"Such as?" said Morry Green, who was to die in a French ditch five years later.

"A sign," said Charlie. "A symbol, Morry—a symbol of our First-ness."

Eddie Temple, who was graduating eleventh in the Class, exhibited his tongue and blew a coarse, fluttery blast.

"That may be the sign *you* want to be remembered by, Ed," began Charlie crossly...

"Shut up, Temple!" growled Van Hamisher.

"Read that bird out of the party!" yelled Ziss Brown, who was suspected of holding radical views because his father had stumped for Teddy Roosevelt in '12.

"Sounds good," said Bill Updike, scowling, "Go on, Charlie."

"What sign?" demanded Rod Black.

"Anything specific in mind?" called Johnnie Cudwise.

Charlie said one word.

"Janus."

And he paused.

"Janus," they muttered, considering him.

"Yes, Janus," said Charlie. "The god of good beginnings—"

"Well, we're beginning," said Morry Green.

"Guaranteed to result in good endings—"

"It certainly applies," nodded Bill Updike.

"Yeah," said Bob Smith. "Eastern's sure on its way to big things."

"Janus of the two faces," cried Charlie Mason mystically. "I wish to point out that he looks in opposite directions!"

"Say, that's right—"

"The past and the future—"

"Smart stuff—"

"Go on, Charlie!"

"Janus," cried Charlie—"Janus, who was invoked by the Romans before any other god at the beginning of an important undertaking!"

"Wow!"

"*This* is certainly important!"

"The beginning of the day, month, and year were sacred to him! *Janus was the god of doorways!*"

"*JANUS!*" they shouted, leaping to their feet; and they raised their tankards and drank deep.

And so from that night forward the annual meeting of the Class of '13 was held on Janus's Day, the first day of January; and the Class of '13 adopted, by unanimous vote, the praenomen of The Januarians. Thus the double-visaged god became patron of Eastern's posterity, and that is why until recently Eastern official stationery was impressed with his two-bearded profiles. It is also why the phrase "to be two-faced," when uttered by Columbia or N.Y.U. men, usually means "to be a student at, or a graduate of, Eastern U."—a development unfortunately not contemplated by Charlie Mason on that historic eve; at least, not consciously.

But let us leave the profounder explorations to psychiatry. Here it is sufficient to record that some time more than thirty years later the phrase suddenly took on a grim verisimilitude; and the Januarians thereupon laid it, so to speak, on the doorstep of one well acquainted with such changelings of chance.

For it was during Christmas week of last year that Bill Updike came—stealthily—to see Ellery. He did not come as young Billy who had presided at the beery board in the Private Party Room of McElvy's Brauhaus on that June night in 1913. He came, bald, portly, and opulently engraved upon a card: Mr. William Updike, President of The Brokers National Bank of New York, residence Dike Hollow, Scarsdale; and he looked exactly as worried as bankers are supposed to look and rarely do.

"Business, business," said Nikki Porter, shaking her yuletide permanent. "It's Christmas week, Mr. Updike. I'm sure Mr. Queen wouldn't consider taking—"

But at that moment Mr. Queen emerged from his sanctum to give his secretary the lie.

"Nikki holds to the old-fashioned idea about holidays, Mr. Updike," said Ellery, shaking Bill's hand. "Ah, the Januarians. Isn't your annual meeting a few days from now—on New Year's Day?"

"How did you know—?" began the bank president.

"I could reply, in the manner of the Old Master," said Ellery with a chuckle, "that I've made an intensive study of lapel buttons, but truth compels me to admit that one of my best friends is Eastern '28 and he's described that little emblem on your coat so often I couldn't help but recognize it at once." The banker figured the disk on his lapel nervously. It was of platinum, ringed with tiny garnets, and the gleaming circle enclosed the two faces of Janus. "What's the matter—is someone robbing your bank?"

"It's worse than that."

"Worse . . . ?"

"Murder."

Nikkie glared at Mr. Updike. Any hope of keeping Ellery's nose off the grindstone until January second was now merely a memory. But out of duty she began: "Ellery . . ."

"At least," said Bill Updike tensely, "I *think* it's murder."

Nikki gave up. Ellery's nose was noticeably honed.

"Who . . ."

"It's sort of complicated," muttered the banker, and he began to fidget before Ellery's fire. "I suppose you know, Queen, that The Januarians began with only eleven men."

Ellery nodded. "The total graduating class of Eastern '13."

"It seems silly now, with Eastern's classes of three and four thousand, but in those days we thought it was all pretty important—"

"Manifest destiny."

"We were young. Anyway, World War I came along and we lost two of our boys right away—Morry Green and Buster Selby. So at our New Year's Day meeting in 1920 we were only nine. Then in the market collapse of '29 Vern Hamisher blew the top of his head off, and in 1930 John Cudwise, who was serving his first term in Congress, was killed in a plane crash on his way to Washington—you probably remember. So we've been just seven for many years now."

"And awfully close friends you must be," said Nikki, curiosity conquering pique.

"Well . . ." began Updike, and he stopped, to begin over again. "For a long time now we've all thought it was sort of juvenile, but we've kept coming back to these damned New Year's Day meetings out of habit or—or something. No, that's not true. It isn't just habit. It's because . . . it's *expected* of us." He flushed. "I don't know—they've— well—deified us." He looked bellicose, and Nikkie swallowed a giggle hastily. "It's got on our nerves. I mean—well, damn it all, we're not exactly the 'close' friends you'd think!" He stopped again, then resumed in a sort of desperation: "See here, Queen. I've got to confess something. There's been a clique of us within The Januarians for years. We've called ourselves . . . The Inner Circle."

"The what?" gasped Nikki.

The banker mopped hs neck, avoiding their eyes. The Inner Circle, he explained, had begun with one of those dully devious phenomena of modern life known as a "business opportunity"—a business opportunity which Mr. Updike, a considerably younger Mr. Updike, had found himself unable to grasp for lack of some essential element, unnamed. Whatever it was that Mr. Updike had required, four other men could supply it; whereupon, in the flush of an earlier camaraderie, Updike had taken four of his six fellow-deities into his confidence, and the result of this was a partnership of five of the existing seven Januarians.

"There were certain business reasons why we didn't want our er . . . names associated with the ah . . . enterprise. So we organized a dummy corporation and agreed to keep our names out of it and the whole thing absolutely secret, even from our—from the remaining two Januarians. It's a secret from them to this day."

"Club within a club," said Nikki. "I think that's cute."

"All five of you in this—hrm!—Inner Circle," inquired Ellery politely, "are alive?"

"We were last New Year's Day. But since the last meeting of The Januarians . . ." the banker glanced at Ellery's harmless windows furtively, "three of us have died. *Three of The Inner Circle.*"

"And you suspect that they were murdered?"

"Yes. Yes, I do!"

"For what motive?"

The banker launched into a very involved and—to Nikki, who was thinking wistfully of New Year's Eve—tiresome explanation. It had something to do with some special fund or other, which seemed to have no connection with the commercial aspects of The Inner Circle's activities—a substantial fund by this time, since each year the five partners put a fixed percentage of their incomes from the dummy corporation into it. Nikki dreamed of balloons and noisemakers. "—now equals a reserve of around $200,000 worth of negotiable securities." Nikki stopped dreaming with a bump.

"What's the purpose of this fund, Mr. Updike?" Ellery was saying sharply. "What happens to it? When?"

"Well, er... that's just it, Queen," said the Banker. "Oh, I know what you'll think . . ."

"Don't tell me," said Ellery in a terrible voice, "it's a form of tontine insurance plan, Updike—*last survivor takes all?*"

"Yes," whispered William Updike, looking for the moment like Billy Updike.

"I knew it!" Ellery jumped out of his fireside chair. "Haven't I told you repeatedly, Nikki, there's no fool like a banker? The financial mentality rarely rises above the age of eight, when life's biggest thrill is to pay five pins for admission to a magic-lantern show in Stinky's cellar. This hard-eyed man of money, whose business it is to deal in safe investments, becomes party to a melodramatic scheme whereby the only way you can recoup your ante is to slit the throats of your four partners. Inner Circles! Januarians!" Ellery threw himself back in his chair. "Where's this silly invitation to murder cached, Updike?"

"In a safe-deposit box at The Brokers National," muttered the banker.

"Your own bank. Very cosy for *you*," said Ellery.

"No, no, Mr. Queen, all five of us have keys to the box—"

"What happened to the keys of the three Inner Circleites who died last year?"

"By agreement, dead members' keys are destroyed in the presence of the survivors—"

"Then there are only two keys to that safe-deposit box now in existence; yours and the key in the possession of the only other living Inner Circular?"

"Yes—"

"And you're afraid said sole-surviving associate murdered the deceased trio of your absurd quintet and has his beady eye on you, Updike?—so that as the last man alive of The Inner Circle he would fall heir to the entire $200,000 boodle?"

"What else can I think?" cried the banker.

"The obvious," retorted Ellery, "which is that your three pals traveled the natural route of all flesh. Is the $200,000 still in the box?"

"Yes. I looked just before coming here today."

"You want me to investigate."

"Yes, yes—"

"Very well. What's the name of this surviving fellow-conspirator of yours in The Inner Circle?"

"No," said Bill Updike.

"I beg pardon?"

"Suppose I'm wrong? If they *were* ordinary deaths, I'd have dragged someone I've known a hell of a long time into a mess. No, you investigate first, Mr. Queen. Find evidence of murder, and I'll go all the way."

"You won't tell me his name?"

"No."

The ghost of New Year's Eve stirred. But then Ellery grinned, and it settled back in the grave. Nikki sighed and reached for her notebook.

"All right, Mr. Updike. Who were the three Inner Circlovians who died this year?"

"Robert Carlton Smith, J. Stanford Jones, and Ziss Brown—Peter Zissing Brown."

"Their occupations?"

"Bob Smith was head of the Kradle Kap Baby Foods Korporation. Stan Jones was top man of Jones-Jones-Mallison-Jones, the ad agency. Ziss Brown was retired."

"From what?"

Updike said stiffly: "Brassières."

"I suppose they do pall. Leave me the addresses of the executors, please, and any other data you think might be helpful."

When the banker had gone, Ellery reached for the telephone.

"Oh dear," said Nikki. "You're not calling . . . Club Bongo?"

"What?"

"You know? New Year's Eve?"

"Heavens, no. My pal Eastern '28. Cully? . . . The same to you. Cully, who are the four Januarians? Nikki, take this down . . . William Updike—yes? . . . Charles Mason? Oh, yes, the god who fashioned Olympus . . . Rodney Black, Junior—um-hm . . . and Edward I. Temple? Thanks, Cully. And now forget I called." Ellery hung up. "Black, Mason, and Temple, Nikki. The only Januarians alive outside of Updike. Consequently one of those three is Updike's last associate in The Inner Circle."

"And the question is which one."

"Bright girls. But first let's dig into the deaths of Smith, Jones, and Brown. Who knows? Maybe Updike's got something."

It took exactly forty-eight hours to determine that Updike had nothing at all. The deaths of Januarians-Inner Circlers Smith, Jones, and Brown were impeccable.

"Give it to him, Velie," said Inspector Queen at Headquarters the second morning after the banker's visit to the Queen apartment.

Sergeant Velie cleared his massive throat. "The Kradle Kap Baby Foods character—"

"Robert Carlton Smith."

"Rheumatic heart for years. Died in an oxygen tent after the third heart attack in eighteen hours, with three fancy medics in attendance and a secretary who was there to take down his last words."

"Which were probably, 'Free Enterprise,' " said the Inspector.

"Go on, Sergeant!"

"J. Stanford Jones, the huckster. Gassed in World War I, in recent years developed t.b. And that's what he died of. Want the sanitarium affidavits, Maestro? I had photostats telephotoed from Arizona."

"Thorough little man, aren't you?" growled Ellery. "And Peter Zissing Brown, retired from brassières?"

"Kidneys and gall-bladder. Brown died on the operatin' table."

"Wait till you see what I'm wearing tonight." said Nikki. "Apricot taffeta—"

"Nikki, get Updike on the phone," said Ellery absently. "Brokers National."

"He's not there, Ellery," said Nikki, when she had put down the Inspector's phone. "Hasn't come into his bank this morning. It has the darlingest bouffant skirt—"

"Try his home."

"Dike Hollow, Scarsdale, wasn't it? With the new back, and a neckline that—Hello?" And after a while the three men heard Nikki say in a strange voice: "*What*?" and then: "Oh," faintly. She thrust the phone at Ellery. "You'd better take it."

"What's the matter? Hello? Ellery Queen. Updike there?"

A bass voice said, "Well—no, Mr. Queen. He's been in an accident."

"Accident! Who's this speaking?"

"Captain Rosewater of the Highway Police. Mr. Updike ran his car into a ravine near his home here some time last night. We just found him."

"I hope he's all right!"

"He's dead."

"Four!" Ellery was mumbling as Sergeant Velie drove the Inspector's car up into Westchester. "Four in one year!"

"Coincidence," said Nikki desperately, thinking of the festivities on the agenda for that evening.

"All I know is that forty-eight hours after Updike asks me to find out if his three cronies of The Inner Circle who died this year hadn't been murdered, he himself is found lying in a gulley with four thousand pounds of used car on top of him."

"Accidents," began Sergeant Velie, "will hap—"

"I want to see that 'accident'!"

A State trooper flagged them on the Parkway near a cutoff and sent them down the side road. This road, it appeared, was a shortcut to Dike Hollow which Updike habitually used in driving home from the City; his house lay some two miles from the Parkway. They found the evidence of his last drive about midway. The narrow blacktop road twisted sharply to the left at this point, but Bill Updike had failed to twist with it. He had driven straight ahead and through a matchstick guardrail into the ravine. As it plunged over, the car had struck the bole of a big old oak. The shock catapulted the banker through his windshield and he had landed at the bottom of the ravine just before his vehicle.

"We're still trying to figure out a way of lifting that junk off him," said Captain Rosewater when they joined him forty feet below the road.

The ravine narrowed in a V here and the car lay in its crotch upside down. Men were swarming around it with crowbars, chains, and acetylene torches. "We've uncovered enough to show us he's mashed flat."

"His face, too, Captain?" asked Ellery suddenly.

"No, his face wasn't touched. We're trying to get the rest of him presentable enough so we can let his widow identify him." The trooper nodded toward a flat rock twenty yards down the ravine on which sat a small woman in a mink coat. She wore no hat and her smart gray hair was whipping in the Christmas wind. A woman in a cloth coat, wearing a nurse's cap, stood over her.

Ellery said, "Excuse me," and strode away. When Nikki caught up with him he was already talking to Mrs. Updike. She was drawn up on the rock like a caterpillar.

"He had a directors' meeting at the bank last night. I phoned one of

125

his associates about 2 A.M. He said the meeting had broken up at eleven and Bill had left to drive home." Her glance strayed up the ravine. "At four-thirty this morning I phoned the police."

"Did you know your husband had come to see me, Mrs. Updike— two mornings ago?"

"Who are you?"

"Ellery Queen."

"No." She did not seem surprised, or frightened, or anything.

"Did you know Robert Carlton Smith, J. Stanford Jones, Peter Zissing Brown?"

"Bill's classmates? They passed away. This year," she added suddenly."This year," she repeated. And then she laughed. "I thought the gods were immortal."

"Did you know that your husband, Smith, Jones, and Brown were an 'inner circle' in the Januarians?"

"Inner Circle." She frowned. "Oh, yes, Bill mentioned it occasionally. No, I didn't know they were in it."

Ellery leaned forward in the wind

"Was Edward I. Temple in it, Mrs. Updike? Rodney Black, Junior? Charlie Mason?

"I don't know. Why are you questioning me? Why—?" Her voice was rising now, and Ellery murmured something placative as Captain Rosewater hurried up and said: "Mrs. Updike. If you'd be good enough . . ."

She jumped off the rock. *"Now?"*

"Please."

The trooper captain took one arm, the nurse the other, and between them they half-carried William Updike's widow up the ravine toward the overturned car.

Nikki found it necessary to spend some moments with her handkerchief.

When she looked up, Ellery had disappeared.

She found him with his father and Sergeant Velie on the road above the ravine. They were standing before a large maple looking at a road-sign. Studded lettering on the yellow sign spelled out *Sharp Curve Ahead*, and there was an elbow-like illustration.

"No lights on this road," the Inspector was saying as Nikki hurried up, "so he must have had his brights on—"

126

"And they'd sure enough light up this reflector sign. I don't get it, Inspector," complained Sergeant Velie. "Unless his lights just weren't workin'."

"More likely fell asleep over the wheel, Velie."

"No," said Ellery.

"What, Ellery?"

"Updike's lights were all right, and he didn't doze off."

"I don't impress when I'm c-cold," Nikki said, shivering. "But just the same, how do you know, Ellery?"

Ellery pointed to two neat holes in the maple bark, very close to the edge of the sign.

"Woodpeckers?" said Nikki. But the air was gray and sharp as steel, and it was hard to forget Mrs. Updike's look.

"This bird, I'm afraid," drawled Ellery, "had no feathers. Velie, borrow something we can pry this sign off with."

When Velie returned with some tools, he was mopping his face. "She just identified him," he said. "Gettin' warmer, ain't it?"

"What d'ye expect to find, Ellery?" demanded the Inspector.

"Two full sets of rivet-holes."

Sergeant Velie said: "Bong," as the road-sign came away from the tree.

"I'll be damned," said Inspector Queen softly. "Somebody removed these rivets last night, and after Updike crashed into the ravine—"

"Riveted the warning sign back on," cried Nikki, "only he got careless and didn't use the same holes!"

"Murder," said Ellery. "Smith, Jones, and Brown died of natural causes. But three of the five co-owners of that fund dying in a single year—"

"Gave Number 5 an idea!"

"If Updike died, too, the $200,000 in securities would . . . Ellery!" roared his father. "Where are you running to?"

"There's a poetic beauty about this case," Ellery was saying restlessly to Nikki as they waited in the underground vaults of The Brokers National Bank. "Janus was the god of entrances. Keys were among his trapping of office. In fact, he was sometimes known as *Patulcius*—'opener'. Opener! I knew at once we were too late."

"You knew, you knew," said Nikki peevishly. "And New Year's Eve only hours away! You can be wrong."

"Not this time. Why else was Updike murdered last night in such a way as to make it appear an accident? Our mysterious Januarian hotfooted it down here first thing this morning and cleaned out that safe-deposit box belonging to The Inner Circle. The securities are gone, Nikki."

Within an hour, Ellery's prophecy was historical fact.

The box was opened with Bill Updike's key. It was empty.

And of *Patulcius*, no trace. It quite upset the Inspector. For it appeared that The Inner Circle had contrived a remarkable arrangement for access to their safe-deposit box. It was gained, not by the customary signature on an admissoin slip, but through the presentation of a talisman. This talisman was quite unlike the lapel button of the Januarians. It was a golden key, and on the key was incised the two-faced god, within concentric circles. The outer circle was of Januarian garnets, the inner of diamonds. A control had been deposited in the files of the vault company. Anyone presenting a replica of it was to be admitted to the The Inner Circle's repository by order of no less a personage, the vault manager informed them, than the late President Updike himself—who, Inspector Queen remarked with bitterness, had been more suited by tempermant to preside over the Delancey Street Junior Spies.

"Anybody remember admitting a man this morning who flashed one of these doojiggers?"

An employee was found who duly remembered, but when he described the vault visitor as great-coated and mufflered to the eyes, wearing dark glasses, walking with a great limp,and speaking in a laryngitical whisper, Ellery said wearily: "Tomorrow's the annual meeting of The Januarians, dad, and *Patulcius* won't dare not to show up. We'd better try to clean it up there."

These, then were the curious events preceding the final meeting of The Januarians in the thirteenth-floor sanctuary of The Eastern Alumni Club, beyond the door bearing the stainless steel medallion of the god Janus.

We have no apocryphal writings to reveal what self-adoring mysteries were performed in that room on other New Year's Days; but on January the first of this year, The Januarians held a most unorthodox service, in that two lay figures—the Queens, *pater et filius*—moved in and administered some heretical sacraments; so there is a full record of the last rites.

It began with Sergeant Velie knocking thrice upon the steel faces of Janus at five minutes past two o'clock on the afternoon of the first of January, and a thoroughly startled voice from within the holy of holies calling: "Who's there?" The Sergeant muttered an *Ave* and put his shoulder to the door. Three amazed, elderly male faces appeared. The heretics entered and the service began.

It is a temptation to describe in loving detail, for the satisfaction of the curious, the interior of the tabernacle—its stern steel furniture seizing the New Year's Day sun and tossing it back in the form of imperious light, the four-legged altar, the sacred vessels in the shape of beakers, the esoteric brown waters, and so on—but there has been enough of profanation, and besides the service is more to our point.

It was chiefly catechistical, proceeding in this wise:

INSPECTOR: Gentlemen, my name is Inspector Queen, I'm from Police Headquarters, this is my son, Ellery, and the big mugg on the door is Sergeant Velie of my staff.

BLACK: Police? Ed, do you know anything about—?

TEMPLE: Not me, Rodeny. Maybe Charlie, Ha-Ha . . . ?

MASON: What is it, Inspector? This is a private clubroom—

INSPECTOR: Which one are *you*?

MASON: Charles Mason—Mason's Theater Chain, Inc. But—

INSPECTOR: The long drink of water—what's *your* name?

TEMPLE: Me. Edward I Temple. Attorney. What's the meaning—?

INSPECTOR: I guess, Tubby, that makes you Rodney Black, Junior, of Wall Street.

BLACK: Sir—!

ELLERY: Which one of you gentlemen belonged to The Inner Circle of The Januarians?

MASON: Inner what, what?

BLACK: Circle, I think he said, Charlie.

TEMPLE: Inner circle? What's that?

SERGEANT: One of 'em's a John Barrymore, Maestro.

BLACK: See here, we're three-fourths of what's left of the Class of Eastern '13 . . .

ELLERY: Ah, then you gentlemen don't know that Bill Updike is dead?

ALL: Dead! *Bill?*

INSPECTOR: Tell 'em the whole story, Ellery.

And so, patiently, Ellery recounted the story of the Inner Circle, William Updike's murder, and the vanished $200,000 in negotiable securities. And as he told this story, the old gentleman from Center Street and his sergeant studied the three elderly faces; and the theater magnate, the lawyer, and the broker gave stare for stare; and when Ellery had finished they turned to one another and gave stare for stare once more.

And finally Charlie Mason said: "My hands are clean, Ed. How about yours?"

"What do you take me for, Charlie?" said Temple in a flat and chilling voice. And they both loked at Black, who squeaked: "Don't try to make *me* out the one, you traitors!"

Whereupon, as if there were nothing more to be said, the three divinities turned and gazed bleakly upon the iconoclasts.

And the catechism resumed:

ELLERY: Mr. Temple, where were you night before last between 11 P.M. and midnight?

TEMPLE: Let me see. Night before last . . . That was the night before New Year's Eve. I went to bed at 10 o'clock.

ELLERY: You're a bachelor, I believe. Do you employ a domestic?

TEMPLE: My man.

ELLERY: Was he—?

TEMPLE: He sleeps out.

SERGEANT: No alibi!

INSPECTOR: How about you, Mr. Black?

BLACK: Well, the fact is . . . I'd gone to see a musical in town . . . and between 11 and 12 I was driving home . . . to White Plains . . .

SERGEANT: Ha! White Plains!

ELLERY: Alone, Mr. Black?

BLACK: Well . . . yes. The family's all away over the holidays . . .

INSPECTOR: No alibi. Mr. Mason?
MASON: Go to hell. (*There is a knock on the door.*)
SERGEANT: Now who would that be?
TEMPLE: The ghost of Bill?
BLACK: You're not funny, Ed!
ELLERY: Come in. (*The door opens. Enter Nikki Porter.*)
NIKKI: I'm sorry to interrupt, but she came looking for you, Ellery. She was terribly insistent. Said she'd just recalled something about The Inner Circle, and—
ELLERY: She?
NIKKI: Come in, Mrs. Updike.

"They're here," said Mrs. Updike. "I'm glad. I wanted to look at their faces."

"I've told Mrs. Updike the whole thing," said Nikki defiantly.

And Inspector Queen said in a soft tone: "Velie, shut the door."

But this case was not to be solved by a guilty look. Black, Mason, and Temple said quick ineffectual things, surrounding the widow and spending their nervousness in little gestures and rustlings until finally silence fell and she said helplessly, "Oh, I don't know, I don't know," and dropped into a chair to weep.

And Black stared out the window, and Mason looked green, and Temple compressed his lips.

Then Ellery went to the widow and put his hand on her shoulder. "You recall something about The Inner Circle, Mrs. Updike?"

She stopped weeping and folded her hands, resting them in her lap and looking straight ahead.

"Was it the names of the five?"

"No. Bill never told me their names. But I remember Bill's saying to me once: 'Mary, I'll give you a hint.' "

"Hint?"

"Bill said that he once realized there was something funny about the names of the five men in The Inner Circle."

"Funny?" said Ellery sharply. "About their *names?*"

"He said by coincidence all five names had one thing in common."

"In common?"

"And he laughed." Mrs. Updike paused. "He laughed, and he said: 'That is, Mary, if you remember that I'm a married man.' I remember saying: 'Bill, stop talking in riddles. What do you mean?' And he

131

laughed again and said: 'Well, you see, Mary, *you're in it, too.*' "

"You're in it, too," said Nikki blankly.

"I have no idea what he meant, but that's what Bill said, word for word." And now she looked up at Ellery and asked, with a sort of ferocious zest: "Does any of this help, Mr. Queen?"

"Oh, yes," said Ellery gently. "All of it, Mrs. Updike." And he turned to the three silent Januarians and said: "Would any of you gentlemen like to try your wits against this riddle?"

But the gentlemen remained silent.

"The reply appears to be no," Ellery said. "Very well; let's work it out *en masse*. Robert Carlton Smith, J. Sanford Jones, Peter Zissing Brown, William Updike. Those four names, according to Bill Updike, have one thing in common. What?"

"Smith," said the Inspector.

"Jones," said the Sergeant.

"Brown," said Nikki.

"Updike!" said the Inspector. "Boy, you've got me."

"Include me in, Maestro."

"Ellery, please!"

"Each of the four names," said Ellery, "has in it, somewhere, the name of well-known college or university."

And there was another mute communion.

"Robert—Carlton—Smith," said the Inspector, doubtfully.

"Smith!" cried Nikki. "*Smith College*, in Massachusetts!"

The Inspector looked startled. "J. Stanford Jones.—That California university, *Stanford!*"

"Hey," said Sergeant Velie. "Brown. *Brown University*, in Rhode Island!"

"Updike," said Nikki, then she stopped. "Updike? There's no college called Updike, Ellery."

"William Updike was his full name, Nikki."

"You mean the 'William' part? There's a Williams, with an *s*, but no William."

"What did Updike tell Mrs. Updike? 'Mary, you're in it, too.' William Updike was in it, and Mary Updike was in it . . ."

"*William and Mary College!*" roared the Inspector.

"So the college denominator checks for all four of the known names. But since Updike told his wife the fifth name had the same thing in common, all we have to do now is test the names of these three gentlemen to see if one of them is the name of a college or university— and we'll have the scoundrel who murdered Bill Updike for the Inner Circle's fortune in securities."

"Black," babbled Rodney Black, Junior. "Rodney Black, Junior. Find me a college in that, sir!"

"Charles Mason," said Charles Mason unsteadily. "Charles? Mason? You see!"

"That," said Ellery, sort of hangs it around your neck, Mr. Temple."

"Temple!"

"*Temple University* in Pennsylvania!"

Of course, it was absurd. Grown men who played at godhead with emblems and talismans, like boys conspiring in a cave, and a murder case which was solved by a trick of nomenclature. Eastern University is too large for that sort of childishness. And it is old enough, we submit, to know the truth:

ITEM: Edward I. Temple, Class of Eastern '13, did not "fall" from the thirteenth floor of The Eastern Alumni Club on New Year's Day this year. He jumped.

ITEM: The Patulcius Chair of Classics, founded this year, was not endowed by a wealthy alumnus from Oil City who modestly chose anonymity. It came into existence through the contents of The Inner Circle's safe-deposit box, said contents having been recovered from another safe-deposit boxrented by said Temple in another bank on the afternoon of December thirty-first under a false name.

ITEM: The Januarian room was not converted to the storage of linen because of the expanded housekeeping needs of The Eastern Alumni Club. It was ordered so that the very name of the Society of the Two-Faced God should be expunged from Eastern's halls; and as for the stainless steel medallion of Janus which had hung on the door, the Chancellor of Eastern University himself scaled it into the Hudson River from the George Washington Bridge, during a sleet storm, one hideous night this January.

THE DAUPHIN'S DOLL

(1948)

THERE IS A LAW among story-tellers, originally passed by Editors at the cries (they say) of their constituents, which states that stories about Christmas shall have children in them. This Christmas story is no exception; indeed, misopedists will complain that we have over-done it. And we confess in advance that this is also a story about Dolls, and that Santa Claus comes into it, and even a Thief; though as to this last, whoever he was—and that was one of the questions—he was certainly not Barabbas, even parabolically.

Another section of the statute governing Christmas stories provides that they shall incline toward Sweetness and Light. The first arises, of course, from the orphans and the never-souring savor of the annual miracle; as for Light, it will be provided at the end, as usual, by that luminous prodigy, Ellery Queen. The reader of gloomier temper will also find a large measure of Darkness, in the person and works of one who, at least in Inspector Queen's harassed view, was surely the winged Prince of that region. His name, by the way, was not Satan, it was Comus; and this is paradox enow, since the original Comus, as everyone knows, was the god of festive joy and mirth, emotions not commonly associated with the Underworld. As Ellery struggled to embrace his phantom foe, he puzzled over this *non sequitur* in vain; in vain, that is, until Nikki Porter, no scorner of the obvious, suggested that he *might* seek the answer where any ordinary mortal would go at once. And there, to the great man's mortification, it was indeed to be found: On page 262b of Volume 6, *Coleb to Damasci,* of the 175th

134

Anniversary edition of the *Encyclopaedia Britannica*. A French conjuror of that name—Comus—performing in London in the year 1789 caused his wife to vanish from the top of a table—the very first time, it appeared, that this feat, uxorial or otherwise, had been accomplished without the aid of mirrors. To track his dark adversary's *nom de nuit* to its historic lair gave Ellery his only glint of satisfaction until that blessed moment when light burst all around him and exorcised the darkness, Prince and all.

But this is chaos.

Our story properly begins not with our invisible character but with our dead one.

Miss Ypson had not always been dead; *au contraire*. She had lived for seventy-eight years, for most of them breathing hard. As her father used to remark, "She was a very active little verb." Miss Ypson's father was a professor of Greek at a small Midwestern university. He had conjugated his daughter with the rather bewildered assistance of one of his brawnier students, an Iowa poultry heiress.

Professor Ypson was a man of distinction. Unlike most professors of Greek, he was a Greek professor of Greek, having been born Gerasymos Aghamos Ypsilonomon in Polykhnitos, on the island of Mytilini, "where," he was fond of recalling on certain occasions, "burning Sappho loved and sung"—a quotation he found unfailingly useful in his extracurricular activities; and, the Hellenic ideal notwithstanding, Professor Ypson believed wholeheartedly in immoderation in all things. This hereditary and cultural background explains the professor's interest in fatherhood—to his wife's chagrin, for Mrs. Ypson's own breeding prowess was confined to the barnyards on which her income was based—a fact of which her husband sympathetically reminded her whenever he happened to sire another wayward chick; he held their daughter to be nothing less than a biological miracle.

The professor's mental processes also tended to confuse Mrs. Ypson. She never ceased to wonder why instead of shortening his name to Ypson, her husband had not sensibly changed it to Jones. "My dear," the professor once replied, "you are an Iowa snob." "But nobody," Mrs. Ypson cried, "can spell it or pronounce it!" "This is a cross," murmured Professor Ypson, "which we must bear with Ypsilanti," "Oh," said Mrs. Ypson.

There was invariably something Sibylline about his conversation.

135

His favorite adjective for his wife was "ypsiliform," a term, he explained, which referred to the germinal spot as one of the fecundation stages in a ripening egg and which was, therefore, exquisitely *aà propos*. Mrs. Ypson continued to look bewildered; she died at an early age.

And the professor ran off with a Kansas City variety girl of considerable talent, leaving his baptized chick to be reared by an eggish relative of her mother's, a Presbyterian named Jukes.

The only time Miss Ypson heard from her father—except when he wrote charming and erudite little notes requesting, as he termed it, *lucrum*—was in the fourth decade of his odyssey, when he sent her a handsome addition to her collection, a terra cotta play doll of Greek origin over three thousand years old which, unhappily, Miss Ypson felt duty-bound to return to the Brooklyn museum from which it had unaccountably vanished. The note accompanying her father's gift had said, whimsically: *"Timeo Danaos et dona ferentes."*

There was poetry behind Miss Ypson's dolls. At her birth the professor, ever harmonious, signalized his devotion to fecundity by naming her Cytherea. This proved the Olympian irony. For, it turned out, her father's philoprogenitiveness throbbed frustrate in her mother's stony womb; even though Miss Ypson interred five husbands of quite adequate vigor, she remained infertile to the end of her days. Hence it is classically tragic to find her, when all passion was spent, a sweet little old lady with a vague if eager smile who, under the name of her father, pattered about a vast and echoing New York apartment playing enthusiastically with dolls.

In the beginning they were dolls of common clay: a Billiken, a kewpie, a Kathe Kruse, a Patsy, a Foxy Grandpa, and so forth. But then, as her need increased, Miss Ypson began her fierce sack of the past.

Down into the land of Pharaoh she went for two pieces of thin desiccated board, carved and painted and with hair of strung beads, and legless—so that they might not run away—which any connoisseur will tell you are the most superb specimens of ancient Egyptian paddle doll extant, far superior to those in the British Museum, although this fact will be denied in certain quarters.

Miss Ypson unearthed a foremother of "Letitia Penn," until her discovery held to be the oldest doll in America, having been brought to

Philadelphia from England in 1699 by William Penn as a gift for a playmate of his small daughter's. Miss Ypson's find was a wooden-hearted "little lady" in brocade and velvet which had been sent by Sir Walter Raleigh to the first English child born in the New World. Since Virginia Dare had been born in 1587, not even the Smithsonian dared impugn Miss Ypson's triumph.

On the old lady's racks, in her plate-glass cases, might be seen the wealth of a thousand childhoods, and some riches—for such is the genetics of dolls—possessed by children grown. Here could be found "fashion babies" from fourteenth century France, sacred dolls of the Orange Free State Fingo tribe, Satsuma paper dolls and court dolls from old Japan, beady-eyed "Kalifa" dolls of the Egyptian Sudan, Swedish birch-bark dolls, "Katcina" dolls of the Hopis, mammoth-tooth dolls of the Eskimos, feather dolls of the Chippewa, tumble dolls of the ancient Chinese, Coptic bone dolls, Roman dolls dedicated to Diana, *pantin* dolls which had been the street toys of Parisian exquisites before Madame Guillotine swept the boulevards, early Christian dolls in their *crèches* representing the Holy Family—to specify the merest handful of Miss Ypson's Briarean collection. She possessed dolls of pasteboard, dolls of animal skin, spool-dolls, crab-claw dolls, eggshell dolls, cornhusk dolls, rag dolls, pine-cone dolls with moss hair, stocking dolls, dolls of *bisque*, dolls of palm leaf, dolls of *papier-mâché*, even dolls made of seed pods. There were dolls forty inches tall, and there were dolls so little Miss Ypson could hide them in her gold thimble.

Cytherea Ypson's collection bestrode the centuries and took tribute of history. There was no greater—not the fabled playthings of Montezuma, or Victoria's, or Eugene Field's; not the collection at the Metropolitan, or the South Kensington, or the royal palace in old Bucharest, or anywhere outside the enchantment of little girls' dreams.

It was made of Iowan eggs and the Attic shore, corn-fed and myrtle-clothed; and it brings us at last to Attorney John Somerset Bondling and his visit to the Queen residence one December twenty-third not so very long ago.

December the twenty-third is ordinarily not a good time to seek the Queens. Inspector Richard Queen likes his Christmas old-fashioned; his turkey stuffing, for instance, calls for twenty-two hours of over-all preparation nd some of its ingredients are not readily found at the corner grocer's. And Ellery is a frustrated gift-wrapper. For a month

before Christmas he turns his sleuthing genius to tracking down unusual wrapping papers, fine ribbons, and artistic stickers; and he
spends the last two days creating beauty.

So it was that when Attorney John S. Bondling called, Inspector
Queen was in his kitchen, swathed in a barbecue apron, up to his
elbows in *fines herbes,* while Ellery, behind the locked door of his study,
composed a secret symphony in glittering fuchsia metallic paper,
forest-green moiré ribbon, and pine cones.

"It's almost useless," shrugged Nikki, studying Attorney Bondling's card, which was as crackly-looking as Attorney Bondling. "You
say you know the Inspector, Mr. Bondling?"

"Just tell him Bondling the estate lawyer," said Bondling neuroti-
cally. "Park Row. He'll know."

"Don't blame me," said Nikki, "if you wind up in his stuffing.
Goodness knows he's used everything else." And she went for Inspector Queen.

While she was gone, the study door opened noiselessly for one inch.
A suspicious eye reconnoitered from the crack.

"Don't be alarmed," said the owner of the eye, slipping through the
crack and locking the door hastily behind him. "Can't trust them, you
know. Children, just children."

"Children!" Attorney Bondling snarled. "You're Ellery Queen,
aren't you?"

"Yes?"

"Interested in youth, are you? Christmas? Orphans, dolls, that sort
of thing?" Mr. Bondling went on in a remarkably nasty way.

"I suppose so."

"The more fool you. Ah, here's your father. Inspector Queen—!"

"Oh, that Bondling," said the old gentleman absently, shaking his
visitor's hand. "My office called to say someone was coming up. Here,
use my handkerchief; that's a bit of turkey liver. Know my son? His
secretary, Miss Porter? What's on your mind, Mr. Bondling?"

"Inspector, I'm handling the Cytherea Ypson estate, and—"

"Nice meeting you, Mr. Bondling," said Ellery. "Nikki, that door is
locked, so don't pretend you forgot the way to the bathroom . . . "

"Cytherea Ypson," frowned the Inspector. "Oh, yes. She died only
recently."

"Leaving me with the headache," said Mr. Bondling bitterly, "of disposing of her Dollection."

"Her what?" asked Ellery, looking up from the key.

"Dolls—collection. Dollection. She coined the word."

Ellery put the key back in his pocket and strolled over to his armchair.

"Do I take this down?" sighed Nikki.

"Dollection," said Ellery.

"Spent about thirty years at it. Dolls!"

"Yes, Nikki, take it down."

"Well, well, Mr. Bondling," said Inspector Queen. "What's the problem? Christmas comes but once a year, you know."

"Will provides the Dollection be sold at auction," grated the attorney, "and the proceeds used to set up a fund for orphan children. I'm holding the public sale right after New Year's."

"Dolls and orphans, eh?" said the Inspector, thinking of Javanese black pepper and Country Gentleman Seasoning Salt.

"That's *nice*," beamed Nikki.

"Oh, is it?" said Mr. Bondling softly. "Apparently, young woman, you've never tried to satisfy a Surrogate. I've administered estates for nine years without a whisper against me, but let an estate involve the interests of just one little ba—little fatherless child, and you'd think from the Surrogate's attitude I was Bill Sykes himself!"

"My stuffing," began the Inspector.

"I've had those dolls catalogued. The result is frightening! Did you know there's no set market for the damnable things? And aside from a few personal possessions, the Dollection constitutes the old lady's entire estate. Sank every nickel she had in it."

"But it should be worth a fortune," protested Ellery.

"To whom, Mr. Queen? Museums always want such things as free and unencumbered gifts. I tell you, except for one item, those hypothetical orphans won't realize enough from that sale to keep them in—in bubble gum for two days!"

"Which item would that be, Mr. Bondling?"

"Number Eight-seventy-four," snapped the lawyer. "This one."

"Number Eight-seventy-four," read Inspector Queen from the fat catalogue Bondling had fished out of a large greatcoat pocket. "The

Dauphin's Doll. Unique. Ivory figure of a boy Prince eight inches tall, clad in court dress, genuine ermine, brocade, velvet. Court sword in gold strapped to waist. Gold circlet crown surmounted by single blue brilliant diamond of finest water, weight approximately 49 carats—"

"How many carats?" exclaimed Nikki.

"Larger than the *Hope* and the *Star of South Africa*," said Ellery, with a certain excitement.

"—appraised," continued his father, "at one hundred and ten thousand dollars."

"Expensive dollie."

"Indecent!" said Nikki.

"This indecent—I mean exquisite royal doll," the Inspector read on, "was a birthday gift from King Louis XVI of France to Louis Charles, his second son, who became dauphin at the death of his elder brother in 1789. The little dauphin was proclaimed Louis XVII by the royalists during the French Revolution while in custody of the *sans-culottes*. His fate is shrouded in mystery. Romantic, historic item."

"*Le prince perdu*. I'll say," muttered Ellery. "Mr. Bondling, is this on the level?"

"I'm an attorney, not an antiquarian," snapped their visitor. "There are documents attached, one of them a sworn statement—holograph —by Lady Charlotte Atkyns, the English actress-friend of the Capet family—she was in France during the Revolution—or purporting to be in Lady Charlotte's hand. It doesn't matter, Mr. Queen. Even if the history is bad, the diamond's good!"

"I take it this hundred-and-ten-thousand dollar dollie constitutes the bone, as it were, or that therein lies the rub?"

"You said it!" cried Mr. Bondling, cracking his knuckles in a sort of agony. "For my money the Dauphin's Doll is the only negotiable asset of that collection. And what's the old lady do? She provides by will that on the day preceding Christmas the Cytherea Ypson Dollection is to be publicly displayed . . . on the main floor of Nash's Department Store! *The day before Christmas, gentlemen!* Think of it!"

"But why?" asked Nikki, puzzled.

"Why? Who knows why? For the entertainment of New York's army of little beggars, I suppose! Have you any notion how many peasants pass through Nash's on the day before Christmas? My cook tells me—she's a very religious woman—it's like Armageddon."

"Day before Christmas," frowned Ellery. "That's tomorrow."

"It does sound chancy," said Nikki anxiously. Then she brightened. "Oh, well, maybe Nash's won't cooperate, Mr. Bondling."

"Oh, won't they!" howled Mr. Bondling. "Why, old lady Ypson had this stunt cooked up with that gang of peasant-purveyors for years! They've been snapping at my heels ever since the day she was put away!"

"It'll draw every crook in New York," said the Inspector, his gaze on the kitchen door.

"Orphans," said Nikki. "The orphans' interests *must* be protected." She looked at her employer accusingly.

"Special measures, Dad," said Ellery.

"Sure, sure," said the Inspector, rising. "Don't you worry about this, Mr. Bondling. Now if you'll be kind enough to excu—"

"Inspector Queen," hissed Mr. Bondling, leaning forward tensely, "that is not all."

"Ah." Ellery briskly lit a cigarette. "There's a specific villain in this piece, Mr. Bondling, and you know who he is."

"I do," said the lawyer hollowly, "and then again I don't. I mean, it's Comus."

"*Comus!*" the Inspector screamed.

"Comus?" said Ellery slowly.

"Comus?" said Nikki. "Who dat?"

"Comus," nodded Mr. Bondling. "First thing this morning. Marched right into my office, bold as day—must have followed me; I hadn't got my coat off, my secretary wasn't even in. Marched in and tossed this card on my desk."

Ellery seized it. "The usual, Dad."

"His trademark," growled the Inspector, his lips working.

"But the card just says 'Comus,' " complained Nikki. "Who—?"

"Go on, Mr. Bondling!" thundered the Inspector.

"And he calmly announced to me," said Bondling, blotting his cheeks with an exhausted handkerchief, "that he's going to steal the Dauphin's Doll tomorrow, in Nash's."

"Oh, a maniac," said Nikki.

"Mr. Bondling," said the old gentleman in a terrible voice, "just what did this fellow look like?"

"Foreigner—black beard—spoke with a thick accent of some sort.

To tell you the truth, I was so thunderstruck I didn't notice details. Didn't even chase him till it was too late."

The Queens shrugged at each other, Gallically.

"The old story," said the Inspector; the corners of his nostrils were greenish. "The brass of the colonel's monkey and when he does show himself nobody remembers anything but beards and foreign accents. Well, Mr. Bondling, with Comus in the game it's serious business. Where's the collection right now?"

"In the vaults of the Life Bank & Trust, Forty-third Street branch."

"What time are you to move it over to Nash's?"

"They wanted it this evening. I said nothing doing. I've made special arrangements with the bank, and the collection's to be moved at seven-thirty tomorrow morning."

"Won't be much time to set up," said Ellery thoughtfully, "before the store opens its doors." He glanced at his father.

"You leave Operation Dollie to us, Mr. Bondling," said the Inspector grimly. "Better give me a buzz this afternoon."

"I can't tell you, Inspector, how relieved I am—"

"Are you?" said the old gentleman sourly. "What makes you think he won't get it?"

When Attorney Bondling had left, the Queens put their heads together, Ellery doing most of the talking, as usual. Finally, the Inspector went into the bedroom for a session with his direct line to Headquarters.

"Anybody would think," sniffed Nikki, "you two were planning the defense of the Bastille. Who is this Comus, anyway?"

"We don't know, Nikki," said Ellery slowly. "Might be anybody. Began his criminal career about five years ago. He's in the grand tradition of Lupin—a saucy, highly intelligent rascal who's made stealing an art. He seems to take a special delight in stealing valuable things under virtually impossible conditions. Master of make-up—he's appeared in a dozen different disguises. And he's an uncanny mimic. Never been caught, photographed, or fingerprinted. Imaginative, daring—I'd say he's the most dangerous thief operating in the United States."

"If he's never been caught,' said Nikki skeptically, "how do you know he commits these crimes?"

"You mean and not someone else?" Ellery smiled pallidly. "The techniques mark the thefts as his work. And then, like Arsène, he leaves a card—with the name 'Comus' on it—on the scene of each visit."

"Does he usually announce in advance that he's going to swipe the crown jewels?"

"No." Ellery frowned. "To my knowledge, this is the first such instance. Since he's never done anything without a reason, that visit to Bondling's office this morning must be part of his greater plan. I wonder if—"

The telephone in the living room rang clear and loud.

Nikki looked at Ellery. ellery looked at the telephone.

"Do you suppose—?" began Nikki. But then she said, "Oh, it's too absurd."

"Where Comus is involved," said Ellery wildly, "nothing is too absurd!' and he leaped for the phone. "Hello!"

"A call from an old friend," announced a deep and hollowish male voice. "Comus."

"Well," said Ellery. "Hello again."

"Did Mr. Bondling," asked the voice jovially, "persuade you to 'prevent' me from stealing the Dauphin's Doll in Nash's tomorrow?"

"So you know Bondling's been here."

"No miracle involved, Queen. I followed him. Are you taking the case?"

"See here, Comus," said Ellery. "Under ordinary circumstances I'd welcome the sporting chance to put you where you belong. But these circumstances are not ordinary. That doll represents the major asset of a future fund for orphaned children. I'd rather we didn't play catch with it. Comus, what do you say we call this one off?"

"Shall we say," asked the voice gently, "Nash's Department Store—tomorrow?"

Thus the early morning of December twenty-fourth finds Messrs. Queen and Bondling, and Nikki Porter, huddled on the iron sidewalk of Forty-third Street before the holly-decked windows of the Life Bank & Trust Company just outside a double line of armed guards. The guards form a channel between the bank entrance and an armored truck, down which Cytherea Ypson's Dollection flows swiftly. And all about gapes New York, stamping callously on the aged, icy face of the street against the uncharitable Christmas wind.

Now is the winter of his discontent, and Mr. Queen curses.

"I don't know what you're beefing about," moans Miss Porter. "You and Mr. Bondling are bundled up like Yukon prospectors. Look at *me*."

"It's that rat-hearted public relations tripe from Nash's," says Mr. Queen murderously. "They all swore themselves to secrecy, Brother Rat included. Honor! Spirit of Christmas!"

"It was all over the radio last night," whimpers Mr. Bondling. "And in this morning's papers."

"I'll cut his creep's heart out. Here! Velie, keep those people away!"

Sergeant Velie says good-naturedly from the doorway of the bank, "You jerks stand back." Little does the Sergeant know the fate in store for him.

"Armored trucks," says Miss Porter bluishly. "Shotguns."

"Nikki, Comus made a point of informing us in advance that he meant to steal the Dauphin's Doll in Nash's Department Store. It would be just like him to have said that in order to make it easier to steal the doll en route."

"Why don't they hurry?" shivers Mr. Bondling. "Ah!"

Inspector Queen appears suddenly in the doorway. His hands clasp treasure.

"Oh!" cries Nikki.

New York whistles.

It is magnificence, an affront to democracy. But street mobs, like children, are royalists at heart.

New York whistles, and Sergeant Thomas Velie steps menacingly before Inspector Queen, Police Positive drawn, and Inspector Queen dashes across the sidewalk between the bristling lines of guards with the Dauphin's Doll in his embrace.

Queen the Younger vanishes, to materialize an instant later at the door of the armored truck.

"It's just immorally, hideously beautiful, Mr. Bondling," breathes Miss Porter, sparkly-eyed.

Mr. Bondling cranes, thinly.

ENTER *Santa Claus, with bell.*

SANTA: Oyez, oyez. Peace, good will. Is that the dollie the radio's been yappin' about, folks?

MR. B: Scram.

144

MISS P: Why, Mr. Bondling.

MR. B: Well, he's got no business here. Stand back, er, Santa. Back!

SANTA: What eateth you, my lean and angry friend? Have you no compassion at this season of the year?

MR. B: Oh . . . Here! (*Clink.*) Now will you *kindly* . . . ?

SANTA: Mighty pretty dollie. Where they takin' it, girlie?

MISS P: Over to Nash's, Santa.

MR. B: You asked for it. Officer!!!

SANTA (hurriedly): Little present for you, girlie. Compliments of Santy. Merry, merry.

MISS P: For *me?* (EXIT *Santa, rapidly, with bell.*) Really, Mr. Bondling, was it necessary to . . . ?

MR. B: Opium for the masses! What did that flatulent faker hand you, Miss Porter? What's in that unmentionable envelope?

MISS P: I'm sure I don't know, but isn't it the most touching idea? Why, it's addressed to *Ellery.* Oh! Elleryyyyyy!

MR. B (EXIT *excitedly*): Where is he? You—! Officer! Where did that baby-deceiver disappear to? A Santa Claus . . . !

MR. Q (*entering on the run*): Yes? Nikki, what is it? What's happened?

MISS P: A man dressed as Santa Claus just handed me this envelope. It's addressed to you.

MR. Q: Note? (*He snatches it, withdraws a miserable slice of paper from it on which is block-lettered in pencil a message which he reads aloud with considerable expression.*) "Dear Ellery, Don't you trust me? I said I'd steal the Dauphin in Nash's emporium today and that's exactly where I'm going to do it. Yours—" Signed . . .

MISS P (*craning*): "Comus." That Santa?

MR. Q: (*Sets his manly lips. An icy wind blows.*)

Even the master had to acknowlede that their defenses against Comus were ingenious.

From the Display Department of Nash's they had requisitioned four miter-jointed counters of uniform length. These they had fitted together, and in the center of the hollow square thus formed they had erected a platform six feet high. On the counters, in plastic tiers, stretched the long lines of Miss Ypson's babies. Atop the platform, dominant, stood a great chair of handcarved oak, filched from the Swedish Modern section of the Fine Furniture Department; and on this Valhalla-like throne, a huge and rosy rotundity, sat Sergeant Thomas Velie of Police Headquarters, morosely grateful for the anonymity endowed by the scarlet suit and the jolly mask and whiskers of his appointed role.

Nor was this all. At a distance of six feet outside the counters shimmered a surrounding rampart of plate glass, borrowed in its various elements from *The Glass Home of the Future* display on the sixth floor rear, and assembled to shape an eight-foot wall quoined with chrome, its glistening surfaces flawless except at one point, where a thick glass door had been installed. But the edges fitted intimately and there was a formidable lock in the door, the key to which lay buried in Mr. Queen's right trouser pocket.

It was 8:54 A.M. The Queens, Nikki Porter, and Attorney Bondling stood among store officials and an army of plainclothesmen on Nash's main floor surveying the product of their labors.

"I think that about does it," muttered Inspector Queen at last. "Men! Positions around the glass partition."

Twenty-four assorted gendarmes in mufti jostled one another. They took marked places about the wall, facing it and grinning up at Sergeant Velie. Sergeant Velie, from his throne, glared back.

"Hagstrom and Piggott—the door."

Two detectives detached themselves from a group of reserves. As they marched to the glass door, Mr. Bondling plucked at the Inspector's overcoat sleeve. "Can all these men be trusted, Inspector Queen?" he whispered. "I mean, this fellow Comus—"

"Mr. Bondling," replied the old gentleman coldly, "you do your job and let me do mine."

"But—"

"Picked men, Mr. Bondling! I picked 'em myself."

"Yes, yes, Inspector. I merely thought I'd—"

"Lieutenant Farber."

A little man with watery eyes stepped forward.

"Mr. Bondling, this is Lieutenant Geronimo Farber, Headquarters jewelry expert. Ellery?"

Ellery took the Dauphin's Doll from his greatcoat pocket, but he said, "If you don't mind, Dad, I'll keep holding on to it."

Somebody said, "Wow," and then there was silence.

"Lieutenant, this doll in my son's hand is the famous Dauphin's Doll with the diamond crown that—"

"Don't touch it, Lieutenant, please," said Ellery. "I'd rather nobody touched it."

"The doll," continued the Inspector, "has just been brought here from a bank vault which it ought never to have left, and Mr. Bondling, who's handling the Ypson estate, claims it's the genuine article. Lieutenant, examine the diamond and give us your opinion."

Lieutenant Farber produced a *loupe*. Ellery held the dauphin securely, and Farber did not touch it.

Finally, the expert said: "I can't pass an opinion about the doll itself, of course, but the diamond's a beauty. Easily worth a hundred thousand dollars at the present state of the market—maybe more. Looks like a very strong setting, by the way."

"Thanks, Lieutenant. Okay, son," said the Inspector. "Go into your waltz."

Clutching the dauphin, Ellery strode over to the glass gate and unlocked it.

"This fellow Farber," whispered Attorney Bondling in the Inspector's hairy ear. "Inspector, are you absolutely sure he's—?"

"He's really Lieutenant Farber?" The Inspector controlled himself. "Mr. Bondling, I've known Gerry Farber for eighteen years. Calm yourself."

Ellery was crawling perilously over the nearest counter. Then, bearing the dauphin aloft, he hurried across the floor of the enclosure to the platform.

Sergeant Velie whined, "Maestro, how in hell am I going to sit here all day without washin' my hands?"

But Mr. Queen merely stood and lifted from the floor a heavy little structure faced with black velvet consisting of a floor and a backdrop, with a two-armed chromium support. This object he placed on the platform directly between Sergeant Velie's massive legs.

Carefully, he stood the Dauphin's Doll in the velvet niche. Then he clambered back across the counter, went through the glass door, locked it with the key, and turned to examine his handiwork.

147

Proudly the prince's plaything stood, the jewel in his little golden crown darting "on pale electric streams" under the concentrated tide of a dozen of the most powerful floodlights in the possession of the great store.

"Velie," said Inspector, "you're not to touch that doll. Don't lay a finger on it.

The Sergeant said, "Gaaaaa."

"You men on duty. Don't worry about the crowds. Your job is to keep watching that doll. You're not to take your eyes off it all day. Mr. Bondling, are you satisfied?" Mr. Bondling seemed about to say something, but then he hastily nodded. "Ellery?"

The great man smiled. "The only way he can get that bawbie," he said, "is by well-directed mortar fire or spells and incantations. Raise the portcullis!"

Then began the interminable day, *dies irae,* the last shopping day before Christmas. This is traditionally the day of the inert, the procrastinating, the undecided, and the forgetful, sucked at last into the mercantile machine by the perpetual pump of Time. If there is peace upon earth, it descends only afterward; and at no time, on the part of anyone embroiled, is there good will toward men. As Miss Porter expresses it, a cat fight in a bird cage would be more Christian.

But on this December twenty-fourth, in Nash's, the normal bedlam was augmented by the vast shrilling of thousands of children. It may be, as the Psalmist insists, that happy is the man that hath his quiver full of them; but no bowmen surrounded Miss Ypson's darlings this day, only detectives carrying revolvers, not a few of whom forbore to use same only by the most heroic self-discipline. In the black floods of humanity overflowing the main floor little folks darted about like electrically charged minnows, pursued by exasperated maternal shrieks and the imprecations of those whose shins and rumps and toes were at the mercy of hot, happy little limbs; indeed, nothing was sacred, and Attorney Bondling was seen to quail and wrap his great-coat defensively about him against the savage innocence of childhood. But the guardians of the law, having been ordered to simulate store employees, possessed no such armor; and many a man earned his citation that day for unique cause. They stood in the millrace of the tide; it churned about them, shouting, "Dollies! *Dollies!*" until the very

148

word lost its familiar meaning and became the insensate scream of a thousand Loreleis beckoning strong men to destruction below the eye-level of their diamond Light.

But they stood fast.

And Comus was thwarted. Oh, he tried. At 11:18 A.M. a tottering old man holding fast to the hand of a small boy tried to wheedle Detective Hagstrom into unlocking the glass door "so my grandson here—he's terrible nearsighted—can get a closer look at the pretty dollies." Detective Hagstrom roared, "Rube!" and the old gentleman dropped the little boy's hand violently and with remarkable agility lost himself in the crowd. A spot investigation revealed that, coming upon the boy, who had been crying for his mommy, the old gentleman had promised to find her. The little boy, whose name—he said—was Lance Morganstern, was removed to the Lost and Found Department; and everyone was satisfied that the great thief had finally launched his attack. Everyone, that is, but Ellery Queen. He seemed puzzled. When Nikki asked him why, he merely said: "Stupidity, Nikki. It's not in character."

At 1:46 P.M., Sergeant Velie sent up a distress signal. He had, it seemed, to wash his hands. Inspector Queen signaled back: "O.K. Fifteen minutes." Sergeant Santa C. Velie scrambled off his perch, clawed his way over the counter, and pounded urgently on the inner side of the glass door. Ellery let him out, relocking the door immediately, and the Sergeant's red-clad figure disappeared on the double in the general direction of the main-floor gentleman's relief station, leaving the dauphin in solitary possession of the dais.

During the Sergeant's recess, Inspector Queen circulated among his men repeating the order of the day.

The episode of Velie's response to the summons of Nature caused a temporary crisis. For at the end of the specified fifteen minutes he had not returned. Nor was there a sign of him at the end of a half hour. An aide dispatched to the relief station reported back that the Sergeant was not there. Fears of foul play were voiced at an emergency staff conference held then and there and countermeasures were being planned even as, at 2:35 P.M., the familiar Santa-clad bulk of the Sergeant was observed battling through the lines, pawing at his mask.

"Velie," snarled Inspector Queen, "where have you been?"

"Eating my lunch," growled the Sergeant's voice, defensively. "I been taking my punishment like a good soldier all this damn day,

Inspector, but I draw the line at starvin' to death even in line of duty."

"Velie—!" choked the Inspector; but then he waved his hand feebly and said, "Ellery, let him back in there."

And that was very nearly all. The only other incident of note occurred at 4:22 P.M. A well-upholstered woman with a red face yelled, "Stop! Thief! He grabbed my pocketbook! Police!" about fifty feet from the Ypson exhibit. Ellery instantly shouted, *"It's a trick! Men, don't take your eyes off that doll!"* "It's Comus disguised as a woman," exclaimed Attorney Bondling, as Inspector Queen and Detective Hesse wrestled the female figure through the mob. She was now a wonderful shade of magenta. "What are you *doing?"* she screamed. "Don't arrest *me!*— catch that crook who stole my pocketbook!" "No dice, Comus," said the Inspector. "Wipe off that make-up." "McComus?" said the woman loudly. "My name is Rafferty, and all these folks saw it. He was a fat man with a mustache." "Inspector," said Nikki Porter, making a surreptitious scientific test. "This is a female. Believe me." And so, indeed, it proved. All agreed that the mustachioed fat man had been Comus, creating a diversion in the desperate hope that the resulting confusion would give him an opportunity to steal the little dauphin.

"Stupid, stupid," muttered Ellery, gnawing his fingernails.

"Sure," grinned the Inspector. "We've got him nibbling his tail, Ellery. This was his do-or-die pitch. He's through."

"Frankly," sniffed Nikki, "I'm a little disappointed."

"Worried," said Ellery, "would be the word for me."

Inspector Queen was too case-hardened a sinner's nemesis to lower his guard at his most vulnerable moment. When the 5:30 bells bonged and the crowds began struggling toward the exits, he barked: "Men, stay at your posts. Keep watching that doll!" So all hands were on the *qui vive* even as the store emptied. The reserves kept hustling people out. Ellery, standing on an Information booth, spotted bottlenecks and waved his arms.

At 5:50 P.M. the main floor was declared out of the battle zone. All stragglers had been herded out. The only persons visible were the refugees trapped by the closing bell on the upper floors, and these were pouring out of elevators and funneled by a solid line of detectives and accredited store personnel to the doors. By 6:05 they were a trickle;

by 6:10 even the trickle had dried up. And the personnel itself began to disperse.

"No, men!" called Ellery sharply from his observation post. "Stay where you are till all the store employees are out!" The counter clerks had long since disappeared.

Sergeant Velie's plaintive voice called from the other side of the glass door. "I got to get home and decorate my tree. Maestro, make with the key."

Ellery jumped down and hurried over to release him. Detective Piggott jeered, "Going to play Santa to your kids tomorrow morning, Velie?" at which the Sergeant managed even through his mask to project a four-letter word distinctly, forgetful of Miss Porter's presence, and stamped off toward the gentlemen's relief station.

"Where are you going, Velie?" asked the Inspector, smiling.

"I got to get out of these x-and-dash Santy clothes somewheres, don't I?" came back the Sergeant's mask-muffled tones, and he vanished in a thunderclap of his fellow-officers' laughter.

"Still worried, Mr. Queen?" chuckled the Inspector.

"I don't understand it." Ellery shook his head. "Well, Mr. Bondling, there's your dauphin, untouched by human hands."

"Yes. Well!" Attorney Bondling wiped his forehead happily. "I don't profess to understand it, either, Mr. Queen. Unless it's simply another case of an inflated reputation . . ." He clutched the Inspector suddenly. "Those men!" he whispered *"Who are they?"*

"Relax, Mr. Bondling," said the Inspector good-naturedly. "It's just the men to move the dolls back to the bank. Wait a minute, you men! Perhaps, Mr. Bondling, we'd better see the dauphin back to the vaults ourselves."

"Keep those fellows back," said Ellery to the Headquarters men, quietly, and he followed the Inspector and Mr. Bondling into the enclosure. They pulled two of the counters apart at one corner and strolled over to the platform. The dauphin was winking at them in a friendly way. They stood looking at him.

"Cute little devil," said the Inspector.

"Seems silly now," beamed Attorney Bondling. "Being so worried all day."

"Comus must have had *some* plan," mumbled Ellery.

"Sure," said the Inspector. "That old man disguise. And that purse-snatching act."

"No, no, Dad. Something clever. He's always pulled something clever."

"Well, there's the diamond," said the lawyer comfortably. "He didn't."

"Disguise . . . " muttered Ellery. "It's always been a disguise. Santa Claus costume—he used that once—this morning in front of the bank . . . Did we see a Santa Claus around here today?"

"Just Velie," said the Inspector, grinning. "And I hardly think—"

"Wait a moment, please," said Attorney Bondling in a very odd voice.

He was staring at the Dauphin's Doll.

"Wait for what, Mr. Bondling?"

"What's the matter?" said Ellery, also in a very odd voice.

"But . . . not possible . . ." stammered Bondling. He snatched the doll from its black velvet repository. *"No!"* he howled. *"This isn't the dauphin! It's a fake—a copy!"*

Something happened in Mr. Queen's head—a little *click!* like the turn of a switch. And there was light.

"Some of you men!" he roared. *"After Santa Claus!"*

"Who, Mr. Queen?"

"What's he talkin' about?"

"After who, Ellery?" gasped Inspector Queen.

"What's the matter?"

"I dunno!"

"Don't stand here! *Get him!*" screamed Ellery, dancing up and down. "The man I just let out of here! The Santa who made for the men's room!"

Detectives started running, wildly.

"But Ellery," said a small voice, and Nikki found that it was her own, "that was Sergeant Velie."

"It was *not* Velie, Nikki! When Velie ducked out just before two o'clock to relieve himself, *Comus waylaid him!* It was Comus who came back in Velie's Santa Claus rig, wearing Velie's whiskers and mask! *Comus has been on this platform all afternoon!*" He tore the dauphin from Attorney Bondling's grasp. "Copy . . . ! Somehow he did it, he did it."

"But Mr. Queen," whispered Attorney Bondling, "his voice. He spoke to us . . . in Sergeant Velie's voice."

"Yes, Ellery," Nikki heard herself saying.

"I told you yesterday Comus is a great mimic, Nikki. Lieutenant Farber! Is Farber still here?"

The jewelry expert, who had been gaping from a distance, shook his head as if to clear it and shuffled into the enclosure.

"Lieutenant," said Ellery in a strangled voice. "Examine this diamond . . . I mean, *is* it a diamond?"

Inspector Queen removed his hands from his face and said froggily, "Well, Gerry?"

Lieutenant Farber squinted once through his *loupe*. "The hell you say. It's strass—"

"It's what?" said the Inspector piteously.

"Strass, Dick—lead glass—paste. Beautiful job of imitation—as nice as I've ever seen."

"Lead me to that Santa Claus," whispered Inspector Queen.

But Santa Claus was being led to him. Struggling in the grip of a dozen detectives, his red coat ripped off, his red pants around his ankles, but his whiskery mask still on his face, came a large shouting man.

"But I tell you," he was roaring, "I'm Sergeant Tom Velie! Just take the mask off—that's all!"

"It's a pleasure," growled Detective Hagstrom, trying to break their prisoner's arm, "we're reservin' for the Inspector."

"Hold him, boys," whispered the Inspector. He struck like a cobra. His hand came away with Santa's face.

And there, indeed, was Sergeant Velie.

"Why, it's Velie," said the Inspector wonderingly.

"I only told you that a thousand times," said the Sergeant, folding his great hairy arms across his great hairy chest. "Now who's the so-and-so who tried to bust my arm?" Then he said, "My pants!" and, as Miss Porter turned delicately away, Detective Hagstrom humbly stooped and raised Sergeant Velie's pants.

"Never mind that," said a cold, remote voice.

It was the master, himself.

"Yeah?" said Sergeant Velie, hostilely.

"Velie, weren't you attacked when you went to the men's room just before two?"

"Do I look like the attackable type?'

"You did go to lunch?—in person?"

"And a lousy lunch it was."

"It was *you* up here among the dolls all afternoon?"

"Nobody else, Maestro. Now, my friends, I want action. Fast patter. What's this all about? Before," said Sergeant Velie softly, "I lose my temper."

While divers Headquarters orators delivered impromptu periods before the silent Sergeant, Inspector Richard Queen spoke.

"Ellery. Son. How in the name of the second sin did he do it?"

"Pa," replied the master, "you got me."

Deck the hall with boughs of holly, but not if your name is Queen on the evening of a certain December twenty-fourth. If your name is Queen on that lamentable evening you are seated in the living room of a New York apartment uttering no falalas but staring miserably into a somber fire. And you have company. The guest list is short, but select. It numbers two, a Miss Porter and a Sergeant Velie, and they are no comfort.

No, no ancient Yuletide carol is being trolled; only the silence sings.

Wail in your crypt, Cytherea Ypson; all was for nought; your little dauphin's treasure lies not in the empty coffers of the orphans but in the hot clutch of one who took his evil inspiration from a long-crumbled specialist in vanishments.

Speech was spent. Should a wise man utter vain knowledge, and fill his belly with the east wind? He who talks too much commits a sin, says the Talmud. He also wastes his breath; and they had now reached the point of conservation, having exhausted the available supply.

ITEM: Lieutenant Geronimo Farber of Police Headquarters had examined the diamond in the genuine dauphin's crown a matter of seconds before it was conveyed to its sanctuary in the enclosure. Lieutenant Farber had pronounced the diamond a diamond, and not merely a diamond, but a diamond worth in his opinion over one hundred thousand dollars.

QUESTION: Had Lieutenant Farber lied?

ANSWER: Lieutenant Farber was (a) a man of probity, tested in a thousand fires, and (b) he was incorruptible. To (a) and (b) Inspector Richard Queen attested violently, swearing by the beard of his personal Prophet.

QUESTION: Had Lieutenant Farber been mistaken?

ANSWER: Lieutenant Farber was a nationally famous police expert in the field of precious stones. It must be presumed that he knew a real diamond from a piece of lapidified glass.

QUESTION: Had it *been* Lieutenant Farber?

ANSWER: By the same beard of the identical Prophet, it had been Lieutenant Farber and no facsimile.

CONCLUSION: The diamond Lieutenant Farber had examined immediately preceding the opening of Nash's doors that morning had been the veritable diamond of the dauphin, the doll had been the veritable Dauphin's Doll, and it was this genuine article which Ellery with his own hands had carried into the glass-enclosed fortress and deposited between the authenticated Sergeant Velie's verified feet.

ITEM: All day—specifically, between the moment the dauphin had been deposited in his niche until the moment he was discovered to be a fraud; that is, during the total period in which a theft-and-substitution was even theoretically possible—no person whatsoever, male or female, adult or child, had set foot within the enclosure except Sergeant Thomas Velie, alias Santa Claus.

> QUESTION: Had Sergeant Velie switched dolls, carrying the genuine dauphin concealed in his Santa Claus suit, to be cached for future retrieval or turned over to Comus or a confederate of Comus's, during one of his two departures from the enclosure?
>
> ANSWER (by *Sergeant Velie*): *
>
> CONFIRMATION: Some dozens of persons with police training and specific instructions, not to mention the Queens themselves, Miss Porter, and Attorney Bondling, testified

*Deleted.—*Editor.*

unqualifiedly that Sergeant Velie had not touched the doll, at any time, all day.

CONCLUSION: Sergeant Velie could not have stolen, and therefore he did not steal, the Dauphin's Doll.

ITEM: All those deputized to watch the doll swore that they had done so without lapse or hindrance the everlasting day; moreover, that at no time had anything touched the doll—human or mechanical—either from inside or outside the enclosure.

> QUESTION: The human vessel being frail, could those so swearing have been in error? Could their attention have wandered through weariness, boredom, *et cetera?*
> ANSWER: Yes; but not all at the same time, by the laws of probability. And during the only two diversions of the danger period, Ellery himself testified that he had kept his eyes on the dauphin and that nothing whatsoever had approached or threatened it.

ITEM: Despite all of the foregoing, at the end of the day they had found the real dauphin gone and a worthless copy in its place.

"It's brilliantly, unthinkably clever," said Ellery at last. "A master illusion. For, of course, it *was* an illusion . . ."

"Witchcraft," groaned the Inspector.

"Mass mesmerism," suggested Nikki Porter.

Two hours later Ellery spoke again.

"So Comus has a worthless copy of the dauphin all ready for the switch," he muttered. "It's a world-famous dollie, been illustrated countless times, minutely described, photographed . . . All ready for the switch, but how did he make it? How? How?"

"You said that," said the Sergeant, "once or forty-two times."

"The bells are tolling," sighed Nikki, "but for whom? Not for us." And indeed, while they were slumped there, Time, which Seneca named father of truth, had crossed the threshold of Christmas; and Nikki looked alarmed, for as that glorious song of old came upon the midnight clear, a great light spread from Ellery's eyes and beatified the whole contorted countenance, so that peace sat there, the peace that approximateth understanding; and he threw back that noble head and laughed with the merriment of an innocent child.

"Hey," said Sergeant Velie, staring.

"Son," began Inspector Queen, half-rising from his armchair; when the telephone rang.

"Beautiful!" roared Ellery. "Oh, exquisite! How did Comus make the switch, eh? Nikki—"

"From somewhere," said Nikki, handing him the telephone receiver, "a voice is calling, and if you ask me it's saying 'Comus.' Why not ask him?"

"Comus," whispered the Inspector, shrinking.

"Comus," echoed the Sergeant, baffled.

"Comus?" said Ellery heartily. "How nice. Hello there! Congratulations."

"Why, thank you," said the familiar deep and hollow voice. "I called to express my appreciation for a wonderful day's sport and to wish you the merriest kind of Yuletide."

"You anticipate a rather merry Christmas yourself, I take it."

"Laeti triumphantes," said Comus jovially.

"And the orphans?"

"They have my best wishes. But I won't detain you, Ellery. If you'll look at the doormat outside your apartment door, you'll find on it—in the spirit of the season—a little gift, with the compliments of Comus. Will you remember me to Inspector Queen and Attorney Bondling?"

Ellery hung up, smiling.

On the doormat he found the true Dauphin's Doll, intact except for a contemptible detail. The jewel in the little golden crown was missing.

"It was," said Ellery later, over pastrami sandwiches, "a fundamentally simple problem. All great illusions are. A valuable object is placed in full view in the heart of an impenetrable enclosure, it is watched hawkishly by dozens of thoroughly screened and reliable trained persons, it is never out of their view, it is not once touched by human hand or any other agency, and yet, at the expiration of the danger period, it is gone—exchanged for a worthless copy. Wonderful. Amazing. It defies the imagination. Actually, it's susceptible—like all magical hocus-pocus—to immediate solution if only one is able—as I was

157

not—to ignore the wonder and stick to the fact. But then, the wonder is there for precisely that purpose: to stand in the way of the fact.

"What is the fact?" continued Ellery, helping himself to a dill pickle. "The fact is that between the time the doll was placed on the exhibit platform and the time the theft was discovered no one and nothing touched it. Therefore between the time the doll was placed on the platform and the time the theft was discovered *the dauphin could not have been stolen*. It follows, simply and inevitably, that the dauphin must have been stolen *outside that period*.

"Before the period began? No. I placed the authentic dauphin inside the enclosure with my own hands; at or about the beginning of the period, then, no hand but mine had touched the doll—not even, you'll recall, Lieutenant Farber's.

"Then the dauphin must have been stolen after the period closed."

Ellery brandished half the pickle. "And, who," he demanded solemnly, "is the only one besides myself who handled that doll after the period closed and before Lieutenant Farber pronounced the diamond to be paste? The only one?"

The Inspector and the Sergeant exchanged puzzled glances, and Nikki looked blank.

"Why, Mr. Bondling," said Nikki, "and he doesn't count."

"He counts very much, Nikki," said Ellery, reaching for the mustard, "because the facts say Bondling stole the dauphin at that time."

"Bondling!" the Inspector paled.

"I don't get it," complained Sergeant Velie.

"Ellery, you must be wrong," said Nikki. "At the time Mr. Bondling grabbed the doll off the platform, the theft had already taken place. It was the worthless copy he picked up."

"That," said Ellery, reaching for another sandwich, "was the focal point of his illusion. How do we know it was the worthless copy he picked up? Why, he said so. Simple, eh? He said so, and like the dumb bunnies we were, we took his unsupported word as gospel."

"That's right!" mumbled his father. "We didn't actually examine the doll till quite a few seconds later."

"Exactly," said Ellery in a munchy voice. "There was a short period of beautiful confusion, as Bondling knew there would be. I yelled to the boys to follow and grab Santa Claus—I mean, the Sergeant here. The detectives were momentarily demoralized. You, Dad, were stunned. Nikki looked as if the roof had fallen in. I essayed an excited explanation. Some detectives ran; others milled around. And while all this was happening—during those few moments when nobody was watching the genuine doll in Bondling's hand because everyone thought it was a fake—Bondling calmly slipped it into one of his greatcoat pockets and from the other produced the worthless copy which he'd been carrying there all day. When I did turn back to him, it was the copy I grabbed from his hand. And the illusion was complete."

"I know," said Ellery dryly. "It's rather on the let-down side. That's why illusionists guard their professional secrets so closely; knowledge is disenchantment. No doubt the incredulous amazement aroused in his periwigged London audience by Comus the French conjurer's dematerialization of his wife from the top of a table would have suffered the same fate if he'd revealed the trap door through which she had dropped. A good trick, like a good woman, is best in the dark. Sergeant, have another pastrami."

"Seems like funny chow to be eating early Christmas morning," said the Sergeant, reaching. Then he stopped. Then he said, "Bondling," and he shook his head.

"Now that we know it was Bondling," said the Inspector, who had recovered a little, "it's a cinch to get that diamond back. He hasn't had time to dispose of it yet. I'll just give downtown a buzz—"

"Wait, Dad," said Ellery.

"Wait for what?"

"Whom are you going to sic the dogs on?"

"What?"

"You're going to call Headquarters, get a warrant, and so on. Who's your man?"

The Inspector felt his head. "Why . . . Bondling, didn't you say?"

"It might be wise," said Ellery, thoughtfully searching with his tongue for a pickle seed, "to specify his alias."

"Alias?" said Nikki. "Does he have one?"

"What alias, son?"

"Comus."

"*Comus!*"

"Comus?"

"Comus."

"Oh, come off it," said Nikki, pouring herself a shot of coffee, straight, for she was in training for the Inspector's Christmas dinner. "How could Bondling be Comus when Bondling was with us all day?—and Comus kept making disguised appearances all over the place . . . that Santa who gave me the note in front of the bank—the old man who kidnapped Lance Morgenstern—the fat man with the mustache who snatched Mrs. Rafferty's purse."

"Yeah," said the Sergeant. "How?"

"These illusions die hard," said Ellery. "Wasn't it Comus who phoned a few minutes ago to rag me about the theft? Wasn't it Comus who said he'd left the stolen dauphin—minus the diamond—on our doormat? Therefore Comus is Bondling.

"I told you Comus never does anything without a good reason," said Ellery. "Why did 'Comus' announce to 'Bondling' that he was *going* to steal the Dauphin's Doll? Bondling told us that—putting the finger on his *alter ego*—because he wanted us to believe he and Comus were separate individuals. He wanted us to watch for *Comus* and take *Bondling* for granted. In tactical execution of this strategy, Bondling provided us with three "Comus'-appearances during the day—obviously, confederates.

"Yes," said Ellery, "I think, Dad, you'll find on backtracking that the great thief you've been trying to catch for five years has been a respectable estate attorney on Park Row all the time, shedding his quiddities and his quillets at night in favor of the soft shoe and the dark lantern. And now he'll have to exchange them all for a number and a grilled door. Well, well, it couldn't have happened at a more appropriate season; there's an old English proverb that says the Devil makes his Christmas pie of lawyers' tongues. Nikki, pass the pastrami."

THE THREE WIDOWS

(1950)

TO THE NORMAL palate the taste of murder is unpleasant. But Ellery is an epicure in these matters and certain of his cases, he deposes, possess a flavor which lingers on the tongue. Among these dangerous delicacies he places high the Case of the Three Widows.

Two of the widows were sisters: Penelope, to whom money was nothing, and Lyra, to whom it was everything, consequently each required large amounts of it. Both having buried thriftless husbands at an early age, they returned to the Murray Hill manse of their father with what everyone suspected was relief, for old Theodore Hood was generously provided with the coin of the republic and he had always been indulgent with his daughters. Shortly after Penelope and Lyra repossessed their maiden beds, however, Theodore Hood took a second wife, a cathedral-like lady of great force of character. Alarmed, the sisters gave battle, which their stepmother grimly joined. Old Theodore, caught in their crossfire, yearned only for peace. Eventually he found it, leaving a household inhabited by widows exclusively.

One evening not long after their father's death Penelope the plump and Lyra the lean were summoned by a servant to the drawing room of the Hood pile. They found waiting for them Mr. Strake, the family lawyer.

Mr. Strake's commonest utterance fell like a sentence from the lips of a judge; but tonight, when he pronounced "Will you be seated, ladies," his tone was so ominous that the crime was obviously a hanging one. The ladies exchanged glances and declined.

161

In a few moments the tall doors squealed into the Victorian walls and Sarah Hood came in feebly on the arm of Dr. Benedict, the family physician.

Mrs. Hood surveyed her stepdaughters with a sort of contempt, her head teetering a little. Then she said, "Dr. Benedict and Mr. Strake will speak their pieces, then I'll speak mine."

"Last week," began Dr. Benedict, "your stepmother came to my office for her semiannual checkup. I gave her the usual thorough examination. Considering her age, I found her in extraordinarily good health. Yet the very next day she came down sick—for the first time, by the way, in eight years. I thought then that she'd picked up an intestinal virus, but Mrs. Hood made a rather different diagnosis. I considered it fantastic. However, she insisted that I make certain tests. I did, and she was right. She had been poisoned."

The plump cheeks of Penelope went slowly pink, and the lean cheeks of Lyra went slowly pale.

"I feel sure," Dr. Benedict went on, addressing a point precisely midway between the sisters, "that you'll understand why I must warn you that from now on I shall examine your stepmother every day."

"Mr. Strake," said old Mrs. Hood, smiling.

"Under your father's will," said Mr. Strake abruptly, also addressing the equidistant point, "each of you receives a small allowance from the income of the estate. The bulk of that income goes to your stepmother for as long as she shall live. But at Mrs. Hood's demise, you inherit the principal of some two million dollars, in equal shares. In other words, you two are the only persons in the world who will benefit by your stepmother's death. As I've informed both Mrs. Hood and Dr. Benedict—if you are not warned by your extremely good fortune in failing in this dastardly murder attempt, I shall devote what remains of my life to seeing that you are punished to the full extent of the law. In fact, it was my advice to call in the police immediately."

"Call them now!" cried Penelope.

Lyra said nothing.

"I could call them now, Penny," said Mrs. Hood with the same faint smile, "but you're both very clever and it might not settle anything. My strongest protection would be to throw the two of you out of this house; unfortunately, your father's will prevents me. Oh, I understand your impatience to be rid of me. You have luxurious tastes which aren't satisfied by my simple way of living. You'd both like to remarry, and with the money you could buy yourselves second husbands." The old lady leaned forward a little. "But I have bad news for you. My mother died at ninety-nine, my father at a hundred and three. Dr. Benedict tells me that I can live another thirty years, and I have every intention of doing so." She struggled to her feet, still smiling. "In fact, I'm taking certain precautions to make sure of it," she said; and she went out.

Exactly one week later Ellery was seated beside Mrs. Hood's great mahogany fourposter, under the anxious eyes of Dr. Benedict and Mr. Strake.

She had been poisoned again. Fortunately, Dr. Benedict had caught it in time.

Ellery bent over the old lady's face, which looked more like plaster than flesh. "These precautions of yours, Mrs. Hood—"

"I tell you," she whispered, "it was impossible."

"Still," said Ellery cheerfully, "it was done. So let's resume. You had your bedroom windows barred and a new lock installed on that door, the single key to which you've kept on your person at all times. You've bought your own food. You've done your own cooking in this room and you've eaten here alone. Clearly, then, the poison could not have been introduced into your food before, during, or after its preparation. Further, you tell me you purchased new dishes, have kept them here, and you and you alone have been handling them. Consequently the poison couldn't have been put on or in the cooking utensils, china, glassware, or cutlery involved in your meals. How then was the poison administered?"

"That's the problem," cried Dr. Benedict.

"A problem, Mr. Queen," muttered Mr. Strake, "that I thought— and Dr. Benedict agreed—was more your sort of thing than the police's."

"Well, my sort of thing is always simple," replied Ellery, "provided you see it. Mrs. Hood, I'm going to ask you a great many questions. Is it all right, Doctor?"

Dr. Benedict felt the old lady's pulse, and he nodded. Ellery began. She replied in whispers, but with great positiveness. She had bought a new toothbrush and fresh tooth paste for her siege. Her teeth were still her own. She had an aversion to medication and took no drugs or palliatives of any kind. She drank nothing but water. She did not smoke, eat sweets, chew gum, use cosmetics. . . .The questions went on and on. Ellery asked every one he could think of, and then he shook up his brain to think of more.

Finally, he thanked Mrs. Hood, patted her hand, and went out with Dr. Benedict and Mr. Strake.

"What's your diagnosis, Mr. Queen?" asked Dr. Benedict.

"Your verdict," said Mr. Strake impatiently.

"Gentlemen," said Ellery, "when I eliminated her drinking water by examining the pipes and faucets in her bathroom and finding they hadn't been tampered with, I'd ruled out the last possibility."

"And yet it's being administered orally," snapped Dr. Benedict. "That's my finding and I've been careful to get medical corroboration."

"If that is a fact, Doctor," said Ellery, "then there is only one remaining explanation."

"What's that?"

"Mrs. Hood is poisoning herself. If I were you I would call in a psychiatrist. Good day!"

Ten days later Ellery was back in Sarah Hood's bedroom. The old lady was dead. She had succumbed to a third poisoning attack.

On being notified, Ellery had promptly said to his father, Inspector Queen, "Suicide."

But it was not suicide. The most painstaking investigation by police experts, utilizing all the resources of criminological science, failed to turn up a trace of the poison, or of a poison container or other possible source, in Mrs. Hood's bedroom or bath. Scoffing, Ellery went over the premises himself. His smile vanished. He found nothing to contradict either the old lady's previous testimony or the findings of the experts. He grilled the servants. He examined with remorseless efficiency Penelope, who kept weeping, and Lyra, who kept snarling. Finally, he left.

It was the kind of problem which Ellery's thinking apparatus, against all the protests of his body, cannot let alone. For forty-six hours he lived in his own head, fasting and sleepless, ceaselessly pacing the treadmill of the Queen apartment floor. In the forty-seventh hour Inspector Queen took him forcibly by the arm and put him to bed.

"I thought so," said the Inspector. "Over a hundred and one. What hurts, son?"

"My whole existence," mumbled Ellery; and he submitted to aspirins, an ice bag, and a rare steak broiled in butter.

In the middle of the steak he shouted like a madman and clawed at the telephone.

"Mr. Strake? Ellery Queen! Meet me at the Hood house immediately!—yes, notify Dr. Benedict!—yes, now I know how Mrs. Hood was poisoned!"

And when they were gathered in the cavern of the Hood drawing room Ellery peered at plump Penelope and lean Lyra and he croaked, "Which one of you is intending to marry Dr. Benedict?"

And then he said, "Oh, yes, it has to be that. Only Penelope and Lyra benefit from their stepmother's murder, yet the only person who could physically have committed the murder is Dr. Benedict. . . . Did you ask how, Doctor?" asked Ellery courteously. "Why, very simply. Mrs. Hood experienced her first poisoning attack the day after her semi-annual medical checkup—by you, Doctor. And thereafter, you announced, *you would examine Mrs. Hood every day.* There is a classic preliminary to every physician's examination of a patient. I submit, Dr. Benedict," said Ellery with a smile, "that you introduced the poison into Mrs. Hood's mouth on the same thermometer with which you took her temperature!"

SNOWBALL IN JULY

(1952)

AT PLAYFUL MOMENTS Diamond Jim Grady liked to refer to himself as a magician, a claim no one disputed—least of all the police. Grady's specialty was jewel robbery at gunpoint, a branch of felonious vaudeville which he had elevated to an art form. His heists were miracles of advance information, timing, teamwork, and deception. And once he got his hands on the loot it vanished with the speed of light, to be seen no more in the shape the manufacturing jeweler had wrought.

Grady's most spectacular trick was keeping himself and his fellow artists out of jail. He would drill his small company without mercy in the wisdom of keeping their mugs covered, their mitts gloved, and their traps shut while on stage. There was rarely a slip in his performances; when one occurred, the slipping assistant disappeared. As Diamond Jim reasonably pointed out, "What witness can identify a slob that ain't here?"

Grady might have gone on forever collecting other people's pretties and driving the law and insurance companies mad, but he pulled one trick too many.

In explanation it is necessary to peep into Diamond Jim's love life. Lizbet had been his big moment for two years and ten months—a slim eyestopper as golden and glittery as any choice piece in his collection. Now in underworld society a romantic attachment of almost three years' duration is equivalent to an epic passion, and Lizbet may be forgiven the folly of having developed delusions of permanence. Unfortunately, that was not all she developed; include an appetite for

166

pizza pies and French ice cream, and along with it her figure. So when one night Grady's bloated eye cased the dainty anatomy of Maybellene, pivot girl of the Club Swahili line, that was all for Lizbet.

One of Grady's staff, a lovelorn lapidary who could grind an ax as well as a diamond, tipped Lizbet the bad news from a phone booth in the Swahili men's room even as Diamond Jim prepared toothily to escort Maybellene home.

Lizbet was revolted at the perfidy of man. She also realized that unless she lammed with great rapidity her life was not worth the crummiest bangle on the junk counter of the nearest Five-and-Dime. She knew far, far too many of Diamond Jim's professional secrets; she even knew where a couple of bodies—of ex-slobs—were buried.

So Lizbet took barely the time to grab an old summer mink and a fistful of unaltered mementoes from Grady's latest personal appearance before she did an impromptu vanishing act of her own.

Immediately Lizbet became the most popular girl in town. Everybody wanted her, especially the police and Grady. The smart money, doping past performances strictly, was on Grady, but this time the smart money took a pratfall. Lizbet was not in town at all. She was in Canada, where—according to every Royal Northwest movie Lizbet had ever seen—the Mounties were large and incorruptible and a girl could think without worrying about stopping a shiv with her back. Having thought, Lizbet slung the summer mink about her plump shoulders, taxied to the nearest police station, and demanded protection and immunity in exchange for a pledge to take the witness stand back home and talk herself, if need be, into lockjaw.

And she insisted on being ushered into a cell while Montreal got in touch with New York.

The long distance negotiations took twenty-four hours. Just long enough for the news to leak out and inundate the front pages of the New York newspapers.

"So now Grady knows where she is," fumed Inspector Queen. He was on special assignment in charge of the case. "He'll go for her sure. She told Piggott and Hesse when they flew up to Montreal that she can even drape a first-degree murder rap around Grady's fat neck."

"Me," said Sergeant Velie gloomily, "I wouldn't give a plugged horse car token for that broad's chances of getting back to New York with a whole hide."

"What is he, a jet pilot?" asked Ellery. "Fly her down."

"She won't fly, has a fear of heights," snapped his father. "It's on the level, Ellery. Lizbet's the only girl friend Grady ever had who turned down a penthouse."

"Train or car, then," said Ellery. "What's the hassle?"

"A train he'd make hash out of," said Sergeant Velie, "and a car he'd hijack some truck to run off the road into a nice thousand-foot hole."

"You're romancing."

"Maestro, you don't know Grady!"

"Then you're tackling this hind end to," said Ellery negligently. "Dad, have Grady and his gang picked up on some charge and locked in a cell. By the time they're sprung this woman can be safe on ice somewhere in Manhattan."

"On ice is where she'll wind up," said Sergeant Velie. "And speaking of ice, who's for a bucket of Thomas Collins?"

When Ellery found that Diamond Jim had anticipated interference and disappeared with his entire company, including Maybellene, a respectful glint came into his eye.

"Let's pull a trick or two of our own. Grady will assume that you'll get Lizbet to New York as quickly as possible. He knows she won't fly and that you wouldn't risk the long trip by car. So he'll figure she'll be brought down by rail. Since the fastest way by rail is through express, it's the crack Montreal train he'll be gunning for. Does he know Piggott and Hesse by sight?"

"Let's say he does," said Inspector Queen, perking up notwithstanding the heat, "and I see what you mean. I'll fly Johnson and Goldberg up there along with a policewoman of Lizbet's build and general appearance. Piggott and Hesse take the policewoman onto the Special, heavily veiled, while Goldie and Johnson hustle Lizbet onto a slow train—"

"You think this Houdini plays with potsies?" demanded Sergeant Velie. "You got to do better than that, my masters."

"Oh, come, Sergeant, he's only flesh and blood," said Ellery soothingly. "Anyway, we're going to do better than that. To befuddle him completely, somewhere along the route we'll have her taken off and complete the trip by automobile. In fact, Dad, we'll take her off ourselves. Feel better, Velie?"

But the Sergeant shook his head. "You don't know Grady."

So Detectives Goldberg and Johnson and an ex-chorus girl named

Policewoman Bruusgaard flew to Montreal, and at the zero hour Detectives Piggott and Hesse ostentatiously spirited Policewoman Bruusgaard—veiled and sweltering in Lizbet's mink—into a drawing room on the Canadian Limited. Thirty minutes after the Limited rolled out of the terminal Detectives Johnson and Goldberg, attired as North Country backwoodsmen and lugging battered suitcases, swaggered behind Lizbet into the smoking car of a sooty, suffocating all-coach local-express entitled laughingly in the timetables The Snowball. Lizbet was in dowdy clothes, her coiffure was now blue-black, and her streaming face—scrubbed clean of heavy makeup—seemed a sucker's bet to fool even Grady, so many wrinkles and crow's-feet showed.

And the game was en route.

For on a sizzling hot morning in July two unmarked squad cars set out from Center Street, Manhattan, for upstate New York. In one rode the Queens and Sergeant Velie, in the other six large detectives.

The Sergeant drove lugubriously. "It won't work," he predicted. "He operates practically by radar. And he can spot and grease an itchy palm from nine miles up. I tell you Grady's got this up his sleeve right now."

"You croak like a witch doctor with bellyache," remarked Inspector Queen, squirming in his damp clothes. "Just remember, Velie, if we don't get to Wapaug with time to spare—"

Wapaug was a whistlestop on the C. & N. Y. Railroad. It consisted of several simmering coal piles, a straggly single street, and a roasted-looking cubby of a station. The two cars drove up to the brown little building and the Inspector and Ellery went inside. No one was in the hotbox of a waiting room but an elderly man wearing sleeve garters and an eyeshade who was poking viciously at the innards of a paralyzed electric fan.

"What's with The Snowball?"

"Number 113? On time, mister."

"And she's due—?"

"10:18."

"Three minutes," said Ellery. "Let's go."

The cars had drawn up close, one to each end of the platform. Two of the six detectives were leaning exhaustedly against an empty handtruck. Otherwise, the baked platform was deserted.

They all squinted north.

169

10:18 came.

10:18 went.

At 10:20 they were still squinting north.

The stationmaster was in the doorway now, also squinting north.

"Hey!" rasped Inspector Queen, swatting a mosquito. "Where was that train on time? In Vermont?"

"At Grove Junction." The stationmaster peered up the tracks, which looked as if they had just come out of a blast furnace. "Where the yards and roundhouse are. It's the all-train stop two stations north."

"Train 113 stops at the next station north, too, doesn't she? Marmion? Did you get a report on her from Marmion?"

"I was just gonna check, mister."

They followed him back into the hotbox and the elderly man put on his slippery headphones and got busy with the telegraph key. "Marmion stationmaster says she pulled in and out on time. Left Marmion 10:12."

"On time at Marmion," said Ellery, "and it's only a six-minute run from Marmion to Wapaug—" He wiped his neck.

"Funny," fretted his father. It was now 10:22. "How could she lose four minutes on a six-minute run? Even on this railroad?"

"Somethin's wrong," said the stationmaster, blowing the sweat off his eyeshade band. He turned suddenly to his key.

The Queens returned to the platform to stare up the local track toward Marmion. After a moment Ellery hurried back into the waiting room.

"Stationmaster, could she have switched to the express track at Marmion and gone right through Wapaug without stopping?" He knew the answer in advance, since they had driven along the railroad for miles in their approach to Wapaug; but his brains were frying.

"Nothin's gone through southbound on these tracks since 7:38 this mornin'."

Ellery hurried out again, fingering his collar. His father was sprinting up the platform toward the squad car. The two detectives had already rejoined their mates in the other car and it was roaring up the highway, heading north.

"Come on!" shouted Inspector Queen. Ellery barely made it before Sergeant Velie sent the car rocketing toward the road. "Somehow Grady got onto the trick—a smear, a leak at headquarters! He's waylaid The Snowball between here and Marmion—wrecked it!"

They kept watching the ties. The automobile road paralleled the railroad at a distance of barely twenty feet, with nothing between but gravel.

And there was no sign of a passenger train, in motion or standing still, wrecked or whole. Or of a freight, or even a handcar. Headed south—or, for that matter, headed north.

They almost zoomed through Marmion before they realized they had covered the entire distance between the two stations. The other car was parked below the weathered eaves of an even smaller shed than the one at Wapaug. As they shot back in reverse, four of the detectives burst out of the little station.

"She left Marmion at 10:12, all right, Inspector!" yelled one. "Stationmaster says we're crazy. We must have missed it!"

The two cars rocked about and raced back toward Wapaug.

Inspector Queen glared at the rails flashing alongside. "Missed it? A whole passenger train? Velie, slow down—!"

"That Grady," moaned Sergeant Velie.

Ellery devoured a knuckle and said nothing. He kept staring at the glittering rails. They winked back, jeering. It was remarkable how straight this stretch of track between Marmion and Wapaug was, how uncluttered by scenery. Not a tree or building beside the right of way. No water anywhere, not so much as a rain puddle. No curves, no grades; no siding, spur line, tunnel, bridge. Not a gully, gorge, or ravine. And no sign of wreckage. . . . The rails stretched, perfect and unburdened, along the hellish floor of the valley. For all the concealment or trickery possible, they might have been a series of parallel lines drawn with a ruler on a sheet of blank paper.

And there was Wapaug's roasted little station again.

And no Snowball.

The Inspector's voice cracked. "She pulls into Grove Junction on time. She gets to Marmion on time. She pulls out of Marmion on time. But she doesn't show up at Wapaug. Then she's got to be between Marmion and Wapaug! What's wrong with that?" He challenged them, hopefully, to find something wrong with it.

Sergeant Velie accepted. "Only one thing," he said in a hollow voice. "She ain't."

That did it. "I suppose Grady's palmed it!" screamed his superior. "That train's between Marmion and Wapaug somewhere, and I'm going to find it or—or buy me a ouija board!"

171

So back they went to Marmion, driving along the railroad at ten miles per hour. And then they turned around and crept Wapaugward again, to shuffle into the waiting room and look piteously at the stationmaster. But that railroad man was sitting in his private oven mopping his chafed forehead and blinking at the shimmering valley through his north window.

And no one said a word for some time.

When the word came, everyone leaped. "Stationmaster!" said Ellery. "Get your Marmion man on that key again. Find out if, after leaving Marmion at 10:12, *The Snowball didn't turn back*."

"Back?" The elderly man brightened. "Sure!" He seized his telegraph key.

"That's it, Ellery!" cried Inspector Queen. "She left Marmion southbound all right, but then she backed up north *past* Marmion again for a repair, and I'll bet she's in the Grove Junction yards or roundhouse right now!"

"Grove Junction says," whispered the stationmaster, "that she ain't in their yards or roundhouse and never was—just went through on time. And Marmion says 113 pulled out southbound and she didn't come back."

And all were silent once more.

But then the Inspector slapped at a dive-bombing squadron of bluebottle flies, hopping on one foot and howling. "But how can a whole train disappear? Snowball! Snowball in July! What did Grady do, melt her down for icewater?"

"And drank her," said Sergeant Velie, licking his lips.

"Wait," said Ellery. "Wait. . . . I know where The Snowball is!" He scuttled toward the door. "And if I'm right we'd better make tracks—or kiss Lizbet goodbye!"

"But *where*?" implored Inspector Queen as the two cars flashed north again, toward Marmion.

"Down Grady's gullet," shouted the Sergeant, wrestling his wheel.

"That's what he wanted us to think," shouted Ellery in reply. "Faster, Sergeant! Train leaves Marmion and never shows up at the next station south, where we're waiting to take Lizbet off. Vanishes without a trace. Between Marmion and Wapaug there's nothing at all to explain what could have happened to her—no bridge to fall from, no water or ravine to fall into, no tunnel to hid in, no anything—just a straight line on flat bare country. Marvelous illusion. Only the same facts that give it the appearance of magic explain it. . . . No, Velie, don't slow down," Ellery yelled as the dreary little Marmion station came into view. "Keep going north—*past* Marmion!"

"North past Marmion?" said his father, bewildered. "But the train came *through* Marmion, Ellery, headed south. . . ."

"The Snowball's nowhere south of Marmion, is it? And from the facts it's a physical impossibility for her to be anywhere south of Marmion. So she *isn't* south of Marmion, Dad. *She never went through Marmion at all.*"

"But the Marmion stationmaster said—"

"What Grady bribed him to say! It was all a trick to keep us running around in circles between Marmion and Wapaug, while Grady and his gang held up the train *between Marmion and Grove Junction*! Isn't that gunfire up ahead? We're still in time!"

And there, four miles north of Marmion, where the valley entered the foothills, cowered The Snowball, frozen to the spot. A huge trailer-truck dumped athwart the local tracks had stopped her, and judging from the gun flashes she was under bombardment of half a dozen bandits hidden in the woods nearby.

Two figures, one lying still and the other crawling toward the woods dragging a leg, told them that the battle was not one-sided. From two of the shattered windows of a railroad car a stream of bullets poured into the woods. What Grady & Co. had not known was that North-woodsman Goldberg and Johnson had carried in their battered suit-cases two submachine guns and a large supply of ammunition.

When the carful of New York detectives broke out their arsenal and cut loose on the run, the Grady gang dropped their weapons and trudged out with their dejected arms up. . . .

Ellery and the Inspector found Lizbet huddled on the floor of the smoking car with assorted recumbent passengers, in a litter of hot cartridge shells, while Detectives Johnson and Goldberg prepared rather shakily to enjoy a couple of stained cigarettes.

"You all right, young woman?" asked the Inspector anxiously. "Anything I can get you?"

Lizbet looked up out of a mess of dyed hair, gunsmoke, sweat, and tears. "You said it, pop," she hissed. "That witness chair!"

MY QUEER DEAN!

(1953)

THE QUEERNESS OF Matthew Arnold Hope, beloved teacher of Ellery's Harvard youth and lately dean of liberal arts in a New York university, is legendary.

The story is told, for instance, of baffled students taking Dr. Hope's Shakespeare course for the first time. "History advises us that Richard II died peacefully at Pontefract, probably of pneumonia," Dr. Hope scolds. "But what does Shakespeare say, Act V, Scene V? That Exton struck him down," and here the famous authority on Elizabethan literature will pause for emphasis, "with a blushing crow!"

Imaginative sophomores have been known to suffer nightmare as a result of this remark. Older heads nod intelligently, of course, knowing that Dr. Hope meant merely to say—in fact, thought he was saying—"a crushing blow."

The good dean's unconscious spoonerisms, like the sayings of Miss Parker and Mr. Goldwyn, are reverently preserved by aficionados, among whom Ellery counts himself a charter member. It is Ellery who has saved for posterity that deathless pronouncement of Dr. Hope's to a freshman class in English composition: "All those who persist in befouling their theme papers with cant and other low expressions not in good usage are warned for the last time: Refine your style or be exiled from this course with the rest of the vanished Bulgarians!"

But perhaps Dean Hope's greatest exploit began recently in the faculty lunchroom. Ellery arrived at the dean's invitation to find him waiting impatiently at one of the big round tables with three members of the English Department.

"Dr. Agnes Lovell, Professor Oswald Gorman, Mr. Morgan Naseby," the dean said rapidly. "Sit down, Ellery. Mr. Queen will have the cute frocktail and the horned beef cash—only safe edibles on the menu today, my boy—well, go fetch, young man! Are you dreaming that you're back in class?" The waiter, a harried-looking freshman, fled. Then Dr. Hope said solemnly, "My friends, prepare for a surprise."

Dr. Lovell, a very large woman in a tight suit, said roguishly: "Wait, Matthew! Let me guess. Romance?"

"And who'd marry—in Macaulay's imperishable phrase—a living concordance?" said Professor Gorman in a voice like an abandoned winch. He was a tall freckled man with strawberry eyebrows and a quarrelsome jaw. "A real surprise, Dr. Hope, would be a departmental salary rise."

"A consummation devoutly et cetera," said Mr. Naseby, immediately blushing. He was a stout young man with an eager manner, evidently a junior in the department.

"May I have your attention?" Dean Hope looked about cautiously. "Suppose I tell you," he said in a trembling voice, "that by tonight I may have it within my power to deliver the death blow—I repeat, the death blow!—to the cockypop that Francis Bacon wrote Shakespeare's plays?"

There were two gasps, a snort, and one inquiring hum.

"Matthew!" squealed Dr. Lovell. "You'd be famous!"

"Immortal, Dean Hope," said Mr. Naseby adoringly.

"Deluded," said Professor Gorman, the snorter. "The Baconian benightedness, like the Marlowe mania, has no known specific."

"Ah, but even a fanatic," cried the dean, "would have to yield before the nature of this evidence."

"Sounds exciting, Doc," murmured Ellery. "What is it?"

"A man called at my office this morning, Ellery. He produced credentials identifying him as a London rare book dealer, Alfred Mimms. He has in his possession, he said, a copy of the 1613 edition of *The Essaies of Sir Francis Bacon Knight the kings solliciter generall*, an item ordinarily bringing four or five hundred dollars. He claims that this copy, however, is unique, *being inscribed on the title page in Bacon's own hand to Will Shakespeare.*"

Amid the cries, Ellery asked: "Inscribed how?"

"In an encomium," quavered Dean Hope, "an encomium to Shakes-

175

peare expressing Bacon's admiration and praise for—and I quote—'*the most excellent plaies of your sweet wit and hand*'!"

"Take that!" whispered Mr. Naseby to an invisible Baconian.

"That does it," breathed Dr. Lovell.

"That would do it," said Professor Gorman, "if."

"Did you actually see the book, Doc?" asked Ellery.

"He showed me a photostat of the title page. He'll have the original for my inspection tonight, in my office."

"And Mimms's asking price is—?"

"Ten thousand dollars."

"Proof positive that it's a forgery," said Professor Gorman rustily. "It's far too little."

"Oswald," hissed Dr. Lovell, "you creak, do you know that?"

"No, Gorman is right," said Dr. Hope. "An absurd price if the inscription is genuine, as I pointed out to Mimms. However, he had an explanation. He is acting, he said, at the instructions of the book's owner, a tax-poor British nobleman whose identity he will reveal tonight if I purchase the book. The owner, who has just found it in a castle room boarded up and forgotten for two centuries, prefers an American buyer in a confidential sale—for tax reasons, Mimms hinted. But, as a cultivated man, the owner wishes a scholar to have it rather than some ignorant Croesus. Hence the relatively low price."

"Lovely," glowed Mr. Naseby. "And so typically British."

"Isn't it," said Professor Gorman. "Terms cash, no doubt? On the line? Tonight?"

"Well, yes." The old dean took a bulging envelope from his breast pocket and eyed it ruefully. Then, with a sigh, he tucked it back. "Very nearly my life's savings. . . . but I'm not altogether senile," Dr. Hope grinned. "I'm asking you to be present, Ellery—with Inspector Queen. I shall be working at my desk on administrative things into the evening. Mimms is due at eight o'clock."

"We'll be here at seven-thirty," promised Ellery. "By the way, Doc, that's a lot of money to be carrying around in yor pocket. Have you confided this business to anyone else?"

"No, no."

"Don't. And may I suggest that you wait behind a locked door? Don't admit Mimms—or anyone else you don't trust—until we get here. I'm afraid, Doc, I share the professor's skepticism."

"Oh, so do I," murmured the dean. "The odds on this being a swindle are, I should think, several thousand to one. But one can't help saying to oneself . . . suppose it's not?"

It was nearly half-past seven when the Queens entered the Arts Building. Some windows on the upper floors were lit up where a few evening classes were in session, and the dean's office was bright. Otherwise the building was dark.

The first thing Ellery saw as they stepped out of the self-service elevator onto the dark third floor was the door of Dean Hope's anteroom . . . wide open.

They found the old scholar crumpled on the floor just inside the doorway. His white hairs dripped red.

"Crook came early," howled Inspector Queen. "Look at the dean's wristwatch, Ellery—smashed in his fall at 7:15."

"I warned him not to unlock his door," wailed Ellery. Then he bellowed. "He's breathing! Call an ambulance!"

He had carried the dean's frail body to a couch in the inner office and was gently wetting the blue lips from a paper cup when the Inspector turned from the telephone.

The eyes fluttered open. "Ellery. . . ."

"Doc, what happened?"

"Book . . . taken. . . ." The voice trailed off in a mutter.

"Book taken?" repeated the Inspector incredulously. "That means Mimms not only came early, but Dr. Hope found the book was genuine! Is the money on him, son?"

Ellery searched the dean's pockets, the office, the anteroom. "It's gone."

"Then he did buy it. Then somebody came along, cracked him on the skull, and lifted the book."

"Doc!" Ellery bent over the old man again. "Doc, who struck you? Did you see?"

"Yes. . . . Gorman. . . ." Then the battered head rolled to one side and Dr. Hope lost conscousness.

"Gorman? Who's Gorman, Ellery?"

"Professor Oswald Gorman," Ellery said through his teeth, "one of the English faculty at the lunch today. *Get him.*"

When Inspector Queen returned to the dean's office guiding the agitated elbow of Professor Gorman, he found Ellery waiting behind the dean's flower vase as if it were a bough from Birnam Wood.

The couch was empty.

"What did the ambulance doctor say, Ellery?"

"Concussion. How bad they don't know yet." Ellery rose, fixing Professor Gorman with a Macduffian glance. "And where did you find this pedagogical louse, Dad?"

"Upstairs on the seventh floor, teaching a Bible class."

"The title of my course, Inspector Queen," said the Professor furiously, "is *The Influence of the Bible on English Literature*."

"Trying to establish an alibi, eh?"

"Well, son," said his father in a troubled voice, "the professor's more than just tried. He's done it."

"Established an alibi?" Ellery cried.

"It's a two-hour seminar, from six to eight. He's alibied for every second from 6 P.M. on by the dozen people taking the course—including a minister, a priest, and a rabbi. What's more," mused the Inspector, "even assuming the 7:15 on the dean's broken watch was a plant, Professor Gorman can account for every minute of his day since your lunch broke up. Ellery, something is rotten in New York County."

"I beg your pardon," said a British voice from the anteroom. "I was to meet Dr. Hope here at eight o'clock."

Ellery whirled. Then he swooped down upon the owner of the voice, a pale skinny man in a bowler hat carrying a package under one arm.

"Don't tell me you're Alfred Mimms and you're just bringing the Bacon!"

"Yes, but I'll—I'll come back," stammered the visitor, trying to hold on to his package. But it was Ellery who won the tug of war, and as he tore the wrappings away the pale man turned to run.

And there was Inspector Queen in the doorway with his pistol showing. "Alfred Mimms, is it?" said the Inspector genially. "Last time, if memory serves, it was Lord Chalmerston. Remember, Dink, when you were sent up for selling a phony First Folio to that Oyster Bay millionaire? Ellery, this is Dink Chalmers of Flatbush, one of the cleverest confidence men in the rare book game." Then the Inspector's geniality faded. "But, son, this leaves us in more of a mess than before."

"No, dad," said Ellery. "This clears the mess up."

From Inspector Queen's expression, it did nothng of the kind.

"Because what did Doc Hope reply when I asked him what happened?" Ellery said. "He replied, 'Book taken.' Well, obviously, the book wasn't taken. The book was never here. Therefore he didn't mean to say 'book taken.' Professor, you're a communicant of the Matthew Arnold Hope Cult of Spoonerisms: What must the dean have meant to say?"

" 'Took . . . Bacon'!" said Professor Gorman.

"Which makes no sense, either, unless we recall, Dad, that his voice trailed off. As if he meant to add a word, but failed. Which word? The word 'money'—'took Bacon *money*.' Because while the Bacon book wasn't here to be taken, the ten thousand dollars Doc Hope was toting around all day to pay for it was.

"And who took the Bacon money? The one who knocked on the dean's door just after seven o'clock and asked to be let in. The one who, when Dr. Hope unlocked the door—indicating the knocker was someone he knew and trusted—promptly clobbered the old man and made off with his life's savings."

"But when you asked who hit him," protested the Inspector, "he answered 'Gorman'."

"Which he couldn't have meant, either, since the professor has an alibi of granite. Therefore—"

"Another spoonerism!" exclaimed Professor Gorman.

"I'm afraid so. And since the only spoonerism possible from the name 'Gorman' is 'Morgan,' hunt up Mr. Morgan Naseby of the underpaid English department, Dad, and you'll have Doc's assailant and his ten grand back, too."

Later, at Bellevue Hospital, an indestructible Elizabethan scholar squeezed the younger Queen's hand feebly. Conversation was forbidden, but the good pedagogue and spoonerist extraordinary did manage to whisper, "My queer Dean. . . ."

GI STORY

(1954)

ELLERY SWUNG OFF the Atlantic State Express in his favorite small town disguised by earlaps, muffler, and skis, resolved that this time nothing should thwart his winter holiday. But he had hardly dumped his gear in Bill York's Bald Mountain lodge when he was called to the phone. Sure enough, it was Wrightsville's chief of police, with a crime.

"I haven't even taken my hat off," Ellery complained. "What do your criminals do, Dakin, watch the Arrivals column in the *Record*?"

"This one's real unorthodox," said Chief Dakin, in the tone of one emotionally involved. "Can I send a car right up?"

The lean old Yank was waiting fretfully on State Street at the side entrance to the County Court House. He pulled himself into the police car with one hand and groped for Ellery with the other.

"I've been up most of the night," croaked Dakin. "Remember Clint Fosdick?"

"Sure. Household Fixtures. Slocum near Upper Whistling. What's old Clint done?"

"Got himself murdered last night," mumbled Dakin, "and I can tell you who did it, only I'm not goin' to. I want *you* to tell *me*."

Ellery stared at the author of this extraordinary statement as the car slid across the icy Square and began to creep up Dade Street. "Why? Aren't you sure?"

"I wish I was as sure of a pew in Heaven," cried Chief Dakin. "I'm not only sure who murdered Clint, I know *how* he murdered Clint, and what's more I've got him dead to rights with the evidence to convict."

"Then what's the problem, Dakin?"

"GI," said Wrightsville's chief of police.

"G-what?"

"GI. Those two letters mean anything to you, Mr. Queen?"

"Well, of course—"

"The only trouble is, it don't fit with my evidence," said Dakin. "And if I can't make it fit with my evidence, a smart lawyer might befuddle a jury with it just enough to put a reasonable doubt in their little minds. So you listen to the facts without prejudice, Mr. Queen," the chief said grimly, "and you make that GI fit. Remember the Smith boys—the brothers we've always called the Presidents?"

"Smith? Presidents?" Ellery looked bewildered.

"Their dad was Jeff Smith—Thomas Jefferson Smith, taught American History at Wrightsville High. Jeff married Martha Higgins and they had three sons. Wash, the eldest, was in the war and he's a lawyer now, when he works at it. Linc was in the service, too, then he went to medical school—he's just finishin' his internship at Wrightsville General. And Woodie, the youngest, was drafted into the Army three months back.

"Well, Clint Fosdick was sweet on Martha Higgins since way before she married Jeff Smith. But Clint was eighteen years Martha's senior, he'd never got past fourth grade in school—never even learned to write Spencerian, just printed his letters—and with Jeff, a college man, in the picture Clint didn't stand a chance.

"But in '37 Jeff Smith drowned in Quetonokis Lake while he was counselin' at a boys' summer camp, Martha found herself a penniless widow with three hungry boys to rear, and there was old faithful Clint, still waitin' . . . Well, Martha married him," growled Dakin, "and Clint bought that big house on Hill Drive—the one with those hundred-and-twenty-year-old shade trees—for them all to live in like he was standin' treat for the ice cream at a Sunday School picnic."

And the chief's Adam's apple jiggled as the police car felt for the top of the ridge and began to skid along Hill Drive between the tombs of Wrightsville's fine old mansions.

"Clint did everything for those boys. He sent 'em to college in style. Gave 'em their own cars, pockets full of allowance money . . . When Martha died in the flu epidemic durin' the war, Clint became father *and* mother to them. He couldn't do enough.

181

"And you'd have said they reciprocated. They called him Dad. They always remembered his birthday and Father's Day and Christmas. Brought their problems to him—real pal stuff. Young Woodie, the one just went in the Army, ran wild as Ivor Crosby's Ayrshire bull for a while, but Clint kept sayin' he'd spoiled the boy; and it's a fact they were mighty close. Linc—the doctor—he's always been kind of studious and intense; Clint said no man had a finer son. As for Wash, the eldest, he was the easygoin' sort—too easygoin' for this world, Clint used to say; he had to bail Wash out of trouble every other Saturday night, a poker debt or a Low Village girl or somethin', or get him down to his law office on time; but Clint claimed there wasn't a mean bone in Wash's body.

"'Well, he was wrong about one of them," said the old police chief, glaring at Ellery, "because one of 'em's poisoned him, and I'll see the murderin' chuck sizzle like pork sausage in a dirty frying' pan—if you'll tell me what GI means, Mr. Queen!"

"Glad to," said Ellery patiently, "If you'll only explain—"

But they were drawing up before the snow-shrouded Fosdick lawns, and Dakin fell silent. They shook the snow from their overshoes in the stained-glass vestibile, and the police chief led the way through the gloom of the broad entrance hall past one of his young officers to Clint Fosdick's library.

"This is where Clint's housekeeper, Lettie Dowling, found him last night when she heard a chair crash and ran in."

It was a wonderful old high-ceilinged, oak-paneled, darkish room, but Ellery found its present musty silence dispiriting. He saw at once where the body must have been lying—the leather-backed swivel chair behind the desk had fallen over on its side, and the Oriental rug beneath was badly wrinkled, as if it had been clawed in agony.

In a litter of papers on the dash lay an overturned cocktail glass. On a tray nearby stood a pitcher half full of an almost colorless liquid. Ellery stooped over the pitcher, sniffing.

"Yep, he got it in the cocktail," nodded Chief Dakin. "Clint used to be a teetotaler, like me, but when Matha died he developed a hankerin' for martinis. He'd sit here in his library nights when he'd get to feelin' lonely for her, gulpin' 'em down."

"Who mixed this?" asked Ellery sharply.

"That won't tell you anythin'. Clint did it himself. I'll cut some corners for you," said Dakin in a deadly voice. "The housekeeper, old Lettie, has her room just off the kitchen. Yesterday mornin', very early—quarter past six—Lettie, who's got a cold and 'd had a bad night, got out of bed for some aspirin. She heard clinky sounds from the pantry, where the liquor's kept, and she opened her door a crack. There was an almost full bottle of gin that Wash had brought home for Clint Wednesday night, and through the open kitchen door Lettie saw one of the Smith brothers monkeyin' with it. He had a little kind of medicine bottle, she says, in his hand. She saw his face plain.

"Then she heard Clint's voice. Clint was comin' down to the kitchen for his mornin' coffee—earlier than usual, but he knew Lettie was sick. She heard Clint ask the boy what he was doin' and the boy mumbled somethin' and went back upstairs. But Lettie'd seen him put the gin bottle back quick when he'd heard Clint comin' and jam the medicine bottle—empty, she says—in the pocket of his bathrobe. And, Mr. Queen, I've got that 'medicine' bottle. Dug it out of the garbage pit in the back yard late last night where it wouldn't have been if the garbage truck had come yesterday afternoon the way it was scheduled to, only the heavy snow and icy roads held 'em up. That bottle contained poison—if it was full, the way Lettie says it was, there was enough to wipe out half of High Village. And it's the same poison, the Connhaven lab says, that's in the bottle of gin. Besides, *his prints are on the poison bottle*. I've got the devil cold."

"Except, apparently," said Ellery, "for GI. Which is—?"

Chief Dakin carefully removed an uncreased sheet of paper from his overcoat pocket. "Clint was makin' out his monthly store bills when he swallowed that cocktail. He must have known right off he was a goner; it's a quick-actin' poison. And the minute he realized he was poisoned he must have known who'd done it. He probably saw the same thing yesterday mornin' that Lettie saw when he was kitchen-bound for his coffee. It must have puzzled him at the time, but what he'd seen told him the answer in a flash when he felt what he'd swallowed. So before he died Clint got hold of his ballpoint pen and wrote on this letterhead in that schoolboy printin' style of his. Then he fell over with the cha ir and died on the floor, like a poisoned dog."

"GI?" Ellery reached.

Chief Dakin handed Ellery the paper.

It was an ordinary business billhead. Below the *Clint Fosdick, House-*

hold Fixtures, High Village, Terms: 30 Days inscription appeared in shaky handprinting the two letters:

$$GI$$

"GI," Ellery repeated. "And they've *all* been in the Army, you say?"

"That's right."

"And they were *all* home yesterday morning?"

"Linc's had a few days off from the hospital. Young Woodie's on leave from Camp Hale. Wash lives here all the time."

Ellery was silent, staring at Clint Fosdick's dying message. Then he said, "Does the guilty one know he's tagged for frying?"

"No. Lettie's told noboby but me what she saw, and I haven't let on because of this piece of paper. I've just made out like all three brothers are under suspicion."

"Well," said Ellery. "Could we have the—what do you call them, Dakin?—the Presidents in for a chat?"

The three tall pale young men brought in by their guards were badly in need of sleep and a shave. Their brotherhood was plain from their dark coloring, deep brown eyes, and the way they huddled.

One, a baby-faced variant of the other two in a rumpled U.S Army' uniform, would be Private Woodie Smith. Private Smith's brown eyes masked fear and confusion; his boyish lips quiviered.

The second had the keen red-rimmed look of hospitals, and hands so scrubbed they looked bleached—obviously the intern, Dr. Linc Smith. He was gaunt and sharpened down and very quiet. He had been, Ellery would have sworn, crying.

So the third was the lawyer brother Wash—Wash the easygoing, with a heavying gray face and a softened body. Wash Smith stood there weakly smiling, like a professional comedian caught in a tragedy and trying desperately to think of a joke.

"GI," murmured Ellery. "That's what your stepfather wrote down, Private Smith, and what does it suggest to you?"

"What am I supposed to do," whispered the boy in uniform, "confess because he wrote down GI? I wouldn't kill Dad—why would I kill Dad?"

"Why would Private Smith kill Dad, Dakin?" asked Ellery.

Dakin said coarsely, "Because he might not want to wait for Clint to die natural so he could collect his one-third of Clint's estate that's willed to the three Smith boys."

"Let me alone!" shrieked the boy.

"Woodie," said his brother Linc gently.

"GI," said Ellery. "Comes into your field in a way, Dr. Smith, doesn't it? GI—gastrointestinal?"

The young intern's fatigued eyes widened. "Are you serious? Of course. You can hardly study internal medicine without covering gastroenterology. I even treated Dad Clint for gastrointestinal flu last spring, at his insistence, although if the Medical Board found out . . . And naturally I have access to any amount of poison. The only thing is, I didn't poison him."

"But the GI, Dr. Smith?" Ellery insisted.

The intern shrugged. "If Dad had thought I'd poisoned him, he'd have written my name. That would make sense. GI doesn't. Not to me, anyway."

"Or to me," cried Wash Smith, as if he could not wait.

So Ellery glanced at the lawyer brother. "Gin begins with the letters GI. And it was the bottle of gin that was poisoned, Mr. Smith—a bottle I understand *you* had brought home for Mr. Fosdick."

"Well, sure, he asked me to," said the eldest brother in a sort of agony. "But what kind of way is that to identify somebody? Linc's right. Whoever Clint though had poisoned him, wouldn't he have written the name?"

Ellery smiled ruefully; he had been chewing on that one for some time. Chief Dakin's face told nothing.

And suddenly Ellery stopped smiling, as if he had recognized the taste in his mouth. "Presidents," he said, "Presidents! Your blood-father, I'm told, gentlemen, was named after President Thomas Jefferson. And he named his three sons after Presidents, too?"

"Why yes," said Wash Smith blankly. "After the three Presidents he always maintained were the greatest. I was named after Washington."

"After Lincoln," said Dr. Linc Smith.

"After Woodrow Wilson," quavered Private Woodie Smith.

And all three said in one voice, "Why?"

But all Ellery replied was, "Thank you. Would you mind stepping out of the room?" It was only when their guards had herded the three Smiths out that Ellery said to Dakin, "Now I can tell you whom old Clint was accusing of murder."

"I'm listening," said Chief Dakin.

Ellery was looking at the fallen chair as if the old man who had toppled it were still with them, gripping a pen and trying to push it along a billhead.

"Because Dr. Smith is right," Ellery said. "Fancy verbal acrobatics are the pleasant preoccupations of detective fiction. In real life they don't happen. A man who will perform the miracle of forcing his dying brain and muscles to commit a message to paper is not trying to be subtle or clever. If he knows who did the job on him his efforts can have only one purpose: to transmit that information as directly as he can. Clint Fosdick, in writing those two letters, GI, was trying to do just one thing: *Name his killer.*"

But Dakin's expression did not change. "GI isn't even a part of any of their names, Mr. Queen. Don't you think I thought of that?"

"Well, Clint did have a problem, Dakin. Suppose the poisoner had been Wash Smith. Clint must have realized that he might start to write down the name Wash, or Washington, *but never get beyond the first letter*—he knew he was going fast. But if all he could manage to write down were the W of Washington, that W would apply equally to young Woodie, named after President Wilson. So, to avoid being misunderstood, Clint simply began to print his poisoner's *first* name."

"First name?" The police chief blinked.

"Thomas Jefferson Smith named his three sons after Presidents. So the boy's full names, like Jeff Smith's own, must begin with the first names of the Presidents they were named for. In fact, Private Smith is actually called Woodie, obviously for Woodrow Wilson Smith. Dr. Linc Smith's full name, then, must be Abraham Lincoln Smith. A for Abraham (or L for Lincoln), W for Woodrow (or for Wilson)—neither fits the GI.

"But how about Wash-for-Washington Smith," said Ellery, "always having to be bailed out of trouble, a lawyer 'when he works at it'— probably over his ears in debt and desperately needing his third of Clint's fortune now? There's your chuck in the woodpile, Dakin—the brother Lettie Dowling saw dosing the gin bottle with poison in the pantry yesterday morning. It was George Washington Smith Lettie saw, wasn't it? It's his fingerprints on the poison bottle?"

"Yes," said Wrightsville's chief of police slowly. "Wash is my man, all right. But Mr.Queen, Clint wrote GI—and Wash's first name, George, starts with GE."

"Tricky," said Ellery, squeezing Dakin's arm. "Poor old Clint got the G down all right, Dakin, but he died just as he completed the downstroke of the E."

MIRACLES DO HAPPEN

(1957)

THE MOMENT HENRY pecked her cheek that night, Claire knew something was wrong. But all she said was a wifely, "How did it go at the office today, dear?"

"All right," Henry Witter said, and Claire knew it was not the office. "What kind of day did Jody have?"

"About the same, dear."

Henry put his coat, hat, and rubbers in the hall closet while the other three children hunted through his pockets for the candy bars he always brought home on paydays.

"It's the teentsy size again," little Sal lisped indignantly.

"I wanna big one!" five-year-old Pete wailed.

Eddie, who was ten and knew the financial facts of life, merely scuttled off with his share of the loot.

"Aren't you two ashamed?" Claire said to Sal and Pete.

But Henry said in a queer voice, "Why should they be? It's true," and he went into the back bedroom to see Jody, who had been lying there for the last three of her eight years.

After dinner, which was beans baked around an irreducible minimum of Mr. Scholte's cheapest shortribs, Claire put Sal and Pete to bed, parked Eddie at the TV set, fixed Jody for the night, and hurried back to the kitchen. She helped Henry finish the dishes, and then the Witters sat down at the kitchen table for their weekly session—Claire with her budget notes, Henry with paper and pencil and his pay check between them.

Claire read off the items in a loud and casual voice, and Henry wrote them down in his bookkeeper's copperplate. The prorated expenses—rent, gas, electricity, telephone, TV installment, life insurance, health plan, personal loans. The running expenses—food, laundry, Henry's allowance. The "extras"—new shoes for Pete, school notebook for Eddie, repairs for the vacuum cleaner. And then—in that dread separate column headed "Jody"—medicines, therapist, installment on surgeon's fee for last operation . . .

Henry added the two columns in silence.

"Expenses, $89.61. Take-home pay, $82.25. Debit balance $7.36." And Henry's tic began to act up.

Claire started to say something, but she swallowed it. It was the Jody column again. Without the Jody column they would be in the black, have a small savings account, and the children could get the clothes they desparately needed . . . Claire shut *those* thoughts off.

Henry cleared his throat. "Claire," he began.

"No," Claire cried. "*No*, Henry! Maybe you've given up hope on Jody, but I haven't. I'm *not* going to send a child of mine to a state institution, no matter what. She needs her family—the love and help we can give her—and maybe some day . . . Hen, we'll have the phone taken out, or send the TV back. You're due for another raise in a few months. We can hold out."

"Who said anything about sending Jody away?" Henry's voice was very queer indeed, and Claire felt a chill. "It's not that, Claire."

"Then what is it? I knew there was something wrong the minute you came home."

"It's Tully. He phoned me at the office this afternoon."

"Tully." Claire sat still. Last year, when Jody had needed her second operation and they had exhausted the annual health plan benefits, Henry had been forced to go to a loan shark for the money. "What's he want?"

"I don't know." Henry reached for his cigarettes. But then he remembered that he had smoked his quota for the day, and he put the pack back in his pocket. "He just said for me to be at his office tomorrow night—at seven o' clock."

"But you paid him last month's interest on the loan, Or—did you, Henry?"

"Of course I did!"

"Then why—?"

"I don't know, I tell you!"

Dear God, Claire thought, nothing more *now*, please. She got up to go over to Henry and put her cracked and reddened hands on his thin shoulders.

"Darling . . . don't worry."

Henry said "Who's worrying?" But he wished his tic would stop.

"Sit down, Witter." Tully indicated the only other chair in the dingy office. He had Henry's folder on his desk and was leafing through it.

Henry sat down. The room held nothing but an old desk and swivel chair, a filing cabinet, a big metal wastebasket, a costumer, and the "client's chair"—yet it always managed to seem crowded. Everything looked cheap, used hard, rubbed off, like Tully himself. The loan shark was a paper-thin man with eyes like rusty razor blades.

"Nice clean file," Tully said, tossing it aside.

"I try to meet my payments on time." Henry though of all the empty-stomached lunch hours, the cigarette rations, Claire's incredible economies, the children's patched clothes, and he felt a gust of anger. "Just what is it you want, Mr. Tully?"

"The principal," Tully said indifferently.

"The . . . "Henry found himself half standing.

The moneylender leaned back with a swivelly creak that crawled up Henry's spine. "I've run into a little recession, you might call it. You know? Overextended. So I'm calling my loans in. Sorry."

"But when I took the loan, Mr. Tully, you assured me—"

"Now don't give me that." Tully flicked some papers from the folder, his murderous eyes suddenly intent. "There's a demand clause in these notes, friend. Want to read it over?"

Henry did not try to focus. He knew what the fine print said. But last year he would have signed anything; he had borrowed the limit from legitimate loan companies and Tully had been his last resort.

Tully lit a big cigar. "You've got forty-eight hours to hand me a certified check for $490."

Henry put his finger on the tic. "I haven't got it, Mr. Tully."

"Borrow it."

"I can't. I can't get any more loans. I have a crippled child—the operations, a therapist who comes in every day—"

The moneylender picked up a letter opener with a sharp point and began to clean his fingernails. "Look, Witter, you got your troubles and I got mine. Be here Thursday night nine o'clock with your check, or I take action."

Henry stumbled out.

Ellery was watching "The Late Show" on TV Thursday night when his doorbell rang. He opened the door and a woman with a worn cloth coat thrown over her housedress fell into his arms. Her eyes were wild.

"Mr. Queen? I'm Claire Witter, Mrs. Henry Witter. I live in the neighborhood—left the children with a neighbor—ran all the way. They say you help people in trouble—"

"Get your breath, Mrs. Witter," Ellery said, supporting her. "Just what kind of trouble are you in?"

"My husband's just been picked up by the police. I understand an Inspector Queen is in charge. He's your father, I'm told. But Henry didn't do it, Mr. Queen—"

"What didn't Henry do?"

"Kill that moneylender! They've taken Henry to the office where Tully's body was found. I don't know what to do." And Claire Witter sobbed like a little girl.

"Now, now," Ellery said. "I'll get my hat."

The Inspector had invited Ellery to trail along when the homicide call came in about 10:30, and Ellery had pleaded fatigue; so the old man was suprised when his son showed up not two hours later.

"I'm representing Mrs. Witter," Ellery told him. "What's the charge against her husband?"

"Suspicion of murder."

"As pat as all that, dad?" Ellery glanced around the crowded office. He had left Claire Witter in the hall in the care of a patrolman. "Is that my client?"

A white-faced man with clerical shoulders was leaning against the wall, his eyes shut, and with Sergeant Velie's beef between him and the possibly tempting open window. Nearby huddled a frowsy old lady, a dumpy woman in a smart suit, and an Italian-looking man with a big gray mustache.

Inspector Queen nodded. "The one next to Velie. And don't tell me Witter doesn't look the type."

"He doesn't."

"Just goes to show. It's Witter, all right."

The basket crew were crating the remains of Mr. Tully. Ellery glimpsed the back of a tan jacket splattered with blood.

"I don't see the weapon. Knife?"

"Tully's letter opener. We couldn't seem to raise a print, so we sent it down to the lab."

Ellery looked around at the bare room, the bare floor. "Those empty desk and file drawers were found open, the way they are now?"

"Nothing's been changed or removed except the letter opener. By the way, the heat was on Tully for a usury charge and he must have got wind of it. He was getting set to skip. Anyway, here's the rundown. Prouty says Tully was knifed tonight between 8:30 and 9:30—"

The inspector paused; Mr. Tully was leaving. Ellery hoped Claire Witter would be crying on the patrolman's shoulder when the basket passed her in the hall. There was blood on it.

"Three people entered this office during that hour," the Inspector resumed. "That dumpy woman next to the man with the mustache—her name is Mrs. Lester. Mr. Mustache came next—he's a barber named Dominini. Finally, Witter."

"Who's the old lady beside Mrs. Lester?"

"The cleaning woman of the building. She found the body." The Inspector raised his voice. "Mrs. Bogan?"

The old woman shuffled forward on her shapeless shoes. She still had her work-apron on and a dust cloth bound around her lifeless white hair.

"Tell your story again, Mrs. Bogan."

"Couple minutes after ten I comes in here to clean." She had badly fitted false teeth, and her words came bubbling and hissing out like water from a rusty faucet. "What do I see but Mr. Tully laying with his face on the desk and a knife sticking outen his back. There was all blood . . ." Her bleary eyes rolled. But there was nothing on the desk now.

"Did you touch anything, Mrs. Bogan?" Ellery asked.

"Me? I run out yelling me head off. Found a cop in the street and that's all I know, Mister. I'll be seeing that knife sticking outen his back in me dreams."

"You didn't hear anything—a fight, an argument—between half-past eight and half-past nine?"

"I wasn't on this floor then. I was cleaning two floors down."

"Mrs. Lester," Inspector Queen called out.

The dumpy woman in the smart suit blanched under her heavy makeup. She was well into her forties, her hair hennaed to a screaming red, her figure fighting a corset. She kept biting her lips, but Ellery saw under her nervousness the expression of chronic restlessness so often worn by women with too little to do.

"You were one of Tully's victims, too?" he asked her.

"Don't tell my husband," Mrs. Lester said in a rapid-fire falsetto. "He'd kick me out, no kidding. I had to get a loan on the q.t., see, because of—well, a bunch of us girls have a little afternoon poker club. We started out sociable, but I don't know, the limit kept getting higher . . . The thing is, I went into the hole for a lot of money, mostly to that Mrs. Carson. If my husband Phil knew—he's a nut against gambling . . . Anyway, she says if I don't pay up she'll go to Phil. So I took a $600 loan from this shark Tully."

"And Tully called the loan in, Mrs. Lester?"

The woman's gloved hands began to writhe. "He said I had to pay off the whole thing by half-past eight tonight. Meantime I'd lost more—I swear to God those harpies play with marked cards! So I came here at half-past eight and I hand Tully two hundred dollars—all I could scrape up between what I could sneak off my household money and a ring I hocked that I told Phil I lost. But Tully says nothing doing. So I start begging him to give me more time, and all he does, the rat, is sit here emptying desk drawers and throwing away papers and ignoring me like I was dirt!"

"Why was he doing that, Mrs. Lester?"

"How should I know? He takes my money and says either I have the other four hundred for him by tomorrow morning or he goes to my husband. I left him still tearing up papers."

"Alive, of course," Ellery smiled.

"Are you kidding? Say, you don't think—" Her bloated eyes began to look terrified.

"Mr. Dominini," Inspector Queen cut in.

The barber bounded forward in bitter excitement. It took a great many haircuts and shaves to keep his ten children in *pasta* and shoe leather, he exclaimed. He had a small neighborhood shop that could accommodate only so many. The neighborhood had run down, lots of poor people had moved in, Mr. Dominini said, and even with the higher prices barbers had to charge these days things got worse and worse. Finally, he had faced the possible loss of his shop.

"I go to bank, bank say Dominini no good risk no more," the barber shouted, brandishing his clean hairy hands. "What can I do? I go to Tully, the blood suck'!"

For a year he had managed to meet Tully's usurious interest charges. Then, on Tuesday, the loan shark had phoned him and demanded payment in full by Thursday night. He named a quarter to nine as the deadline.

"Where Dominini get fifteen hundred dollar?" the mustachioed barber cried. "I bring him five hundred sixty-five, it's a best I can do. He say, Dominini, that's a no good. I say okay, Mr. Tully, you run barber shop, I work for you. He call me bad name, take my money, say get out, I sue you. Couple hour later, the policeman he pick me up. For what? My wife she cry, *bambini* run under bed . . . I no kill Tully!"

"Then he was alive when you left this office tonight, Mr. Dominini?" Ellery said. "That's your story?"

"It's a true!"

"Clearing Mrs. Lester," Inspector Queen murmured.

Ellery frowned. "What was Tully doing, if anything," he asked the barber, "while you were here?"

"Like a that lady say. He take a things out of file cabinet. Tear up paper, folder."

"Bringing us," the Inspector said, "to Henry Witter."

Sergeant Velie had to assist Henry forward. The bookkeeper sank into the chair, his tic working overtime. Suddenly his nostrils expanded. He looked up. Ellery was lighting a cigarette.

"Might I have one?" Henry asked. "I've run out."

"Sure. No, that's all right. Keep the pack."

"Oh, no—"

"I have another, Mr. Witter."

"Thanks. Thanks a million." Henry inhaled hungrily. "I should have cut them out long ago." He puffed and puffed.

"Mr. Witter, you found Tully alive at nine?"

"Oh, yes," Henry said.

"Alive and alone?"

Henry nodded.

"Clearing Dominini," the Inspector murmured. "Neat?"

"Even gaudy," Ellery murmured back. "Tell me just what happened, Mr. Witter, after you got here."

Henry lit a fresh cigarette from the butt of the old one, looked around, hesitated, then tossed the smoldering butt into the wastebasket.

"I told Tully I hadn't been able to raise the money. I said, you can do what you want, Mr. Tully, sue me, have me arrested, beaten up, killed, it won't do you any good, you can't get blood from a stone. He kept sitting there behind the desk tearing up papers and records as if he didn't hear me. But he was paying attention, all right." Henry gulped in a lungful of smoke. "Because as soon as I got through he started to chew me out. What he called me—"

Henry choked over the smoke. After a moment Ellery said "Yes, Mr. Witter?"

"I've never raised my hand in anger to anybody in my life. But Tully said some things to me no man could take. Real nasty things. And while he was saying them I kept getting sorer and sorer." Henry's tic was hopping around now like a flea. "I thought of all the months we'd scrimped to pay him his blood money and at the same time pay for the medical care my little girl Jody needs so maybe some day she'll walk again. I though of the stockings my wife couldn't buy, the baseball cards my Eddie couldn't collect, the complaints we didn't make to the Health Department about the cockroaches because the landlord might get mad and somehow chisel us out of the apartment and we'd have to rent another place at a bigger rent . . . I thought of a lot of things like that, and then I leaned over the desk and let Tully have it."

"With the paper knife?" Ellery asked gently.

"Huh?" Henry Witter came back to the present. "No, with this." Henry made a skinny fist and looked at it. "I pasted him one right on the button. Socko!" The memory of it gave him a momentary pleasure; a spark of life came into his eyes. "I didn't know I could hit that hard. He went out like a light."

"How did he fall, Mr. Witter?"

"On his face on the desk. I certainly was surprised. But I felt better, too. So then I walked out."

"Leaving Tully unconscious but alive?"

"Sure. He was breathing like a walrus."

"Did you notice anyone in the hall, or downstairs?"

"Just the night man mopping in the lobby."

"And that's how we know, " Inspector Queen said to his son, "that nobody else entered the building between Witter's leaving and Mrs. Bogan's finding the body. The porter saw Witter come and go, and he was in the lobby working the whole time afterward. Yes, Velie?"

The Sergeant, who had been summoned into the hall, came back to rumble into the Inspector's ear.

"That cinches it," the Inspector snapped. "The lab's found three partially smeared prints on Tully's letter knife. One is Tully's. The other two have been identified, Witter, as yours."

Henry Witter sat there with his mouth open. But then he yelped as the cigarette burned his fingers. He flung it into the wastebasket and covered his face with his hands. Ellery, fearing a fire, walked over to the basket, but he saw that it was empty except for the two butts.

"So, Witter," Inspector Queen began.

"Hold it, Dad." Ellery stooped over Henry. "Mr. Witter, while you were seated here across the desk from Tully, did you happen to handle the letter knife?"

Henry looked up dully. "I must have, if my fingerprints are on it. I don't remember. But I didn't use it on Tully. I'd remember that. God, yes. Don't you believe me, Inspector?"

"No," Inspector Queen said. "No, Witter, I don't. Take my advice and come clean. Maybe the D.A. would consent to a lesser plea—"

"Maybe the D.A. would, but I won't," Ellery said. "My client will not plead guilty."

Sergeant Velie remarked with some bitterness to no one in particular, "And the beauty of it is, he does it all with his little sleeves rolled up."

The Inspector's glance at the Sergeant was a terrible thing. "How come, Ellery?"

"Because they aren't here," Ellery said, waving vaguely.

"Because *what* aren't here?"

"The papers."

"*What* papers?"

"Look," Ellery said. "Mrs. Lester, Dominini, Witter—all three say Tully was cleaning out his desk and file, throwing away papers and records. You told me, Dad, that nothing has been removed from this office except Tully's letter knife. Yet the file and desk drawers are cleaned out, the floor is bare, there's nothing on the desk—*and the wastebasket is empty*. I ask you: Where are all the papers and records Tully was throwing out?"

His father looked as if he had been struck by lightning. He turned toward the old cleaning woman cowering in her corner, but Ellery was there before him. "You'd been inside this office earlier tonight than you claimed, Mrs. Bogan," Ellery was saying "—right after Witter left, in fact. And you found Tully just recovering from Witter's haymaker."

The old woman blinked.

"You owed Tully money, too, didn't you, Mrs. Bogan? And he put the screws on you tonight as well, while you were cleaning his office—right? You'd already emptied the wastebasket and taken the contents outside when you killed him. By the way, how did you come to owe Tully money?"

The old woman blinked and blinked. Finally she touched her liverish old lips with her old tongue, and she said, "Me boy Jim. Jim's a three-time loser. Next time he gets sent up, it's for life. And then what's he do but hook a wad outen the till in the garage where he's working. The boss says he won't send Jimmy up if I pays back the money, so I borries it offen Tully . . . I paid him his interest faithful.

"But tonight Tully says he wants all the money or he'll have me pinched. I didn't care about meself, I've had it, but if I wasn't around to keep an eye on Jim . . . I had me cleaning gloves on . . . I sees the knife on Tully's desk . . . I was in back of him . . . " Her old face settled, but it was hard to tell whether the lines told of remorse, resignation, or indifference. But then she said, "Now who'll be keeping me Jimmy out of trouble?"

Inspector Queen said furiously, "Maybe you, mother, maybe you. Just tell that story of yours to a jury."

When they had taken the old lady out, Ellery nudged Henry Witter, whose mouth was open. "You still here? Don't you know there's a lady waiting for you in the hall?"

"Claire." Henry hauled himself out of the chair.

"Oh, and you might remember," Ellery said severely, "—I'm thinking of your little girl, Mr. Witter—that miracles do happen."

Henry shook himself like a dog coming out of a mud hole. "You bet, Mr. Queen," he said. "Thanks for reminding me."

LAST MAN TO DIE

(1963)

FOR WELL OVER once around the clock Ellery tried to breathe life
into The Butler who was lying in the way of the new Queen novel's
progress.

In the fourteenth futile hour Ellery detected the difficulty; it was so
long since he had seen a real live butler that it was like trying to bring a
brontosaurus to life.

The situation obviously called for research; and making a haggard
mental note to start looking for a specimen—assuming the breed was
not extinct—Ellery collapsed.

He had no sooner closed his eyes, it seemed, than the alarm clock
brought him up with a leap, groping. Noting blearily that the time was
8:07 A.M. and the alarm was off, he concluded: It's the doorbell ringing.
And he staggered to the apartment door to find himself blinking out at
a girl, 38-23-36, with eyes of blue, and red hair, too. Oh, brother!

"Mr. Queen?" asked a voice like temple bells, eying the Queen
dishevelment doubtfully. "Am I inconvenient?"

"Not even after only two hours and eleven minutes' sleep," said Mr.
Queen, quickly showing her in. "With whom do I have the pleasure?"

"Edie Burroughs," said the belle with the bell voice, turning pink
and pleased, "and I have a problem."

"Haven't we all? Mine concerns a butler."

"Well, isn't that weird!" she cried. "So does mine. In fact, two of
them. Did you ever hear of The Butlers Club?"

"May we make haste slowly, Miss Burroughs?" begged Ellery, drag-

198

ging over a chair. "*Two* butlers? The Butlers *Club*? Where? When? In short, what?"

The goddess graciously explained. Aphrodite-like, The Butlers Club had risen out of the golden foam of the '20s. Hoity-toitier than even the Union, Century, or Metropole clubs, its membership had been restricted to the thirty noblest butlers of them all, who pooled their considerable resources and leased a haughty brownstone in the Sixties, just off Fifth Avenue, for their clubrooms.

By 1939 the depression and natural causes had lopped the membership to a butler's dozen. But the club treasury took on a hideous life of its own, for the survivors—privy to the financial secrets of their multi-millionaire employers—invested in common stocks for $5 and less a share, and by 1963 the club owned the brownstone and $3,000,000 worth of blue-chip securities besides.

Today a mere two members, long since retired from butling, survived. Both were in their 80s-William Jarvis (who had, it appeared, a repulsive grandson named Benzell Jarvis), and Peter Burroughs, Edie's grandfather, both of whom lived at the club.

"Ben Jarvis and I lead lives of our own elsewhere and," Miss Burroughs added grimly, "apart, thank goodness. But under the bylaws the members must live at the club or forfeit their rights of survivorship."

"Rights of *survivorship*?" Mr. Q was sniffing like an enchanted hound dog. "Do you mean to say this association of majordomos created a tontine? That wonderful old stupidity in which everything goes to the last beneficiary left alive?"

"Yes, Mr. Queen."

"I'm amazed. Butlers are supposed to be the most conservative group on earth."

"You evidently don't know much about butlers," chimed Miss Burroughs. "They're all born gamblers. Anyway, by now those two old ninnies have only one thought—to outlive the other and so fall heir to the club treasury. It's all pretty silly, and it would be amusing if not for the fact . . ." She hesitated.

"If not for what fact?"

"Well, that's really why I'm here, Mr. Queen. Last evening I dropped by for my weekly visit to grandfather . . ."

THE NIGHT BEFORE, 7 P.M.: Edie found the pair of octogenarians in the oak-and-leather "silence room," engaged in making a great deal of what, in any but butlers, would have been unseemly noise.

"And you, Jarvis," Edie heard her grandfather shout in an undertone, "have a narsty mind!" Peter Burroughs was a long withered root of a man, all crooked with age, and he was vibrating as in a high wind.

"Really, Burroughs?" chortled William Jarvis. Jarvis was little and bald and livid, and the chortle sounded remarkably evil. "Can you deny trying to put me out of the way in order to be able to leave the club fortune to your granddaughter?"

"I can, Jarvis, and I do!"

"*Mr.* Jarvis, really," said Edie, shocked. "Nobody's trying to put you out of the way."

"No, indeed, you doddering scullion," said old Burroughs to old Jarvis in a refined shriek. "The boot is quite on the other foot! It is *you* who are planning to kill *me* for the tontine, to pass it over to that playboy grandson of yours!"

And the two old men tottered toward each other's throats, claws at the ready.

At that moment, fortunately, Benzell Jarvis arrived on *his* weekly visit, which always seemed to coincide with Edie's, and stepped between the bristling gaffers. For once Edie was glad to see him (young Jarvis, who was an exemplary Dr. Jekyll in company, became an instant Mr. Hyde when he could catch Edie alone).

"Here, Edie," said Ben Jarvis, who was as little and bald as his grandfather, "you take your old fool, and I'll take my old fool, and we'll put 'em away—I wish there were locks on their bedroom doors— and then . . . you and me . . .?"

" . . . but I'm worried half to death, Mr. Queen," Edie concluded, not mentioning the judo chop she had had to resort to in escaping from young Mr. Jarvis. "Each thinks the other is out to murder him, and they might do each other real harm in imagined self-defense. It seems ridiculous to go to the police, and yet—what shall I do?"

"Don't they employ anyone to take care of them?"

"The houseman and the cook work afternoons only; they sleep out. Nobody's there at night if one of them should get a senile notion."

"Then what is required in this emergency," said Ellery with gravity, "is an unofficial show of authority. My father is a police inspector, Miss

Burroughs, and this is just the kind of crime-prevention work he dotes on. Excuse me while I telephone him."

LATER: For a man who doted on crime prevention, Inspector Queen seemed extraordinarily unenamored of this particular opportunity. The Inspector glared at his son as they waited with edie Burroughs on the sidewalk in front of The Butlers Club for Ben Jarvis (the Inspector had insisted on phoning him to join them); he glowered at Jarvis as that young man, clearly suffering from hangover, crawled out of a cab; and as they all mounted the brownstone steps he muttered to Ellery, "What in the so-and-so is the goldang idea?"

But he pressed the bell. And again. And again, and again. "Are they deaf as well as mush-headed?" the Inspector growled.

"It's a very loud bell," said Edie Burroughs nervously. "Oh, do you suppose—?"

"Allow me," said Ellery, whipping out his trusty picklock gun. He unlocked the door and they stepped through a time machine into a living past of dark woods, altitudinous ceilings, vast stained-glass chandeliers, brassy firedogs, and many many oil paintings of—incredibly—butlers.

And, oddly, a continuous trilling sound.

"That's grandfather's alarm clock," Edie exclaimed, "in his bedroom. Why doesn't he turn it off?"

She bounded like Artemis toward the rear of the main floor, explaining on the fly that her grandfather could no longer climb stairs. And as she burst into the old butler's bedroom the girl wailed, and stopped and turned away; and just as the Queens sprang to the big brass bed to stoop over Peter Burroughs, the old-fashioned single-alarm clock on the nightstand uttered a last peevish screek and went as dead as its owner.

Old Burroughs, fully dressed, was sprawled across the bed. There were several ugly scratches on his barklike cheeks, but no other signs of violence.

"From the condition of the body, he's been dead since last night," said Inspector Queen after a while. "Did he have those face scratches when you two left here?"

"No," said Ben Jarvis, absently embracing Edie. "Tough luck, sugar. My condolences."

"Thank you, Ben," said Edie, "but no hands? Please?"

"I think, Jarvis," said Ellery, eying Ben coldly, "we had better look in on your grandfather, too. Where is his bedroom? Upstairs? No, Miss Burroughs, you'd better wait for us down here."

So they found little old William Jarvis crumpled on his bedroom floor, fully clothed also; and *his* cheeks were badly scratched; and he was just as dead as his fellow butler below.

"When," asked young Jarvis wildly, "did *he* die?"

And the Inspector rose and said, "Last night, too."

"At 7:46," Ellery nodded, pointing to the bedside electric clock. In falling, the old man's body had jerked the cord out of the wall socket, stopping the clock. "What time did you and Miss Burroughs leave here last night, Jarvis?"

"Not quite 7:30."

They found Edie in the big clubroom downstairs, weeping quietly. She looked up and said, "Dear God, what happened?"

"I'd say they waited until you two left," Inspector Queen said, "and then headed for each other again. The only damage they were able to do was scratch each other's faces, but the exertion and excitement must have been too much for both of them. They managed to get back to their bedrooms, collapsed, and died. I'm betting the postmortems show simple heart failure in both cases."

"There, there," Ellery was crooning to the flooded blue eyes. "They were very old, Edie."

"Thus endeth The Butlers club, and high time, too," said Benzell Jarvis. "All I want to know is, which one died first? Or rather, second?"

"No autopsy can determine the exact moment of death," the Inspector said, regarding him as if he were a strange bug, "although I'm positive they died around the same time. You know, Ellery, it makes an interesting problem at that."

"What, dad?" said Ellery. "Oh! Yes. It does, indeed."

"You're damned right it does!" snarled Jarvis. "If old Burroughs died first, my grandfather inherited the tontine and I get the jackpot. If it was the other way around, Edie gets it. There's got to be some way of telling which survived the other, even if it was only for ten seconds!"

"Oh," said Ellery, "there is, Jarvis, there is."

As Ellery explained it: "We know what time William Jarvis fell dead last night. The electric clock he stopped in falling says it was 7:46.

"The question, then, is how to determine what time Peter Burroughs died. His alarm clock provides the answer.

"If you want an alarm clock to ring at, say 8 o'clock in the morning, you must set the alarm *after* 8 o'clock the night before. Because if you set the alarm before 8, it will obviously ring at 8 the same night, not at 8 the next morning.

"It was a few minutes past 8 A.M. when Edie Burroughs came to me for help this morning. I had to call you, dad; you called Ben Jarvis; we all had to meet on 60th street—it was therefore long past 8 A.M. when we entered The Butlers Club. And what did we hear when we entered? The ringing of Peter Burroughs's alarm clock, which ran down just as we got into his bedroom.

"Therefore Peter Burroughs must have set his alarm long past 8 o'clock last night. To have been able to do that, he had to have been alive long past 8 P.M.

"But your grandfather, Jarvis, died at 7:46 P.M.

"Miss Burroughs, may I shake the hand of the loveliest multimillionaire of my acquaintance?"

ABRAHAM LINCOLN'S CLUE

(1965)

FOURSCORE AND EIGHTEEN years ago, Abraham Lincoln brought forth (in this account) a new notion, conceived in secrecy and dedicated to the proposition that even an Honest Abe may borrow a leaf from Edgar A. Poe.

It is altogether fitting and proper that Mr. Lincoln's venture into the detective story should come to its final resting place in the files of a man named Queen. For all his life Ellery has consecrated Father Abraham as the noblest projection of the American dream; and, insofar as it has been within his poor power to add or detract, he has given full measure of devotion, testing whether that notion, or any notion so conceived and so dedicated, deserve to endure.

Ellery's service in running the Lincoln clue to earth is one the world has little noted nor, perhaps, will long remember. That he shall not have served in vain, this account:

The case began on the outskirts of an upstate-New York city with the dreadful name of Eulalia, behind the flaking shutters of a fat and curlicued house with architectural dandruff, recalling for all the world some blowsy ex-Bloomer Girl from the Gay Nineties of its origin.

The owner, a formerly wealthy man named DiCampo, possessed a grandeur not shared by his property, although it was no less fallen into ruin. His falcon's face, more Florentine than Victorian, was—like the house—ravaged by time and the inclemencies of fortune; but haughtily so, and indeed DiCampo wore his scurfy purple velvet house jacket like the prince he was entitled to call himself, but did not. He was proud, and stubborn, and useless; and he had a lovely daughter named Bianca, who taught at a Eulalia grade school and, through marvels of economy, supported them both.

How Lorenzo San Marco Borghese-Ruffo DiCampo came to this decayed estate is no concern of ours. The presence there this day of a man named Harbidger and a man named Tungston, however, is to the point: they had come, Harbidger from Chicago, Tungston from Philadelphia, to buy something each wanted very much, and DiCampo had summoned them in order to sell it. The two visitors were collectors, Harbidger's passion being Lincoln, Tungston's Poe.

The Lincoln collector, an elderly man who looked like a migrant fruit picker, had plucked his fruits well: Harbidger was worth about $40,000,000, every dollar of which was at the beck of his mania for Lincolniana. Tungston, who was almost as rich, had the aging body of a poet and the eyes of a starving panther, armament that had served him well in the wars of Poeana.

"I must say, Mr. DiCampo," remarked Harbidger, "that your letter surprised me." He paused to savor the wine his host had poured from an ancient and honorable bottle (DiCampo had filled it with California claret before their arrival). "May I ask what has finally induced you to offer the book and document for sale?"

"To quote Lincoln in another context, Mr. Harbidger," said DiCampo with a shrug of his wasted shoulders, " 'the dogmas of the quiet past are inadequate to the stormy present.' In short, a hungry man sells his blood."

"Only if it's of the right type," said old Tungston, unmoved. "You've made that book and document less accessible to collectors and historians, DiCampo, than the gold in Fort Knox. Have you got them here? I'd like to examine them."

"No other hand will ever touch them except by right of ownership." Lorenzo DiCampo replied bitterly. He had taken a miser's glee in his lucky finds, vowing never to part with them; now forced by his need to sell them, he was like a suspicion-caked old prospector who, stumbling at last on pay dirt, draws cryptic maps to keep the world from stealing the secret of its location. "As I informed you gentlemen, I represent the book as bearing the signatures of Poe and Lincoln, and the document as being in Lincoln's hand; I am offering them with the customary proviso that they are returnable if they should prove to be not as represented; and if this does not satisfy you," and the old prince actually rose, "let us terminate our business here and now."

"Sit down, sit down, Mr. DiCampo," Harbidger said.

"No one is questioning your integrity," snapped old Tungston. "It's just that I'm not used to buying sight unseen. If there's a money-back guarantee, we'll do it your way."

Lorenzo DiCampo reseated himself stiffly. "Very well, gentlemen. Then I take it you are both prepared to buy?"

"Oh, yes!" said Harbidger. "What is your price?"

"Oh, no," said DiCampo. "What is your bid?"

The Lincoln collector cleared his throat, which was full of slaver. "If the book and document are as represented, Mr. DiCampo, you might hope to get from a dealer or realize at auction—oh—$50,000. I offer you $55,000."

"$56,000," said Tungston.

"$57,000," said Harbidger.

"$58,000," said Tungston.

"$59,000," said Harbidger.

Tungston showed his fangs. "$60,000," he said.

Harbidger fell silent, and DiCampo waited. He did not expect miracles. To these men, five times $60,000 was of less moment than the undistinguished wine they were smacking their lips over; but they were veterans of many a hard auction-room campaign, and a collector's victory tastes very nearly as sweet for the price as for the prize.

So the impoverished prince was not surprised when the Lincoln collector suddenly said, "Would you be good enough to allow Mr. Tungston and me to talk privately for a moment?"

DiCampo rose and strolled out of the room, to gaze somberly through a cracked window at the jungle growth that had once been his Italian formal gardens.

It was the Poe collector who summoned him back. "Harbidger has convinced me that for the two of us to try to outbid each other would simply run the price up out of all reason. We're going to make you a sporting proposition."

"I've proposed to Mr. Tungston, and he has agreed," nodded Harbidger, "that our bid for the book and document be $65,000. Each of us is prepared to pay that sum, and not a penny more."

"So that is how the screws are turned," said DiCampo, smiling. "But I do not understand. If each of you makes the identical bid, which of you gets the book and document?"

"Ah," grinned the Poe man, "that's where the sporting proposition comes in."

"You see, Mr. DiCampo," said the Lincoln man, "we are going to leave that decision to you."

Even the old prince, who had seen more than his share of the astonishing, was astonished. He looked at the two rich men really for the first time. "I must confess," he murmured, "that your compact is an amusement. Permit me?" He sank into thought while the two collectors sat expectantly. When the old man looked up he was smiling like a fox. "The very thing, gentlemen! From the typewritten copies of the document I sent you, you both know that Lincoln himself left a clue to a theoretical hiding place for the book which he never explained. Some time ago I arrived at a possible solution to the President's little mystery. I propose to hide the book and document in accordance with it."

"You mean whichever of us figures out your interpretation of the Lincoln clue and finds the book and document where you will hide them, Mr. DiCampo, gets both for the agreed price?"

"That is it exactly."

The Lincoln collector looked dubious. "I don't know . . ."

"Oh, come, Harbidger," said Tungston, eyes glittering. "A deal is a deal. We accept, DiCampo! Now what?"

"You gentlemen will of course have to give me a little time. Shall we say three days?"

Ellery let himself into the Queen apartment, tossed his suitcase aside, and set about opening windows. He had been out of town for a week on a case, and Inspector Queen was in Atlantic City attending a police convention.

Breathable air having been restored, Ellery sat down to the week's accumulation of mail. One envelope made him pause. It had come by air-mail special delivery, it was postmarked four days earlier, and in the lower left corner, in red, flamed the word URGENT. The printed return address on the flap said; *L.S.M.B.-R. DiCampo, Post Office Box 69, Southern District, Eulalia, N.Y.* The initials of the name had been crossed out and "Bianca" written above them.

The enclosure, in a large agitated female hand on inexpensive notepaper, said:

> Dear Mr. Queen,
> The most important detective book in the world has disappeared. Will you please find it for me?
> Phone me on arrival at the Eulalia RR station or airport and I will pick you up.
>
> Bianca DiCampo

A yellow envelope then caught his eye. It was a telegram, dated the previous day:

WHY HAVE I NOT HEARD FROM YOU STOP AM IN DESPERATE NEED YOUR SERVICES

BIANCA DICAMPO

He had no sooner finished reading the telegram than the telephone on his desk trilled. It was a long-distance call.

"Mr. Queen?" throbbed a contralto voice. "Thank heaven I've finally got through to you! I've been calling all day—"

"I've been away," said Ellery, "and you would be Miss Bianca DiCampo of Eulalia. In two words, Miss DiCampo: Why me?"

"In two words, Mr. Queen: Abraham Lincoln."

Ellery was startled. "You plead a persuasive case," he chuckled. "It's true, I'm an incurable Lincoln addict. How did you find out? Well, never mind. Your letter refers to a book, Miss DiCampo. Which book?"

The husky voice told him, and certain other provocative things as well. "So will you come, Mr. Queen?"

"Tonight if I could! Suppose I drive up first thing in the morning. I ought to make Eulalia by noon. Harbidger and Tungston are still around, I take it?"

"Oh, yes. They're staying at a motel downtown."

"Would you ask them to be there?"

The moment he hung up Ellery leaped to his bookshelves. He snatched out his volume of *Murder for Pleasure,* the historical work on detective stories by his good friend Howard Haycraft, and found what he was looking for on page 26:

> And ... young William Dean Howells thought it significant praise to assert of a nominee for President of the United States:
>
> > The bent of his mind is mathematical and metaphysical, and he is therefore pleased with the absolute and logical method of Poe's tales and sketches, in which the problem of mystery is given, and wrought out into everyday facts by processes of cunning anaysis. It is said that he suffers no year to pass without a perusal of this author.
>
> Abraham Lincoln subsequently confirmed this statement, which appeared in his little-known "campaign biography" by Howells in 1860... The instance is chiefly notable, of course, for its revelation of a little-suspected affinity between two great Americans ...

Very early the next morning Ellery gathered some papers from his files, stuffed them into his briefcase, scribbled a note for his father, and ran for his car, Eulalia-bound.

He was enchanted by the DiCampo house, which looked like something out of Poe by Charles Addams; and, for other reasons, by Bianca, who turned out to be a genetic product supreme of northern Italy, with titian hair and Mediterranean blue eyes and a figure that needed only some solid steaks to qualify her for Miss Universe competition. Also, she was in deep mourning; so her conquest of the Queen heart was immediate and complete.

"He died of a cerebral hemorrhage, Mr. Queen," Bianca said, dabbing at her absurd little nose. "In the middle of the second night after his session with Mr. Harbidger and Mr. Tungston."

So Lorenzo San Marco Borghese-Ruffo DiCampo was unexpected'y dead, bequeathing the lovely Bianca near-destitution and a mystery.

"The only things of value father really left me are that book and the Lincoln document. The $65,000 they now represent would pay off father's debts and give me a fresh start. But I can't find them, Mr.

Queen, and neither can Mr. Harbidger and Mr. Tungston—who'll be here soon, by the way. Father hid the two things, as he told them he would; but where? We've ransacked the place."

"Tell me more about the book, Miss DiCampo."

"As I said over the phone, it's called *The Gift: 1845*. The Christmas annual that contained the earliest appearance of Edgar Allan Poe's *The Purloined Letter*."

"Published in Philadelphia by Carey & Hart? Bound in red?" At Bianca's nod Ellery said, "You understand that an ordinary copy of *The Gift: 1845* isn't worth more than about $50. What makes your father's copy unique is that double autograph you mentioned."

"That's what he said, Mr. Queen. I wish I had the book here to show you—that beautifully handwritten *Edgar Allan Poe* on the flyleaf, and under Poe's signature the signature *Abraham Lincoln*."

"Poe's own copy, once owned, signed, and read by Lincoln," Ellery said slowly. "Yes, that would be a collector's item for the ages. By the way, Miss DiCampo, what's the story behind the other piece—the Lincoln document?"

Bianca told him what her father had told her.

One morning in the spring of 1865, Abraham Lincoln opened the rosewood door of his bedroom in the southwest corner of the second floor of the White House and stepped out into the red-carpeted hall at the unusually late hour—for him—of 7:00 A.M.; he was more accustomed to beginning his work day at six.

But (as Lorenzo DiCampo had reconstructed events) Mr. Lincoln that morning had lingered in his bedchamber. He had awakened at his usual hour but, instead of leaving immediately on dressing for his office, he had pulled one of the cane chairs over to the round table, with its gas-fed reading lamp, and sat down to reread Poe's *The Purloined Letter* in his copy of the 1845 annual; it was a dreary morning, and the natural light was poor. The President was alone; the folding doors to Mrs. Lincoln's bedroom remained closed.

Impressed as always with Poe's tale, Mr. Lincoln on this occasion was struck by a whimsical thought; and, apparently finding no paper handy, he took an envelope from his pocket, discarded its enclosure, slit the two short edges so that the envelope opened out into a single sheet, and began to write on the blank side.

"Describe it to me, please."

"It's a long envelope, one that must have contained a bulky letter. It is addressed to the White House, but there is no return address, and father was never able to identify the sender from the handwriting. We do know that the letter came through the regular mails, because there are two Lincoln stamps on it, lightly but unmistakably canceled."

"May I see your father's transcript of what Lincoln wrote out that morning on the inside of the envelope?"

Bianca handed him a typewritten copy and, in spite of himself, Ellery felt goose flesh rise as he read:

Apr. 14, 1865

Mr. Poe's The Purloined Letter is a work of singular originality. Its simplicity is a master-stroke of cunning, which never fails to arouse my wonder.

Reading the tale over this morning has given me a "notion." Suppose I wished to hide a book, this very book, perhaps? Where best to do so? Well, as Mr. Poe in his tale hid a letter *among letters,* might not a book be hidden *among books?* Why, if this very copy of the tale were to be deposited in a library and on purpose not recorded—would not the Library of Congress make a prime depository!—well might it repose there, undiscovered, for a generation.

On the other hand, let us regard Mr. Poe's "notion" turn-about: Suppose the book were to be placed, not amongst other books, but *where no book would reasonably be expected?* (I may follow the example of Mr. Poe, and, myself, compose a tale of "ratiocination"!)

The "notion" beguiles me, it is nearly seven o'clock. Later to-day, if the vultures and my appointments leave me a few moments of leisure, I may write further of my imagined hiding-place.

In self-reminder: The hiding-place of the book is in 30d, which

Ellery looked up. "The document ends there?"

"Father said that Mr. Lincoln must have glanced again at his watch, and shamefacedly jumped up to go to his office, leaving the sentence unfinished. Evidently he never found the time to get back to it."

Ellery brooded. Evidently indeed. From the moment when Abraham Lincoln stepped out of his bedroom that Good Friday morning, fingering his thick gold watch on its vest chain, to bid the still-unrelieved night guard his customary courteous "Good morning" and make for his office at the other end of the hall, his day was spoken for. The usual patient push through the clutching crowd of favor-seekers, many of whom had bedded down all night on the hall carpet; sanctuary in his sprawling office, where he read official correspondence; by 8:00 A.M. having breakfast with his family—Mrs. Lincoln chattering away about plans for the evening, 12-year-old Tad of the cleft palate lisping a complaint that "nobody asked me to go," and young Robert Lincoln, just returned from duty, bubbling with stories about his hero Ulysses Grant and the last days of the war; then back to the presidential office to look over the morning newspapers (which Lincoln had once remarked he "never" read, but these were happy days, with good news everywhere), sign two documents, and signal the soldier at the door to admit the morning's first caller, Speaker of the House Schuyler Colfax (who was angling for a Cabinet post and had to be tactfully handled); and so on throughout the day—the historic Cabinet meeting at 11:00 A.M., attended by General Grant himself, that stretched well into the afternoon; a hurried lunch at almost half-past two with Mrs. Lincoln (had this 45-pounds-underweight man eaten his usual midday meal of a biscuit, a glass of milk, and an apple?); more visitors to see in his office (including the unscheduled Mrs. Nancy Bushrod, escaped slave and wife of an escaped slave and mother of three small children, weeping that Tom, a soldier in the Army of the Potomac, was no longer getting his pay: "You are entitled to your husband's pay. Come this time tomorrow," and the tall President escorted her to the door, bowing her out "like I was a natural-born lady"); the late afternoon drive in the barouche to the Navy Yard and back with Mrs. Lincoln; more work, more visitors, into the evening... until finally, at five minutes past 8:00 P.M., Abraham Lincoln stepped into the White House formal coach after his wife, waved, and sank back to be driven off to see a play he did not much want to see, *Our American Cousin*, at Ford's Theatre...

Ellery mused over that black day in silence. And, like a relative hanging on the specialist's yet undelivered diagnosis, Bianca DiCampo sat watching him with anxiety.

212

Harbidger and Tungston arrived in a taxi to greet Ellery with the fervor of castaways grasping at a smudge of smoke on the horizon.

"As I understand it, gentlemen," Ellery said when he had calmed them down, "neither of you has been able to solve Mr. DiCampo's interpretation of the Lincoln clue. If I succeed in finding the book and paper where DiCampo hid them, which of you gets them?"

"We intend to split the $65,000 payment to Miss DiCampo," said Harbidger, "and take joint ownership of the two pieces."

"An arrangement," growled old Tungston, "I'm against on principle, in practice, and by plain horse sense."

"So am I," sighed the Lincoln collector, "but what else can we do?"

"Well," and the Poe man regarded Bianca DiCampo with the icy intimacy of the cat that long ago marked the bird as its prey, "Miss DiCampo, who now owns the two pieces, is quite free to renegotiate a sale on her own terms."

"Miss DiCampo," said Miss DiCampo, giving Tungston stare for stare, "considers herself bound by her father's wishes. His terms stand."

"In all likelihood, then," said the other millionaire, "one of us will retain the book, the other the document, and we'll exchange them every year, or some such thing." Harbidger sounded unhappy.

"Only practical arrangement under the circumstances," grunted Tungston, and *he* sounded unhappy. "But all this is academic, Queen, unless and until the book and document are found."

Ellery nodded. "The problem, then, is to fathom DiCampo's interpretation of that *30d* in the document. 30d . . . I notice, Miss Di-Campo—or, may I? Bianca?—that your father's typewritten copy of the Lincoln holograph text runs the 3 and 0 and *d* together—no spacing in between. Is that the way it occurs in the longhand?"

"Yes."

'Hmm. Still . . . 30d . . . Could *d* stand for *days* . . . or the British *pence* . . . or *died*, as used in obituaries? Do any of these make sense to you, Bianca?"

"No."

"Did your father have any special interest in, say, pharmacology? chemistry? physics? algebra? electricity? Small *d* is an abbreviation used in all those." But Bianca shook her splendid head. "Banking? Small *d* for *dollars, dividends*?"

213

"Hardly," the girl said with a sad smile.

"How about theatricals? Was your father ever involved in a play production? Small *d* stands for *door* in playscript stage directions."

"Mr. Queen, I've gone through every darned abbreviation my dictionary lists, and I haven't found one that has a point of contact with any interest of my father's."

Ellery scowled. "At that—I assume the typewritten copy is accurate—the manuscript shows no period after the *d*, making an abbreviation unlikely. 30d . . . let's concentrate on the number. Does the number 30 have any significance for you?"

"Yes, indeed," said Bianca, making all three men sit up. But then they sank back. "In a few years it will represent my age, and that has enormous significance. But only for me, I'm afraid."

"You'll be drawing wolf whistles at twice thirty," quoth Ellery warmly. "However! Could the number have cross-referred to anything in your father's life or habits?"

"None that I can think of, Mr. Queen. And," Bianca said, having grown roses in her cheeks, "thank you."

"I think," said old Tungston testily, "we had better stick to the subject."

"Just the same, Bianca, let me run over some 'thirty' associations as they come to mind. Stop me if one of them hits a nerve. The Thirty Tyrants—was your father interested in classical Athens? Thirty Years' War—in Seventeenth Century European history? Thirty all—did he play or follow tennis? Or . . . did he ever live at an address that included the number 30?"

Ellery went on and on, but to each suggestion Bianca DiCampo could only shake her head.

"The lack of spacing, come to think of it, doesn't necessarily mean that Mr. DiCampo chose to view the clue that way," said Ellery thoughtfully. "He might have interpreted it arbitrarily as 3-space-*O-d*."

"Three od?" echoed old Tungston. "What the devil could that mean?"

"Od? Od is the hypothetical force or power claimed by Baron von Reichenbach—in 1850, wasn't it?—to pervade the whole of nature. Manifests itself in magnets, crystals, and such, which according to the excited Baron explained animal magnetism and mesmerism. Was your father by any chance interested in hypnosis, Bianca? Or the occult?"

"Not in the slightest."

"Mr. Queen," exclaimed Harbidger, "are you serious about all this —this semantic sludge?"

"Why, I don't know," said Ellery. "I never know till I stumble over something. Od ... the word was used with prefixes, too—*biod*, the force of animal life; *elod*, the force of electricity; and so forth. *Three* od ... or *triod*, the triune force—it's all right, Mr. Harbidger, it's not ignorance on your part, I just coined the word. But it does rather suggest the Trinity, doesn't it? Bianca, did your father tie up to the Church in a personal, scholarly, or any other way? No? That's too bad, really, because Od—capitalized—has been a minced form of the word God since the Sixteenth Century. Or ... you wouldn't happen to have three Bibles on the premises, would you? Because—"

Ellery stopped with the smashing abruptness of an ordinary force meeting an absolutely immovable object. The girl and the two collectors gaped. Bianca had idly picked up the typewritten copy of the Lincoln document. She was not reading it, she was simply holding it on her knees; but Ellery, sitting opposite her, had shot forward in a crouch, rather like a pointer, and he was regarding the paper in her lap with a glare of pure discovery.

"That's it!" he cried.

"What's it, Mr. Queen?" the girl asked, bewildered.

"Please—the transcript!" He plucked the paper from her. "Of course. Hear this: 'On the other hand, let us regard Mr. Poe's "notion" turn-about.' *Turn-about*. Look at the 30d 'turn-about'—as I just saw it!"

He turned the Lincoln message upside down for their inspection. In that position the 30d became:

POƐ

"*Poe!*" exploded Tungston.

"Yes, crude but recognizable," Ellery said swiftly. "So now we read the Lincoln clue as: 'The hiding-place of the book is in *poe*'!"

There was a silence.

"In Poe," said Harbidger blankly.

"In Poe?" muttered Tungston. "There are only a couple of trade editions of Poe in DiCampo's library, Harbidger, and we went through those. We looked in every book here."

"He might have meant among the Poe books in the *public* library. Miss DiCampo—"

"Wait." Bianca sped away. But when she came back she was drooping. "It isn't. We have two public libraries in Eulalia, and I know the head librarian in both. I just called them. Father didn't visit either library."

Ellery gnawed a fingernail. "Is there a bust of Poe in the house, Bianca? Or any other Poe-associated object, aside from books?"

"I'm afraid not."

"Queer," he mumbled. "Yet I'm positive your father interpreted 'the hiding-place of the book' as being 'in Poe.' So he'd have hidden it 'in Poe' . . ."

Ellery's mumbling dribbled away into a tormented sort of silence: his eyebrows worked up and down, Groucho Marx fashion; he pinched the tip of his nose until it was scarlet; he yanked at his unoffending ears; he munched on his lip . . . until, all at once, his face cleared; and he sprang to his feet. "Bianca, may I use your phone?"

The girl could only nod, and Ellery dashed. They heard him telephoning in the entrance hall, although they could not make out the words. He was back in two minutes.

"One thing more," he said briskly, "and we're out of the woods. I suppose your father had a key ring or a key case, Bianca? May I have it, please?"

She fetched a key case. To the two millionaires it seemed the sorriest of objects, a scuffed and dirty tan leatherette case. But Ellery received it from the girl as if it were an artifact of historic importance from a newly discovered IV Dynasty tomb. He unsnapped it with concentrated love; he fingered its contents like a scientist. Finally he decided on a certain key.

"Wait here!" Thus Mr. Queen; and exit, running.

"I can't decide," old Tungston said after a while, "whether that fellow is a genius or an escaped lunatic."

Neither Harbidger nor Bianca replied. Apparently they could not decide, either.

They waited through twenty elongated minutes; at the twenty-first they heard his car, champing. All three were in the front doorway as Ellery strode up the walk.

He was carrying a book with a red cover, and smiling. It was a compassionate smile, but none of them noticed.

"You—" said Bianca. "—found—" said Tungston. "—the book!" shouted Harbidger. "Is the Lincoln holograph in it?"

"It is," said Ellery. "Shall we all go into the house, where we may mourn in decent privacy?"

"Because," Ellery said to Bianca and the two quivering collectors as they sat across a refectory table from him, "I have foul news. Mr. Tungston, I believe you have never actually seen Mr. DiCampo's book. Will you now look at the Poe signature on the flyleaf?"

The panther claws leaped. There, toward the top of the flyleaf, in faded inkscript, was the signature *Edgar Allan Poe*.

The claws curled, and old Tungston looked up sharply. "DiCampo never mentioned that it's a full autograph—he kept referring to it as 'the Poe signature.' Edgar *Allan* Poe . . . Why, I don't know of a single instance after his West Point days when Poe wrote out his middle name in an autograph! And the earliest he could have signed this 1845 edition is obviously when it was published, which was around the fall of 1844. In 1844 he'd surely have abbreviated the 'Allan,' signing 'Edgar *A.* Poe,' the way he signed everything! This is a forgery."

"My God," murmured Bianca, clearly intending no impiety; she was as pale as Poe's Lenore. "Is that true, Mr. Queen?"

"I'm afraid it is," Ellery said sadly. "I was suspicious the moment you told me the Poe signature on the flyleaf contained the 'Allan.' And if the Poe signature is a forgery, the book itself can hardly be considered Poe's own copy."

Harbidger was moaning. "And the Lincoln signature underneath the Poe, Mr. Queen! DiCampo never told me it reads *Abraham* Lincoln—the full Christian name. Except on official documents, Lincoln practically always signed his name '*A.* Lincoln.' Don't tell me this Lincoln autograph is a forgery, too?"

Ellery forbore to look at poor Bianca. "I was struck by the 'Abraham' as well, Mr. Harbidger, when Miss DiCampo mentioned it to me, and I came equipped to test it. I have here"—and Ellery tapped the pile of documents he had taken from his briefcase—"facsimiles of Lincoln signatures from the most frequently reproduced of the historic documents he signed. Now I'm going to make a precise tracing of the Lincoln signature on the flyleaf of the book."—he proceeded to do so—"and I shall superimpose the tracing on the various signatures of the authentic Lincoln documents. So."

He worked rapidly. On his third superimposition Ellery looked up. "Yes. See here. The tracing of the purported Lincoln signature from the flyleaf fits in minutest detail over the authentic Lincoln signature on this facsimile of the Emancipation Proclamation. It's a fact of life that's tripped many a forger that *nobody ever writes his name exactly the same way twice.* There are always variations. If two signatures are identical, then, one must be a tracing of the other. So the 'Abraham Lincoln' signed on this flyleaf can be dismissed without further consideration as a forgery also. It's a tracing of the Emancipation Proclamation signature.

"Not only was this book not Poe's own copy; it was never signed—and therefore probably never owned—by Lincoln. However your father came into possession of the book, Bianca, he was swindled."

It was the measure of Bianca DiCampo's quality that she said quietly, "Poor, poor father," nothing more.

Harbidger was poring over the worn old envelope on whose inside appeared the dearly beloved handscript of the Martyr President. "At least," he muttered, "we have *this.*"

"Do we?" asked Ellery gently. "Turn it over, Mr. Harbidger."

Harbidger looked up, scowling. "No! You're not going to deprive me of this, too!"

"Turn it over," Ellery repeated in the same gentle way. The Lincoln collector obeyed reluctantly. "What do you see?"

"An authentic envelope of the period! With two authentic Lincoln stamps!"

"Exactly. And the United States has never issued postage stamps depicting living Americans; you have to be dead to qualify. The earliest U.S. stamp showing a portrait of Lincoln went on sale April 15, 1866—a year to the day after his death. Then a living Lincoln could scarcely have used this envelope, with these stamps on it, as writing paper. The document is spurious, too. I am so very sorry, Bianca."

Incredibly, Lorenzo DiCampo's daughter managed a smile with her *"Non importa, signor."* He could have wept for her. As for the two

218

collectors, Harbidger was in shock; but old Tungston managed to croak, "Where the devil did DiCampo hide the book, Queen? And how did you know?

"Oh, that," said Ellery, wishing the two old men would go away so that he might comfort this admirable creature. "I was convinced that DiCampo interpreted what we now know was the forger's, not Lincoln's, clue as *30d* read upside down; or, crudely, *Poe*. But 'the hiding-place of the book is in Poe' led nowhere.

"So I reconsidered, P, o, e. If those three letters of the alphabet didn't mean Poe, what could they mean? Then I remembered something about the letter you wrote me, Bianca. You'd used one of your father's envelopes, on the flap of which appeared his address: *Post Office Box 69, Southern District, Eulalia, N.Y.* If there was a Southern District in Eulalia, it seemed reasonable to conclude that there were post offices for other points of the compass, too. As, for instance, an Eastern District. Post Office Eastern, P.O. East. P.O.E."

"Poe!" cried Bianca.

"To answer your question, Mr. Tungston: I phoned the main post office, confirmed the existence of a Post Office East, got directions as to how to get there, looked for a postal box key in Mr. DiCampo's key case, found the right one, located the box DiCampo had rented especially for the occasion, unlocked it—and there was the book." He added, hopefully, "And that is that."

"And that *is* that," Bianca said when she returned from seeing the two collectors off. "I'm not going to cry over an empty milk bottle, Mr. Queen. I'll straighten out father's affairs somehow. Right now all I can think of is how glad I am he didn't live to see the signatures and documents declared forgeries publicly, as they would surely have been when they were expertized."

"I think you'll find there's still some milk in the bottle, Bianca."

"I beg your pardon?" said Bianca.

Ellery tapped the pseudo—Lincolnian envelope. "You know, you didn't do a very good job describing this envelope to me. All you said was that there were two canceled Lincoln stamps on it."

"Well, there are."

"I can see you misspent your childhood. No, little girls don't collect things, do they? Why, if you'll examine these 'two canceled Lincoln stamps,' you'll see that they're a great deal more than that. In the first place, they're not separate stamps. They're a vertical pair—that is, one stamp is joined to the other at the horizontal edges. Now look at this upper stamp of the pair."

The Mediterranean eyes widened. "It's upside down, isn't it?"

"Yes, it's upside down," said Ellery, "and what's more, while the pair have perforations all around, there are no perforations between them, where they're joined.

"What you have here, young lady—and what our unknown forger didn't realize when he fished around for an authentic White House cover of the period on which to perpetrate the Lincoln forgery—is what stamp collectors might call a double printing error: a pair of 1866 black 15-cent Lincolns imperforate horizontally, with one of the pair printed upside down. No such error of the Lincoln issue has ever been reported. You're the owner, Bianca, of what may well be the rarest item in U.S. philately, and the most valuable."

The world will little note, nor long remember.

But don't try to prove it by Bianca DiCampo.

WEDDING ANNIVERSARY

(1967)

IN SPITE OF his passion for Wrightsville, hardly a visit of Ellery's does not turn up some major crime, as if in savage welcome to his gifts. Compelled to use them against the objects of his affection, he yet goes back, again and again and again, hopefully turning the other cheek. It is no reward for his devotion.

On this occasion he was beguiled by the season. The magnolias were in their improbable New England bloom, the syringa enriched the town with outcroppings of gold, the grass in Memorial Park stretched in greenest innocence, the ancient maples along State Street were in their infant leaf. It was simply not a day for death.

Or so Ellery told himself.

He cut across the Square (which is round), passed the Town Hall and the American Legion Bandstand, and turned into the alley of the County Court House building, whose downstairs west wing houses the Wrightsville Police Department.

"I'm dodderin'," Chief Anselm Newby said, pumping Ellery's hand. "When you called from the Hollis to ask me to supper, I clean forgot about Mr. B.'s anniversary blowout. So I phoned him and he said, 'Sure, bring Mr. Queen along.' I hope you don't mind, Ellery."

It appeared that Ellery did not mind; to the contrary. Ernst Bauenfel was one of the few prominent Wrightsvillians whose path had never happened to intersect his, even though he kept running across the name in the news and advertising columns of the *Wrightsville Record*, to which he was a mail subscriber.

As the town reckoned such things, Bauenfel was a newcomer to the

221

community. But what he lacked in local ancestry he more than made up by good works. As one of the leading merchants of High Village— he was a jeweler, with branches strewn about the state—Bauenfel's was to Wright County what Cartier's is to Fifth Avenue. He was a past president of the Chamber of Commerce, he held high office in most of the benevolent societies, he had twice been elected to the Board of Selectmen, he was regularly asked to take charge of the Red Cross, Community Chest, and other important drives, and his private bene-factions had earned him the title of "Mr. Bountiful," which the *Record* abbreviated to Mr. B. It was said that no one ever came to Mr. B. in genuine need and went away empty-handed.

"From all I read about him," Ellery said as Chief Newby drove him up toward Hill Drive, "he's the nearest thing to a civic saint that Wrightsville's ever had."

"There isn't a living soul in Low Village or High," the police chief said, "who doesn't swear by him."

"Aren't you forgetting some juicy rumors a year ago, Anse?"

"You mean when he remarried?" Newby grunted. "You know small towns. They even talked when he got married the first time. Hester, his first wife, was a lot younger than Mr.B.—she was twenty-five when she gave birth to Amy, their only child, and Ernst was more than double that, fifty-five—and it made a lot of tongues go clickety-clack in the ladies' auxiliaries, especially since Hester was a Dade, and you know how far back the Dades go in this town. But the gabble soon died out, and there wasn't another unkind word said about Mr. B. until last year, after Hester died in that auto smashup. I mean, when he married Zelda Brown, Al Brown's youngest—the ice-cream parlor Brown— less than a month after Hester's funeral."

"What's the scoop?" Ellery asked in his nosiest Wrightsville tone. "The *Record* was annoyingly tactful."

"Well, for one thing, Zelda was Mr. B.'s secretary-bookkeeper in his Wrightsville branch store; they were together a lot. And Zelda's pretty sexy-looking. So as soon as Mr. B. married her the ladies began whispering that they'd been having an affair behind Hester's back. The damn flapmouths! I know Mr. B., and in my book he's as straight as they come. Of course, the short time between Hester's death and Ernst's remarrying helped the gossip along—"

"Some men are born for marriage," said Ellery, with the authority of one who was not.

"—but it wasn't only that. Ernst pulled the boner, or maybe in the excitement he just forgot, of marrying Zelda on what would have been Hester's birthday."

"The most generous of men," the sage pointed out, "is often the least tactful."

"Anyway, Ellery, that's ancient history. The biddies haven't found a thing to rip Zelda up the back for in the year she and Ernst have been hitched. She's raising Hester's kid—Amy is five now—as if she were her own flesh and blood, and that sort of thing goes a long way in this town. They're good people, Ellery. You'll like 'em."

As, indeed, Ellery did. He liked everything about the Bauenfels, from their chalet-type house with its squared-timber construction and steeply projecting eaves (evidently built by Mr. B. in an early nostalgia for his native Switzerland, to what must have been the astonishment of its Colonial neighbors on Hill Drive) to the solid *bürgerstand* furnishings of the interior.

They were simple, hearty folk, like a peasant soup. Mr. B. was portly and florid, with a gray Teutonic brush and eyes with a malty sparkle; he wore a brocaded vest festooned with a heavy gold watch-chain; and Ellery thought he needed only a tray and a white apron tied around his girth to step into a *Züricher* beer garden. As for Zelda Bauenfel, nee Brown, Ellery almost failed to recognize her. He had last seen Zelda as a nubile teen-ager working after school hours in her father's ice cream emporium on Lower Main. Now she was a well-fleshed, handsome *hausfrau* in a struggling girdle, cheerful and authoritative and obviously well-loved.

It took no seer, either, to divine the affection between Zelda and her husband's first wife's child. At the approach of the stranger, little Amy clung to her stepmother's skirt, her pale Dade eyes enormous. Zelda briskly soothed her, Ellery went to work on her, and in a few minutes the child was on his lap.

"We used to love you," Amy lisped.

"Really, Amy?" Ellery said. "When was that?"

"When my mommy was bery young?"

"And that, young lady," said Zelda, pink as a geranium, "is the last time I'm ever going to tell you any of my girlish secrets! Kiss Mr. Queen and Chief Newby and your papa good night, and off to bed."

"I ought to feel jealous, Mr. Queen," chuckled Ernst Bauenfel as his wife took the little girl upstairs. "That is a secret my Zelda never confided in *me*." He had a slight German accent.

"Or me, worse luck."

"But I am not a jealous man; it is one of the things for which I thank God. Too many waste their lives envying and hating. And I am being a Saturday-night philosopher! I think that is our other guests—excuse me." And Mr. B. hastily went to the front door.

"I told you," Newby laughed.

"I'm glad I came, Anse."

But Ellery's gladness was within a half hour of destruction.

The three other guests were men also. At first Ellery suspected that the absence of ladies might be significant. But it turned out that Franklin Lang was a bachelor, Rob Packard was a widower, and Martin Overbrook's wife was entertaining an uninvited spring virus and had insisted on her husband not disappointing the Bauenfels on their anniversary party.

Of the three, Ellery had met only Lang. A tall weedy man with an occupational tic under his eye and bottle-fed veins in his nose, Lang was managing editor of the *Record*; Ellery's visits to Wrightsville, which the *Record* considered news, had brought them into contact from time to time. The newspaperman had always struck Ellery as rather indrawn. There was nothing indrawn about Franklin Lang this evening. He punched Mr. B's heavy shoulder and then threw a long arm around it.

Ellery knew Rob Packard by hearsay. He was a one-time real estate broker who had blossomed overnight into a general building contractor and had actually succeeded in supplanting that hardy Wrightsville perennial, J.C. Pettigrew, as chairman of the town's Realty Board. Packard was a redhaired man in an Italian silk suit and a bow tie, with a handshake like an oil salesman.

He, too, embraced his host.

Martin Overbrook Ellery did not know at all, although he recalled that one of the old red-brick buildings in Low Village bore the white-on-black stencil, *Overbrook Paperbox Factory*, on its grimy side walls.

Overbrook was a feisty little fellow who came bursting in like the White Rabbit, glancing at this watch and crying, "Am I late, Mr. B.? I hope I'm not late—Jinny couldn't come, she's down sick—oh, she phoned Zelda, I forgot—congratulations," beaming all the while, the reports of his Yankee voice bouncing around the room like shellfire.

There were hail-fellow introductions and lively conversation, a good deal of it concerned with the unexpected presence of Wrightsville's self-adopted son; then Zelda Bauenfel came flying downstairs, everything bobbing, and there was more embracing, and some jokes about first anniversaries, and much laughter; whereupon Mrs. B. dug her elbow into Mr. B.'s meaty ribs and said, "You're a fine host, you are! Weren't you supposed to do something the very first thing?"; and Ernst Bauenfel seized his head and exclaimed, "*Ach*, I forgot! Excuse me a minute," and trotted out to return a moment later pushing a bar cart with a bucketed bottle of champagne on it and a queerly shaped liqueur bottle, six wine glasses and a liqueur glass (and now he does look like a *biergarten* waiter, Ellery grinned to himself).

"Well, open it, Ernst," said Mrs. B., "what are you standing there for?"; and Mr. B. with a sly smile said, "Before the very first thing comes the *very* first thing, Zelda," and he took from the pocket of his jacket a jewel box and offered it to her, saying, "As a jeweler, I know that the first anniversary gift should be a clock. But how could a clock express my feeling? Open it, *liebchen*"; and Zelda Bauenfel opened a box, and gasped, and held high a magnificent emerald bracelet, and burst into tears. Then she rushed into her husband's arms, and he said softly, "I wish I could give you the whole world, Zelda," and it was said with such simplicity that no one was embarrassed, not even Ellery, who was allergic to clichés.

And when Zelda had blown her nose, and tried on the bracelet, and everyone had exclaimed over it, Ernst Bauenfel cried, "To work!" and he began struggling with the champagne cork, popping it unexpectedly and drenching himself, his young wife laughing so hard that every curve in her body described a parabola.

Then Mr. B. was filling the wine glasses and passing them around; and when Ellery said, "You've left yourself out, Mr. Bauenfel," Mr. B. shook his head and said "Zelda will tell you I am no drinker, Mr. Queen. I never drink anything but the liqueur, and this only on very special occasions, like tonight," and he opened the liqueur bottle and poured himself a critical quantity of its topaz-colored contents, as if each drop was precious; and then he held up his glass and said, "My friends, a toast, I give you a German proverb: When an old man marries a young wife, death laughs. To my Zelda!" and the guests echoed, "Zelda!", and drank their champagne, and Ernst Bauenfel raised his liqueur glass to his lips and looked at his blushing wife over the rim, and chuckled, and threw his head back and drained the glass—which was not, in Ellery's view, the respectful way to imbibe a prized liqueur, even in a toast—and then the jeweler's eyes opened wide, and he clutched his throat with a hoarse cry and groped with the other hand as if seeking something to hang onto, and finally fell heavily to the floor, where he lay, incredibly, writhing.

And Ellery found himself on his knees beside the stricken man, saying, "Poison, poison. Anse, call Conk Farnham—hurry!" and while Chief Newby ran to phone Dr. Farnham, Franklin Lang led an open-mouthed young wife away, and Rob Packard and Martin Overbrook hovered over their recumbent friend with popping eyes. The writhings had stilled and the breathing had become shallow and very rapid. The complexion was already that of a corpse.

"Mr. Bauenfel—Ernst," Ellery said urgently. "Can you hear me? Do you know who did this? Who poisoned your liqueur?"

The cyanosing lips tried desparately to tell him. But they could not. Then an odd thing happened. The dying man's left hand fumbled its way to his abdomen and found the lower left-hand pocket of his brocaded vest. With his forefinger and thumb he made his way in little stabs into the pocket. Then he withdrew his fingers and stretched out his hand as if offering something, and his heavy body arched like a drawn bow, and released its arrow.

And there he lay.

"Dead," said Ellery bitterly. "I swear I'll never set foot in Wrightsville again."

But then he opened Ernst Bauenfel's left hand.

In it lay a large unset diamond.

"What was he trying to tell you?" Packard, the building contractor, muttered.

"With a diamond, of all things," said little Overbrook, the paperbox manufacturer. "Why a diamond?"

But before Ellery could reply, Chief Newby came back.

"Dr. Farnham will be over as soon as they locate him," said the police chief, and then he stopped. "He's *dead?*" he said, looking down at his friend. "Mr. B.?"

"I'm sorry, Anse."

"You're sorry. We were his best friends."

"I know." And after a moment Ellery said, "A quick-acting poison. It can only have been in that bottle of whatever it is—the liqueur."

"Who could have wanted to kill Ernst?" said Packard. There were tears in his eyes; and Overbrook turned away.

The police chief picked up the bottle by the neck, sniffed its contents, and set it softly down. He was one of those occasional small compact men who contrive to look as if they are made of rock. His sensitive face was now as hard as the rest of him. He went over to the settee, unfolded an afghan, and draped it carefully over Ernst Bauenfel's body. Then he turned away, saying, "I never heard of this stuff,"jerking his head toward the liqueur bottle. "What is it?"

Ellery came to. He inspected the label. "It's new to me, too. Made at a monastery in Switzerland. Zelda should know."

"Zelda does know," said Zelda; and the newly made widow appeared in the archway, followed by Lang, who was shaking his head as if to say, "I couldn't keep her away." The young woman's face was blotched from weeping, but it was set in as rocky planes as Newby's. She went over to the corner of the settee, near her husband's body, and sat down. "No, I'm all right," she said as Ellery and Newby stepped toward her. "I want to help. I've got to help. Mr. Queen, what do you want to know?"

"All about the liqueur. I've never heard of it."

"It's never been sold outside Switzerland, because the monks could only make small quantities. Ernst adored it—it's the only alcohol he could drink, as he told you. Then the monastery was disbanded. Ernst bought up as many bottles as he could find—about half a dozen, I think it was—and brought them with him from the old country when he came to the United States."

"How many bottles are left?"

"This is the last one. He kept hoarding it. It's the only thing Ernst was selfish about."

"That's true, Ellery," Franklin Lang said. "Ernst would give you the socks off his feet, but in all the years I knew him he never offered me a drink out of this bottle. Did he ever offer you any, Rob?"

Packard shook his head, and Martin Overbrook said "Mr B. dead. It's not possible," and again turned away.

"In other words, no one ever drank from this bottle except your husband, Zelda? Not even you?"

"That's right, Mr. Queen." Now she was struggling to control her voice. "In fact, tonight is the first time I've seen even Ernst drink any, there's so little left in the bottle. He was trying to make it last as long as possible."

"Then the poison could only have been intended for him,"Chief Newby said in harsh tones. "And what's this I heard about a diamond, Ellery?"

"When you went to phone Farnham, I asked Bauenfel if he knew who poisoned him. He tried to talk but couldn't. The last act of his life was to take the diamond out of his vest pocket."

The police chief examined it. "I don't see anything special about it except its size. Do you know anything about this, Zelda?"

The young widow shook her hed. "I didn't even know he was carrying it. Ernst often had unset gems in his pockets. Most jewelers do."

"He was trying to answer your question, Mr. Queen. Is that what you think?" asked the contractor.

"I don't see what other construction we can put on the last responsive act of a dying man," Ellery said. "Who killed you? I ask him, and he answers with a diamond. So we have to start from the diamond."

"A diamond," said the paperbox man, "is a diamond."

"Yes, Mr. Overbrook, but is also stands for something. Remember the occasion. This was his wedding anniversary party; the anniversay was uppermost on Ernst Bauenfel's mind. So let's think of a diamond in relation to wedding anniversaries.

"In the traditional listing," said Ellery, "the diamond is associated with the sixtieth and seventy-fifth wedding anniversaries. In that list the gift for a first anniversary is paper. But when Ernst, earlier this evening, mentioned the gift *he* associated withfirst anniversaries, he didn't say paper, he said a clock. Well, the clock as a first-anniversary gift happens to head the official list authorized by the jewelry industry. In the jewelers' list a diamond represents the thirtieth wedding anniversary. Ernst was a jeweler. We have the right to assume that, in answering my question as to who poisoned him, he replied with the jeweler's symbol for thirty."

"Thirty," muttered Chief Newby. "Who the devil could he have meant by thirty? It makes no sense."

Ellery was silent. Suddenly he said, "I hope no one will mind if I make an experiment? Mr. Overbrook, do you have a connection with anything associated with thirty?"

The little manufacturer jumped. "You mean you suspect me of having poisoned Mr. B.'s bottle?" he sputtered. "I don't like your experiment, Mr.Queen! Or your questions!"

"Why don't you answer it, Martie?" said Zelda Bauenfel quietly.

"What do you mean, Zelda? I couldn't have been closer to Ernst if I'd been his brother!"

"Yes, Martie, " she said, "but have you forgotten about the loan?"

"Loan?" Overbrook licked his lips. "I don't see what that has to do with anything . . ."

"What loan?" asked Ellery.

"This is ridiculous! Three years ago I was foreman of the paperbox factory. The owner decided to retire. He offered me the chance to buy him out, but I didn't have nearly enough cash to put down, and I couldn't give the bank the collateral they wanted. Ernst came to my rescue. Without a cent of collateral he loaned me enough to finance my purchase of the factory."

"How much was the loan?"

Overbrook licked his lips again. "Thirty thousand dollars." He went on quickly, "But that's just a coincidence—"

"It may well be, because at least one other thirty is represented here." And Ellery swung about to face Franklin Lang.

"Me?" said Lang.

"I'm afraid so, Frank. As a newspaperman and managing editor of the *Record*, you don't have to be reminded that the numeral 30 written at the end of newspaper copy means 'the end'; it's a trade-wide symbol in journalism, at least in this country. I merely point it out, Frank."

The newspaperman snapped, "I felt toward Ernst the way Martie Overbrook and Rob Packard did, and everyone else in town. Four years ago I was hospitalized for eight months after an operation. I had no savings, and the medical expenses were enormous. Well, for almost that entire period Mr. B. paid my bills. Does it stand to reason I'd repay him with poison? It wasn't even a loan—Ernst wouldn't hear of my paying him back. Besides, about this thirty nonsense—how many people outside the newspaper field have ever heard of it?"

"A point," Ellery conceded. He looked at the building contractor. "I wonder, Mr. Packard, about you."

"And thirty?"Rob Packard nodded slowly. "It's a queer thing, Mr. Queen, but there's a tie between me and Ernst, too, in that regard. It was Ernst who got me out of the realty brokerage game. He owned a parcel out in Hill Valley, near the airport, and he came to me with a proposition. He foresaw that Wrightsville housing was going to expand in that direction, and he offered to put up the land and financing, with me providing the know-how and the management, on a partnership basis. I snapped at it like a trout. It started me out as a building contractor. We named the development Thirty Acres, from the amount of land we built on. You'll find it on all the newer maps of Wrightsville." Then Packard said, "Does that sound as if I'd want to kill Ernst Bauenfel?"

Ellery said ruefully, "I admit, motive in this case is the tough one. Probably half of Wrightsville could come up with similar favors that Mr. B. did for them. By the way, Zelda," he said suddenly, turning to her, "your husband was a wealthy man. And you're young enough to have been his daughter. Forgive me, but it's happened before. At the least, his death would mean to you—"

"In terms of gain, Mr. Queen," said Zelda Bauenfel, examining him as if he were a germ under a microscope, "absolutely nothing. When we got married a year ago, I insisted that Ernst write a will to leave Amy everything he had. I had reasons for this which aren't anyone's business, but in view of what's happened I'll tell you.

"In the first place there was the talk, as I suppose you've heard. Well, I didn't want Ernst—when he heard the gossip—to think I'd married him for his money.

"In the second place I wanted to protect Amy and, incidentally, reassure Ernst about her future. After all, I wasn't her real mother, and if Ernst died before I did, which was likely, he being so much older than I, Amy would be left to my care. We had quite an argument about the will. Finally, Ernst compromised. He made it out in such a way that, after three years, Amy and I would share his estate equally.

"With Ernst dead now, after only one year, I'm left with nothing. Why would I kill him? As unthinkable as that is."

"Not unthinkable," said Ellery gently. "Here's a possible reason, as old as the hills and as new as this spring: another man."

Her chin came up. "You look for one, Mr. Queen. You, too, Anse. Look all you want, You won't find any. I love my husband, and I've been faithful to him."

Ellery half turned away, frowning.

"Don't any of you blame Mr. Queen." said Chief Newby in a mumble. "Questions like these have to be asked . . . Zelda, Ernst kept the liqueur bottle in the liquor cabinet in the dining room, didn't he? Did he keep the cabinet locked?"

"Ernst never locked anything here, Anse. You know that."

"Then anybody could have got to that bottle! I don't know how many people in town have been entertained in this house at one time or another. We'll fingerprint the bottle, but my hunch is this is going to be a long, long job."

"Maybe not so long," said Ellery; and he turned to the widow again. "Zelda, you and Ernst weren't married in Wrightsville, were you?"

The question took her by suprise. 'Well, no, Mr. Queen. We thought it . . . best to do it in Connhaven, and we went straight on to New York, where we spent our honeymoon. We left Amy with my mother while we were away."

"Then that could be it." Unaccountably, Ellery looked relaxed and relieved. "There's no legal proof, Anse, but I can give you a theory that covers all the facts."

"Earlier this evening," said Ellery, "Zelda said that she had never seen Ernst take a drink of his private-stock liqueur before tonight. In recalling this, I wondered why he hadn't dipped into it when he and Zelda were married, which would surely be one of those extra-special occasions on which he could be expected to indulge. Zelda just gave us the reason: they weren't married in Wrightsville, and they spent their honeymoon in New York. So Mr. B. had no access to the bottle when he and Zelda married.

"Since only three or four weeks elapsed between his first wife's funeral and his remarriage, it's reasonable to assume that Ernst had last taken a drink from that bottle during his first marriage—*that is, while Hester Dade was still alive.*

"Put that together," said Ellery swiftly, "with the climate in this town a year ago. There was plenty of talk, you told me, Anse, when Mr. B. and Zelda Brown married. Zelda was working for Ernst up to

231

that time. Suppose before her fatal automobile accident Hester had got a jump on the gossips—suspected that there was something going on between her husband and his secretary-bookkeeper. Suppose, true or not, it became an *idée fixe* in Hester's mind. Suppose, in her jealousy, Hester poured poison into the bottle of liqueur from which only her husband ever drank."

"Hester," Zelda Bauenfel whispered.

"Tonight, when he realized he had been poisoned," Ellery went on, "Mr. B. remembered something, just what we'll never learn. But it was enough to convince him that his liqueur had been poisoned by Hester. Unable to speak, he used his last strength and took out the diamond to leave us a clue—the 'thirty' clue. He was too far gone to realize that it might point to his three best friends as well."

"I still don't get it," complained the police chief. "How does this thirty thing tag Hester for the poisoning?"

"You told me yourself, Anse, on our drive up here. Hester, you said, was twenty-five years old when she gave birth to Amy. Amy is now five. You also told me that Ernst married Zelda on Hester's birthday. So today is not only Ernst's and Zelda's first wedding anniversary, *it would have been Hester's thirtieth birthday.*"

Chief Anslem Newby was never able to prove that Hester Dade Bauenfel reached out from the grave to kill Mr. Baountiful, but then Newby never pinned the murder on anyone else, either. To tell the truth, he didn't try very hard.

As for Ellery, while it is to be doubted that his absence will remain permanent, the fact is that he has not yet paid another visit to his favorite scene of the crime, Wrightsville.

AN ELLERY QUEEN
SHORT STORY CHECKLIST

Francis M. Nevins, Jr.

NOTE: Almost all of Ellery Queen's short stories and novelets were published in one or more collections between 1934 and 1968. The following story checklist is arranged by collection, and the title of each tale within a collection is followed by information on its first publication in a magazine. The stories that remain uncollected are covered chronologically at the end of the checklist. For more information both bibliographic and critical, please see my *Royal Bloodline: Ellery Queen, Author and Detective* (Bowling Green University Popular Press, 1974).

THE ADVENTURES OF ELLERY QUEEN. New York: Stokes, 1934. London: Gollancz, 1935. First paperback: Pocket Books pb #99, 1941.

"The Adventure of the African Traveler" (no prior magazine publication)

"The Adventure of the Hanging Acrobat" (*Mystery*, May 1934, as "The Girl on the Trapeze")

"The Adventure of the One-Penny Black" (*Great Detective*, April 1933, as "The One-Penny Black")

"The Adventure of the Bearded Lady" (*Mystery*, August 1934, as "The Sinister Beard")

"The Adventure of the Three Lame Men" (*Mystery*, April 1934, as "The Three Lame Men")

"The Adventure of the Invisible Lover" (*Mystery*, September 1934, as "Four Men Loved a Woman")

"The Adventure of the Teakwood Case" (*Mystery*, May 1933, as "The Affair of the Gallant Bachelor")

"The Adventure of 'The Two-Headed Dog' " (*Mystery*, October 1934, as "The 'Two-Headed Dog' ")

"The Adventure of the Glass-Domed Clock" (*Mystery League*, October 1933, as "The Glass-Domed Clock")

"The Adventure of the Seven Black Cats" (*Mystery*, October 1934, as "The Black Cats Vanished")

"The Adventure of the Mad Tea-Party" (*Redbook*, October 1934, as "The Mad Tea-Party")

THE NEW ADVENTURES OF ELLERY QUEEN. New York: Stokes, 1940. London: Gollancz, 1940. First paperback: Pocket Books pb #134, 1941.

"The Lamp of God" (*Detective Story*, November 1935, as "House of Haunts")

"The Adventure of the Treasure Hunt" (*Detective Story*, December 1935, as "The Treasure Hunt")

"The Adventure of the Hollow Dragon" (*Redbook*, December 1936, as "The Hollow Dragon")

"The Adventure of the House of Darkness" (*American Magazine*, February 1935, as "The House of Darkness")

"The Adventure of the Bleeding Portrait" (*American Cavalcade*, September 1937, as "The Gramatan Mystery")

"Man Bites Dog" (*Blue Book*, June 1939)

"Long Shot" (*Blue Book*, September 1939, as "The Long Shot")

"Mind Over Matter" (*Blue Book*, October 1939)

"Trojan Horse" (*Blue Book*, December 1939, as "The Trojan Horse")

CALENDAR OF CRIME. Boston: Little Brown, 1952. London: Gollancz, 1952. First paperback: Pocket Books pb #960, 1953.

"The Inner Circle" (*Ellery Queen's Mystery Magazine*, January 1947)

"The President's Half Disme" (*Ellery Queen's Mystery Magazine*, February 1947)

"The Ides of Michael Magoon" (*Ellery Queen's Mystery Magazine*, March 1947)

"The Emperor's Dice" (*Ellery Queen's Mystery Magazine*, April 1951)

"The Gettysburg Bugle" (*Ellery Queen's Mystery Magazine*, May 1951, as "As Simple as ABC")

"The Medical Finger" (*Ellery Queen's Mystery Magazine*, June 1951)

"The Fallen Angel" (*Ellery Queen's Mystery Magazine*, July 1951)

"The Needle's Eye" (*Ellery Queen's Mystery Magazine*, August 1951)

"The Three R's" (*Ellery Queen's Mystery Magazine*, September 1946)

"The Dead Cat" (*Ellery Queen's Mystery Magazine*, October 1946)

"The Telltale Bottle" (*Ellery Queen's Mystery Magazine*, November 1946)

"The Dauphin's Doll" (*Ellery Queen's Mystery Magazine*, December 1948)

QBI: QUEEN'S BUREAU OF INVESTIGATION. Boston: Little Brown, 1955. London: Gollancz, 1955. First paperback: Pocket Books pb #1118, 1956.

"Money Talks" (*This Week*, April 2, 1950, as "The Sound of Blackmail")

"A Matter of Seconds" (*This Week*, August 9, 1953)

"The Three Widows" (*This Week*, January 29, 1950, as "Murder Without Clues")

"My Queer Dean!" (*This Week*, March 8, 1953)

"Driver's Seat" (*This Week*, March 25, 1951, as "Lady, You're Dead!")

"A Lump of Sugar" (*This Week*, July 9, 1950, as "The Mystery of the 3 Dawn Riders")

"Cold Money" (*This Week*, March 20, 1952)

"The Myna Birds" (*This Week*, December 28, 1952, as "The Myna Bird Mystery")

"A Question of Honor" (*This Week*, September 13, 1953)

"The Robber of Wrightsville" (*Today's Family*, February 1953)

"Double Your Money" (*This Week*, September 30, 1951, as "The Vanishing Wizard")

"Miser's Gold" (*This Week*, June 30, 1950, as "Love Hunts a Hidden Treasure")

"Snowball in July" (*This Week*, August 31, 1952, as "The Phantom Train")

"The Witch of Times Square" (*This Week*, November 5, 1950)

"The Gamblers' Club" (*This Week*, January 7, 1951)

"GI Story" (*Ellery Queen's Mystery Magazine*, August 1954)

"The Black Ledger" (*This Week*, January 26, 1952, as "The Mysterious Black Ledger")

"Child Missing!" (*This Week*, July 8, 1951, as "Kidnaped!")

QUEENS FULL. New York: Random House, 1965. London: Gollancz, 1966. First paperback: Signet pb #D2894, 1966.

"The Death of Don Juan" (*Argosy*, May 1962)

"E = Murder" (*This Week*, August 14, 1960)

"The Wrightsville Heirs" (*Better Living*, January-February 1956)

"Diamonds in Paradise" (*Ellery Queen's Mystery Magazine*, September 1954)

"The Case Against Carroll" (*Argosy*, September 1958)

QED: QUEEN'S EXPERIMENTS IN DETECTION. New York: New American Library, 1968. London: Gollancz, 1969. First paperback: Signet pb #T4120, 1970.

"Mum Is the Word" (*Ellery Queen's Mystery Magazine*, April 1966)

"Object Lesson" (*This Week*, September 11, 1955, as "The Blackboard Gangsters")

"No Parking" (*This Week*, March 18, 1956, as "Terror in a Penthouse")

"No Place to Live" (*This Week*, June 10, 1956, as "The Man They All Hated")

"Miracles Do Happen" (*Ellery Queen's Mystery Magazine*, July 1957)

"The Lonely Bride" (*This Week*, December 4, 1949, as "The Lady Couldn't Explain")

"Mystery at the Library of Congress" (*Argosy*, June 1960, as "Enter Ellery Queen")

"Dead Ringer" (*Diner's Club Magazine*, March 1965)

"The Broken T" (*This Week*, July 27, 1963, as "Mystery in Neon Red")

"Half a Clue" (*This Week*, August 25, 1963, as "Half a Clue to Murder")

"Eve of the Wedding" (*Ellery Queen's Mystery Magazine*, August 1955, as "Bride in Danger")

"Last Man to Die" (*This Week*, November 3, 1963)

"Payoff" (*Cavalier*, August 1964, as "Crime Syndicate Payoff")

"The Little Spy" (*Cavalier*, January 1965)

"The President Regrets" (*Diner's Club Magazine*, September 1965)

"Abraham Lincoln's Clue" (*MD*, June 1965)

THE BEST OF ELLERY QUEEN. Edited by Francis M. Nevins, Jr. and Martin H. Greenberg. New York: Beaufort Books, 1985.

"The Glass-Domed Clock" (THE ADVENTURES OF ELLERY QUEEN)

"The Bearded Lady" (THE ADVENTURES OF ELLERY QUEEN)

"The Mad Tea-Party" (THE ADVENTURES OF ELLERY QUEEN)

"Man Bites Dog" (THE NEW ADVENTURES OF ELLERY QUEEN)

"Mind Over Matter" (THE NEW ADVENTURES OF ELLERY QUEEN)

"The Inner Circle" (CALENDAR OF CRIME)

"The Dauphin's Doll" (CALENDAR OF CRIME)

"The Three Widows" (QBI: QUEEN'S BUREAU OF INVESTIGATION)

"Snowball in July" (QBI: QUEEN'S BUREAU OF INVESTIGATION)

"My Queer Dean!" (QBI: QUEEN'S BUREAU OF INVESTIGATION)

"GI Story" (QBI: QUEEN'S BUREAU OF INVESTIGATION)

"Miracles Do Happen" (QED: QUEEN'S EXPERIMENTS IN DETEC-
TION)

"Last Man to Die" (QED: QUEEN'S EXPERIMENTS IN DETECTION)

"Abraham Lincoln's Clue" (QED: QUEEN'S EXPERIMENTS IN
DETECTION)

"Wedding Anniversary" (*Ellery Queen's Mystery Magazine*, September
1967)

UNCOLLECTED STORIES

"Terror Town" (*Argosy*, August, 1956)

"Uncle from Australia" (*Diner's Club Magazine*, June 1965)

"The Three Students" (*Playboy*, March 1971)

"The Odd Man" (*Playboy*, June 1971)

"The Honest Swindler" (*Saturday Evening Post*, Summer 1971)

"The Reindeer Clue" (*National Enquirer*, December 23, 1975)